EVERYMAN,
I WILL GO WITH THEE,
AND BE THY GUIDE,
IN THY MOST NEED
TO GO BY THY SIDE

JOSEPH ROTH

*The Radetzky
March*

Translated from the German by
Joachim Neugroschel

with an Introduction by
Alan Bance

EVERYMAN'S LIBRARY

197

Joseph Roth: Radetzkymarsch
Copyright © 1932 by Gustav Kiepenheuer Verlag, Berlin
Copyright © 1950 by Verlag Allert de Lange, Amsterdam and
Verlag Kiepenheuer & Witsch, Cologne
Translation by Joachim Neugroschel copyright © 1995
Published by arrangement with The Overlook Press

First included in Everyman's Library, 1996
Introduction, Bibliography and Chronology © Everyman's Library,
1996

ISBN 1-85715-197-6

A CIP catalogue record for this book is available from the
British Library

Published by Everyman's Library,
Gloucester Mansions, 140A Shaftesbury Avenue,
London WC2H 8HD

Distributed by Random House (UK) Ltd.,
20 Vauxhall Bridge Road, London SW1V 2SA

Printed and bound in Germany
by GGP Media, Pössneck

THE RADETZKY MARCH

INTRODUCTION

On 2 July 1859, the correspondent of *The Times* reported back to London on the Austrian defeat at the Battle of Solferino in northern Italy, at the hands of the French under Napoleon III. In his account, the *Times* man makes a particular point of deploring the presence on the battlefield of the Emperor Franz Joseph of Austria, whose anachronistic gallantry in leading his men from the front endangered rather than advanced the Austrian cause, for 'every one thought himself bound to take care of the EMPEROR's safety, and Solferino ... would probably have been better defended if he had been away'.

This is precisely the defining moment in Austrian history which Joseph Roth chooses as the point of departure for his great novel of the decline of Austria. Its action takes place between 1859 and 1916, encompassing that other and opposite defining moment, the assassination of Archduke Franz Ferdinand, heir to the Imperial Austrian throne, at Sarajevo in 1914. In 1859 the Emperor's safety is the concern of all, and in the novel he is indeed rescued by 'the Hero of Solferino', founder of the Trotta dynasty. The last scion of the family, Carl Joseph Trotta von Sipolje, dies in battle in 1914 as a direct result of the insult offered to Austria–Hungary by a Serbian assassin. From first to last, the history of the Trottas is intimately bound up with that of Austria and the house of Hapsburg. The reiterated contrast between the sturdy, simple Hero of Solferino and the complex, neurasthenic modern anti-hero, Carl Joseph Trotta, provides the loom upon which is woven the myth of a lost golden age – the late Hapsburg Empire – which gained ever more elegiac poignancy during the 1930s when the first Austrian Republic was threatened, and finally absorbed, by Nazi Germany.

It is as a celebration of the Austrian myth that Joseph Roth's novel is best known. *The Radetzky March* bears at first sight the signs of an old man's dream of his youth, the perennial conviction of the old that giants walked the earth in those

ix

days. Yet in 1932, when the novel appeared, Roth was no more than thirty-eight years old – surely too young to match, say, the geriatric vision of the seventy-nine-year old H. G. Wells, in whose eyes nowadays 'old men behave ... meanly and disgustingly and the young are spasmodic, foolish and all too easily misled'. Besides, Roth would not be a true Austrian (who rejects all that presents itself in too definitive a form) if he could be so definite and dogmatic; and sure enough, the novel incorporates some correctives to his undeniable tendency to idealize the past. These correctives, though, tend not to carry as much weight as the idealizing. It was not lost on Roth, for example, that the Battle of Solferino, finest heroic hour of the Trottas, was a defeat that meant the imminent end of the hated Austrian presence in Italy, and the beginning of the end of the Hapsburgs. He is aware that he is creating an illusion, but in the Austrian way treats reality and the past as malleable or plastic enough to be adjusted. The title of his novel also reflects the lost cause of the Italian territories, for it derives from a popular march tune written to celebrate the achievements of Field Marshal Count Radetzky, who checked the Italian national revolution of 1848–9, but died just over a year before all his good work was undone at the Battle of Solferino. These are inconvenient facts such as Austria, right down to the present and the Waldheim affair, has had no little practice in forgetting.

Roth's own life story was subject to the same fictional adjustment by the author. He was a notorious 'mythomaniac' when it came to accounting for his origins, and until the 1970s, when the facts were finally established, you could take your pick from a number of versions he put about. The facts are that he was born Moses Joseph Roth in 1894, in Brody in Austrian Galicia (now in the Ukraine), on the frontier with Russia. The model for all the border towns described in his novels, Brody had a large Jewish population (when he visited it, the Emperor Franz Joseph I is supposed to have said 'Now I know why I'm called King of Jerusalem!'). It was an important centre for smuggling, and a narrow provincial town with a cosmopolitan mixture of races and tongues. What Roth tells us about his mother, that she was 'a Jewess, strong, earthy and Slavic in her make-up', can be allowed to stand uncorrected: she was never the object of his fantasy, presumably because she was always present and therefore prosaic – 'earthy'. His stories about his father are a different matter. The least extravagant account gave him the status of Austrian railway official. In the most colourful versions, Roth was 'the natural son of a Polish Count with whom his mother had enjoyed a brief affair', or of an artist, a converted Jew, a Viennese munitions manufacturer, or an officer with a woman in every garrison town. The true facts about his parentage can be summarized as follows: his mother was born in Brody into a large Jewish family. Linguistically they reflected the polyglot mixture of the border area, where Polish, Yiddish and German were all standard: at home, German was the main language spoken. (On his journalistic trip to the Soviet Union in the 1920s, Roth got by very well in Russian.) The brothers of the family all left Brody to take up careers elsewhere: some became wealthy and later helped to support Maria – or Miriam, to give Roth's mother her Jewish name – and her son Moses Joseph.

The father, Nachum Roth, was a Hamburg businessman, originally from West Galicia, who grew up among the Hasidim, an Eastern Orthodox Jewish sect characterized by mysticism and religious euphoria. Introduced to Maria by her brothers, he married her in the Brody synagogue in 1892. Roth's birth was, therefore, quite legitimate. But it was not long before disaster struck in the life of the Roths: after a business calamity, Nachum developed signs of insanity, and was committed to an asylum in Germany. Eventually he found refuge in the home of a Hasidic rabbi in Russian Poland. Maria was left to bring up her son alone. A divorce was impossible under Jewish law, as Nachum was mentally unfit to give the necessary consent. But aside from the acutely felt absence of a father figure – and the theme of the absent father was to provide his richest vein of autobiographical and fictional fantasy – Roth does not appear to have suffered greatly as a result. He attended a state-supported, all-Jewish school in Brody, and received a good grounding especially in German language and literature: it was the Jews of the Eastern provinces who above all represented and preserved German culture there.

After beginning his university studies in the provincial capital, Lemberg, with family support Roth moved to the University of Vienna in 1914, living at first in the Leopoldstadt area, which was the centre for the large Jewish element in the city – some 100,000 in number, the biggest Jewish population of any in central Europe. Vienna before the First World War was many things to many outstanding spirits: Robert Musil, Hermann Broch, Arthur Schnitzler, Hugo von Hofmannsthal, Stefan Zweig, Karl Kraus, not to mention Sigmund Freud and even Adolf Hitler. For Kraus, the capital was 'the Austrian experimental site for Doomsday', and the leftish student Roth must have experienced this negative side of the city, too, although retrospectively in *The Radetzky March* his by now desperately conservative imagination summons up the essence of Vienna in the brilliant Corpus Christi procession of Chapter 13. His nostalgia is understandable: the first spring he enjoyed in the city was also the last of pre-war days, when his own future lay bright before him. His German studies under the eminent Professor Walter Brecht were successful: there was talk of a scholarship (a rare distinction in those days), and Roth was planning an academic career, while also beginning to publish some poems and articles.

The war intervened drastically. On the national level, Austria was never to recover from the terrible losses she sustained in the autumn of 1914 at the hands of the Russians in Galicia, Roth's home province. In 1914 he was a complete pacifist, and the news from home must have distressed him deeply, yet for the time being he remained caught up in his own affairs: his studies, his writing, his chronic poverty. It was only in 1916 that, having initially been rejected by the military on health grounds, he decided to 'arrange' his conscription; although such was the war-weariness and disillusion in Vienna that even an army doctor advised him against enlisting! Austria in any case traditionally much preferred the glamour of the military to the too distinct reality of war, and for the soldiers of *The Radetzky March* the famous words of Prince Eugene of Savoy, who led the Austrian army in a number of battles around the turn of the seventeenth century, certainly seem appropriate: 'The Austrian soldier fights with great courage, but without conviction.' The spring of 1917 took Roth to the Galician front. He was later to embroider upon his military record as he did upon his family background, but it seems unlikely that he was involved in any fighting, let alone decorated, or captured only to escape and trek back home across Russia, as his tall tales were later to recount. In fact he worked in the army press office, and continued to write poetry, although it is clear that the horrors of war did not leave him untouched. Later, however, he was to award himself full officer rank and adopt the bearing of a 'k. und k. Kavalier', a dignified veteran of the old Royal and Imperial Army. In the unstable postwar world following the abolition of the monarchy, the army hierarchy offered security and simplicity, as it had for the first Trotta, the Hero of Solferino. The theme of return from the war was a particularly productive one for Roth, occurring in a number of his novels and stories; and in a sense *Heimkehr*, the return home, is the central motif of all his work.

After his own return to post-Hapsburg Vienna, he shared the bleak state of mind of the war generation. Nonetheless, he met in 1919 his future wife, Friederike (Friedl) Reichler, a shy and attractive Jewish girl from Leopoldstadt, whom he was to marry in 1922 in Berlin; and he began to make his way in journalism, publishing at first mainly in the left-wing Viennese paper *Der Neue Tag*. The move to Berlin, a livelier city for journalism, but one which he never grew to love, took place in 1920. His preferred form of composition was still the very Austrian one of the *Feuilleton* article. A highly cultivated form associated with such masters as Karl Kraus, Peter Altenberg, and Alfred Polgar, the *Feuilleton* is a vehicle for Viennese impressionism. It consists of a short article for the literary section of a paper (which properly speaking is the *Feuilleton* or literary supplement): it has little news value, needs no detailed preparation or study, but is built around a brilliant original *Einfall* or inspiration. The necessary economy and conciseness require an ability to evoke character by a few gestures and atmosphere by the invocation of representative objects. The

Feuilletonist is not expected to be an objective reporter, but to embellish what he sees and turn the mundane into uncommon experience. Clearly the techniques of the *Feuilleton* relate closely to the style of *The Radetzky March*. There is the same love of the set-piece description (for instance, the Corpus Christi procession already mentioned) and the tableau, the same impressionism, the feeling for the nuances of atmosphere, the use of a naive point of view, the tendency to see human figures as marionettes in the hands of fate, and to take the part for the whole in a way which makes reality disjointed and unintegrated. Roth's earliest novels are connected in a very practical sense to his journalism, not only in terms of content but also because *The Spider's Web*, *Hotel Savoy* and *The Rebellion* were all first serially published in newspapers in the 1920s.

Roth's political sympathies were broadly left-wing at this time, but the term may be too categorical for him. He disliked abstract thinking, and never accepted an ideology: he was anti-war, but unable to sustain pacifism; he loved the underdog but could never be a Marxist. Nonetheless, he was sensitive enough to political atmosphere in those days to abandon, after 1922, the right-wing Berlin *Borsen-Courier* and move towards the radical *Vorwarts*, for which he occasionally wrote under the name of 'der rote Joseph' (Red Joseph), and the liberal *Frankfurter Zeitung*. His association with the latter became the dominant one and continued rather unevenly up to 1932, shortly before Hitler's seizure of power. After 1925 he travelled widely in Europe on behalf of the paper, indulging in the nomadic existence which was obviously congenial to him and not merely forced upon him later by exile. His visit to the Soviet Union in 1926 only served to confirm his anti-ideological stance.

When Germany fell into the hands of Hitler, Roth left the country for ever. He was at the height of his fame as a novelist, *The Radetzky March* having gained him universal respect, except of course among Germany's new masters. On 10 May 1933, his books were consigned to the flames along with those of other great writers in Nazi book-burning ceremonies throughout the Reich. This was the first of a series of blows cutting him off from his readership, including the annexation of Austria in 1938 and the German invasion of the Netherlands in 1940, when the Nazis destroyed the stocks of Dutch publishing houses who had been hospitable to German *émigré* writers. One result of exile (based in Paris) was loss of income from journalism, so that Roth was forced to regard his literary work as his primary source of income. There were frequent complaints of poverty, isolation and depression, though he constantly expended effort and money on helping fellow exiles worse off than himself. His drinking – an addiction so well described in its effects on Lieutenant Trotta in *The Radetzky March* – did not begin with exile, but gradually intensified until it became a kind of slow method of committing suicide. In these years his political views moved steadily to the right; as early as 1933 he was already denying any left-wing past. His position as a Jew from the margins of the Empire had always disposed him towards conservatism with a small 'c'; for him the greatest disaster was the loss of order. In this, the Jewish experience of the need for protection probably played its part. The supranational authority of the Emperor was a first and last line of defence for Eastern Judaism. Hence the fervour of their personal homage to the monarch when he meets 'his' Jews in Chapter 15 of *The Radetzky March*, and Roth's irritation with the 'German' Austrians and the Viennese who do not sufficiently value the Crown Lands and the periphery of the Empire, and so eventually forfeit the supranational Austro-Hungarian Dual Monarchy which has for so long (since 1867) maintained peace and stability in Central Europe. With hindsight, we can see that this analysis was not entirely wrong.

The turn to the right was accelerated in the 1930s as barbarity broke out around him, one of the first to foresee the horrifying future of Nazism. He retreated ever further into the only order he had known, embracing both Catholicism (though it is not recorded that he was ever baptized) and the lost cause of the restoration of the Hapsburg monarchy: two powerful totems brought together in the image of the Capuchin Crypt, the vault in Vienna where the Hapsburgs were laid to rest. This vault lends its name to the title of one of

Roth's last novels: a kind of sequel to *The Radetzky March*, published in Holland in 1938, *The Capuchin Crypt* takes us through the life story of another Lieutenant Trotta – cousin to Carl Joseph of *The Radetzky March* – up to 12 March 1938, when Nazi troops marched into Austria. Roth's health in exile was progressively deteriorating, and he was ageing visibly – a phenomenon strangely prefigured by the premature ageing of characters such as District Captain Trotta and Frau von Taussig in *The Radetzky March*. His wife's mental health had given way, and she was in a Viennese asylum whose fees he was always hard pressed to find. From 1931 to 1936 he lived with the exotic Frau Andrea Manga Bell: her mother was from Hamburg, her father Cuban, and she had two children from her marriage with Manga Bell, Prince of Douala in West Cameroon. Roth's treatment of her was reputedly very repressive, but despite his physical deterioration he was still able to exercise a sexual spell over her, until the relationship finally became intolerable. Subsequently his partner was Irmgard Keun, a vivacious and brilliant young exile novelist who, if not precisely a feminist in a modern sense, certainly had a sharply critical eye for the pretensions of men. After about eighteen months of living with Roth, she went off to Nice with a French naval officer.

Except for a brief period in Berlin in the early 1920s, Roth had no fixed abode, but preferred hotel rooms and writing at café tables. This he continued to do, a potent liquid always to hand, six to eight hours a day to the very end, although he complained that shortage of time and the need to earn money would never again allow the same fastidious care in the writing of his novels which he had lavished upon *The Radetzky March* in the days when he had been free to spend a morning composing a single sentence. Alcoholism was a slow but certain death sentence, however, and he died in a Parisian charity hospital in May 1939, of pneumonia following delirium tremens.

Between 1923 and 1939, Roth had published some fourteen novels or novellas. In the 1930s *The Radetzky March* was required reading for any student of modern Austrian literature. Exile deprived him of most of the enjoyment of this acclaim, and it was only in the 1960s that a small number of readers began to rediscover him. Although *The Radetzky March* now has the status of an undisputed classic, even in 1989 a German publisher's blurb for a book about him opened with the statement that 'strictly speaking, Joseph Roth must still be classed as a forgotten writer'. If that is true (and I believe it to be somewhat exaggerated by now), the present edition may help to remedy the situation, at least in the English-speaking world.

*

Joseph Roth is above all a great story-teller, and in a world increasingly deprived of magic his narrative seems to work to restore the spell that has been broken, above all the enchantment of the old monarchy. His stories have an elemental quality that sometimes suggests the magical world of the fairy tale: but it is an ambiguous quality. The tale told in *The Radetzky March*, with its long inventories of past glories, of objects, peoples and places in the old Dual Monarchy, evokes an age of simple truths where everyday things acquire a special magic simply because they belong to the past. Yet it is a story which is also replete with disturbing elemental requisites of the fairy tale, like mirrors and pictures and the associated *Doppelgänger* motif, brought to a head in the uncanny scene in Chapter 18 where the Emperor and District Captain Trotta each meet their double (each other): 'And while the Kaiser pointed his left hand at the window, the district captain stretched his right hand in the same direction. And the Kaiser felt he was standing in front of his own mirror image.' For both of them it turns out to be true that to meet your double, as in the old tales, is a harbinger of imminent death.

Drawing upon ancient resources of the story-teller's art, Roth creates a monumental style which is natural, with which we feel at home, but which is in tension with the subject-matter of the book – the modern destabilizing and displacement of the Trottas and their tenuous relationship to their roots in the Slovenian past. For this 'homelessness' and consequent loss of identity the Empire and the Emperor provide a substitute 'home' (of the district captain it is said at one point that he 'was homesick for the Kaiser'!), only to disappear in their turn like God absenting himself from the twentieth-century world, leaving no further points of reference. The fairy-tale 'founding event' of the novel, the rescue of the Emperor from a bullet at Solferino, not only draws down the curse of the Emperor's favour upon the Trottas, making them rather 'fey' in a manner reminiscent of fairy-tale characters placed in the situation of having all their wishes granted (we might think of the Grimm Brothers' 'The Fisherman and his Wife', for example): it also rebounds upon the Emperor himself, who lives long enough to wish that he had not survived Solferino. In making the Hero of Solferino object so vehemently to his own action being turned into an instant legend by the authorities (supposedly for children, though the sub-text is that the subjects of the mon-archy are all meant to be kept in a condition of childlike trust), Roth indicates his own modern awareness of the mythopœic processes at work in the self-creation of the Hapsburg myth, to which he is nonetheless retrospectively contributing. It is this irony and ambiguity which make the novel so different from a mere self-indulgent exercise in nostalgia.

Not that the book lacks a certain indulgence of another kind, particularly in the voluptuousness of its very Austrian awareness of death, reflected overtly in baroque reminders of the Great War just around the corner ('And not one of the Czar's officers and not one of His Apostolic Majesty's officers knew that Death was already crossing his haggard invisible hands over the glass beakers from which the men drank'), and implicitly in the sad fact that Carl Joseph Trotta's attempts to find life, in the form of love and friendship, culminate in the deaths of his lover Frau Slama and his only friend, Dr Demant. There is, further, a sense that all the characters in the novel are going through the motions of living, that their world is already dead but that they are forced to live on in it without conviction until outer events catch up with inner ones and the monarchy is officially declared defunct. While deluding themselves that they are still at home in an intact world, they are already living in a kind of exile, a dreamlike state with which Roth himself was familiar long before his official exile began. (The sense of life as a dream, as shadow or spectacle as much as substance, is also a part of the Austrian tradition, from Grillparzer with his play *A Dream is Life* (1834) to Schnitzler's avowed debt to the Austrian baroque intermingling of life and theatre.) As Count Chojnicki, in many ways the spokesman for the most nihilistic side of Joseph Roth, expresses it in the moment of truth in Chapter 11 where he brings the district captain face to face with his real post-mortem condition: 'the Fatherland no longer exists ... We are all no longer alive!' His words are almost a direct echo of the famous and damning verdict of the North German character, Baron Neuhoff, concerning the 'effete' Viennese in Hugo von Hofmannsthal's comedy *The Difficult Man* (1921): 'All these people in reality no longer exist.'

The death-in-life theme culminates in the regimental party at Chojnicki's country house, where upon the news of the assassination at Sarajevo drunken guests perform a macabre Dance of Death to Chopin's Funeral March, whose tempo accelerates in the hands of the equally drunken musicians. Where all are whirling carelessly towards the impending mass slaughter of the war, the certainty of death clearly has an ironic relish for Roth, as it does in the baroque tradition of the grotesque and often humorous 'memento mori' and its grim satisfaction in the knowledge that the only constant thing is inconstancy itself. (There is an element of retrospective *schadenfreude* in Roth's writing here, for the pace-setters in the irreverent response to the news from Sarajevo are the Hungarian contingent: the Hungarians historically disliked Franz Ferdinand because of his alleged pro-Slav stance, and Roth in turn heartily disliked the Hungarians for this reason.) In this scene, ominously, an individual death has already lost its dignity, a quality which – as the narrator of *The Radetzky March* comments – is going to be rendered ludicrously archaic by the sheer quantity of death in the Great War. I am reminded of the child rescued from a concentration camp at the end of the Second World War who found the sight of a funeral hilarious – so much significance attached to a single death!

A constant in *The Radetzky March*, however, as a counterpoint to death and the inconstancy of human affairs, is the realm of nature. There are many indications that all would have been well for the Trottas if they had not been banished from their Garden of Eden in Sipolje; that the earth and its rhythms outlive empires, and that empires last only as long as they maintain their roots in the soil from which they sprang. The centralizing Austrian system deliberately severs the connections between its most loyal servants and their roots: when Lieutenant Trotta transfers from the cavalry to the infantry, he is not allowed to return to Sipolje, which was his aim in making the transfer. The natural motifs in the novel, however, are a constant subliminal reminder to the reader of a scale of values not dictated by Vienna. The permanent blue of summer skies from a remembered pre-war past, the gently dripping rain that conveys a sense of unendingness, the treacherous, untamed marshlands of the remote border country, to be negotiated safely only by countrymen like the sturdy peasant-soldier Onufrij, provide a backdrop that places momentous political events within a metaphysical perspective. Birdsong is a constant reminder of the natural order of things, symbolically refusing to be drowned out even by the hubbub of the Corpus Christi procession in the heart of Vienna, and ominously leading into the motif of the ravens which suddenly appear on the eve of war and refuse to be put to flight.

Nature references are a part of the music of the novel, which weaves together change and changelessness, movement and stasis, near and yet far, homely and alien – these are concepts that create a kind of *basso continuo* in the novel's composition. In particular, the combination of familiarity and distance is incorporated in the Emperor and in the portrait of the Hero of Solferino hanging in the Trotta home. Similarly, the appeal for Roth of small provincial towns out in the Wild East of the frontier territory is precisely their indefinable position between nature and civilization, the imperceptible merging of town and country at their limits, and their boundless horizons blending near and far in a play on liminality which suggests an outlook truer to the verities of human life than that of the capital.

The relationship of town and landscape implies both the unity and the unlimited vision which is the essence of Roth's ideal monarchy. But it also implies a kind of spiritual unity that we find in the Emperor himself, with his combination of childlike simplicity and far-sighted vision fixed upon the limits of the humanly knowable, where divine knowledge begins: '[his eyes] gazed straight at that soft, fine line that is the frontier between life and death – gazed at the edge of the horizon, which is always seen by the eyes of the old ...'. In the original German this dividing line is referred to as 'Grenze', border or frontier, reinforcing the connection with the frontier towns of Galicia. A metaphor for Roth's existence as a writer is the liminal homeliness of the border areas where, though constantly marginalized as a Jew and a provincial, he feels a sense of belonging, strongly rooted as he is in the spiritual qualities of his native country. Perhaps it was in part that powerful synthesis of marginality and secure roots that appealed to Nadine Gordimer when she wrote a pioneering essay on Roth for the *New York Review of Books* in December 1991, at a time when the search for ethnic origins – as exemplified by the television series, *Roots* – had become a well-established American preoccupation. Is it simply coincidence that the death-bed legacy of old Jacques to the last offspring of the Trottas is precisely a root? 'There's ... a piece of root, for fever. Give that to your son, Carl Joseph. My best regards to him. He can use the root, that area's swampy.' When the district captain travels up to Galicia to visit his son, he is afraid of the frontier and takes with him his old service revolver. But instead of the bears and wolves he had half expected, he finds nothing he can fight, only the nameless fears of liminality itself and a terrifying vision of the death of Austria (and therefore, as far as he is concerned, of the death of meaning) not perceptible from Vienna.

The sense of not being 'at home in the interpreted world', in Rilke's famous phrase, is very much an Austrian one, and in Roth's case leads to a constant reassuring reference back to his roots, as well as to a cult of the simple old Emperor as transcendent symbol of the better Austria, instinctively in touch with the peasant basis of his state, and providing a living testament to the existence of an intact world not yet brought low by the cynics and string-pullers of Vienna who only serve to come between base and pinnacle. The symbiotic relationship of monarch and peasant, the two-way relationship by virtue of which each is really the servant of the other, can very easily be criticized (and has been) as ideologically naive, if not dangerous, because it obscures the real relations of power in the state. It might appear especially dangerous in the context of the early 1930s, when a Führer waited in the wings to step in and establish exclusive rights to understanding the will of the people: but the contemporary context serves if anything to bring out the harmlessness of Roth's retrospective wish-fulfilment and the poetic nature of his vision of an intact and integrated world.

The symbols of the integrity of the old Dual Monarchy are many in the novel. The ubiquitous portrait of the monarch is one of them, but so is the railway network that with utter uniformity links every corner of the Empire; or the weight of shared history (which can also be stifling, as epitomized by the case of Carl Joseph Trotta, who cannot escape from his ancestors) evoked by the strains of the *Radetzky March* itself; or the way that a whole culture can be caught in the description of food (as in modern 'food movies' like *Babette's Feast*), as more than once happens with descriptions of the district captain's – a Spartan and yet an Austrian in his enjoyment of food – meal-time ceremonies. But the symbol *par excellence* of the principle that binds the old world together is the idealized master–servant relationship, linking the district captain, his servant Jacques, and the Emperor in a moment of chill insight when Trotta senior realizes that the death of Jacques is no isolated event: 'If Jacques dies, it occurred to the district captain, then in a sense the Hero of Solferino will die once again and perhaps – and here Herr von Trotta's heart skipped a beat – the man whom the Hero of Solferino had rescued from death.' The master–servant relationship is all too easy to sentimentalize, as Roth is well aware (he foregrounds the point himself in his comments on the touching, doglike loyalty of the army servant, Onufrij, to his officer, Carl Joseph), but it is a topos that throughout the history of literature has been used as a touchstone for the level of civilization prevailing in a given society, from the comedies of Plautus or Terence, down to *The Marriage of Figaro*, Hofmannsthal's *The Difficult Man* – closer to *The Radetzky March*, set in Vienna in the same period, and opening with a brilliant comic scene of a brash, modern servant attempting to displace the faithful family retainer – and, a recent example, Kazuo Ishiguro's prize-winning novel *The Remains of the Day*, analysing late- and post-imperial England through its treatment of a dedicated butler.

At the heart of *The Radetzky March* is an implicit criticism of the Hapsburg military-bureaucratic, centralized system for its failure, through no fault of the Emperor himself, to value sufficiently the loyalty of its servants outside the charmed Imperial circle, and above all to use the loyalty of the Slavs of the Empire to create a truly equal system of partnership in a triple monarchy along with the Germans and Hungarians. Here, indeed, in Roth's view lies the real reason for the decline and collapse of the supranational Empire. One of the most savagely honest moments in the novel occurs at the outbreak of war, when the demoralized Austrian army retreats across Galicia, viciously compensating for the military débâcle by murdering its 'own' population, which, it is now clear, it has neither really trusted nor felt any kinship with. The real alienation between the Austro-Hungarian officer class and the provincial subjects of the Emperor, suggested throughout the novel, now appears in undisguised form, as 'the shots of executioners carrying out hasty sentences rang from the church squares of hamlets and villages, and the somber rolls of drums accompanied the monotonous decisions of judges, and the wives of victims lay shrieking for mercy before the mud-caked boots of officers'. Lieutenant Carl Joseph Trotta expresses his own, typically silent and private protest by burying single-handed three of these Slav victims, and later dies a death which 'takes back' Austrian history – and the heroic deed of his grandfather at Solferino – by suicidally attempting under fire to fetch water for his thirsty platoon. It is a useless gesture, and one 'not suitable for textbooks in the elementary schools and high schools of Imperial and Royal Austria'. But it is also a noble gesture, the spirit of which has survived in Roth's novel long after all the Imperial and Royal textbooks have been swept away. It is significant, metaphorically speaking, that the fierce thirst of Carl Joseph's men (the physical equivalent of a long-standing Slav thirst for justice?) arises precisely out of the murderous actions of Austrian officers on their own territory, for 'the wells were stuffed with corpses of people who had been shot or strung up'. The dying Carl Joseph receives absolution from his Slav troops: 'From below the Ukrainian peasants in his platoon chorused, "Praised be Jesus Christ!".' It is an undeservedly generous absolution for the whole of the Empire.

The moment of Carl Joseph's death is the culmination of the novel's questioning of conventional notions of heroism, and the apotheosis of an alternative, modern and in many ways much more difficult heroic stance: a life lived stoically in confusion and isolation, and above all in increasing self-reflection and self-consciousness. The one impulsive reflex action immortalized in legend was so much easier for the Hero of Solferino, and a seductively simple model for his descendants. Contemplating his son's fate, Herr von Trotta muses that 'he [himself] was all alone in this world. And this world too was going under ... and his son was likewise alone and perhaps, being younger, was closer to the collapse of the world. How simple the world had always looked! the district captain mused. There were rules of conduct for every situation in life.' In terms of political history, this is precisely the feeling that fascist parties have fed upon (we are seeing its equivalent in the confusion of Russia and Eastern Germany today). But Roth carefully distances himself from any such seductive promises of a return to simplicity, just as, however reactionary he may have become in his later years, he always expressed the utmost loathing for Nazism. On the few occasions when Lieutenant Trotta tries to take decisive action in the spirit of his heroic grandfather, the results are either farcical or disastrous, and he increasingly grows to dislike the anachronistic certainties of army life, exposed for him as particularly inadequate when in Chapter 14 he is given the task of leading a squad of soldiers in putting down a legitimate strike demonstration.

Interestingly, the supposedly reactionary Roth of 1932 encourages sympathy for the plight of the workers, and does not demonize the angry crowd of strikers as a bestial mob, the standard literary treatment of riots and political crowds in bourgeois writing, from Dickens (*A Tale of Two Cities*) to Disraeli (*Sybil*), Hugo (*Les Misérables*), Zola (*Germinal*) and Manzoni (*I promessi sposi*), right up to Elias Canetti's *Crowds and Power*, where the crowd is seen as a unitary phenomenon stripped of all social and historical specificity. It is striking that Roth has none of this, and indeed characteristically breaks the crowd down into impressionistic isolated fragments. If the crowd is not an abstract unity, neither does Lieutenant Trotta have ready a single, abstract answer to the terrible conundrum of his situation. Crushed between two imperatives, 'he saw the times rolling toward one another like two rocks, and he himself, the lieutenant, was smashed between them ...': 'tangled voices in his heart enjoined him to show now pity, now cruelty, reminded him of what his grandfather would have done in this situation, predicted that he himself would die the next moment, and also presented his own death as the only possible and desirable outcome of this battle'.

Trotta's failure to measure up to the anachronistic certainties of the army is built into this 'no win' situation, which is an echo of famous instances in German history when the military supplied brutal answers to legitimate civilian questions about the misuse of state power by governments: the putting down of starving Silesian weavers in 1844, for instance, or the scandal of harsh treatment of civilians by the military in Zabern in Prussian Alsace as late as 1913. Roth's perception of the true, insulated position of the army *vis à vis* the strikers is shown by the fact that at precisely the moment when the working population is at breaking point, and strikes and political unrest hit the headlines, gambling fever breaks out among the bored and redundant military of the remote garrison town. One of the worst faults of Trotta's fellow officers is the opposite of his own: whereas he cannot forget the past, they cannot remember it, thanks to their criminal frivolity and to 'their natural faculty for forgetting'. The frivolity and short-sightedness of the pre-war officer class is a theme Roth will stress especially in his late novel, *The Capuchin Crypt*.

The dominance of the military mentality over civic life is a fact of German and Austrian history up until the First World War, and is well reflected in the novel in the subservience of civilians in the face of the military ethos. The institution of duelling which kills the essentially civilian Dr Demant and, even worse, simultaneously leads him to commit an offence against the hippocratic oath by killing his opponent, was the most obviously anachronistic of devices (tolerated even longer in the Austrian than in the Prussian army) to maintain awareness among the population of the army's monopoly of violence. The duel was neither a just nor a suitable means to convey to society a dignified picture of the officer corps. But it was useful to the military authorities, intent upon the isolation of the officer from society and its dangerous influences, and – to quote a social historian – 'preferring an unpleasant image of the officer to one which might invite fraternization with other social classes'.

In contrast to the static outlook of the army, the movement in the novel in general is away from the rigid routines, rituals and stability of the old Austrian world, so fixed and permanent for the district captain that his routine appears to have become part of the natural order of things and any alteration to it seems monstrous. At the beginning of the book, change has been firmly ruled out: and yet it was always there in the lives of the Trottas. Rather as in *Buddenbrooks*, Thomas Mann's classic turn-of-the-century novel depicting the decline of a family, circumstances force upon the dynasty an increasing awareness of the problematical nature of existence, expressed in increasing self-reflection and self-consciousness. So, for example, the district captain eventually follows his son in the experience of gazing interrogatively upon the portrait of the Hero of Solferino, his father, and seeing it dissolve into the brush strokes of which it is constituted. As his father – along with the Emperor, another father figure – is the district captain's main point of reference, the metaphor of disintegration includes himself. A recurrent motif signifying their loss of confidence and growing introspection is the characters' difficulty in knowing how to 'inscribe' themselves. What starts out as a formal prescribed task, the dutiful exchange of letters between father and son, becomes progressively harder to perform as events have the temerity to intervene, bringing the disturbingly complex nature of life into ever greater prominence. The consequent embarrassment each finds in writing reflects the gradual erosion of a personal sense of authenticity. There is an almost comic variation on the theme when, as the war is about to engulf the world they inhabit, the officers of the dragoon regiment agonize for many man-hours over the form of their invitation to the regimental centenary celebration.

And yet the unquestioning sense of authenticity that was present in the first of the Trotta line was not truly a personal one, but derived from a system where by common consent society agreed to set the Emperor up as signifier of the state's patriarchal values. What is remarkable is that Roth, unlike many writers of the modern period in his part of the world (Kafka above all) on one level mourns the demise of the patriarchy. Psychoanalysts will no doubt draw their own conclusions from the vagueness or even the absence of mother figures in *The Radetzky March*; the misogynist aspects of the novel reflected in the harsh treatment meted out to Frau Demant and the district captain's housekeeper, Fräulein Hirschwitz; and the fact that the women with whom Carl Joseph becomes involved are explicitly turned into mother substitutes. Perhaps by way of compensation for and reflection of his own lack of a father figure, Roth creates a world in which the father is all-important, and then follows through the process of the father's gradual disappearance. Carl Joseph initially feels himself to be the son of his grandfather (whom he physically resembles) and only in adult life becomes truly his father's son as the father's patriarchal claims are dissipated and the collapsing order around them brings them closer together. By the end of the novel the process has gone so far that Trotta junior feels more adult and wiser than his father. Yet Roth also shows that the patriarchal figure *par excellence*, the Emperor, original source of all patriarchy, is a simple soul whose real freedom of action is severely curtailed and who is reduced to childish subterfuges in order to outwit his court officials and enjoy even a moment's semblance of real life. At the heart of the system is a vacuum supported only by the willing suspension of disbelief among the Empire's subjects.

Seen in a more positive perspective, Trotta's development cannot only be regarded as a decline, since he effectively sets out on a path to emancipation from tutelage and towards individualism. A milestone on that path is his unilateral decision to quit the army. It is one of his first steps to a genuinely individual existence, in contrast to the life at second hand he has previously lived, in which his army career was decided for him by his father (who would have made a better soldier, and wants to do so vicariously); his first passion for a woman involved another man's wife, and after her death his father discreetly settled the affair behind Carl Joseph's back; his mistress really belonged to another man (Frau von Taussig, Chojnicki's long-standing paramour); and even his gambling debts are incurred at second hand, through Captain Wagner, Trotta not being bold enough to enter into anything so full-blooded. It is noteworthy that the generation to which Carl Joseph belongs are addictive and compulsive by nature, and this too is perhaps a sign of their incomplete emancipation. The lieutenant himself is compelled to repeat history, paro-distically, by 'saving the Emperor' time after time in the form of the famous portrait, which is rescued from the most undignified places. He also lapses into alcoholism. The latter is wonderfully described by Roth, clearly from first-hand knowledge; but so are the gambling fever of Captain Wagner and the compulsive serial acquisition by Frau von Taussig of fresh young lieutenants as lovers, and as a kind of constantly renewed elixir of youth. Such symptoms of decline and deca-dence in one way resemble the last involuntary convulsions of a dying body. But decline is never a permanent state, and in the case of Carl Joseph genuine emancipation and free will (with all their attendant terrors) are also in prospect, except that the war intervenes to prevent him reaching such a point of maturity.

The texture of a book is as important in its achievement of classic status as its subject-matter, and this is emphatically the case with *The Radetzky March*. All of Roth's training as a *Feuilletonist* goes into set-piece descriptions like the atmospheric scene in Chapter 4 at Sergeant Slama's house when Carl

Joseph goes with a bad conscience to offer his condolences for
the death of Slama's wife; or the careful milieu-description of
old Jacques' house, as unfamiliar as an undiscovered land for
his master, who has never before crossed that threshold; or
the thunderstorm at the regimental party, when the news of
Sarajevo arrives almost as though it were a scene from a
second-rate melodrama. His skill and subtlety as a writer are
apparent in the retrospective exposition in Chapter 6 of Carl
Joseph's fatal relationship with Frau Demant, and in the
parallels in the text which establish links between the two
visits of condolence he carries out to Sergeant Slama and
Frau Demant respectively; or between the collarbone injury
sustained by the Hero of Solferino while saving his Emperor,
and the identical injury suffered by Carl Joseph during the
ugly strike episode; or between the fate of the Trottas and that
of the unfortunate barber who by pleasing the Emperor earns
a promotion he does not want, since it means he must serve
longer in the army.

A delicate feature of the text is the way that various aspects
of what we take to be reality are refracted or toned down,
sensitively rendered so that a veil is interposed between us
and the world of the senses. Time can play tricks, become
variable, and be frozen in certain moments like a tableau or
a scene in a waxworks. In the descriptions of interiors, sunlight
is typically filtered and diffused, so that culture retains the
upper hand over nature, and nothing is too precisely presented
or too crassly picked out. The impressionism of the style
likewise filters experience through an individual's perceptions,
for the most part those of Carl Joseph Trotta, an intriguingly
silent and inarticulate personality who is sadly but perfectly
attuned to the mood of a declining world. He seems forever
to tremble on the verge of explicit, overt verbalization, but
never quite achieves it; his sensitivity emerges with difficulty
from the repressive influence of his stern, bureaucratic father
and his narrow religion of duty to the monarchy. Although
the novel never collapses into subjectivity, it has much in
common with the Austrian experimental novel of subjectivity
such as Robert Musil's *Törless* or Rainer Maria Rilke's *Malte
Laurids Brigge*. On the other hand, it also has something of the

epic scale and leisurely pace of the nineteenth-century realist novel. It achieves a coming to terms with the past in the sense that the stately tempo of the monarchy's decline is reflected in its pages and abruptness avoided, except at the very end as the war explodes upon the scene. The sharpness is taken out of historical events by concentration on the interest of the personal: the personal tragedy is dulled by its impersonal setting in the wider panoramic setting of history.

One consolation that never fails in Roth's vision of a faltering, increasingly alienated reality is the *ultimate* reality, the perpetual round of the seasons and the life which is in tune with them and the demands of the earth. All the Trottas instinctively strive to return to the 'earthy' life of their fore-bears (and of Roth's mother, as he describes her), from which service to the father figure – be it a real father, or the Emperor – deflects them, but to which in two cases they do manage to return: the grandfather permanently, and the grandson only temporarily, until history in the form of the Great War summons him back to the army to die for it. As with *Budden-brooks*, in the end nothing matters except that the earth continues to turn and be peopled. In *The Radetzky March*, District Captain Trotta returns to the *Volk*, to the crowd from which his family came before the stigma of Solferino, and under a steadily weeping sky waits patiently with them in the grounds of Schönbrunn Castle for news of the dying Emperor. Fittingly, a gardener from the Schönbrunn Park momentarily interrupts his ceaseless business, and, spade in hand, comes to ask them, ' "How's he doing?" And the onlookers – foresters, coachmen, minor officials, janitors, and war veterans like the father of the Hero of Solferino – replied: "No news. He's dying!".' The gardener took off, went with his spade to dig up the flower beds, the eternal earth. Rain was falling, quiet, dense, and increasingly denser.' There is nothing more to be said.

Alan Bance

SELECT BIBLIOGRAPHY

WORKS IN ENGLISH

CHAMBERS, HELEN, ed., *Co-existent Contradictions. Joseph Roth in Retrospect* (Leeds University Symposium, 1989), Ariadne Press, Riverside, CA, 1991.

GORDIMER, NADINE, 'The Empire of Joseph Roth', *New York Review of Books*, 5 December 1991, 16–21. The best general introduction for the non-specialist reader.

MATHEW, CELINE, *Ambivalence and Irony in the Works of Joseph Roth*, Peter Lang, Frankfurt am Main, 1984.

WORKS IN GERMAN

ARNOLD, HEINZ LUDWIG, ed., *Joseph Roth*, Edition Text + Kritik, Richard Boorberg, Munich, 1974.

BRONSEN, DAVID, *Joseph Roth: eine Biographie*, abridged version ed. Katharina Ochse, Kiepenheuer & Witsch, Cologne, 1993. Bronsen's biography represents a massive scholarly achievement. Helen Chambers' English translation of the abridged version is currently in progress, and will appear with Chatto & Windus.

HACKERT, FRITZ, *Kulturpessimismus und Erzählform. Studien zu Joseph Roths Leben und Werk*, Peter Lang, Bern, 1967.

KESSLER, MICHAEL and HACKERT, FRITZ, eds., *Joseph Roth: Interpretation, Kritik, Rezeption*, Stauffenberg, Tübingen, 1990.

KRASKE, BERND M., ed., *Joseph Roth: Werk und Wirkung*, Bouvier, Bonn, 1988.

MUELLER-FUNK, WOLFGANG, *Joseph Roth*, C. H. Beck, Munich, 1989.

NÜRNBERGER, HELMUT, *Joseph Roth. Mit Selbstzeugnissen und Bilddokumenten*, Rowohlt Taschenbuch, Reinbek bei Hamburg, 1981. Non-readers of German may still be fascinated by the wealth of pictorial material.

CHRONOLOGY

DATE	AUTHOR'S LIFE	LITERARY CONTEXT
1894	Born (2 September) in Brody, Austrian Galicia, of Jewish parents. As a boy, Roth lived in his grandfather's house in Brody with his mother after the father was committed to an asylum; spent summer holidays with an uncle (mother's brother) in Lemberg.	Rilke: *Leben und Lieder.* H. Mann: *In einer Familie.* Schnitzler: *Das Märchen.* Hamsun: *Pan.* Kipling: *The Jungle Book.*
1895		Fontane: *Effi Briest.* Schnitzler: *Light-o'-Love.* Wedekind: *Earth Spirit.* Crane: *The Red Badge of Courage.*
1896		Altenberg: *Wie ich es sehe.* Fontane: *Die Poggenpuhls.* Sudermann: *Morituri.* Chekhov: *The Seagull.*
1897		Rilke: *Traumgekrönt.* Strindberg: *Inferno.*
1898		Schnitzler: *Die Frau des Weisen.* T. Mann: *Little Herr Friedemann.* Zola: *J'accuse.*
1899		Rilke: *Mir zur Feier.* Schnitzler: *Leutnant Gustl; Frau Berta Gartan.* Hauptmann: *Fuhrmann Henschel.* Fontane: *Der Stechlin.* Tolstoy: *Resurrection.* Ibsen: *When We Dead Awaken.* James: *The Awkward Age.*
1900	Attends Jewish community school in Brody (to 1905).	Schnitzler: *Reigen.*
1901		T. Mann: *Buddenbrooks.* Strindberg: *Dance of Death.* Chekhov: *Three Sisters.*
1902		Wedekind: *Pandora's Box.* Rilke: *The Book of Pictures.* Gide: *L'Immoraliste.* James: *The Wings of the Dove.*

Franz Joseph I Austrian Emperor since 1848. Dreyfus trial begins in France. Resignation of Gladstone in Britain. Death of Alexander III in Russia; accession of Nicholas II.

Lumière brothers invent cinematograph. Marconi invents wireless telegraphy. Freud's *Studien über Hysterie* inaugurates psychoanalysis. X-rays discovered (Röntgen).

Wilhelm II announces German pursuit of 'world politics'. Theodor Herzl, founder of modern political Zionism, publishes *Der Judenstaat*, putting forward the idea of a Jewish national home in Palestine.

Assassination of Elisabeth, wife of Franz Joseph I, in Geneva. First Zionist Congress in Basel. Vienna *Sezession* led by painter Gustav Klimt and architect Otto Wagner, to further modern (*Jugendstil*) movement. German Navy Law begins the arms race. Death of Bismarck. Curies discover radium.

Renewal of *Ausgleich* of 1867 (established Dual Monarchy of Austria–Hungary) following agitation for its repeal and (in 1897) breakdown in constitutional government and rule by Imperial decree. *Die Fackel* (edited by Karl Kraus) founded. Berlin *Sezession* founded by *avant-garde* artists under Max Liebermann. Schoenberg: *Verklärte Nacht*.

Beginning of severe recession in Austria–Hungary (to 1907). Bülow Chancellor of Germany. Freud: *The Interpretation of Dreams*. First Zeppelin. Death of Queen Victoria; accession of Edward VII. Roosevelt US President after McKinley's assassination. First wireless communication between Europe and US. Picasso's 'blue period' (to 1904).
Triple Alliance (Germany, Austria, Italy) renewed to 1914. Klimt's revolutionary 'Beethovenfries' at the Vienna *Sezession* Exhibition.

DATE	AUTHOR'S LIFE	LITERARY CONTEXT
1903		T. Mann: *Tristan*; *Tonio Kröger*. Hauptmann: *Rosa Bernd*. Shaw: *Man and Superman*. Butler: *The Way of all Flesh*. James: *The Ambassadors*.
1904		Hofmannsthal: *Elektra*. Pirandello: *The Late Mattia Pascal*. Conrad: *Nostromo*.
1905	Attends grammar school in Brody (to 1913).	Rilke: *The Book of Hours*. H. Mann: *Professor Unrat*.
1906		Hofmannsthal: *Oepidus and the Sphinx*. Wedekind: *Spring Awakening*. Musil: *Young Törless*. Galsworthy: *The Man of Property*.
1907		Rilke: *New Poems* (to 1908). Strindberg: *The Ghost Sonata*. Conrad: *The Secret Agent*.
1908		Altenberg: *Märchen des Lebens*. Schnitzler: *Der Weg ins Freie*. Maeterlinck: *L'Oiseau bleu*.
1909		Rilke: *Requiem*. H. Mann: *Die kleine Stadt*. Bely: *The Silver Dove*. Gide: *La Porte étroite*.
1910	Death of father who had been insane since before Roth's birth.	Rilke: *Sketches of Malte Laurids Brigge*. Forster: *Howards End*.
1911		Altenberg: *Neues Altes*. Hauptmann: *Die Ratten*. Conrad: *Under Western Eyes*. Pound: *Canzoni*.
1912		T. Mann: *Death in Venice*. Kafka: *Amerika*. Hesse: *Rosshalde*. Hofmannsthal: *Everyman*. Pound: *Ripostes*.
1913	Gains school-leaving certificate with distinction. Enrols at University of Lemberg (winter semester).	Trakl: *Gedichte*. Alain Fournier: *Le Grand Meaulnes*. Proust: *Remembrance of Things Past* (to 1927). Gorky: *Childhood*. Lawrence: *Sons and Lovers*.

CHRONOLOGY

DATE	AUTHOR'S LIFE	LITERARY CONTEXT
1914	Enrols at University of Vienna and studies German literature.	Rilke: *Fünf Gesänge.* Bahr: *Expressionism.* Joyce: *Dubliners.*
1915		H. Mann: *Emile Zola.* Kafka: *Metamorphosis.* Ford: *The Good Soldier.*
1916	Volunteers in Austrian rifle regiment.	Brod: *Tycho Brahes Weg zu Gott.* Bahr: *Himmelfahrt.* Joyce: *A Portrait of the Artist as a Young Man.*
1917	Is sent to the army press office in Galicia.	Eliot: *Prufrock and other Observations.* Pound: *Cantos 1–3.*
1918	Back in Vienna during December; then returns east, becoming involved in the Czech–Ukrainian war.	Altenberg: *Vita ipsa.* Kaiser: *Gas.* Kraus: *The Last Days of Mankind.* H. Mann: *Der Untertan* (1st of *Kaiserreich* trilogy). T. Mann: *Reflections of an Unpolitical Man.* Spengler: *The Decline of the West.*
1919	Returns to Vienna, taking up journalism.	Altenberg: *Mein Lebensabend.* Dos Passos: *One Man's Initiation.* Hesse: *Demian.* Kafka: *A Country Doctor.*
1920	Moves to Berlin.	Döblin: *Wallenstein.* Zamyatin: *We.* S. Zweig: *Drei Meister.* Lawrence: *Women in Love.* Wharton: *The Age of Innocence.*
1921		Hašek: *The Good Soldier Švejk.* Hofmannsthal: *The Difficult Man.* Pirandello: *Six Characters in Search of an Author.* Dos Passos: *Three Soldiers.*
1922	Marries Friederike Reichler.	Brecht: *Baal; Drums in the Night.* S. Zweig: *Amok.* Hesse: *Siddhartha.* Bely: *Petersburg.* Valéry: *Charmes.* Eliot: *The Waste Land.* Joyce: *Ulysses.* Woolf: *Jacob's Room.*

CHRONOLOGY

Heir to Austro-Hungarian throne, Archduke Franz Ferdinand d'Este and his wife, Sophie, assassinated in Sarajevo (June). Austria–Hungary declares war on Serbia (July). World War I breaks out (August). Austrian armies suffer heavy defeats (1914–15) when Russia invades Galicia. President Wilson proclaims US neutrality.

Serbia and Poland overrun by Austro-Hungarian and German troops. Entry of Italy into the war. Heavy fighting at Gallipoli. Sinking of the *Lusitania*.

Death of Emperor Franz Joseph; accession of Charles I. Murder of Austrian premier Stürgh; growing unpopularity of war leads to rioting. Tzara founds Dada movement in Zürich. Jung: *The Psychology of the Unconscious*.

US enters war on Allied side. February Revolution in Russia; fall of monarchy. Lenin's return to Russia; October (Bolshevik) Revolution. Italians defeated by Austrian army at Caporetto (October). Balfour Declaration promises a Jewish homeland in Palestine. Freud: *Introductory Lectures*.

Wilson's Fourteen Points (January); point 10 includes notion of self-determination for the nationalities of Austria–Hungary. Russia signs peace of Brest-Litovsk with Germany and Austria–Hungary (March). Italian troops overwhelm Austrian forces (October). End of World War I (November). Collapse of Austrian Empire; abdication of Charles I; Austrian republic declared. Balkan countries declare independence. Abdication of Wilhelm II in Germany. Assassination of Nicholas II in Russia. Russian Civil War (to 1921).

Treaty of Versailles. Weimar Republic constituted; a 'Soviet Republic' established in Munich and swiftly repressed. Bauhaus founded by Walter Gropius. Rutherford splits the atom.

New Austrian constitution. Socialist leader Renner first Chancellor (to 1924). Struggle between Social Democrats and Christian Socialists dominates Austrian politics. The Kapp *putsch* defeated by Berlin workers. First meeting of League of Nations. Irish Civil War. Prohibition in US.

New Economic Policy in Russia. Rise of Fascism in Italy. Schoenberg's Suite Op. 25, his first work wholly in the 12-note method. Serialist composers Webern and Berg also working in Vienna at this time.

Mussolini's march on Rome; Italian Fascists come to power. USSR founded. Stalin General Secretary of Russian Communist Party Central Committee. In Germany, political assassinations of Erzberger and Rathenau by right-wing extremists. Max Weber: *Economy and Society*. Wittgenstein: *Tractatus Logico-Philosophicus*.

DATE	AUTHOR'S LIFE	LITERARY CONTEXT
1923	*Das Spinnennetz* (*The Spider's Web*).	Rilke: *Sonnets to Orpheus; Duino Elegies.* T. Mann: *Von deutscher Republik.* Svevo: *The Confessions of Zeno.* Gorky: *My Universities.*
1924	*Hotel Savoy; Die Rebellion.*	T. Mann: *The Magic Mountain.* Musil: *Drei Frauen.* Trotsky: *Literature and Revolution.* Ford: *Parade's End* (to 1928).
1925	In Paris as correspondent of the *Frankfurter Zeitung*.	Kafka: *The Trial.* Hitler: *Mein Kampf.* S. Zweig: *Volpone.* Zuckmayer: *Der fröhliche Weinberg.* Bulgakov: *The White Guard.* Fitzgerald: *The Great Gatsby.*
1926	Visits Soviet Union, after loss of Paris post.	Kafka: *The Castle.* Brecht: *Mann ist Mann.* Schnitzler: *Traumnovelle.* Babel: *Red Cavalry.*
1927	Leaves *Frankfurter Zeitung* where he worked as reporter, then editor. *Die Flucht ohne Ende* (*Flight Without End*); *Juden auf Wanderschaft* (essays).	Hesse: *Der Steppenwolf.* A. Zweig: *The Case of Sergeant Grischa.* S. Zweig: *Verwirrung der Gefühle.* Brod: *Eine Frau, nach der man sich sehnt.* Woolf: *To the Lighthouse.*
1928	*Zipper und sein Vater* – heralds his success as a novelist. Beginning of his wife's schizophrenia.	Hofmannsthal: *The Tower.* H. Mann: *Eugénie oder Die Bürgerzeit.* Nabokov: *King, Queen, Knave.* Waugh: *Decline and Fall.*
1929	*Der Stumme Prophet* (*The Silent Prophet*); *Rechts und Links* (*Right and Left*). Meets Andrea Manga Bell. Works for Munich paper (to 1930).	Remarque: *All Quiet on the Western Front.* Döblin: *Berlin Alexanderplatz.* Kraus: *Literatur und Lüge.* Sholokhov: *And Quiet Flows the Don.* Faulkner: *The Sound and the Fury.* Hemingway: *A Farewell to Arms.* Graves: *Goodbye to All That.*

CHRONOLOGY

Failure of Hitler's Munich *putsch*. French occupy Ruhr. Rampant inflation in Germany. In Austria, years of economic instability, poverty and unemployment give rise to extremist groups, both Leftist and Pan-German (Nazi). Ottoman Empire ends. Le Corbusier: *Towards a New Architecture*.

Death of Lenin. First Labour government in Britain under Ramsay MacDonald. André Breton: Surrealist Manifesto.

Hindenburg elected as second Chancellor of German Republic, in succession to Elbert. Berg: *Wozzek*. Eisenstein: *The Battleship Potemkin*.

General strike in Britain. Germany admitted to League of Nations.

Social Democrat riots in Vienna following acquittal of Nazis for political murder. Formation of *Heimwehr*, or bourgeois private army, to challenge the activities of Socialists' illegal armed bands. Trotsky expelled from Russian Communist Party. Lindbergh flies Atlantic solo.

Stalin de facto dictator in USSR: first Five Year Plan. Brecht/Weill: *Threepenny Opera*. Heidegger: *Time and Being*. Discovery of penicillin by A. Fleming.

Wall Street Crash: world economic crisis. Stalin's collectivization of agriculture of USSR begins. Yugoslavia formed.

DATE	AUTHOR'S LIFE	LITERARY CONTEXT
1930	*Hiob* (*Job*); *Panoptikum* (essays). *Die Flucht ohne Ende* (*Flight Without End*) published in English translation by Hutchinson (UK) and Doubleday (US).	T. Mann: *Mario and the Magician*; *Die Forderung des Tages*. Hesse: *Narziss and Goldmund*. Musil: *The Man without Qualities*. Sudermann: *The Dance of Youth*.
1931		H. Mann: *Geist und Tat*. Zuckmayer: *The Captain of Köpenick*. Horváth: *Tales from the Vienna Woods*.
1932	*Radetzkymarsch* (*The Radetzky March*).	Broch: *The Sleepwalkers*. Hesse: *Morgenlandfahrt*. Huxley: *Brave New World*. Céline: *Journey to the End of the Night*.
1933	Roth's work burnt by Nazis. Emigrates to Paris: works on journals and newspapers for exiles.	Mann: *The Tales of Jakob* (first of *Joseph* tetralogy). Lorca: *Blood Wedding*.
1934	Lives in South of France (to June 1935).	Broch: *The Unknown Quantity*. Weinheber: *Adel und Untergang*. Fitzgerald: *Tender is the Night*.
1935	*Die Büste des Kaisers*; *Tarabas, ein Gast auf dieser Erde* (*Tarabus: A Guest on Earth*). Returns to Paris.	Klausmann: *Symphonie pathétique*. H. Mann: *Die Jugend des Königs Henri Quatre* (2nd vol. 1938). Brecht: *Furcht und Elend des Dritten Reiches* (to 1938). Döblin: *Pardon wird nicht gegeben*. Canetti: *Auto da Fé*.
1936	*Die hundert Tage*; *Beichte eines Mörders*. Amsterdam (March–June), Ostend (July), Paris (late 1936).	K. Mann: *Mephisto*. H. Mann: *Es kommt der Tag*. Lorca: *La Casa de Bernarda Alba*. Faulkner: *Absalom, Absalom!*
1937	*Das falsche Gewicht* (*Weights and Measures*). Travels to Poland, stays in Vienna. Paris again.	Brecht: *The Life of Galileo* (to 1939). Nabokov: *The Gift*. Hemingway: *To Have and Have Not*.

CHRONOLOGY

HISTORICAL EVENTS

In Austria Social Democrats replace Christian Socialists as largest single party but are still obliged to rely for support on the pan-German groups. Freud: *Civilization and its Discontents*. Brecht/Weill: *Aufstieg und Fall der Stadt Mahagonny*.

Austrian customs union with Germany; failure of largest bank in Austria. Collapse of government. Christian Socialists returned to power and customs union renounced.

Roosevelt President of the US: New Deal. Dollfuss becomes Austrian Chancellor; allies with *Heimwehr* group and pursues a line independent from both pan-Germans and Socialists, antagonizing both. First autobahn, Cologne–Bonn, opened.

In Germany, Nazis under Hitler come to power by constitutional means but swiftly establish one-party state with violent suppression of opponents; beginning of the Third Reich. Jung: *Modern Man in Search of a Soul*.

Socialists rise against *Heimwehr*; for one week Vienna and other Austrian cities in state of civil war. Rebels crushed and leaders executed. Dollfuss murdered. Succeeded by Schuschnigg. Stringent laws against political violence; under new constitution Austrian independence effectively surrendered to Germany.
Nuremberg Laws depriving Jews in Germany of citizenship. Italy invades Abyssinia. Berg: *Lulu*.

Outbreak of Spanish Civil War. Abdication of Edward VIII in Britain. Stalin's Great Purges in Russia (to 1938).

Religious persecution in Germany. Rome–Berlin axis formed. Japanese invade China. Orff: *Carmina Burana*.

DATE	AUTHOR'S LIFE	LITERARY CONTEXT
1938	*Die Kapuzinergruft* (*The Capuchin Crypt*). Last visit to Vienna; last visit to Amsterdam. Declining health.	Beckett: *Murphy.* Sartre: *Nausea.*
1939	*Die Legende vom heiligen Trinker*; *Die Geschichte der 1002. Nacht.* Dies as a result of alcoholism (May).	T. Mann: *Lotte in Weimar.* S. Zweig: *Beware of Pity.* Joyce: *Finnegans Wake.* Isherwood: *Goodbye to Berlin.* Steinbeck: *The Grapes of Wrath.*

CHRONOLOGY

PART ONE

Chapter 1

THE TROTTAS WERE a young dynasty. Their progenitor had been knighted after the Battle of Solferino. He was a Slovene. Sipolje—the German name for his native village—became his title of nobility. Fate had elected him for a special deed. But he then made sure that later times lost all memory of him.

At the Battle of Solferino, he, as an infantry lieutenant, commanded a platoon. The fighting had been raging for half an hour. Three paces ahead of him, he could see the white backs of his soldiers. The front line of his platoon was kneeling, the second line standing. All the men were cheery and confident of victory. They had lavishly devoured food and liquor at the expense of and in honor of the Kaiser, who had been in the field since yesterday. Here and there, a soldier fell from the line. Trotta swiftly leaped into every gap, shooting from the orphaned rifles of the dead or wounded. By turns he serried the thinned rank or widened it, his eyes sharpened a hundredfold, peering in many directions, his ears straining in many directions. Right through the rattling of guns, his quick ears caught his captain's few, loud orders. His sharp eyes broke through the blue-gray fog curtaining the enemy's lines. He never shot without aiming, and his every last bullet struck home. The men sensed his hand and his gaze, heard his shouts, and felt confident.

The enemy paused. The command scurried along the interminable front rank: "Stop shooting!" Here and there a ramrod still clattered, here and there a shot rang out, belated and lonesome. The blue-gray fog between the fronts lifted slightly. All at once, they were in the noonday warmth of the cloudy, silvery, thundery sun. Now, between the lieutenant and the backs of the soldiers, the Kaiser appeared with two staff officers.

He held a field glass supplied by one of his escorts and was about to place it on his eyes. Trotta knew what that meant: even assuming that the enemy was retreating, the rear guard must still be facing the Austrians, and anyone raising binoculars was marking himself as a worthy target. And this was the young Kaiser! Trotta's heart was in his throat. Terror at the inconceivable, immeasurable catastrophe that would destroy Trotta, the regiment, the army, the state, the entire world drove burning chills through his body. His knees quaked. And the eternal grudge of the subaltern frontline officer against the high-ranking staff officers, who haven't the foggiest sense of bitter reality, dictated the action that indelibly stamped the lieutenant's name on the history of his regiment. Both his hands reached toward the monarch's shoulders in order to push him down. The lieutenant probably grabbed too hard; the Kaiser promptly fell. His escorts hurled themselves upon the falling man. That same instant, a shot bored through the lieutenant's left shoulder, the very shot meant for the Kaiser's heart. As the emperor rose, the lieutenant sank. Along the entire front, a tangled and irregular rattling awoke from the terrified guns, which had been startled from their slumber. The Kaiser, impatiently urged by his escorts to leave this perilous zone, nevertheless leaned over the prostrate lieutenant and, mindful of his imperial duty, asked the unconscious man, who could hear nothing, what his name was. A regimental surgeon, an ambulance orderly, and two stretcher bearers came galloping over, backs bent, heads stooped. The staff officers first yanked the Kaiser down and then threw themselves on the ground. "Here—the lieutenant!" the Kaiser shouted up at the breathless medic.

Meanwhile the firing had petered out. And while the acting cadet officer stepped in front of the platoon and announced in a clear voice, "I am taking command," Franz Joseph and his escorts stood up, the orderlies gingerly strapped the lieutenant to the stretcher, and they all withdrew toward the regimental command post, where a snow-white tent spread over the nearest clearing station.

Trotta's left clavicle was shattered. The bullet, lodged right under the left shoulder blade, was removed in the presence of the

Supreme Commander in Chief, amid the inhuman bellowing of the wounded man, who was revived by his pain.

Trotta recovered within four weeks. By the time he returned to his south Hungarian garrison, he possessed the rank of captain, the highest of all decorations—the Order of Maria Theresa—and a knighthood. Now he was called Captain Joseph Trotta von Sipolje.

Every night before retiring and every morning upon awakening, as if his own life had been traded for a new and alien life manufactured in a workshop, he would repeat his new rank and his new status to himself and walk up to the mirror to confirm that his face was the same. Despite the awkward heartiness of army brethren trying to bridge the gulf left by a sudden and incomprehensible destiny, and in spite of his own vain efforts to encounter everyone as unabashedly as ever, the ennobled Captain Trotta seemed to be losing his equilibrium; he felt he had been sentenced to wear another man's boots for life and walk across a slippery ground, pursued by secret talking and awaited by shy glances. His grandfather had been a little peasant, his father an assistant paymaster, later a constable sergeant on the monarchy's southern border. After losing an eye in a fight with Bosnian smugglers, he had been living as a war invalid and groundskeeper at the Castle of Laxenburg, feeding the swans, trimming the hedges, guarding the springtime forsythias and then the elderberry bushes against unauthorized, thievish hands, and, in the mild nights, shooing homeless lovers from the benevolent darkness of benches.

To the son of a noncommissioned officer, the rank of an ordinary infantry lieutenant had seemed natural and suitable. But to the decorated, aristocratic captain, who went about in the alien and almost unearthly radiance of imperial favor as in a golden cloud, his own father had suddenly moved far away, and the measured love that the offspring showed the old man seemed to require an altered conduct and a new way for father and son to deal with each other. The captain had not seen his father in five years; but every other week, while doing his rounds in the eternally unalterable rotation, he had written the old man a brief letter in the meager and fickle glow of the guardroom candle, after first inspecting the sentries, recording the time of each relief, and, in the column labeled UNUSUAL INCIDENTS, penning a clear and assertive *None* that virtually denied even the remotest possibility of unusual incidents. These letters to his father, on yellowish and pulpy octavo, resembled one another like furlough orders and regulation forms. After the salutation *Dear Father* at the left, four fingers from the top and two from the side, they began with the terse news of the writer's good health, continued with his hope for the recipient's good health, and closed with an indentation for the perpetual formula drawn at the bottom right at a diagonal interval from the salutation: *Very humbly yours, your loyal and grateful son, Lieutenant Joseph Trotta.*

But now, especially since his new rank exempted him from the old rotation, how should he refashion the official epistolary form, which was designed for a whole military lifetime, and how should he intersperse the standardized sentences with unusual statements about conditions that had become unusual and that he himself had barely grasped? On that silent evening when, for the first time since his recovery, Captain Trotta, in order to perform the correspondence duty, sat down at the table, which was lavishly carved up and notched over by the playful knives of bored men, he realized he would never get beyond the salutation *Dear Father*. Leaning the barren pen against the inkwell, he twisted off the tip of the wick on the guttering candle as if hoping for a happy inspiration and an appropriate phrase from its soothing light, and he gently rambled off into memories of childhood, village, mother, and military school. He gazed at the gigantic shadows cast by small objects upon the bare blue lime-washed walls, at the slightly curved, shimmering outline of the saber on the hook by the door, and, tucked into the saber guard, at the dark neckband. He listened to the tireless rain outside and its drumming chant on the tin-plated windowsill. And he finally stood up, having resolved to visit his father the week after the prescribed thank-you audience with the Kaiser, for which he would be detailed during the next few days.

One week later, right after an audience of barely ten minutes, not more than ten minutes of imperial favor and those ten or twelve questions read from documents and at which, standing at attention, one had to fire a "Yes, Your Majesty!" like a gentle but definite gunshot, he took a fiacre to see his father in Laxenburg. He found the old man in shirtsleeves, sitting in the kitchen of his official apartment over a spacious cup of steaming, fragrant coffee on the naked, shiny, planed table, on which lay a dark-blue handkerchief trimmed in red. At the table's edge, the knotty russet cherrywood cane hung on its crook, swaying gently. A wrinkled leather pouch thickly swollen with fibrous shag lay half open next to a long pipe of white clay, now a brownish-yellow color. It matched the hue of the father's tremendous white moustache. Captain Joseph Trotta von Sipolje stood amid this shabby governmental homeyness like a military god, wearing a gleaming officer's scarf, a lacquered helmet emanating virtually its own black sunshine, smooth fiery waxed riding boots with glittering spurs, two rows of lustrous, almost blazing buttons on his coat, and the blessing of the ethereal power of the Order of Maria Theresa. There the son stood in front of the father, who rose slowly as if the slowness of his greeting were to make up for the boy's splendor. Captain Trotta kissed his father's hand, lowered his head, and received a kiss on the brow and a kiss on the cheek.

"Sit down!" said the old man. The captain unbuckled parts of his splendor. "Congratulations!" said the father, his voice normal, in the hard German of army Slavs. The consonants boomed like thunderstorms and the final syllables were loaded with small weights. Just five years ago he had still been speaking Slovenian to his son, although the boy understood only a few words and never produced a single one himself. But today it might strike the old man as an audacious intimacy to hear his mother tongue used by his son, who had been removed so far by the grace of Fate and Emperor, while the captain focused on the father's lips in order to greet the first Slovenian sound as a familiar remoteness and lost homeyness. "Congratulations, congratulations!" the sergeant thunderously repeated. "In my day it never went this fast. In my day Radetzky gave us hell!"

It's really over! thought Captain Trotta. His father was separated from him by a heavy mountain of military ranks.

"Do you still have rakia, sir?" he asked, addressing him formally while trying to confirm the last remnant of family togetherness. They drank, clinked glasses, drank again; the father moaned after every gulp, floundered in endless coughing, turned purple, spat, gradually calmed down, then launched into old chestnuts about his own military time, with the unmistakable goal of deflating his son's merits and career. Finally, the captain stood up, kissed the paternal hand, received the paternal kiss on brow and cheek, buckled on his saber, donned his shako, and left—secure in the knowledge that this was the last time he would ever see his father in this life.

It *was* the last time. The son wrote his father the routine letters—there was no other visible link between them; Captain Trotta was severed from the long procession of his Slavic peasant forebears. A new dynasty began with him.

The round years rolled by, one by one, like peaceful, uniform wheels. In keeping with his status, Trotta married his colonel's not-quite-young well-off niece, the daughter of a district captain in western Bohemia; he fathered a boy, enjoyed the uniformity of his healthy military life in the small garrison, rode horseback to the parade ground every morning, and played chess every afternoon with the lawyer at the café, eventually feeling at home in his rank, his station, his standing, and his repute. He had an average military gift, of which he provided average samples at maneuvers every year; he was a good husband, suspicious of women, no gambler, grouchy, but a just officer, a fierce enemy of all deceit, unmanly conduct, cowardly safety, garrulous praise, and ambitious self-seeking. He was as simple and impeccable as his military record, and only the anger that sometimes took hold of him would have given a judge of human nature some inkling that Captain Trotta's soul likewise contained the dim nocturnal abysses where storms slumber and the unknown voices of nameless ancestors.

He read no books, Captain Trotta, and secretly pitied his growing son, who had to start handling slate, pencil, and sponge, paper, ruler, and arithmetic, and for whom the unavoidable primers were already waiting. The captain was convinced his boy had to become a soldier. It never crossed his mind that—

from now until the extinction of his dynasty—a Trotta could follow any other calling. Had he had two, three, four sons (but his wife was sickly, needed doctors and treatments, and pregnancy was risky for her), they would all have become soldiers. That was what Captain Trotta still thought. There was talk of another war; Trotta was ready any day. Yes, it struck him as almost certain that he was destined to die in combat. His unshakable simplicity viewed death in the field as a necessary consequence of warrior fame. Until one day, out of idle curiosity, he picked up the first reader assigned to his son, who had just turned five and who, because of his mother's ambition, had far too prematurely tasted the ordeals of school, thanks to a private tutor. Trotta read the rhymed morning prayer. It had been the same for decades; he could still remember it. He read "The Four Seasons," "The Fox and the Hare," "The King of the Beasts." Then he opened to the table of contents and found the title of a selection that seemed to refer to him, for it was called "Franz Joseph I at the Battle of Solferino"; he read and had to sit down. "In the Battle of Solferino," the piece began, "our Emperor and King, Franz Joseph I, was beset by great danger." Trotta himself appeared, but how utterly transformed!

> The monarch [it said] had ventured so far ahead in the heat of fighting that he suddenly found himself ringed by a throng of enemy troopers. At that moment of supreme need, a lieutenant of tender years galloped over at full speed on a sweat-covered sorrel, swinging his saber. Oh, how the blows rained upon the heads and necks of the enemy riders!

And further:

> An enemy lance bored through the young hero's chest, but most of the foes were already slain. Gripping his naked sword in his hand, our young undaunted monarch could easily fend off the ever-weakening attacks. The entire enemy cavalry was taken prisoner. And the young lieutenant—Sir Joseph von Trotta was his name—was awarded the highest distinction that our Fatherland has to bestow on its heroic sons, the Order of Maria Theresa.

Captain Trotta, clutching the reader, stepped into the small orchard behind the house, where his wife busied herself on balmier afternoons, and, his lips pale, his voice very low, he asked her whether she had read the vile selection. She nodded with a smile.

"It's a pack of lies!" shouted the captain and hurled the book upon the damp soil.

"It's for children," his wife gently answered.

The captain turned his back on her. Anger shook him like a storm shaking a flimsy shrub. He hurried indoors, his heart pounding. It was time for his chess game. He took the saber from its hook, buckled the strap around his waist with a nasty and violent jerk, and loped wildly out of the house. To anyone who saw him he looked as if he were out to massacre a drove of enemies. With four deep furrows in his narrow brow under the rough short hair, he lost two games at the café without saying a word, knocked the clattering figures over with a fierce hand, and said to his opponent, "I have to confer with you!" Pause. "I've been abused," he resumed, peering straight into the lawyer's sparkling glasses, and noticed after a while that words were failing him. He should have brought the primer along. With that odious object in hand, he would have had a far easier time explaining things.

"What kind of abuse?" asked the lawyer.

"I never served with the cavalry." That was how Captain Trotta felt he might best begin, although he himself realized he was not making himself clear. "And here these shameless writers write in the children's books that I galloped up on a sorrel, they write, on a sweat-covered sorrel, to rescue the monarch, they write."

The lawyer understood. He knew the piece himself from his sons' books. "You're taking it too seriously, captain," he said. "Don't forget, it's for children."

Trotta looked at him aghast. At that instant, the entire world seemed allied against him: the authors of primers, the lawyer, his wife, his son, the tutor.

"All historic events," said the lawyer, "are rewritten for school use. And to my mind this is proper. Children need examples that they can grasp, that sink in. They can find out the real truth later on."

"Check!" cried the captain, standing up. He went over to the barracks, surprised the officer on duty, Lieutenant Amerling, with a woman in the assistant paymaster's office, personally inspected the sentries, sent for the sergeant, commanded the junior officer on duty to report, had the company fall in, and ordered rifle drill on the parade ground.

The men obeyed, confused and trembling. A few were missing from each platoon; they were nowhere to be found. Captain Trotta ordered their names read out. "All absentees are to report to me tomorrow!" he told the lieutenant. Panting and gasping, the troops did their rifle exercises. Ramrods clattered, straps flew, hot hands clapped upon cool metal barrels, huge gun butts stamped upon the dull, soft ground.

"Load!" commanded the captain. The air quivered with the hollow rattling of the blank cartridges. "Half an hour of salute drilling!" commanded the captain. Ten minutes later, he changed the order. "Kneel down for prayers!" Appeased he listened to the numb thud of hard knees on soil, sand, and gravel. He was still captain, master of his company. He would show those writers.

That night he did not go to the officers' mess; he didn't even eat, he went to bed. His sleep was heavy and dreamless. The next morning, at the officers' roll call, he submitted his complaint, terse and sonorous, to the colonel. It was passed on. And now began the martyrdom of Captain Joseph Trotta von Sipolje, the Knight of Truth. It took weeks for the Ministry of War to notify him that his complaint had been forwarded to the Ministry of Religion, Culture, and Education. And more weeks dragged by until one day the minister's answer arrived. It read:

Your Lordship,
Dear Captain Trotta,
   In reply to Your Lordship's complaint regarding Text No. 15 in the authorized readers written and edited by Professors Weidner and Srdcny for Austrian elementary and secondary schools in accordance with the Law of 21 July 1864, the Minister of Religion, Culture, and Education most

*respectfully takes the liberty of calling Your Lordship's attention to the
circumstance that, in accordance with the Edict of 21 March 1840, the
primer selections of historic significance, in particular those relating to the
august person of His Majesty Emperor Franz Joseph as well as other
members of the Supreme Imperial House, are to be adjusted to the intellectual capacities of the pupils and kept consistent with the best possible
pedagogic goals. The text in question, No. 15, as mentioned in Your
Lordship's complaint, was submitted personally to His Excellency the
Minister of Religion, Culture, and Education, who approved the use thereof
in the school system. It was the intention of the higher educational
authorities and no less that of the lower educational authorities to introduce
the pupils in the Monarchy to the heroic deeds performed by members of the
Armed Forces and to depict them in accordance with the juvenile character,
imagination, and patriotic sentiments of the developing generation without
altering the veracity of the events portrayed, but also without rendering them
in a dry tone devoid of any spur to the imagination and any patriotic
sentiments. In consequence of the above and similar considerations, the
undersigned most respectfully begs Your Lordship to be so good as to
withdraw his complaint.*

This document was signed by the Minister of Religion,
Culture, and Education. The colonel handed it to Captain
Trotta with the fatherly words, "Let it be!"

Trotta took it and remained silent. One week later, through
official channels, he petitioned for an audience with His Majesty, and one morning three weeks later he stood in the palace,
face-to-face with the Supreme Commander in Chief.

"Listen, my dear Trotta!" said the Kaiser. "The whole business is rather awkward. But neither of us comes off all that badly.
Let it be!"

"Your Majesty," replied the captain, "it's a lie!"

"People tell a lot of lies," the Kaiser confirmed.

"I can't, Your Majesty," the captain choked forth.

The Kaiser inched closer to the captain. The monarch was
scarcely taller than Trotta. They locked eyes.

"My ministers," Franz Joseph began, "must know what they're
doing. I have to rely on them. Do you catch my drift, my dear
Trotta?" And after a while. "We'll do something. You'll see!"

The audience was over.

His father was still alive. But Trotta did not go to Laxenburg. He returned to the garrison and requested his discharge from the army.

He was discharged as a major. He moved to Bohemia, to his father-in-law's small estate. Imperial favor did not abandon him. A few weeks later, he was notified that the Kaiser had seen fit to contribute five thousand guldens from the privy purse to the education of the son of the man who had saved his life. At the same time, Trotta was raised to the barony.

Baron Joseph von Trotta und Sipolje accepted these imperial gifts sullenly, as insults. The campaign against the Prussians was waged and lost without him. His resentment simmered. His temples were already turning silvery, his eyes dim, his steps slow, his hands heavy, his words fewer than ever. Though a man in the prime of life, he appeared to be aging swiftly. He had been driven from the paradise of simple faith in Emperor and Virtue, Truth, and Justice, and, now fettered in silence and endurance, he may have realized that the stability of the world, the power of laws, and the glory of majesties were all based on deviousness. Thanks to the Kaiser's casually expressed wish, Reading Text No. 15 disappeared from the monarchy's schoolbooks. The Trotta name survived only in the unknown annals of the regiment.

The major now vegetated as the unknown bearer of ephemeral fame, like a fleeting shadow that a secret object sends into the bright world of the living. On his father-in-law's estate, he puttered about with watering cans and garden shears: similar to his father at the castle park in Laxenburg, the baron trimmed the hedges and mowed the lawn, guarded the forsythia in early spring and then the elderberry bushes against thievish and unauthorized hands; he supplanted the rotten pickets with fresh, smoothly planed ones, repaired tools and tackling, bridled and saddled his bay horses himself, replaced rusty locks on gates and portals, carefully wedged neatly carved slats in worn-out sagging hinges, spent days on end in the forest, shot small game, slept in the gamekeeper's hut, looked after poultry, manure, and harvest, fruit and espalier flowers, groom and coachman.

Penny-pinching and distrustful, he made his purchases, his sharp fingers fishing coins from the stingy leather pouch and slipping it back upon his chest. He became a little Slovenian peasant.

At times, his old anger would overcome him, shaking him like a powerful storm shaking a flimsy shrub. He would then whip the servant and the flanks of the horses, smash the doors into the locks that he himself had repaired, threaten to maim and murder the farmhands, shove his luncheon plate away in a nasty swing, and fast and grumble. Next to him lived his feeble, sickly wife, in a separate room; the boy, who saw his father only at meals and whose report cards were submitted to him twice a year, eliciting neither praise nor reproach; the father-in-law, who blithely frittered his pension and had a weakness for young girls, who stayed in town for long weeks and feared his son-in-law. He was a little old Slovenian peasant, that Baron Trotta. Twice a week, late in the evening, by flickering candlelight, he still wrote his father a letter on yellowish octavo, the salutation *Dear Father* four male fingers from the top, two male fingers from the side. He very seldom received an answer.

The baron did occasionally think of visiting his father. He had long since begun missing the sergeant of the frugal government poverty, the fibrous shag, and the homemade brandy. But the son dreaded the travel expenses just as his father, his grandfather, and his great-grandfather would have done. Now he was closer to the war invalid at Laxenburg Castle than years ago, when, in the fresh glory of his newly bestowed nobility, he had sat in the blue lime-washed kitchen of the small official apartment, drinking rakia. He never discussed his background with his wife. He sensed that an embarrassed pride would come between the daughter of the older dynasty of civil servants and a Slovenian sergeant, so he never asked his father to visit him.

Once, on a bright day in March, when the baron was trudging across the hard clods to see his steward, a farmhand brought him a letter from the administration of the Castle of Laxenburg. The invalid was dead; he had passed away painlessly at the age of eighty-one. The baron said only, "Go to the baroness; my bag is to be packed; I'm going to Vienna tonight." He walked on, entered the steward's house, inquired about the sowing, discussed the weather, instructed him to order three new plows and send for the veterinarian on Monday and the midwife for a pregnant serving girl today, and then added, when leaving, "My father has died; I'm spending three days in Vienna," saluted with a casual finger, and left.

His bag was packed, the horses were harnessed to the carriage; the station was an hour's drive. He bolted down the soup and the meat. Then he told his wife, "I can't go on! My father was a good man. You never met him." Was it an obituary? Was it a lament? "You're coming along!" he told his frightened son. His wife stood up to pack the boy's things. While she busied herself on the next floor, Trotta said to the child, "Now you'll see your grandfather." The boy trembled and lowered his eyes.

The sergeant was lying in state by the time they arrived. Guarded by eight candles three feet high and by two war veterans, he lay on a bier in his living room, sporting a tremendous bristly moustache, a dark-blue uniform, and three twinkling medals on his chest. An Ursuline nun was praying in the corner by the single curtained window. The veterans stood at attention when Trotta came in. He wore his major's uniform with the Order of Maria Theresa. He knelt down; his son likewise fell to his knees at the dead man's feet, the tremendous soles of those boots in front of the young face. For the first time in his life, Baron Trotta felt a thin, sharp jab in the region of his heart. His tiny eyes remained dry. He murmured one, two, three Lord's Prayers out of pious embarrassment, stood up, leaned over the dead man, kissed the tremendous moustache, waved at the veterans, and said to his son, "Come on!

"Did you see him?" he asked outside.

"Yes," said the boy.

"He was only a constable sergeant," said the father. "I saved the Kaiser's life at the Battle of Solferino—and then we got the barony."

The boy said nothing.

The pensioner was buried in the small cemetery at Laxenburg, military section. Six dark-blue veterans carried the coffin from the chapel to the grave. Major Trotta, in shako and full dress, kept his hand on his son's shoulder the whole time. The boy sobbed. The sad music of the military band, the priests' doleful and monotonous singsong, audible whenever the music paused, the gently drifting incense—it all made the boy choke with incomprehensible pain. And the rifle shots discharged over the grave by a demi-platoon shook him with their long-echoing relentlessness. They fired martial salutes for the dead man's soul, which went straight to heaven, vanishing from this earth forever and always.

Father and son headed back. The baron remained silent the entire trip. It was only when they got off the train and climbed into the carriage awaiting them behind the station garden that the major said, "Don't forget your grandfather!"

The baron resumed his daily routine, and the years rolled away like mute, peaceful, uniform wheels. The sergeant was not the last corpse that the baron had to inter. First he buried his father-in-law, a few years later his wife, who had died a quick, discreet death without saying goodbye after a severe case of pneumonia. He sent his son to boarding school in Vienna, making sure the boy could never become a regular soldier. He remained alone on the estate, in the white, spacious house through which the breath of the deceased still passed, and he spoke only with the gamekeeper, the steward, the groom, and the coachman. His rage exploded in him less and less. But the servants constantly felt his peasant fist, and his seething hush lay like a hard yoke on their necks. Dreadful silence wafted from him as before a storm.

Twice a month he received obedient letters from his child. Once a month he replied in two brief sentences, on small, thrifty scraps torn from the respectful margins of the letters he had gotten. Once a year, on the eighteenth of August, the Kaiser's birthday, he donned his uniform and drove to the nearest garrison town. Twice a year his son visited him, during Christmas break and summer vacation. On every Christmas Eve the boy was handed three hard silver guldens, for which he had to sign a receipt and which he could never take along. That same evening, the guldens landed in a cashbox inside the old man's chest. Next to the guldens lay the report cards. They testified to the son's thorough diligence and his middling but always adequate capacities. Never was the son given a toy, never an allowance, never a book, aside from the required schoolbooks. He did not seem deprived. His mind was neat, sober, and honest. His meager imagination provided him with no other wish than to get through the school years as fast as possible.

He was eighteen years old when his father said to him on Christmas Eve, "This year you'll no longer get your three guldens. You may take nine from the cashbox if you sign for them. Be careful with women! Most of them are diseased." And, after a pause: "I've decided that you're going to be a lawyer. It will take two years. There'll be time enough for the army. It can be deferred until you're done."

The boy took the nine guldens as obediently as he took his father's wish. He seldom visited women, chose among them carefully, and had six guldens left when he came home again in the summer holidays. He asked his father for permission to invite a friend. "Fine," said the major, somewhat astonished. The friend came with little baggage but a huge paint box, which did not appeal to the master of the house.

"He paints?" asked the old man.

"Very nicely," said Franz, the son.

"Don't let him splatter up the house. He can paint the landscape."

The guest did paint outdoors, but not the landscape. He was painting Baron Trotta from memory. At every meal he memorized his host's features.

"Why are you staring at me?" asked the baron. Both boys turned red and peered at the tablecloth. Nevertheless the portrait was finished, framed, and presented to the old man when the boys left. He studied it thoughtfully and with a smile. He turned it over as if seeking further details perhaps left out on the front; he held it up to the window, then far from his eyes, gazed at himself in the mirror, compared himself with the portrait, and finally said, "Where should it hang?" It was his first joy in many years. "You can lend your friend money if he needs something," he murmured to Franz. "Get along with each other!" The portrait was and remained the only one ever done of old Trotta. Later it hung in his son's study and even haunted his grandson's imagination.

Meanwhile the portrait kept the major in a rare mood for several weeks. He hung it now on one, now on another wall, feeling flattered delight as he scrutinized his hard, jutting nose, his clean-shaven jaw, his pale, narrow lips, his gaunt cheekbones rising like hills in front of the tiny black eyes, and the low, heavily creased forehead covered by the awning of close-cropped, bristly, thorny hair. Only now did he grow acquainted with his features; he sometimes had a mute dialogue with his own face. It aroused unfamiliar thoughts and memories, baffling, quickly blurring shadows of wistfulness. He had needed the portrait to experience his early old age and his great loneliness; from the painted canvas loneliness and old age came flooding toward him. Has it always been like this? he wondered. Has it been like this always?

Now and then, aimlessly, he went to the cemetery, to his wife's grave, peered at the gray pedestal and the chalky-white cross, the dates of her birth and death: he calculated that she had died too early and he admitted that he could not remember her clearly. He had forgotten, say, her hands. Quinquina Martial Wine flashed into his mind, a medicament she had taken for many long years. Her face? Shutting his eyes, he could still evoke it, but soon it vanished, blurring into the reddish circular twilight. He became mild-mannered in the house and on the farm, sometimes stroking a horse, smiling at the cows, drinking liquor more often than before, and one day he wrote a brief letter to his son outside the normal schedule. People began greeting him with smiles; he nodded pleasantly. Summer came. The holidays brought the son and the friend; the old man drove them to town, entered a restaurant, had a few gulps of slivovitz, and ordered a lavish meal for the boys.

The son became a lawyer, visited home more frequently, looked around the estate, felt one day that he wanted to manage it and abandon his law career. He confessed his wish to his father. The major said, "It's too late. You'll never become a farmer or manage an estate in your lifetime. You'll make an able official, that's all." The matter was settled. The son obtained a political office, becoming a district commissioner in Austrian Silesia. While the Trotta name may have disappeared from the authorized schoolbooks, it had not vanished from the secret files of the higher political authorities, and the five thousand guldens allotted by the Kaiser's favor assured Trotta the official a constant benevolence and furtherance from anonymous higher places. He advanced swiftly. Two years before the son's promotion to district captain, his father died.

He left a surprising will. Since he was certain—he wrote—that his son was not a good farmer, and since he hoped that the Trottas, grateful to the Kaiser for his continual favor, could advance to high ranks in government service and live more happily than he, the author of the testament, he had decided, in memory of his late father, to bequeath the estate, made over to him years earlier by his father-in-law, together with all his movable and immovable chattel, to the Military Invalid Fund, whereby the beneficiaries of this last will and testament would have no further obligation than to bury the testator as modestly as possible in the cemetery where his father had been interred and, if it was convenient, near the deceased. He, the testator, requested that they refrain from any ostentation. All residual moneys, fifteen thousand florins plus accrued interest placed with the Efrussi Bank in Vienna, as well as any other money, silver and copper, to be found in the house, and also the late mother's ring, watch, and necklace, belonged to the testator's only son, Baron Franz von Trotta und Sipolje.

A Viennese military band, an infantry company, a representative of the Knights of the Order of Maria Theresa, a few officers of the south Hungarian regiment whose modest hero the major had been, all military invalids capable of marching, two officials of the Royal and Cabinet Chancellery, an officer of the Military Cabinet, and a junior officer carrying the Order of Maria Theresa on a black-draped cushion: they formed the official cortège. Franz, the son, walked, black, thin, and alone. The band played the same march they had played at the grandfather's funeral. The salvos fired this time were louder and faded out with longer echoes.

The son did not weep. No one wept for the deceased. Everyone remained dry and solemn. No one spoke at the grave. Near the constable sergeant lay Major Baron von Trotta und Sipolje, the Knight of Truth. They set up a plain military headstone on which, beneath name, rank, and regiment, the proud epithet was engraved in thin black letters: THE HERO OF SOLFERINO.

Now little was left of the dead man but this stone, a faded glory, and the portrait. That is how a farmer walks across the soil in spring—and later, in summer, the traces of his steps are obscured by the billowing richness of the wheat he once sowed. That same week, the Imperial and Royal High Commissioner Trotta von Sipolje received a letter of condolence from His Majesty, which spoke twice about the forever "unforgotten services" rendered by the late deceased.

Chapter 2

NOWHERE IN THE entire jurisdiction of the division was there a finer military band than that of Infantry Regiment No. Ten in the small district town of W in Moravia. The bandmaster was one of those Austrian military musicians who, thanks to an exact memory and an ever-alert need for new variations on old melodies, were able to compose a new march every month. All the marches resembled one another like soldiers. Most of them began with a roll of drums, contained a tattoo accelerated by the march rhythm and a shattering smile of the lovely cymbals, and ended with the rumbling thunder of the kettledrum, the brief and jolly storm of military music. What distinguished Kapellmeister Nechwal from his colleagues was not so much his extraordinarily prolific tenacity in composing as his rousing and cheerful severity in drilling the music. Other bandmasters had the negligent habit of letting a drum major conduct the first march, only picking up the baton for the second item on the program, but Nechwal viewed that slovenly practice as a clear symptom of the decline of the Austro-Hungarian Empire. By the time the band had stationed itself in the prescribed round and the dainty little feet of the frail music desks had dug into the black soil of the cracks between the wide paving stones on the square, the bandmaster was already standing at the center of his musicians, discreetly holding up his ebony baton with the silver pommel.

Every one of these outdoor concerts—they took place under the Herr District Captain's balcony—began with "The Radetzky March." Though all the band members were so thoroughly familiar with it that they could have played it without a conductor, in the dead of night, and in their sleep, the kapellmeister

nevertheless required them to read every single note from the
sheets. And every Sunday, as if rehearsing "The Radetzky
March" for the first time with his musicians, he would raise his
head, his baton, and his eyes in military and musical zeal and
concentrate all four on any segments that seemed needful of his
orders in the round at whose midpoint he was standing. The
rugged drums rolled, the sweet flutes piped, and the lovely
cymbals shattered. The faces of all the spectators lit up with
pleasant and pensive smiles, and the blood tingled in their legs.
Though standing, they thought they were already marching.
The younger girls held their breath and opened their lips. The
more mature men hung their heads and recalled their maneuvers. The elderly ladies sat in the neighboring park, their small
gray heads trembling. And it was summer.

Yes, it was summer. The old chestnut trees opposite the
district captain's house moved their dark-green crowns with
rich, broad foliage only mornings and evenings. During the day
they remained motionless, exhaling a pungent breath and sending their wide cool shadows all the way to the middle of the
road. The sky was a steady blue. Invisible larks warbled incessantly over the silent town. Sometimes a fiacre rolled across the
bumpy cobblestones, transporting a stranger from the railroad
station to the hotel. Sometimes the hooves of the two horses
taking Lord von Winternigg for a ride clopped along the broad
road from north to south, from the landowner's castle to his
immense hunting preserve. Small, ancient, and pitiful, a little
yellow oldster with a tiny wizened face in a huge yellow blanket,
Lord von Winternigg sat in his barouche. He drove through the
brimming summer like a wretched bit of winter. On high,
soundless, resilient rubber wheels whose delicate brown spokes
mirrored the sunshine, he rolled straight from his bed to his
rural wealth. The big dark woods and the blond green game-
keepers were already waiting for him. The townsfolk greeted
him. He did not respond. Unmoved, he drove through a sea of
greetings. His dark coachman loomed steeply aloft, his top hat
almost grazing the boughs of the chestnut trees, the supple whip
caressing the brown backs of the horses, and at very definite,
regular intervals the coachman's firm-set mouth emitted a

snappy clicking, louder than the clopping of the hooves and similar to a melodious rifle shot.

Summer vacation began around this time. Carl Joseph von Trotta, the fifteen-year-old son of the district captain, a pupil at the Cavalry Military School in Hranice, Moravia, regarded his native town as a summery place; it was as much the summer's home as his own. Christmas and Easter he spent at his uncle's. He came home only during summer holidays. He always arrived on a Sunday. This accorded with the wishes of his father, Herr District Captain Franz, Baron von Trotta und Sipolje. At home, summer vacation, no matter when it commenced at school, had to begin on a Saturday. On Sundays, Herr von Trotta was off duty. He reserved the entire morning, from nine to twelve, for his son. Punctually at ten minutes to nine, a quarter hour after early mass, the boy stood in his Sunday uniform outside his father's door. At five minutes to nine, Jacques, in his gray butler's livery, came down the stairs and said, "Young master, your Herr Papá is coming." Carl Joseph gave his coat a last tug, adjusted the waist belt, took off the cap, and, as prescribed by regulations, propped it against his hip.

The father arrived; the son clicked his heels; the noise snapped through the hushed old house. The old man opened the door and with a slight wave of his hand motioned for his son to precede him. The boy stood still; he did not respond to the invitation. So the father stepped through the door. Carl Joseph followed but paused on the threshold. "Make yourself comfortable!" said the district captain after a while. It was only now that Carl Joseph walked over to the large red-plush armchair and sat down opposite his father, his knees drawn up stiffly and the cap and white gloves upon them. Through the narrow cracks of the green Venetian blinds, narrow stripes of sunshine fell upon the dark-red carpet. A fly buzzed, the wall clock began to strike. After the nine golden strokes faded, the district captain began.

"How is Herr Colonel Marek?"

"Thank you, Papá, he's fine."

"Still weak in geometry?"

"Thank you, Papá, a little better."

"Read any books?"

"Yessir, Papá!"

"How's your horsemanship? Last year, it wasn't special."

"This year—" Carl Joseph began, but was promptly interrupted. His father had stretched out his narrow hand, which lay half hidden in the round shiny cuff. The huge square cuff link glittered golden.

"It wasn't special, I just said. It was—"here the district captain paused and then said in a toneless voice, "a disgrace."

Father and son remained silent. As soft as the word "disgrace" had been, it was still wafting through the room. Carl Joseph knew that a pause had to be observed after a severe critique from his father. The censure had to be absorbed in its full significance, pondered, stamped upon the mind, and imprinted on the heart and the brain. The clock ticked, the fly buzzed.

"This year it was a lot better," Carl Joseph began in a clear voice. "The sergeant often said so himself. I also received praise from Herr First Lieutenant Koppel."

"Glad to hear it," the Herr District Captain remarked in a doomsday voice. Using the edge of the table, he pushed the cuff back into the sleeve; there was a harsh rattle. "Keep talking!" he said, lighting a cigarette. It was the signal for the start of relaxation. Carl Joseph put his cap and his gloves on a small desk, got to his feet, and began reciting all the events of the last year. The old man nodded. Suddenly he said, "You're a big boy, my son. Your voice is changing. Are you in love yet?"

Carl Joseph turned red. His face burned like a red lantern, but he held it bravely toward his father.

"So, not yet!" said the district captain. "Don't let me disturb you. Carry on!"

Carl Joseph gulped, the redness faded, he was suddenly freezing. He reported slowly and with many pauses. Then he produced the reading list from his pocket and handed it to his father.

"Quite an impressive list!" said the district captain. "Please give me a plot summary of *Zriny*."

Carl Joseph outlined the drama act by act. Then he sat down, weary, pale, with a dry tongue.

He stole a glance at the clock, it was only ten-thirty. The examination would drag on for another hour and a half. It might occur to the old man to test him in ancient history or German mythology. The father walked through the room, smoking, his left hand behind his back. The cuff rattled on his right hand. The sunny stripes kept growing stronger and stronger on the carpet; they kept edging closer and closer to the window. The sun must be high by now. The church bells started clanging; they tolled all the way into the room as if swinging just beyond the thick blinds. Today the old man tested him only in literature. He articulated his detailed opinion of Grillparzer's significance and recommended Adalbert Stifter and Ferdinand von Saar as "light vacation reading" for his son. Then the father jumped back to military topics: guard duty, Military Regulations Part Two, makeup of an army corps, wartime strength of the various regiments. All at once he asked, "What is subordination?"

"Subordination is the duty of unconditional obedience," Carl Joseph declaimed, "which every inferior and every lower rank—"

"Stop!" the father broke in, correcting him. "*As well as* every lower rank." And Carl Joseph went on.

"—is obligated to show a superior when—"

"As soon as," the old man rectified. "As soon as the latter takes command."

Carl Joseph heaved a sigh of relief. The clock struck twelve.

Only now did his vacation begin. Another quarter hour, and he heard the first rattling drumroll from the band leaving the barracks. Every Sunday at noontime it played outside the official residence of the district captain, who, in this little town, represented no lesser personage than His Majesty the Emperor. Carl Joseph, concealed behind the dense foliage of the vines on the balcony, received the playing of the military band as a tribute. He felt slightly related to the Hapsburgs, whose might his father represented and defended here and for whom he himself would some day go off to war and death. He knew the names of all the members of the Imperial Royal House. He loved them all sincerely, with a child's devoted heart—more than anyone else the Kaiser, who was kind and great, sublime and just, infinitely remote and very close, and particularly fond of the officers in the army. It would be best to die for him amid military music, easiest with "The Radetzky March." The swift bullets whistled in cadence around Carl Joseph's ears, his naked saber flashed, and, his heart and head brimming with the lovely briskness of the march, he sank into the drumming intoxication of the music, and his blood oozed out in a thin dark-red trickle upon the glistening gold of the trumpets, the deep black of the drums, and the victorious silver of the cymbals.

Jacques stood behind him and cleared his throat. So lunch was starting. Whenever the music paused, a soft clattering of dishes could be heard from the dining room. It lay three large rooms away from the balcony, at the exact midpoint of the second floor. During the meal, the music resounded, far but clear. Unfortunately, the band did not play every day. It was good and useful; it entwined the solemn ceremony of the luncheon, mild and conciliatory, allowing none of the terse, harsh, embarrassing conversations that the father so often loved to start. One could remain silent, listening and enjoying. The plates had narrow, fading, blue-and-gold stripes. Carl Joseph loved them. He often recalled them throughout the year. They and "The Radetzky March" and the wall portrait of his deceased mother (whom the boy no longer remembered) and the heavy silver ladle and the fish tureen and the scalloped fruit knives and the tiny demitasses and the wee frail spoons as thin as thin silver coins: all these things together meant summer, freedom, home.

He handed Jacques his cape, belt, cap, and gloves and went to the dining room. The old man walked in at the same time, smiling at the son. Fräulein Hirschwitz, the housekeeper, came a bit later in her Sunday gray silk, with her head aloft, her heavy bun at her nape, a huge curved brooch across her bosom like some kind of scimitar. She looked armed and armor-plated. Carl Joseph breathed a kiss on her long hard hand. Jacques pulled out the chairs. The district captain gave the signal for sitting. Jacques vanished and reappeared after a time with white gloves, which seemed to alter him thoroughly. They shed a snowy glow upon his already white face, his already white whiskers, his already white hair. But after all, their brightness also surpassed just about anything that could be called bright in this world. With these gloves he held a dark tray. Upon it lay the steaming soup tureen.

Soon he had placed it at the center of the table, gingerly, soundlessly, and very quickly. Following an old custom, Fräulein Hirschwitz ladled out the soup. She offered the plates, and the diners approached them with hospitably stretching arms and grateful smiles in their eyes. She smiled back. A warm golden shimmer hovered in the plates; it was the soup, noodle soup: transparent, with thin, tender, entwined, golden-yellow noodles. Herr von Trotta und Sipolje ate very swiftly, sometimes fiercely. He virtually destroyed one course after another with a noiseless, aristocratic, and rapid malice; he was wiping them out. Fräulein Hirschwitz took small portions at the table, but after a meal she re-ate the entire sequence of food in her room. Carl Joseph fearfully and hastily swallowed hot spoonfuls and huge mouthfuls. In this way, they all finished in tandem. No word was spoken when Herr von Trotta und Sipolje held his tongue.

After the soup the *Tafelspitz* was served, boiled fillet of beef with all the trimmings, the old man's Sunday entrée for countless years. The delighted contemplation he devoted to this dish took more time than half the meal. The district captain's eyes caressed first the delicate bacon that silhouetted the colossal chunk of meat, then each small individual plate on which the vegetables were bedded: the glowing violet beets, the lush-green earnest spinach, the bright cheery lettuce, the acrid white of the horseradish, the perfect oval of new potatoes swimming in melting butter and recalling delicate baubles. The baron had a bizarre relationship with food. He ate the most important morsels with his eyes, so to speak; his sense of beauty consumed above all the essence of the food—its soul, as it were; the vapid remainders that then reached mouth and palate were boring and had to be wolfed down without delay. The beauteous appearance of the victuals gave the old man as much pleasure as their simplicity. For he set store by good solid fare, a tribute he paid to both his taste and his conviction; the latter, you see, he called Spartan. With felicitous skill, he thus combined the sating of his desire with the demands of duty. He was a Spartan. But he was also an Austrian.

Now, as on every Sunday, he set about carving the beef. He jammed his cuffs into his sleeves, raised both hands, set knife and

fork to the meat, and began, while saying to Fräulein Hirschwitz, "You see, my dear lady, it is not enough to ask the butcher
for a tender piece. One must heed the way it is cut. I mean, with
or against the grain. Nowadays butchers no longer understand
their craft. The finest meat is ruined by merely a wrong cut.
Look here, my dear lady! I can barely save it. It's disintegrating
into threads, it's simply crumbling. As a whole, it can be labeled
'tender.' But the individual pieces will be tough, as you yourself
shall soon see. As for the trimmings, which the Germans call
Beilage, I would prefer the horseradish, which the Germans call
Meerrettich, to be somewhat drier. It must not lose its pungency
in the milk. It should also be prepared just before it reaches the
table. It's been wet far too long. A mistake!"

Fräulein Hirschwitz, who had lived in Germany for many
years and always spoke High German, and to whose predilec-
tion for literary usage Herr von Trotta's Germanisms had al-
luded, nodded slowly and heavily. It was obviously a great effort
for her to detach the considerable weight of her bun from the
back of her neck and induce her head to nod in acquiescence.
This added a touch of reserve to her assiduous amiability—
indeed, it even seemed to contain resistance. And the district
captain felt prompted to say, "Surely I am not off the mark, my
dear lady!"

He spoke the nasal Austrian German of higher officials and
lesser nobles. It vaguely recalled distant guitars twanging in the
night and also the last dainty vibrations of fading bells; it was a
soft but also precise language, tender and spiteful at once. It
suited the speaker's thin, bony face, his curved, narrow nose, in
which the sonorous, somewhat rueful consonants seemed to be
lying. His nose and mouth, when the district captain spoke,
were more like wind instruments than facial features. Aside
from the lips, nothing moved in his face. The dark whiskers that
Herr von Trotta wore as part of his uniform, as insignia demonstrating his fealty to Franz Joseph I, as proof of his dynastic
conviction—these whiskers likewise remained immobile when
Herr von Trotta und Sipolje spoke. He sat upright at the table, as
if clutching reins in his hard hands. When sitting he appeared to
be standing, and when rising he always surprised others with his

full ramrod height. He always wore dark blue, summer and winter, Sundays and weekdays: a dark-blue jacket with gray striped trousers that lay snug on his long legs and were tautened by straps over the smooth boots. Between the second and third course, he would usually get up in order to "stretch my legs." But it seemed more as if he wanted to show the rest of the household how to rise, stand, and walk without relinquishing immobility.

Jacques cleared away the meat, catching a swift glance from Fräulein Hirschwitz to remind him to have it warmed up for her. Herr von Trotta walked over to the window with measured paces, lifted the shade slightly, and returned to the table.

At that moment, the cherry dumplings appeared on a spacious platter. The district captain took only one, sliced it with his spoon, and said to Fräulein Hirschwitz, "This, dear lady, is a paragon of a cherry dumpling. It has the necessary consistency when it is cut open, yet it nevertheless yields instantly on the tongue." And, turning to Carl Joseph, "I advise you to take two today!" Carl Joseph took two. He wolfed them down in a flash, was finished one second earlier than his father, and gulped down a glass of water (for wine was served only at dinner) to wash them from his gullet, where they might still be stuck, down into his stomach. He folded his napkin in the same rhythm as the old man.

They all stood up. The band outside played the *Tannhäuser* overture. Amid its sonorous strains, they walked into the study with Fräulein Hirschwitz in the lead. There Jacques brought the coffee. They were expecting Herr Kapellmeister Nechwal. While down below his musicians fell in to march off, he came, in a dark-blue full-dress uniform, with a shining sword and two small, golden, sparkling harps on his collar. "I am delighted with your concert," said Herr von Trotta today as on every Sunday. "It was quite extraordinary today." Herr Nechwal bowed. He had already lunched in the officers' mess an hour ago, unable to wait for the black coffee: the taste of the food was still in his mouth; he craved a Virginia cigar. Jacques brought him a packet of cigars. The bandmaster drew and drew on the light that Carl Joseph steadfastly held at the end of the long cigar, running the risk of burning his fingers.

They sat in broad leather armchairs. Herr Nechwal talked about the latest Lehár operetta in Vienna. He was a man of the world, the kapellmeister. He went to Vienna twice a month, and Carl Joseph sensed that the musician hid many secrets of the great nocturnal demimonde in the depths of his soul. He had three children and a wife "from a simple background," but he himself stood in the brightest splendor of the world, quite separate from his family. He relished and told Jewish jokes with impish gusto. The district captain did not understand them, nor did he laugh, but he said, "Very good, very good!"

"How is Frau Nechwal?" Herr von Trotta would inquire regularly. He had been asking that question for years. He had never seen her, nor did he wish ever to meet the wife "from a simple background." Whenever Herr Nechwal would be leaving, the baron would always say to him, "My very best to Frau Nechwal, whom I do not know!" And Herr Nechwal promised to give her the message and assured the baron that his wife would be delighted.

"And how are your children?" asked Herr von Trotta, who could never remember whether they were sons or daughters.

"The eldest boy is doing well at school," said the kapellmeister.

"So he'll be a musician too?" asked Herr von Trotta und Sipolje with a smidgen of condescension.

"No," replied Herr Nechwal, "another year and he'll be entering military school."

"Ah, an officer!" said the district captain. "That's good. Infantry?"

Herr Nechwal smiled. "Of course! He's capable. Maybe someday he'll join the general staff."

"Certainly, certainly!" said the district captain. "Such things have happened."

A week later, he had forgotten everything. One did not recall the bandmaster's children.

Herr Nechwal drank two demitasses, no more, no less. With regret he stubbed out the final third of the cigar. He had to go; one did not leave with a smoking cigar.

"It was especially wonderful today. My very best to Frau Nechwal. Unfortunately I have not yet had the pleasure!" said Herr von Trotta und Sipolje.

Carl Joseph clicked his heels. He accompanied the kapell-meister down to the first landing. Then he returned to the study. Presenting himself to his father, he said, "I'm taking a walk, Papá!"

"Fine, fine! Have a relaxing time!" said Herr von Trotta and waved his hand.

Carl Joseph left. He meant to saunter slowly; he wanted to amble, prove to his feet that they were on vacation. But he "shaped up," as the army term goes, when he encountered the first soldier. He began to march. He reached the town limits, the big yellow tax office broiling leisurely in the sun. The sweet fragrance of the fields came surging toward him, the throbbing song of the larks. To the west, the blue horizon was cut off by gray-blue hills; the first peasant huts emerged with shingled or thatched roofs; the clucking of poultry thrust like fanfares into the summery hush. The countryside was sleeping, wrapped in day and brightness.

Behind the railroad embankment lay the constabulary head-quarters, commanded by a sergeant. Carl Joseph knew him, Sergeant Slama. He decided to knock. He entered the broiling veranda, knocked, rang the bell; no one answered. A window opened. Frau Slama leaned over the geraniums and called, "Who's there?" Catching sight of little Trotta, she said, "Coming!" She opened the front door; the interior smelled cool and a bit fragrant. Frau Slama had dabbed a drop of scent on her dressing gown.

Carl Joseph thought of the Viennese nightclubs. He said, "The sergeant isn't here, ma'am?"

"He's on duty, Herr von Trotta," the wife replied. "Do come in!"

Now Carl Joseph sat in the Slama parlor. It was a low, reddish room, very cool; this was like sitting in an icebox. The high backs of the upholstered chairs were stained brown and richly carved into leafy vines that hurt the back. Frau Slama brought in some cool lemonade; she sipped it daintily, her pinkie cocked and one leg crossing the other. She sat next to Carl Joseph, turning toward him and jiggling one foot, which was trapped in a red velvet slipper, naked, without a stocking. Carl Joseph eyed the foot, then the lemonade. He did not look at Frau Slama's face. His cap lay on his knees. He kept them stiff. He sat upright in front of the lemonade as if drinking it were an official obligation.

"You haven't been here in a long time, Herr von Trotta," said the sergeant's wife. "You've really grown! Are you past fourteen?"

"Yes, ma'am, long ago." He thought of leaving the house as fast as possible. He would have to bolt down the lemonade, bow nicely, tell her to give his best to her husband, and leave. He gazed helplessly at the lemonade; there was no finishing it. Frau Slama refilled his glass. She brought cigarettes. He was not allowed to smoke. She lit a cigarette for herself and drew on it indolently, with flaring nostrils, and jiggled her foot. Suddenly, without a word, she took the cap from his knees and put it on the table. Then she thrust her cigarette into his mouth. Her hand was redolent with smoke and cologne; the bright sleeve of her dressing gown with its pattern of summery flowers shimmered before his eyes. He politely puffed the cigarette, its tip wet from her mouth, and gazed at the lemonade. Frau Slama reinserted the cigarette between her teeth and placed herself behind Carl Joseph. He was afraid to turn around. All at once, both her shimmering sleeves were around his neck, and her face bore down on his hair. He did not stir. But his heart pounded; a huge tempest burst inside him, convulsively held back by his petrified body and the solid buttons of the uniform.

"Come on!" whispered Frau Slama. She sat on his lap, kissed him hurriedly, and eyed him roguishly. A tuft of blond hair accidentally dropped into her forehead; she peered upward, trying to puff it away with puckered lips. He began feeling her weight on his legs; at the same time new energy gushed through him, tensing the muscles in his thighs and arms. He embraced the woman and felt the soft coolness of her breasts through the tough cloth of the uniform. A soft chuckle erupted from her throat, a bit like a sob and a bit like a warble. Tears formed in her eyes. Then she leaned back and with delicate precision began undoing button after button on his tunic. She placed a cool, tender hand on his chest, kissed his mouth with prolonged and systematic relish, and suddenly rose as if startled by some noise. He promptly leaped up, she smiled and slowly drew him along, stepping backward, with both hands outstretched and her head thrown back, a radiance in her face, moving toward the door, which she opened by kicking behind her. They glided into the bedroom.

As if helplessly fettered, he watched her through half-shut eyelids while she undressed him, slow, thorough, and motherly. Somewhat dismayed, he noticed his full-dress uniform falling slackly to the floor, piece by piece; he heard the thudding of his shoes and instantly felt Frau Slama's hand on his foot. From below, a new billow of warmth and coolness swept up to his chest. He let himself go slack. He received the woman like a huge soft wave of bliss, fire, and water.

He woke up. Frau Slama stood before him, handing him his clothing piece by piece; he began to dress hastily. She hurried into the parlor, brought him his gloves and cap. She straightened his tunic. He felt her constant glances on his face but avoided looking at her. He banged his heels together, shook the woman's hand while gazing stubbornly at her right shoulder, and went off.

A bell-tower clock struck seven. The sun was nearing the hills, which were now as blue as the sky and barely distinguishable from clouds. Sweet fragrance flowed from the trees along the way. The evening wind combed the small grasses of the sloping meadows on both sides of the road; he could see the grasses quivering and billowing under the wind's broad, quiet, invisible hand. In distant marshes, the frogs began to croak. At an open window of a bright yellow cottage on the edge of town, a young woman stared at the empty road. Although Carl Joseph had never seen her before, he greeted her, stiff and reverential. She nodded back, rather surprised and grateful. It was as if he had said goodbye to Frau Slama only now. The strange, familiar woman stood at the window like a border guard between love and life. After greeting her, he felt restored to the world. He quickened his pace. At the stroke of seven-forty-five he was home, announcing his return to his father, pale, terse, and resolute, as is appropriate for men.

The sergeant had patrol duty every other day. Every other day, he came to the district captain's headquarters with a stack of documents. He never ran into the district captain's son. Every other day at four in the afternoon, Carl Joseph marched to the constabulary headquarters. He left it at 7 P.M. The fragrance he brought along from Frau Slama blended with the smells of the dry summer evenings, lingering on his hands day and night. At meals, he made sure never to get closer to his father than necessary.

"It smells of autumn here," the old man said one evening. He was generalizing. Frau Slama always used mignonette.

Chapter 3

IN THE DISTRICT captain's study, the portrait hung opposite the windows and so high on the wall that hair and forehead blurred into the dark-brown shadow under the old wooden ceiling. The grandson's curiosity constantly focused on his grandfather's blurring figure and vanished fame. Sometimes, on still afternoons (the windows open, the dark-green shadows of the chestnut trees in the town park filling the room with the entire mellow and powerful calm of the summer, the district captain heading one of his commissions outside the town, old Jacques's ghostly steps shuffling from distant stairs as he trudged through the house in felt slippers, gathering shoes, clothes, ashtrays, candelabras, and floor lamps for cleaning and polishing), Carl Joseph would climb on a chair and view his grandfather's portrait up close. It splintered into countless deep shadows and bright highlights, into brush strokes and dabs, into a myriad weave of the painted canvas, into a hard colored interplay of dried oil. Carl Joseph got down from the chair. The green shade of the trees flashed on the grandfather's brown coat, the dabs and brush strokes merged back into the familiar but unfathomable physiognomy, and the eyes regained their usual remote look that blurred toward the darkness of the ceiling. The grandson's mute conversations with the grandfather took place every summer vacation. The dead man revealed nothing; the boy learned nothing. From year to year, the portrait seemed to be growing paler and more otherworldly, as if the Hero of Solferino were dying once again and a time would come when an empty canvas would stare down upon the descendant even more mutely than the portrait.

In the courtyard below, in the shade of the wooden balcony, Jacques sat on a stool in front of an orderly military line of waxed boots. Whenever Carl Joseph returned home from Frau Slama, he would go over to Jacques in the courtyard and perch on a ledge. "Tell me about Grandfather, Jacques." And Jacques would put down brush, shoe wax, and brass polish and rub his hands as if cleansing them of work and dirt before starting to talk about the deceased. And as usual, like a good twenty times in the past, he would begin.

"I always got on fine with him. I wasn't so young when I came to the farm. I never married; the baron wouldn't have liked that. He never cared much for women, aside from his own Frau Baroness, but she soon died—her lungs. Everyone knew he had saved the Kaiser's life at the Battle of Solferino, but he kept mum about it, never a peep out of him. That was why they wrote 'The Hero of Solferino' on his gravestone. He wasn't so old when he died; it was in the evening, around nine, in November. It was already snowing. That afternoon he'd been standing in the courtyard, and he said, 'Jacques, where did you put my fur-lined boots?' I didn't know where, but I said, 'I'll get them, Herr Baron.' 'Tomorrow's soon enough!' he says—and tomorrow he no longer needed them. I never got married."

That was all.

Once—it was the last summer vacation; a year from now Carl Joseph was to join the regiment—when the boy was leaving, the district captain said, "I hope everything goes smoothly. You are the grandson of the Hero of Solferino. Think about it, then nothing can happen to you!"

The colonel, all the teachers, and all the junior officers likewise thought about it, and so indeed nothing could happen to Carl Joseph. Although he was not an excellent horseman, was weak in topography, and had utterly failed trigonometry, he was graduated "with a good average," given a lieutenant's commission, and assigned to the Tenth Lancers.

His eyes intoxicated with his own new glory and the commencement mass, his ears ringing with the colonel's thunderous farewell speeches, his body sporting the azure tunic with gold buttons, the silver bandolier with its august golden two-headed eagle on its back, the *czapka* with a metal chinstrap, the horsehair plume in his left hand, bright-red jodhpurs, mirrorlike boots, and singing spurs, and on his hip the broad-hilted saber: that was how Carl Joseph presented himself to his father one hot summer day. This time it was not a Sunday. A lieutenant could also arrive on a Wednesday.

The district captain was sitting in his study. "Make yourself comfortable!" he said. He took off the pince-nez, squinted, stood up, scrutinized his son, and found everything in order. He hugged Carl Joseph. They kissed one another casually on the cheek. "Sit down!" said the district captain, pressing the lieutenant into a chair. He himself then paced up and down the room. He was casting about for a suitable approach. A rebuke was not appropriate this time, nor could one start on a note of satisfaction.

"You should now," he finally said, "study the history of your regiment and read a bit in the history of the regiment in which your grandfather fought. I have to spend two days in Vienna on business. You'll be accompanying me." Then he swung the handbell. Jacques came. "Fräulein Hirschwitz," the district captain commanded, "is to have some wine brought up today and, if possible, prepare beef and cherry dumplings. Today we're lunching twenty minutes later than usual."

"Yessir, Herr Baron," said Jacques. He looked at Carl Joseph and whispered, "Congratulations!"

The district captain went to the window; the scene threatened to turn poignant. Behind his back he heard his son shaking the butler's hand, Jacques scraping his feet, murmuring something unintelligible about the deceased lord. The father turned around only after Jacques left the room.

"It's hot, isn't it?" the old man began.

"Yessir, Pápa!"

"I think we out to go out."

"Yessir, Pápa!"

The district captain took the black ebony stick with the silver pommel, not the yellow cane that he ordinarily liked to carry on bright mornings. Nor did he hold his gloves in his left hand, he slipped them on. He donned his silk hat and left the room, followed by the boy. Slowly and without exchanging a word, they walked through the summery stillness of the town park.

The town policeman saluted. Men rose from the banks and greeted them. Next to the old man's dark gravity, the boy's jingling colorfulness seemed even noisier and more radiant. At the park promenade, where a light-blond girl under a red sunshade was pouring soda water with raspberry juice, the old man halted and said, "A cool drink couldn't hurt!" He ordered two sodas plain and, with stealthy dignity, observed the blond girl, who, lustful and will-less, seemed utterly absorbed in Carl Joseph's colorful effulgence. They drank and walked on. Sometimes the district captain swung his cane slightly; it hinted at an exuberance that knows where to stop. Though his usual silent and earnest self, today he struck his son as almost breezy. From his cheery interior, a slight coughing occasionally broke forth, a kind of laughter. If someone greeted him, he briefly raised his hat. There were moments when he even ventured to come out with bold paradoxes: for example, "Politeness too can become burdensome!" He preferred to say something daring rather than betray his delight at the astonished looks from passersby. As they were approaching the front gates of the house, he halted once again. Turning his face to his son, he said, "In my youth, I would have liked to become a soldier. Your grandfather explicitly prohibited it. Now I'm glad that you're not a government official."

"Yessir, Pápa!" replied Carl Joseph.

There was wine; they had also managed to muster up beef and cherry dumplings. Fräulein Hirschwitz came in her gray Sunday silk and, upon seeing Carl Joseph, relinquished most of her severity without further ado. "I am utterly delighted," she said, "and congratulate you from the bottom of my heart"—using the German word *beglückwünschen* for "congratulate." The district captain translated it into the Austrian word *gratulieren*. And they began to eat.

"You don't have to hurry!" said the old man. "If I finish first, I'll wait a little."

Carl Joseph looked up. He realized his father must have always known what an effort it was to keep up with him. And for the first time he felt he could see through the old man's armor, into his living heart and into the web of his secret thoughts. Though he was already a lieutenant, Carl Joseph turned red. "Thank you, Pápa," he said. The district captain kept eating his soup. He seemed not to hear.

A few days later, they boarded the train for Vienna. The son was reading a newspaper, the old man documents. At one point the district captain glanced up and said, "We'll have to order you a pair of dress trousers in Vienna, you've only got two."

"Thank you, Pápa!" They continued reading.

They were just fifteen minutes from Vienna when the father put away the documents. The son instantly folded the newspaper. The district captain peered at the windowpane, then for a few seconds at the son. All at once, he said, "You know Constable Sergeant Slama, don't you?"

The name banged against Carl Joseph's memory, a cry from lost times. He instantly saw the road leading to the constabulary headquarters, the low room, the flowery dressing gown, the wide well-upholstered bed; he caught the scent of meadows and also Frau Slama's mignonette. He listened.

"Unfortunately he was widowed this year," the old man went on. "Sad. His wife died in childbirth. You should call on him."

All at once the train compartment was unbearably hot. Carl Joseph tried to loosen his collar. As he vainly struggled for appropriate words, a hot, foolish, childish desire to weep rose up in him, strangling him; his palate was dry as if he had drunk nothing for days. He felt his father's eyes, peered strenuously at the countryside, sensed the nearness of the destination toward which they were heading inexorably, felt it as a sharpening of his torment, longed to be at least in the corridor, and simultaneously realized that he could not escape the old man's eyes and news. He quickly gathered a bit of weak, temporary strength and said, "I'll call on him."

"The train ride doesn't seem to be agreeing with you," the father remarked.

"Yessir, Pápa"

Mute and upright, plagued by a torment that he could not have named, that he had never known, that was like an enigmatic disease from distant climes, Carl Joseph went to the hotel. He

barely managed to say, "Excuse me, Pápa!" Then he locked his
door, unpacked his suitcase, and pulled out the folder containing
a few letters from Frau Slama in their envelopes, as they had
come, with the encoded address: *General Delivery, Hranice, Moravia*. The blue pages were the color of the sky and had a hint of
mignonette, and the black, dainty letters soared off like an
orderly flight of sleek swallows. Letters from a dead Frau Slama!
To Carl Joseph they seemed like early harbingers of her sudden
end, with the spectral grace that emanates only from doomed
hands, anticipatory greetings from the beyond. He had not
answered her last letter. The induction, the speeches, the leave-
taking, the mass, his commission, his new rank, and the new
uniforms lost their meaning before the dark, weightless procession of the letters sweeping across the blue background. The
traces of the dead woman's caressing hands still lay upon his
skin, and his own warm hands still contained the memory of her
cool breasts, and with closed eyes he saw the blissful weariness in
her love-sated face, the parted red lips and the white shimmer of
the teeth, the indolently bent arm, in every line of the body the
flowing reflection of contented dreams and happy sleep. Now
the worms were crawling over her breasts and thighs, and decay
was thoroughly devouring her face. The more intense the
dreadful images of rot before the young man's eyes, the more
vehemently they kindled his passion. It seemed to be reaching
out into the incomprehensible boundlessness of those regions
where the dead woman had vanished. I probably would never
have visited her again, the lieutenant mused. I would have
forgotten her. Her words were tender, she was a mother, she
loved me, she died! It was clear that her death was his fault. She
lay on the threshold of his life, a beloved corpse.

It was Carl Joseph's first encounter with death. He did not
remember his mother. All he knew of her was a grave and
flowerbed and two photographs. But now death flashed up
before him like a black lightning bolt, striking his harmless joys,
scorching his youth, and hurling him to the brink of the gloomy
abyss that divides the living from the dead. Ahead of him lay a
life of grief. He braced himself to endure it, pale and resolute, as
befits a man. He packed away her letters. He shut the suitcase.

He stepped into the corridor, knocked on his father's door, entered, and heard the old man's voice as if through a thick glass wall: "You seem to have a soft heart!" The district captain adjusted his tie at the mirror. He had some business at the governor's residence, the police headquarters, the Higher Regional Court. "You're accompanying me," he said.

They drove in the two-horse carriage on rubber wheels. The streets looked more festive than ever to Carl Joseph. The vast summery gold of the afternoon flowed over houses and trees, trolleys, pedestrians, policemen, green benches, monuments, and gardens. You could hear the swift clippity-clop of the hooves on the cobblestones. Young women glided by like bright, dainty lights. Soldiers saluted. Shopwindows glistened. The summer wafted gently through the big city.

But all the beauties of summer glided unseen past Carl Joseph's indifferent eyes. His father's words banged against his ears. The old man was noting hundreds of changes: relocated tobacco shops, new kiosks, extended bus lines, shifted stops. A lot had been different in his day. But his loyal memory clung to all that had vanished as well as all that was preserved; with soft and unusual tenderness his voice raised tiny treasures from buried times; his thin hand moved to greet the places where his youth had once blossomed. Carl Joseph kept silent. He too had just lost his youth. His love was dead, but his heart was open to his father's nostalgia, and he began to sense that behind the district captain's bony hardness someone else was hidden, a mysterious yet familiar man, a Trotta, descendant of a Slovenian war invalid and of the singular Hero of Solferino. And the livelier the old man's cries and remarks, the sparser and softer the boy's obedient and habitual confirmations, and the smart and dutiful "Yessir, Pápa," drilled into his tongue since infancy, now sounded different: brotherly and confidential. The father seemed to be growing younger and the son older.

They stopped off at several government buildings, where the district captain looked for earlier comrades, witnesses to his youth. Brandl had become a police superintendent, Smekal a department head, Monteschitzky a colonel, and Hasselbrunner an embassy councilor. Father and son went to shops: at Reitmeyer on

Die Tuchlauben they ordered a pair of formal ankle boots, matte, kidskin, for court balls and official audiences; a pair of formal trousers at Ettlinger, a royal and military tailor on Die Wieden. And then something unbelievable happened at Schafransky, jeweler to the Emperor: the district captain picked out a silver cigarette case, solid and with a fluted back—a de luxe item, to be engraved with the words *In periculo securitas. Your Father.*

They landed at the Volksgarten and had coffee. The round tables on the terrace shone white in the dark-green shade, the siphons turned blue on the tablecloths. When the band paused, they heard the jubilant singing of the birds. The district captain raised his head and, as if drawing memories from above, he began, "I once met a girl here. How long ago was it?" He got lost in mute calculations. Long, long years seemed to have waned since then; Carl Joseph felt as if it were not his father sitting next to him, but a distant forebear. "Her name was Mizzi Schinagl," said the old man. In the dense crowns of the chestnut trees, he looked for the vanished portrait of Fräulein Schinagl as if she had been a bird.

"Is she still alive?" Carl Joseph asked out of courtesy, and as though to find a clue for assessing bygone eras.

"I hope so! In my day, you know, we weren't sentimental. We said goodbye to girls and also to friends—"

He broke off suddenly. A stranger stood at their table, a man with a trilby and a flowing tie, a very old gray cutaway with slack ends, and thick long hair down the back of his neck, his broad gray face poorly shaved—a painter obviously, with that exaggerated clarity of the traditional artistic physiognomy that seems unreal and clipped from old illustrations. The stranger put his portfolio on the table and was about to hawk his works with the arrogant equanimity that poverty and a sense of mission seemed to inspire in him in equal parts.

"Why, Moser!" said Herr von Trotta.

The painter slowly rolled his heavy lids up from his large bright eyes, perused the district captain for a few seconds, then held out his hand and said, "Trotta!"

The next moment he had doffed both amazement and gentleness. He hurled the portfolio down so hard the glasses trembled, and he shouted "Damn it!" three times in a row as mightily as if damning were in his power; he scanned the neighboring tables triumphantly as if expecting applause from the patrons; he sat down, removed his trilby and tossed it on the gravel by the chair, shoved the portfolio from the table with his elbows, described his work as "garbage," poked his head toward the lieutenant, frowned, leaned back again, and said, "Your son, Herr Governor?"

"This is my boyhood friend, Herr Professor Moser," explained the district captain.

"Damn it, Herr Governor!" Moser repeated. He simultaneously reached for a waiter's tuxedo tails, stood up and whispered an order like a secret, sat down, and lapsed into silence, fixing his eyes on the direction from which the waiter would carry the drinks. Finally a seltzer glass stood in front of him, half filled with slivovitz as clear as water; he passed it to and fro several times under his flaring nostrils, brought it to his mouth with a tremendous sweep of his arm as if to drain a huge tankard chugalug, but finally took only a small sip and then stuck out his tongue to gather the drops from his lips.

"You've been here two weeks and you haven't come by!" he began, with the prying severity of a higher rank.

"My dear Moser," said Herr von Trotta. "I arrived yesterday and I'm going back tomorrow morning."

The painter stared into the district captain's face for a long time. Then he set the glass to his lips again and drained it without stopping, like water. When he tried to put it down, he missed the saucer, and so he let Carl Joseph take the glass from his hand. "Thank you!" said the painter and leveled his forefinger at the lieutenant. "Extraordinary, the resemblance to the Hero of Solferino! Only a little softer. A weakish nose. Soft mouth. But things may change in time. . . ."

"Professor Moser did a portrait of Grandfather," remarked old Trotta. Carl Joseph looked at his father and at the painter, and his grandfather's portrait emerged in his memory, blurring under the ceiling of the study. His grandfather's relationship to this professor seemed incomprehensible; his father's intimacy with Moser startled him. He saw the stranger's broad, dirty hand drop with a friendly smack on the district captain's striped trousers, and he saw the gentle, defensive retreat of his father's thigh. There the old man sat, dignified as ever, leaning back, virtually deterred by the smell of alcohol aimed at his chest and his face, and yet he smiled and put up with it all.

"You should get an overhaul," said the painter. "You've grown shabby! Your father looked very different."

The district captain stroked his whiskers and smiled.

"Yes, old Trotta!" the painter resumed.

"Check," the district captain said abruptly and quietly. "Do forgive us, Moser, we have an appointment."

The painter remained seated; father and son left the garden.

The district captain tucked his arm under his son's. This was the first time that Carl Joseph felt his father's gaunt arm on his chest. The paternal hand in the dark-gray kid glove rested in slightly bent familiarity on the blue sleeve of his uniform. It was the same hand that, haggard and wrathful, encased in the stiff clattering cuff, could admonish and warn, leaf through papers with sharp, quiet fingers, shove drawers into their compartments with grim jolts, twist keys so resolutely that the locks seemed locked for all eternity. It was the hand that drummed on the table's edge with lurking impatience if things were not to the master's liking and on the windowpane if something awkward had occurred in the room. This hand could raise its thin forefinger if someone had neglected something in the house; it could clench into a mute, never-striking fist, settle tenderly around the forehead, remove the pince-nez gingerly, bend lightly around the wineglass, bring the black Virginia cigar caressingly to the lips. It was his father's left hand, long familiar to the son. And yet he sensed he was only just learning that it was the father's hand, the paternal hand. Carl Joseph felt a desire to press this hand to his chest.

"You know, Moser—" the district captain began, paused a while, cast about for a fair judgment, and finally said, "He could have made something of himself."

"Yes, Pápa!"

"When he did Grandfather's picture, he was sixteen years old. We were both sixteen years old. He was my only friend at school. Then he enrolled at the academy. Well, liquor got hold of him. But he's still . . . ." The district captain paused, then said, only after a few minutes; "Among all the people I saw today, he's still my friend."

"Yes—Father."

This was the first time Carl Joseph had ever pronounced the word *father*. "Yessir, Papá!" he quickly corrected himself.

It was getting dark. The evening fell vehemently into the street.

"Are you cold, Papá?"

"Not a bit!"

But the district captain strode faster. Soon they were near the hotel.

"Herr Governor!" someone boomed behind them. Moser, the painter, had clearly followed them. They turned. There he stood, hat in hand, lowering his head, humble, as if to undo his ironic salutation. "Please excuse me, gentlemen," he said. "I noticed too late that my cigarette case is empty." He displayed an open, empty tin container. The district captain pulled out his cigar case, "I don't smoke cigars," said the painter.

Carl Joseph held out a pack of cigarettes.

Moser awkwardly put his portfolio on the pavement, at his feet, filled his cigarette case, asked for a light, curved both hands around the small blue flame. His hands were red and sticky, too large for their wrists; they trembled softly, recalled senseless tools. His nails were like small, flat, black spades that had just been grubbing in soil, feces, colored pulp, and tobacco juice. "We won't be meeting again," he said, bending over for his portfolio. He stood up, thick tears rolling down his cheeks. "Won't be meeting again!" he blubbered.

"I have to go up to my room for a moment," said Carl Joseph and entered the hotel.

He ran up the stairs to his room, leaned out the window, anxiously observed his father, saw the old man producing his wallet, the rejuvenated painter putting his ghastly hand on the baron's shoulder two seconds later, and heard Moser exclaiming, "Well, Franz, on the third, as usual!"

Carl Joseph ran back down, feeling he had to protect his father; the professor saluted, stepped back, and left with a final greeting, his head high; he walked with somnambular self-confidence straight across the roadway and waved once again from the opposite pavement before vanishing in a side street. An instant later, however, he reemerged, shouting "Hold on!" so loudly that the silent street reverberated; he bounded across the roadway with incredibly sure, huge leaps and stood in front of the hotel, as casual and virtually newly arrived as if he had not taken his leave just minutes ago. And as though seeing his boyhood friend and the latter's son for the first time, he began in a plaintive voice, "How sad it is to meet again like this! Do you still remember that we sat side by side in the third row? You were bad in Greek; I always let you copy. If you're really honest, then say so yourself in front of your scion! Didn't I always let you copy everything?" And to Carl Joseph: "He was a good guy, your father, but a scaredy-cat. He only started going to prostitutes very late, I had to boost his courage, otherwise he'd never have managed. Be fair, Trotta! Admit I took you!"

The district captain smirked and held his tongue.

Moser the painter geared up for a long lecture. He deposited his portfolio on the sidewalk, doffed his hat, put one foot forward, and began. "When I first met the old man, it was summer vacation; you remember, don't you?" He suddenly broke off and felt all his pockets with flurried hands. Sweat formed thick beads on his forehead. "I've lost it!" he cried, trembling and reeling. "I've lost the money!"

At that instant, the doorman stepped out of the hotel. He greeted the district captain and the lieutenant with a vigorous sweep of his gold-braided cap but showed an angry face. He glared as if about to order the painter Moser to stop loitering, making noise, and insulting the guests in front of the hotel. Old Trotta reached into his breast pocket; the painter lapsed into silence.

"Can you help me out?" the father asked his son.

The lieutenant said, "I'll accompany Professor Moser a bit of the way. Goodbye, Pápa!"

The district captain raised his silk hat and went into the hotel. The lieutenant handed the professor a banknote and followed his father. Moser the painter picked up his portfolio and retreated with a gravely tottering dignity.

The deep evening had already settled in the streets; the hotel lobby was also dark. The district captain, dimming into the twilight, sat in the leather chair, the room key in his hand, his cane and silk hat at his side. His son halted at a respectful distance as if wanting to submit an official report on the resolution of the Moser affair. The lamps were not lit as yet. Out of the twilit silence came the old man's voice. "We're leaving tomorrow afternoon at two-fifteen."

"Yessir, Papá!"

"It occurred to me during the music that you should call on Kapellmeister Nechwal. After visiting Sergeant Slama, of course. Do you have anything to take care of in Vienna?"

"Send for the trousers and the cigarette case."

"What else?"

"Nothing, Papá"

"Tomorrow morning you will pay your respects to your uncle. Evidently you've forgotten. How often have you been his guest?"

"Twice a year, Papá!"

"There you are! Give him my best. Apologize for me. Incidentally, how's he looking, my good Stransky?"

"Very well, last time I saw him."

The district captain reached for his cane and propped his outstretched hand upon the silver crook—his habit when standing—as if even when sitting he required a special support once Stransky's name popped up.

"The last time *I* saw him was nineteen years ago. He was still a first lieutenant. Already in love with that Koppelmann woman. Incurably! The whole thing was quite deplorable. Simply in love with a Koppelmann." He pronounced this name louder than anything else and with a sharp caesura between the two parts. "Naturally they couldn't scrape up the dowry. Your mother nearly talked me into coming up with half."

"He left the army?"

"Yes, that he did. And joined the Northern Railroad. How far has he gotten today? Railroad official, I believe, right?"

"Yessir, Papá!"

"There you are. Didn't he let his son become a pharmacist?"

"No, Papá, Alexander is still in high school."

"I see. Limps slightly, I've heard, right?"

"One leg's shorter than the other."

"Oh, well!" The old man finished contentedly, as if he had foreseen nineteen years ago that Alexander would limp.

He stood up. The lamps in the lobby flared, illuminating his pallor. "I'm getting some money," he said. He approached the stairs.

"I'll get it, Papá!" said Carl Joseph.

"Thank you," said the district captain.

Then, while they were eating pastry, he said, "I recommend the Bacchus Hall. It's supposed to be the latest thing. You may run into Smekal there."

"Thank you, Papá! Good night!"

From 11 P.M. to midnight, Carl Joseph visited Uncle Stransky's home. The railroad official was still at the office; his wife, née Koppelmann, sent her best to the district captain. Carl Joseph walked slowly along the Ring Promenade to the hotel. He turned into Die Tuchlauben, had the trousers delivered to the hotel, and picked up the cigarette case. The metal was cool; he felt the coolness on his skin through the pocket of his thin blouse. He thought of the condolence visit he would have to pay Sergeant Slama and made up his mind not to enter that room no matter what. My sincerest condolences, Herr Slama! he would say, out on the veranda. The larks are warbling invisibly in the blue vault. You can hear the drawling whispers of the crickets. You can smell the hay, the late fragrance of acacias, the burgeoning buds in the small garden of the constabulary headquarters. Frau Slama is dead. Kathi—Katharina Luise, according to her baptismal certificate—she is dead.

They took the train home. The district captain put away the documents, cradled his head between the red velvet cushions in the window corner, and closed his eyes.

This was the first time that Carl Joseph saw the district captain's head in a supine position, the flaring nostrils of his narrow, bony nose, the delicate cleft in the clean-shaven powdered chin, and the whiskers calmly splayed into two small wide black wings. Their extreme corners were already silvering; old age had already grazed him there and also on the temples. He's going to die someday, thought Carl Joseph. He's going to die and be buried. I'm going to remain.

They were alone in the compartment. The father's slumbering countenance swayed peacefully in the reddish twilight of the upholstery. Under the black moustache, the pale tight lips formed a single line, the bald Adam's apple on the narrow throat jutted out between the shiny corners of the stand-up collar, the infinitely wrinkled, bluish skin of the closed eyelids quivered steadily and quietly, the wide burgundy tie rose and sank evenly, and the hands were also asleep, buried in the armpits, the arms crisscrossed on the chest. A vast stillness emanated from the sleeping father. Unconscious and appeased, his severity was slumbering too, embedded in the silent vertical furrow between nose and forehead, the way a storm sleeps in the jagged fissure between mountains. Carl Joseph was familiar with this furrow, even intimate. It adorned his grandfather's face on the portrait in the study: the same furrow, the angry insignia of the Trottas, the legacy of the Hero of Solferino.

His father opened his eyes. "How much longer?"

"Two hours, Papá!"

It began to rain. It was Wednesday. The condolence visit to Slama was scheduled for Thursday afternoon. It rained again on Thursday morning. A quarter hour after lunch, when they were having coffee in the study, Carl Joseph said, "I'm going to the Slamas, Papá"

"There's only one, unfortunately," replied the district captain. "You'll most likely find him in at four."

At that instant, they heard two clear strokes from the church tower; the district captain raised his forefinger and pointed toward the window, in the direction of the bells. Carl Joseph turned red. It seemed as if his father, the rain, the clocks, people, time, and nature itself were determined to make his trip even more difficult. On those afternoons when he had managed to visit the living Frau Slama, he had also listened for the golden stroke of the bells, as impatient as today, but intent on *not* finding the sergeant in. Those afternoons seemed buried behind many decades. Death overshadowed and concealed them, Death stood between then and now, inserting his entire timeless darkness between past and present. And yet the golden stroke of the hours was still unchanged—and today, exactly as then, they were sitting in the study and drinking coffee.

"It's raining," said his father, as if first noticing it now. "Are you taking a carriage?"

"I like walking in the rain, Papá." He wanted to say, The road I take must be long, long. Perhaps I should have taken a carriage back then, when she was alive.

It was still. The rain was drumming against the window. The district captain got to his feet. "I have to go over there." He meant his office. "I'll see you later." He shut the door more gently than usual. Carl Joseph felt as if his father were standing outside for a while, eavesdropping.

Now the church bell struck quarter past, then half past. Two-thirty: another hour and a half. He stepped into the hall, took his coat, adjusted the prescribed creases in the back for a long time, tugged his saber hilt through the slit in his pocket, donned the cap mechanically in front of the mirror, and left the house.

Chapter 4

HE TOOK THE habitual route, under the open railroad barriers, past the sleeping yellow tax office. From here one could already see the lonesome constabulary headquarters. He walked on. The small cemetery with the wooden gate lay ten minutes beyond the headquarters. The veil of rain seemed to cover the dead more densely. The lieutenant touched the wet iron handle; he entered. An unknown bird was warbling desolately. Where might it be hiding? Wasn't it singing from a grave? He unlatched the cemetery office door; an old woman with spectacles on her nose was peeling potatoes. She let both peels and potatoes drop from her lap into the pail and stood up.

"I would like to see Frau Slama's grave."

"Next to last row, Fourteen, Grave Seven!" the woman said promptly, as if she had been expecting this question for the longest time.

The grave was still fresh: a tiny mound, a small temporary wooden cross, and a rain-drenched wreath of glass violets reminiscent of bonbons and pastry shops. KATHARINA LUISE SLAMA, BORN, DIED. She lay below; the fat curling worms were just starting to gnaw cozily on her round white breasts. The lieutenant shut his eyes and doffed his cap. The rain caressed his parted hair with wet tenderness. He paid no heed to the grave; the decaying body under this mound had nothing to do with Frau Slama: dead, she was dead—beyond reach, even though he was standing at her grave. The flesh buried in his memory was closer to him than the corpse beneath this mound. Carl Joseph donned his cap and pulled out his watch. Another half hour. He left the cemetery.

He reached the constabulary headquarters, rang the bell, no one came. The sergeant was not home yet. The rain gurgled over the dense wild grape leaves shrouding the veranda. Carl Joseph paced to and fro, to and fro, lit a cigarette, tossed it away, felt he must look like a sentry, turned his head whenever his eyes encountered that right-hand window from which Katharina had always looked; he pulled out his watch, pressed the white bell button once again, waited.

Four muffled strokes came slowly from the town's church tower. Now the sergeant appeared. He saluted mechanically before he even saw who was there. As if responding not to a greeting but to a threat from the sergeant, Carl Joseph exclaimed, louder than he intended, "Good day, Herr Slama!" He stretched out his hand, virtually plunging into the greeting as into an entrenchment, and with the impatience of a man bracing himself for an attack he awaited the sergeant's clumsy preparations, his strenuous effort in stripping off his wet cotton glove and his sedulous devotion to this enterprise and his lowered gaze. At last, the bare hand settled, damp, broad, and slack, into the lieutenant's hand.

"Thank you for calling, Herr Baron!" said the sergeant, as if the lieutenant had not just arrived but were about to leave. The sergeant pulled out the key. He unlocked the door. A gust of wind lashed the pattering rain against the veranda. It seemed to be driving the lieutenant into the house. The hallway was gloomy. Didn't a narrow streak light up, narrow, silvery, an earthly trace of the dead woman?

The sergeant opened the kitchen door; the streak drowned in the flooding light. "Please take off your coat," said Slama. He was still in his, the belt still buckled.

My sincere condolences! thinks the lieutenant. I'll say it fast and then leave. Slama's arms are already widening to remove Carl Joseph's coat. Carl Joseph yields to the courtesy, Slama's hand momentarily grazes the back of the lieutenant's neck, the hairline above the collar, the very place where Frau Slama's hands used to interlock, a tender clasp of the beloved chain. When, at which exact point, can you finally unload the condolence formula? When entering the parlor or only after sitting down? Do you then have to stand up again? It's as if you couldn't utter the slightest sound until you say those stupid words—

something you've brought along and carried in your mouth the whole time. It lies on the tongue, burdensome and useless, with a stale taste.

The sergeant pushes down the door handle; the parlor is locked. He says, "Excuse me!" although it is not his fault. He reaches back into the pocket of the coat, which he has already taken off—it seems very long ago—and jingles the keys. This door was never locked when Frau Slama was alive.

So she's not here! the lieutenant suddenly thinks, as if he had not come here because she simply is not here anymore, and he notices that all this time he has secretly believed that she could be here, sitting in a room and waiting. Now she is undeniably no longer here. She is truly lying outside, in the grave he has just seen.

A damp smells lingers in the parlor. Of the two windows one is curtained; the gray light of the dreary day floats through the other. "Please step in," the sergeant says. He is right behind the lieutenant.

"Thank you," says Carl Joseph. And he steps in and walks to the round table; he is quite familiar with the pattern of the ribbed cloth covering it, and the small jagged stain in the middle, the brown finish, and the curlicues of the grooved feet. There stands the sideboard with its glass doors, nickel-silver beakers behind them and small porcelain figures and a yellow clay pig with a slot for coins on its back.

"Please do me the honor of having a seat," the sergeant murmurs. He stands behind a chair, his hands clutching its back; he holds it out like a shield.

Carl Joseph last saw him over four years ago. The sergeant was on duty then. He wore a scintillating panache on his black helmet; straps crisscrossed his chest; he stood with ordered arms, waiting outside the district captain's office. He was Sergeant Slama, his name was like his rank, both the panache and the blond moustache were part of his physiognomy. Now the sergeant stands there bareheaded, no saber, no strap or belt; one sees the greasy luster of the ribbed uniform cloth on the slight curve of the belly over the back of the chair, and he is no longer the Sergeant Slama of those days, he is Herr Slama, a constable sergeant on duty, once the husband of Frau Slama and now a widower and master of this house. His close-cropped blond hair lies, parted down the middle, like a small double brush over the uncreased chin with the horizontal reddish stripes left by the permanent pressure of the hard cap. Without cap or helmet, his head is orphaned. The face without the shade of the visor is a perfect oval, filled out with cheeks, nose, moustache, and small, blue, stubborn, guileless eyes. He waits for Carl Joseph to sit down, then shifts his own chair, likewise sits down, and pulls out his cigarette case. Its lid is made of particolored enamel. The sergeant puts the case in the center of the table, between him and the lieutenant, and says, "Would you care for a cigarette?"

It is time to express my condolences, Carl Joseph thinks to himself. He stands up and says, "My sincere condolences, Herr Slama!"

The sergeant sits with both hands in front of him on the edge of the table, appears not to grasp what is happening, tries to smile, rises too late just as Carl Joseph is about to sit down again; the sergeant takes his hands from the table and puts them on his trousers, lowers his head, raises it, looks at Carl Joseph as if asking what to do. They sit down again. It is over. They are silent.

"She was a fine woman, Frau Slama; may she rest in peace!" says the lieutenant.

The sergeant puts his hand on his moustache and says, with a wisp of it between his fingers, "She was beautiful. The Herr Baron knew her, didn't you?"

"I knew her, your wife. Was her death easy?"

"It took two days. By the time we sent for the doctor it was too late. Otherwise she would've survived. I had night duty. When I got home, she was dead. The financier's wife across the road was with her." And hard upon it: "Would you care for a raspberry drink?"

"Thank you, yes!" says Carl Joseph in a clearer voice, as if the raspberry drink could entirely alter the situation, and he sees the sergeant stand up and go to the sideboard, and he knows there is no raspberry drink there. It is in the kitchen, in the white cabinet, behind glass; that was where Frau Slama always got it. He closely watches all the sergeant's movements, the short strong arms in the tight sleeves, stretching to find the bottle on the top shelf, then sinking helplessly as his tiptoeing feet drop back on their soles; and Slama, virtually coming home from a foreign territory to which he has gone on a superfluous and, alas, unsuccessful expedition, turns around and with touching despair in his shiny blue eyes makes a simple announcement: "Please forgive me, I'm afraid I can't find it."

"It doesn't matter, Herr Slama," the lieutenant consoles him.

But, as if not hearing this solace or as if obeying a command that, expressly issued by a higher authority, can brook no interference from subalterns, the sergeant leaves the room. He can be heard rummaging in the kitchen; he comes back, bottle in hand, removes glasses with matte rim decorations from the sideboard, places a carafe of water on the table, pours the viscous ruby-red liquid from the dark-green bottle, and repeats, "Please do me the honor, Herr Baron!" The lieutenant pours water from the carafe into the raspberry juice; they remain silent. The water plunges from the sinuous mouth of the carafe, splashes a bit, and is like a small response to the tireless pouring of the rain outside, which they have been hearing all along. The rain, they know, envelops the lonesome house and seems to make the two men even more lonesome. They are alone. Carl Joseph raises his glass, the sergeant does likewise; the lieutenant tastes the sweet, sticky liquid. Slama drains his glass at one draught, he's thirsty, a strange, inexplicable thirst on this cool day.

"Joining the Tenth Lancers?" asks Slama.

"Yes. I don't know which regiment."

"I know a sergeant there, Zenower, he's in the audit department. He and I served with the riflemen, then he transferred. A great guy, very educated! He's sure to pass the officer's exam. People like us stay put. There are no prospects in the constabulary."

The rain has grown more intense, the gusts are more vehement, the drops keep pelting the window. Carl Joseph says, "It's generally difficult in our profession—I mean the military!" The sergeant bursts into a puzzling laughter; he seems utterly delighted that the profession practiced by him and the lieutenant is a difficult one. He laughs a bit harder than he intends. You can tell by his mouth, which is wider open than his laughter requires and which remains open longer than it lasts. So for an instant the sergeant, if only for physical reasons, might seem to have trouble regaining his normal earnest self. Is he truly delighted that he and Carl Joseph have such a difficult life?

"Herr Baron," the sergeant begins, "is good enough to speak of 'our' profession. Please do not take it amiss, but it's quite different for our kind."

Carl Joseph does not know how to respond. He feels—vaguely—that the sergeant is nursing a grudge toward him, perhaps toward the overall conditions in the army and the constabulary. At military school they never learned anything about how an officer is to conduct himself in this kind of situation. At any rate, Carl Joseph smiles, a smile that pulls down and squeezes his lips together like an iron clamp; he looks as if he is being chary with expressing pleasure, which the sergeant heedlessly fritters away. The raspberry drink, so sweet upon the tongue, sends a bitter, vapid taste back from the throat; it would call for a brandy chaser. The reddish parlor seems lower and smaller than usual; perhaps it is being squashed by the rain.

On the table lies the familiar album with the hard, shiny brass mountings. Carl Joseph is well acquainted with each and every picture. Sergeant Slama says, "May I?" and opens the album and offers it to the lieutenant. The sergeant is photographed here in mufti, as a young bridegroom at his wife's side. "In those days I was a still a platoon commander," he says somewhat bitterly, as if he would rather say that a higher rank would have been more befitting by then. Frau Slama sits next to him in a snug light-colored summer frock with a wasp waist as in an airy armor, a white broad-brimmed hat slanting across her hair. What is this? Has Carl Joseph never seen this picture before? Then why does it look so new to him today? And so old? And so alien? And so ridiculous? Yes, he smiles as if he were viewing a quaint picture from times long gone and as if Frau Slama had never been close and dear to him and as if she had died, not just a few months ago but years ago.

"She was very pretty! You can tell!" says Carl Joseph, no longer out of embarrassment, as before, but in honest flattery.

You have to say something nice about a dead woman in front of the widower you're condoling with.

He instantly feels liberated, and also severed from the dead woman, as if everything were snuffed out. It was all a fantasy! He finishes the raspberry drink, stands, and says, "I'll be going now, Herr Slama!" He does not wait, he wheels around, the sergeant barely has time to get up, they are already in the hallway, Carl Joseph already has his coat on, he slowly and luxuriously slips on his left glove, he suddenly has more time for that; and, upon saying, "Well, *auf Wiedersehn*, Herr Slama," Carl Joseph is gratified to catch an alien, haughty sound in his own voice.

Slama stands there with downcast eyes and helpless hands, which are suddenly empty as if after holding something until this very moment they had only just dropped it and lost it forever. They shake hands. Does Slama have something to say? No matter. "Perhaps another time, Herr Lieutenant!" he nevertheless says. No, he probably doesn't mean it, but Carl Joseph has already forgotten Slama's face. All he sees are the golden-yellow braids on the collar and the three golden chevrons on the black sleeve of his constable tunic.

"Goodbye, sergeant!"

The rain is still falling, mild, tireless, with sporadic warm mountain gusts. It feels as if evening should have come long ago, and yet evening cannot come. Eternal, this wet gray hatchwork. For the first time since he began wearing a uniform—indeed, for the first time since he began thinking—Carl Joseph feels he ought to pull his coat collar up. He even raises his hands for an instant, then recalls that he is in uniform and drops them again. It is as if he had forgotten his profession for a second. He walks slowly and jingly over the wet, crunching gravel of the front yard and delights in his slowness. He has no need to hurry; nothing has happened, it was all a dream. What time might it be? His watch is buried too deep under his tunic in the small trouser pocket. Not worth unbuttoning his coat. The church clock will be striking soon anyway.

He opens the garden gate, he steps into the road. "Herr Baron!" the constable suddenly says behind him. Mystifying how silently he has followed him. Yes, Carl Joseph is startled. He halts but cannot make up his mind to turn straightaway. Perhaps a pistol barrel is resting right in the hollow between the regulation creases in his coat. A grisly and childish idea! Is everything starting all over again?

"Yes?" he says, still with an arrogant casualness that almost arduously prolongs his leave-taking and is a great strain on him—and he wheels around.

Coatless and bareheaded, the sergeant stands in the rain, with his wet, small, double brush and thick beads of water on his blond, smooth forehead. He holds a small blue packet tied crosswise with a thin silver ribbon. "This is for you, Herr Baron," he says, with downcast eyes. "Please excuse me. I have orders from the district captain. I took it to him right away. The district captain skimmed it and said I should give it to you personally!"

The hush lasts for an instant. Only the rain pelts down on the poor little pale-blue packet, staining it utterly dark; it can no longer wait—the packet. Carl Joseph takes it, plunges it deep into his coat pocket, reddens, thinks momentarily about stripping the glove from his right hand, changes his mind, holds his leather-clad hand out to the sergeant, says, "Thank you very much," and leaves quickly.

He can feel the letters in his pocket. From there, through his hand, along his arm, an unknown heat swells up, turning his face a deeper red. He now feels that he should loosen his collar, just as he believed earlier that he should turn it up. The bitter aftertaste of the raspberry drink is back in his mouth. Carl Joseph takes out the packet. Yes, there is no doubt. These are his letters.

Evening should finally come and the rain stop. A number of things should change in the world: the evening sun perhaps send a final beam here. Through the rain the meadows exhale the familiar fragrance, and an alien bird lets out a lonesome cry; it has never been heard here before; this is like an alien land. He hears five o'clock striking: so it was exactly one hour ago—no more than one hour. Should one walk fast or slow? Time has an alien, enigmatic motion, an hour is like a year. The bell strikes a quarter past five. He has barely gone a few paces. Carl Joseph starts tramping faster. He crosses the rails; here is where the town's outlying houses begin. He walks past the town café; this is the only place with a modern revolving door. It might be good to go in, have a brandy at the bar, and then leave. Carl Joseph goes in.

"Quick, a brandy," he says at the counter. He keeps on his cap and coat, a few patrons stand up. You can hear the clattering of the pool balls and the chess figures. Garrison officers sit in the alcove shadows; Carl Joseph does not see them, does not salute them. Nothing is more urgent than the brandy. He is ashen. The pale-blond cashier smiles maternally from her lofty seat and, with a kind hand, places a sugar cube next to the cup. Carl Joseph drains it at one swoop. He instantly orders a refill. All he sees of the cashier's face is a light-blond shimmer and two gold caps in the corners of her mouth. He feels he is doing something forbidden, and he has no idea why drinking two brandies should be forbidden. After all, he is no longer a cadet. Why is the cashier ogling him with such a bizarre smile? Her navy-blue gaze disconcerts him, as does the charred blackness of her eyebrows. He turns and peers into the room. There in the corner by the window sits his father.

Yes, he is the district captain—and what's so amazing about that? He sits there every day, from five to seven, reading the *Foreign News* and the *Civil Service Gazette* and smoking a Virginia cigar. The whole town knows, it has known for three decades. The district captain sits there, watching his son, and he seems to be smiling. Carl Joseph doffs his cap and walks over to his father. Old Herr von Trotta glances up from his newspaper without putting it down and says, "Are you coming from Slama?"

"Yessir, Papá!"

"He gave you your letters?"

"Yessir, Papá!"

"Sit down, please."

"Yessir, Papá!"

The district captain finally lets go of the newspaper, props his elbows on the table, turns to his son, and says, "She's given you a cheap brandy. I always drink Hennessy."

"I'll remember that, Papá!"

"I seldom drink anyway."

"Yessir, Papá!"

"You're still pale. Take off your coat. Major Kreidl is over there, just look."

Carl Joseph stands up and bows to the major.

"Was Slama unpleasant?"

"No, quite a nice guy."

"There you are!"

Carl Joseph takes off his coat.

"Where are the letters?" asks the district captain. His son removes them from his coat pocket. Old Herr von Trotta takes hold of them. He weighs them in his right hand, puts them down, and says, "Quite a lot of letters!"

"Yessir, Papá!"

It is still, one hears the clatter of the pool balls and the chess figures, and the rain is pouring outside.

"The day after tomorrow you're reporting for duty!" says the district captain, glancing toward the window. All at once, Carl Joseph feels his father's gaunt hand on his right hand. The district captain's hand, cool and bony, a hard shell, lies on the lieutenant's.

Carl Joseph lowers his eyes to the tabletop. He turns red. He says, "Yessir, Papá!"

"Check!" calls the district captain, removing his hand. "Tell the girl," he remarks to the waiter, "that we only drink Hennessy."

In a dead-straight diagonal they veer across the café to the door, the father and, behind him, the son.

Now it is only dripping in a gentle singsong from the trees as they slowly walk home through the humid garden. From the entrance to the district headquarters, Sergeant Slama emerges in a helmet, with a rifle and a fixed bayonet plus a rule book under his arm.

"Good day, my dear Slama!" says old Herr von Trotta. "No news, eh?"

"No news," the sergeant echoes.

Chapter 5

THE BARRACKS LAY in the northern part of town. It closed off the broad well-kept highway, which started a new life behind the red brick construction, where it led far into the blue countryside. The barracks looked as if it had been thrust into the Slavic province by the Imperial and Royal Army as an emblem of the Hapsburg might. The ancient highway itself, which had become so broad and roomy after centuries of migrating Slavic generations, was blocked by the barracks. The highway had to yield. It looped around the barracks. If on a clear day you stood at the extreme northern edge of town at the end of the highway, where the houses grew smaller and smaller, finally becoming peasant huts, you could spy, in the distance, the broad, arched, black-and-yellow entrance to the barracks, a gate brandished like a mighty Hapsburg shield against the town: a threat, a protection, and both at once. The regiment was stationed in Moravia. But its troops were not Czechs, as might be expected; they were Ukrainians and Rumanians.

Twice a week, military exercises took place on the southern terrain. Twice a week, the regiment galloped through the streets of the little town. The clear blaring peal of the trumpets interrupted the regular clopping of the horses' hooves at regular intervals, and the red trousers of the men astride the glossy brown bodies of the chargers filled the little town with gory splendor. The citizens paused on the curbs. The shopkeepers left their shops, the idle café patrons their tables, the town policemen their customary beats, and the farmers, coming from the villages and bringing fresh produce to the marketplace, their horses and wagons. Only the coachmen on the few fiacres lined up near the town park remained immobile on their boxes. From up above, they had an even better view of the military spectacle than the people standing at the curbs. And the old nags seemed to greet the splendid arrival of their younger and healthier brethren with dull indifference. The cavalry steeds were very distant relatives of the bleak horses that for fifteen years now had done nothing but pull droshkies to the station and back.

Carl Joseph, Baron von Trotta, was unconcerned about the animals. At times he believed he felt the blood of his forebears inside himself: they had not been horsemen. With combing harrows in their hard hands, they had placed foot after foot on the ground. They had shoved the furrowing plows into the succulent clods of soil and trudged with buckling knees behind the massive pair of oxen. They had goaded the beasts with willow rods, not spurs and whips. And with arms raised high they had swung the polished scythes like flashes of lightning and harvested the rich crops they had sown themselves. His grandfather's father had been a peasant. Sipolje was the village they came from. Sipolje: the name had an ancient meaning. No one, not even today's Slovenes, really knew what it meant. But Carl Joseph felt he knew the village. He saw it whenever he recalled his grandfather's portrait, which hung blurring under the ceiling of the study. The village lay cradled between unknown mountains, under the golden glow of an unknown sun, with squalid huts of clay and thatch. A lovely village, a good village! He would have given his whole career as an officer for it.

Ah, he was no peasant, he was a baron and a lieutenant in the lancers! Unlike the other officers, he had no room of his own in town. Carl Joseph lived in the barracks. His window faced the parade ground. Across from him were the troop rooms. Whenever he returned home to the barracks in the afternoon, and the huge double gate closed behind him, he felt trapped; never again would the gates open before him. His spurs jingled frostily on the bare stone staircase, and the tread of his boots echoed on the brown caulked wooden floor of the corridor. The whitewashed walls clung to a bit of vanishing daylight, radiating it now, as if making sure in their bleak thrift that the government kerosene lamps in the corners were not lit until evening had thickened completely, as if they had collected the day at the right time in order to dole it out in the destitution of darkness.

Carl Joseph did not turn on the light. Pressing his forehead against the window, which seemed to separate him from the darkness but was actually the cool, familiar outer wall of the darkness itself, he peered into the bright yellow coziness of the troop rooms. He would have gladly traded places with any of the privates. There they sat, half undressed, in their coarse yellowish army shirts, dangling their bare feet over the edges of their bunks, singing, talking, and playing harmonicas. Around this time of day—autumn was already well advanced—an hour after lockup and an hour and a half before taps, the entire barracks resembled a gigantic ship. And Carl Joseph also felt as if it were rocking gently and the chary yellow kerosene lamps with the broad white shades were bobbing in the steady rhythm of waves on an unknown ocean. The men were crooning in an unknown language, a Slavic language. The old peasants of Sipolje would have probably understood them. Carl Joseph's grandfather might still have understood them! His enigmatic portrait blurred under the ceiling of the study. Carl Joseph's memory clung to this portrait as the sole and final emblem bequeathed to him by the long line of his unknown forebears. He was their offspring. Since joining the regiment, he felt he was his grandfather's grandson, not his father's son; indeed, he was the son of his strange grandfather. They kept playing their harmonicas over there nonstop. He could clearly see sporadic glints of the metal and the movements of the coarse brown hands pushing the metal instruments back and forth in front of red mouths. The vast melancholy of these instruments poured through the closed windows into the black rectangle of the parade ground, filling the darkness with vague inklings of home and wife and child and farm. Back home they lived in dwarfed huts, making their wives fertile by night and their fields by day. White and high, the snow piled around their huts in winter. Yellow and high, the grain billowed around their hips in summer. They were peasants. Peasants! And the Trotta dynasty had lived no differently. No differently!

The autumn was already well advanced. When he sat up in bed in the morning, the sun emerged like a blood-red orange on the eastern rim of the sky. And when physical training began on the water meadow, in the wide greenish glade framed by blackish firs, the silvery mists rose clumsily, torn apart by the vehement, regular motions of the dark-blue uniforms. Pale and dismal, the sun then rose. Its matte silver, cool and alien, broke through the black branches. Frosty shudders passed like a cruel comb over the russet skins of the horses, and their whinnying emerged from the nearby glade—painful cries for home and stable. The soldiers were doing "carbine exercises." Carl Joseph could hardly wait to get back to the barracks. He dreaded the fifteen-minute break, which started punctually at ten, and the conversations with his fellow officers, who sometimes gathered in the nearby tavern to have a beer and wait for Colonel Kovacs. Even more awkward was the evening at the officers' club. It would soon begin. Attendance was mandatory. Taps was fast approaching. The dark-blue jingling shadows of returning men flitted through the murky rectangle of the parade ground. Sergeant Reznicek was already stepping from his door, clutching his yellowly blinking lantern, and the buglers were gathering in the darkness. The yellow brass instruments shimmered against the dark shiny blue of the uniforms. From the stables came the drowsy whinnying of the horses. In the sky, the stars twinkled golden and silvery.

Someone knocked on the door. Carl Joseph did not stir. It's his orderly; he'll come in all the same. He'll come in right away. His name is Onufrij. How long did it take to learn this name, Onufrij? Grandfather would have been familiar with this name!

Onufrij came in. Carl Joseph was pressing his forehead against the window. Behind him he heard the orderly clicking his heels. Today was Wednesday. Onufrij had leave. The light had to be switched on and a pass signed.

"Switch on the light!" Carl Joseph ordered without looking around. Across the square the men were still playing harmonicas.

Onufrij switched on the light. Carl Joseph heard the click of the switch on the door molding. Behind him the room lit up. But outside the window the rectangular darkness was still gaping, and across the square the cozy yellow light of the troop rooms was flickering. (Electric light was a privilege reserved for officers.)

"Where are you going tonight?" asked Carl Joseph, still gazing at the troop rooms.

"To see a girl," said Onufrij. This was the first time the lieutenant had used the familiar form with him.

"What girl?" asked Carl Joseph.

"Katharina!" said Onufrij. His tone indicated that he was standing at attention.

"At ease!" Carl Joseph ordered. Onufrij audibly put his right foot in front of his left. Carl Joseph turned around. Before him stood Onufrij, big horse teeth shimmering between his full red lips. He could never stand at ease without smiling. "What does she look like, your Katharina?" asked Carl Joseph.

"Lieutenant, sir, if I may say so, big white breast!"

"Big white breast!" The lieutenant's hands became hollows and he felt a cool memory of Kathi's breasts. She was dead. Dead!

"The pass!" Carl Joseph ordered. Onufrij held out the pass. "Where is Katharina?" asked Carl Joseph.

"Maid, works for rich people," replied Onufrij. "Big white breast!" he added happily.

"Let me see it!" said Carl Joseph. He took the pass, smoothed it, signed. "Go to Katharina!" said Carl Joseph. Onufrij once again clicked his heels. "Dismissed!" Carl Joseph ordered.

He switched off the light. He groped for his coat in the darkness. He stepped out into the corridor. The instant he shut the door downstairs, the buglers launched into the final part of taps. The stars flickered in the sky. The sentry at the gate presented arms. The gate closed behind Carl Joseph. The road shimmered silvery in the moonlight. The yellow lights of the town greeted him like fallen stars. His steps rang hard on the freshly frozen ground, autumnal and nocturnal.

In back of him he heard Onufrij's boots. The lieutenant walked faster so his orderly would not catch up with him. But Onufrij likewise quickened his pace. And so, one behind the other, they hurried along the hard, lonesome, reverberating road. Plainly, Onufrij enjoyed the idea of overtaking his lieutenant. Carl Joseph stood still and waited. Onufrij loomed clearly in the moonlight. He seemed to be growing; he raised his head against the stars as if drawing new strength for his encounter with his superior. His arms jerked in the same rhythm as his legs; it was as if his hands were treading air. Three paces ahead of Carl Joseph he halted, flinging his chest out once more, with a dreadful bang of his boot heels, and his hand saluted with five consolidated fingers. Flustered, Carl Joseph smiled. Anyone else, he mused, would have found something nice to say. It was touching the way Onufrij followed him. He had never really looked at him closely. So long as Carl Joseph had failed to recall his name, it had also been impossible to see his face. It was as if he had had a different orderly every day. Other officers talked about their orderlies with meticulous expertise, the way they talked about girls, clothes, favorite dishes, and horses. But whenever conversation turned to servants, Carl Joseph thought about old Jacques at home—old Jacques, who had even served Carl Joseph's grandfather. Aside from old Jacques, there was no other servant in the world! Now Onufrij stood in front of him on the moonlit highway, with a tremendously pumped-up chest, glittering buttons, and boots polished like mirrors, his broad face convulsively suppressing his glee at running into the lieutenant. "Stand! At ease!" said Carl Joseph.

He would have liked to say something pleasant. Grandfather would have said something pleasant to Jacques. Onufrij loudly put his right foot in front of his left. His chest remained pumped up; the order had no effect.

"Stand comfortably," said Carl Joseph, a bit sad and impatient.

"Sir, I *am* standing comfortably," replied Onufrij.

"Does she live far from here, your girl?" asked Carl Joseph.

"Lieutenant, sir, not far, an hour's march!"

No, it was not working. Carl Joseph was tongue-tied. He was choking on some kind of unknown affection. He could not deal with orderlies. Whom *could* he deal with? His helplessness ran deep; he was tongue-tied even with his fellow officers. Why did they all start whispering whenever he left them or was about to join them? Why did he sit a horse so badly? Ah, he knew himself. As if watching himself in a mirror, he could see the figure he cut; it was no use pretending. The other officers whispered behind his back. He understood their answers only after they were explained to him, and even then he could not laugh: especially then! Yet Colonel Kovacs really liked him. And his record was certainly excellent. He lived in his grandfather's shadow. That was it! He was the grandson of the Hero of Solferino, the only grandson. He constantly felt his grandfather's dark enigmatic gaze on the back of his neck. He was the grandson of the Hero of Solferino!

For a couple of minutes, Carl Joseph and his orderly, Onufrij, stood facing each other silently on the milky, shimmering highway. The hush and the moonlight lengthened the minutes. Onufrij did not stir. He stood like a monument, all aglow in the silvery moonlight. Suddenly Carl Joseph turned and began to march. Onufrij followed exactly three paces behind him. Carl Joseph heard the regular banging of the heavy boots and the iron ringing of the spurs. It was allegiance itself following him. Every bang of the boots was like a terse stamped repeat of an orderly's oath of allegiance. Carl Joseph was afraid to turn around. He wished that this dead-straight highway would suddenly branch off into an unexpected, unknown side road, offering escape from Onufrij's obstinate officiousness. The orderly followed him in step. The lieutenant tried to keep pace with the boots in back of him. He was afraid of disappointing Onufrij by heedlessly changing pace. Onufrij's allegiance lay in those reliably tramping boots. And every single bang stirred Carl Joseph anew. It was as if a clumsy man behind him were trying to knock on his master's heart with heavy soles—the helpless tenderness of a spurred and booted bear.

At last they reached the edge of town. Carl Joseph had thought of an apt phrase to say goodbye with. He turned and said, "Have fun, Onufrij!" And he swiftly cut into a side street. The orderly's thank-you reached him only as a remote echo.

He had to take a detour. He reached the club ten minutes later. It was on the second floor of one of the finest mansions on the Old Ring. All windows, as on every evening, were pouring light upon the square, upon the promenade of the townsfolk. It was late; he had to thread his way adroitly through the dense swarms of burghers taking their constitutionals with their wives.

Day after day he endured the same unspeakable agony of emerging in jingly colorfulness among the dark civilians, encountering nosy, spiteful, or lustful looks, and finally plunging like a god into the bright entrance of the club. Today he quickly wound through the strollers. It took two minutes to get through the rather lengthy Promenade, a disgusting two minutes! He climbed the steps two at a time. Meet no one! You had to avoid meeting anyone on the stairs: bad omens. Warmth, light, and voices came toward him in the hallway.

He entered, he exchanged greetings. He looked for Colonel Kovacs in his usual corner. Every evening, the colonel played dominoes there, every evening with a different man. He was a domino enthusiast—perhaps out of an immoderate dread of cards. "I've never held a card in my hand," he would say. It was not without malevolence that he pronounced the word *card*; and he would glance at his hands as if they held his sterling character. "Gentlemen," he would sometimes add, "I advise you all to play dominoes. They are clean and they teach moderation." And now and then he would lift up one of the many-eyed black-and-white dominoes like a magic instrument for freeing depraved cardplayers of their demon.

Tonight it was Captain Taittinger's turn for domino duty. The colonel's face cast a purple reflection on the rittmaster's haggard, yellowish features. With a faint jingle, Carl Joseph halted in front of the colonel.

"Hi!" said the colonel without looking up from the dominoes. He was an easygoing man, that Colonel Kovacs. For years now, he had been cultivating a fatherly manner. And only once a month did he work himself up into an artificial rage that struck more fear in him than in the regiment. Any pretext would do. He yelled so loud that the barrack walls shook, as did the old trees around the water meadow. His purple face blanched down to the lips, and his riding crop, quivering and untiring, lashed against his boot shaft. He shrieked a torrent of gobbledygook in which only the ever-recurring and incoherent words, "in my regiment," were softer than anything else. He would finally stop, for no reason, just as he had started, and leave the office, the club, the parade ground, or whatever setting he had chosen for his thunderstorm. Yes, they all knew him, that Colonel Kovacs—a good egg! His outbursts were as regular and as reliable as the phases of the moon. Each time, Captain Taittinger, who, after already transferring twice in his career, had an accurate knowledge of officers, would assure everyone that there wasn't a more harmless corporal in the entire army.

Colonel Kovacs finally looked up from the domino game and shook Trotta's hand. "Dined already?" he asked. "Too bad," he went on, his eyes melting into an enigmatic distance. "The schnitzel was excellent today." And "Excellent!" he repeated a bit later. He was sorry that Trotta had missed the schnitzel. He would have gladly chewed a second one for the lieutenant—or at least watched it being eaten with gusto. "Well, have fun!" he eventually said, turning back to the dominoes.

The chaos was intense by now, and a comfortable seat was nowhere to be found. In the course of time, Captain Taittinger, who had been in charge of the mess hall since time immemorial and whose only passion was the consumption of pastries, had transformed the club into a replica of the pastry shop where he spent every afternoon. He could be viewed sitting there behind the glass door, as somber and static as a bizarrely uniformed advertising mannequin. He was the best regular customer in the pastry shop, and probably its hungriest. Without the slightest twitch in his careworn face, he would wolf down one plate of goodies after another, taking a sip of water from time to time, peering fixedly through the glass door and into the street, and nodding gravely whenever a passing soldier saluted him, and simply nothing appeared to be happening inside his big lean skull with its sparse hair. He was a gentle and very lazy officer. Among all his official functions, his only pleasant duty was his supervision of the officers' mess: its kitchen, the cooks, the orderlies, the wine cellar. And his extensive correspondence with wine dealers and liqueur makers kept no fewer than two army clerks busy full-time. Over the years, he had managed to furnish the officers' club exactly like his beloved pastry shop, placing dainty little tables in the corners and garbing the table lamps with reddish shades.

Carl Joseph glanced around. He was looking for a tolerable place to sit. Relative safety might be found between Reserve

Ensign Sir Bärenstein von Zaloga, a wealthy and recently
knighted attorney, and Lieutenant Kindermann, a rosy man of
German extraction. The ensign's youthful rank was so inconsistent with his slight paunch and dignified age that he looked like
a civilian in military disguise, and his face with its small coal-
black moustache was off-putting because it lacked an utterly
indispensable pince-nez. Emanating a dependable dignity in this
officers' club, he reminded Carl Joseph of a family doctor or an
uncle. In these two rooms, he was the only one who sat truly,
honestly, believably, while the others seemed to be hopping
around on their chairs. Aside from his uniform, the only con-
cession that Reserve Ensign Doctor Bärenstein made to the
military was his monocle when on duty; for in civilian life he did
indeed sport a pince-nez.

Lieutenant Kindermann was likewise more reassuring than
the rest, no doubt about it. He consisted of a blond, rosy,
transparent substance; one could almost have reached through
him as through an airy haze in evening sunlight. Everything he
said was airy and transparent and was breathed from his being
without diminishing him. And there was something like a
sunny smile in his earnest way of following the earnest conversations. A cheerful nonentity, he sat at the little table. "Hello
there!" he squealed in his high voice, which Colonel Kovacs
described as one of the wind instruments of the Prussian army.
Reserve Ensign Bärenstein stood up appropriately but solemnly.
"Good evening, Herr Lieutenant," he said.

Carl Joseph almost replied reverently, Good evening, Herr
Doctor! But all he said was "May I?" and sat down.

"Dr. Demant is coming back tonight," Bärenstein began. "I
ran into him this afternoon."

"A charming fellow," Kindermann squealed; behind Bärenstein's powerful forensic baritone it sounded like a gentle zephyr
grazing a harp. Kindermann, ever intent on making up for his
scant interest in women by feigning a special attentiveness to
them, announced, "And his wife—do you know her?—a
charming creature, a delight!" And at the word *delight* he raised
his hand, his limp fingers capering in the air.

"I've known her since she was a girl," said the ensign.

"Interesting," said Kindermann. He was blatantly shamming.

"Her father used to be one of the richest hat manufacturers," the ensign went on. It sounded as if he were reading from a document. Terrified by his own remark, he paused. The words *hat manufacturers* struck him as too civilian; after all, he was not sitting with lawyers. He swore to himself that from now on he would think about every statement before uttering it. He did owe the cavalry that much. He tried to catch Lieutenant Trotta's reaction. But Trotta was sitting to the left, and Bärenstein's monocle was on his right eye. The lawyer could see only Lieutenant Kindermann clearly, and he didn't matter. To determine whether his familiar mention of the hat manufacturer had had a devastating impact on Lieutenant Trotta, Bärenstein produced his cigarette case and held it out to his left, recollected Kindermann's seniority in time, and, turning right, hastily said, "Excuse me!"

Now all three men were smoking in silence. Carl Joseph's gaze focused on the portrait of the Kaiser on the opposite wall. There was Franz Joseph in a sparkling-white general's uniform, the wide blood-red sash veering across his chest and the Order of the Golden Fleece at his throat. The big black field marshal's helmet with its lavish peacock-green aigrette lay next to the Emperor on a small, wobbly-looking table. The painting seemed to be hanging very far away, farther than the wall. Carl Joseph remembered that during his first few days in the regiment that portrait had offered him a certain proud comfort. He had felt that the Kaiser might step out of the narrow black frame at any moment. But gradually the Supreme Commander in Chief developed the indifferent, habitual, and unheeded countenance shown on his stamps and coins. His picture hung on the wall of the club, a strange kind of sacrifice that a god makes to himself. His eyes—earlier they had recalled a summer vacation sky—were now a hard blue china. And it was still the same Kaiser! This painting also hung at home, in the district captain's study. It hung in the vast assembly hall at military school. It hung in the colonel's office at the barracks. And Emperor Franz Joseph was scattered a hundred thousand times throughout his vast empire, omnipresent among his subjects as God is omnipresent in the world. His life had been saved by the Hero of Solferino. The Hero of Solferino had grown old and died. Now the worms were devouring him. And his son, the district captain, Carl Joseph's father, was also growing old. Soon the worms would be devouring him too. But the Kaiser—the Kaiser seemed to have aged suddenly, within a single day, within a very specific hour, and since that hour he had remained locked in his eternal, silvery, and dreadful senility as in an armor of awe-inspiring crystal. The years did not dare approach him. His eyes kept growing bluer and harder. His very favor, which rested upon the Trotta dynasty, was a load of cutting ice. And Carl Joseph felt chills under his Emperor's blue gaze.

At home during vacation, he recalled, and on Sundays, before lunch, when Kapellmeister Nechwal had set up his military band in the regulation circle, Carl Joseph had been ready to perish for his Kaiser in a warm, sweet, blissful death. Grandfather's legacy, to save the Emperor's life, was alive in him. And if you were a Trotta, you kept saving the Emperor's life over and over.

Now he had been in the regiment for barely four months. All at once it was as if the Kaiser, unapproachably secure in his crystal armor, no longer needed Trottas. Peace had worn on for too long. Death lay far away for a young cavalry lieutenant, as far as the highest grade of regulated advancement. You became colonel someday and then you died. Meanwhile you went to the officers' club every evening, you saw the Kaiser's picture. The longer Lieutenant Trotta perused it, the more remote the Kaiser grew.

"Just look!" Lieutenant Kindermann's voice simpered. "Trotta can't take his eyes off the old man!"

Carl Joseph smiled at Kindermann. Reserve Ensign Bären-stein had started a game of dominoes long since and he was losing. He considered it his bounden duty to lose when playing with the regulars. Back in civilian life, he always won. He was a feared player even among lawyers. But when he reported for the annual military exercises, he shelved his superiority and tried to act the fool. "He keeps losing nonstop," Kindermann said to Trotta. Lieutenant Kindermann was convinced that "civilians" were inferior beings. They could not even win at dominoes.

The colonel still sat in the corner with Captain Taittinger. A few bored officers wandered between the tables. They did not dare leave the club so long as the colonel was playing. The gentle pendulum clock whined every quarter hour very clearly and slowly, its rueful melody interrupting the clatter of dominoes and chess figures. Sometimes one of the orderlies clicked his heels, dashed into the kitchen, and returned with a small snifter of brandy on a ridiculously large salver. Sometimes somebody guffawed resoundingly, and if you glanced toward the source of the mirth you spied four heads huddling together and you realized they were telling jokes. These jokes! These anecdotes with which you could instantly tell whether the laughter was polite or genuine! The jokes separated the natives from the foreigners. Any man who did not understand was not an insider. No, Carl Joseph was not among them!

He was just about to propose a three-way game when the door opened and an orderly saluted with a conspicuously loud bang of his boot heels. The room instantly hushed. Colonel Kovacs leaped from his chair and peered at the door. It was none other than Demant, the regimental surgeon. He himself was taken aback by the agitation he had triggered. He halted at the door and smiled. Next to him the orderly was still at attention, which plainly embarrassed the physician. He waved his hand. But the orderly did not notice. The doctor's thick spectacles were faintly misted by the autumnal evening fog outside. Normally he would remove his spectacles and polish them when he stepped from the cold air into the warmth. But here he did not have the nerve. It took him awhile to leave the threshold.

"Why, look, it's the doctor!" cried the colonel. He was yelling for all he was worth, as if straining to make himself heard in the tumult of a county fair. The good man believed that shortsighted people were also deaf and that their spectacles would become clearer if their ears heard more sharply. The colonel's voice blazed a passage. The officers stepped back. The few officers still sitting at tables stood up. The regimental surgeon gingerly placed one foot before the other as if walking on ice. His spectacles seemed to be clearing gradually. Greetings showered upon him from all sides. He painstakingly recognized the officers. He leaned over to read the faces the way one pores over books. He finally halted in front of Colonel Kovacs, squaring his chest. His posture looked strongly exaggerated as he tossed back his eternally bowing head on his thin neck and attempted to jerk up his narrow, sloping shoulders. He had almost been forgotten during his long sick leave: he and his unmilitary bearing. Now the men stared at him not without surprise.

The colonel hastened to end the official ritual of greeting. He shouted loud enough to make the glasses tremble, "He looks good, our doctor!"—as if trying to inform the entire army. He slapped Demant on the shoulder as though to restore it to its natural position. He really liked the regimental surgeon. But the guy was unmilitary, damn it all to hell! If only he'd act just a little more like an officer, they wouldn't have to make such efforts to be nice to him. And, damn it all, they could've sent Kovacs a different doctor. Why *his* regiment? Those endless battles that the colonel's heart had to fight with his military sensibilities on behalf of this goddamn nice guy were enough to grind down an old soldier. This doctor's gonna be the death of me! mused the colonel whenever he saw the regimental surgeon on horseback. And one day he had even asked him if he would mind not riding through town.

I have to say something nice to him, he thought frantically. In his haste, it flashed through his mind: The schnitzel was excellent today! And say it he did. The doctor smiled. The guy has a totally civilian smile! the colonel thought. And suddenly he recalled that there was an officer here who did not know the doctor. Trotta, of course! He had joined while the doctor was on sick leave. The colonel thundered, "This is Trotta, our youngest! You haven't met him!" And Carl Joseph went over to the regimental surgeon.

"Grandson of the Hero of Solferino?" asked Dr. Demant.

No one would have expected him to be so conversant with military history.

"He knows everything, our doctor!" cried the colonel. "He's a bookworm."

And for once in his life, he liked the suspicious word "book-worm" so much that he repeated it—"a bookworm!"—in the caressing tone that he normally used for "a lancer!"

They sat down again, and the evening took its usual course.

"Your grandfather," said the regimental surgeon, "was one of the most singular men in the army. Did you know him?"

"I didn't know him," replied Carl Joseph. "His picture is in our study at home. When I was little, I used to look at it frequently. And his butler, Jacques, is still with us."

"What's the picture like?" asked the regimental surgeon.

"It was painted by my father's boyhood friend," said Carl Joseph. "It's a strange portrait. It's hung fairly high. When I was little, I had to climb on a chair to look at it."

They paused for a moment. Then the doctor said, "My grandfather was an innkeeper, a Jewish innkeeper in Galicia. Galicia—have you ever been there?" Dr. Demant was a Jew. All the jokes had Jewish regimental surgeons. There had also been two Jews at military school. They had joined the infantry.

"Let's go to Resi's, Aunt Resi's!" a voice suddenly shouted.

And they all repeated, "To Resi's! We're going to Resi's!"

"To Aunt Resi's!"

Nothing could have frightened Carl Joseph more than that shout. He had been dreading it for weeks. He still had sharp memories of everything about his last visit to Frau Horwath's brothel: everything! The champagne, consisting of camphor and lemonade; the soft, fleshy dough of the girls, the blinding red and demented yellow of the wallpaper, the smell of cats, mice, and lilies of the valley in the corridor, and his heartburn twelve hours later. He had scarcely been in the regiment a week, and that had been his first visit to a brothel.

"Love maneuvers!" said Taittinger. He was the ringleader. It was one of the duties of an officer who had been in charge of the mess hall since time immemorial. Pale and haggard, his saber hilt in his arm, he would take long, thin, softly jingling steps from table to table in Frau Horwath's parlor—a stealthy admonisher to sour joys. Kindermann felt faint whenever he smelled naked women; the female sex nauseated him. Major Prohaska had stood in the toilet, earnestly striving to thrust his stubby finger down Kindermann's throat. Frau Resi Horwath's silk petticoats rustled in every nook of the house at once. Her big black eyeballs rolled aimlessly and haphazardly in her broad, mealy face; as white and large as piano keys, her false teeth shimmered in her broad mouth. Trautmannsdorff, from his corner, followed all her movements with quick, squinting, greenish glances. Eventually he got up and lunged one hand into Frau Horwath's bosom. The hand disappeared inside like a white mouse among white mountains. And Pollak, the pianist, a slave to the music, sat hunched over at the grand piano with its blackish reflections, and on his hammering hands the hard cuffs clattered like hoarse cymbals accompanying the tinny sounds.

To Aunt Resi's! They were going to Aunt Resi's. The colonel wheeled around downstairs. He said, "Have fun, gentlemen," and twenty voices chorused through the silent street—"Good night, sir!"—and forty spurs jingled against one another. Dr. Max Demant, the regimental surgeon, made a shy attempt to likewise take his leave. "Do you have to go with them?" he softly asked Lieutenant Trotta.

"I really do!" whispered Carl Joseph. And the regimental surgeon wordlessly tagged along. They brought up the rear in the straggly line of officers walking and rattling through the hushed, moonlit streets of the small town. The two men did not converse. They felt bonded by the whispered question and the whispered answer; there was nothing more to say. Both were cut off from the entire regiment. And yet they had met barely half an hour ago.

Suddenly, without knowing why, Carl Joseph said, "I loved a woman named Kathi. She died."

The regimental surgeon halted and turned to the lieutenant full face. "You will love other women," he said.

And they walked on.

Late trains could be heard whistling from the distant station, and the regimental surgeon said, "I'd like to go away, go far away!"

Now they stood by Aunt Resi's blue lantern. Captain Taittinger knocked on the bolted door. Someone opened. Inside, the piano instantly began to tinkle: "The Radetzky March."

The officers marched into the parlor. "Fall out singly!" Taittinger commanded. The naked girls thronged toward them, a
bustling cluster of white hens.

"God be with you!" said Prohaska. This time Trautmanns-
dorf, still standing, promptly reached into Frau Horwath's
bosom. He would not let go. She had kitchen and cellar to
supervise, and though she visibly suffered under the first lieutenant's caresses, hospitality imposed sacrifices. She allowed herself
to be seduced. Lieutenant Kindermann blanched. He was
whiter than the powder on the girls' shoulders.

Major Prohaska ordered soda water. Anyone who knew him
well could predict that he would get very drunk tonight. He
simply used water to clear the way for liquor, the way streets are
cleaned before an official visit. "Has the doctor come along?" he
asked loudly.

"He has to study diseases at their source!" said Captain
Taittinger with scientific gravity, as pale and haggard as ever.

Ensign Bärenstein's monocle was now on the eye of an ash-
blond girl. He sat there with small, black, blinking eyes, his hairy
brown hands creeping across her like bizarre animals. Little by
little, everyone had taken a seat. On the red sofa, two girls, perching stiffly with drawn knees between the doctor and Carl
Joseph, were intimidated by the despairing faces of these two
men. When the champagne arrived—ceremoniously brought in
by the strict housekeeper in black taffeta—Frau Horwath, for love
of order, resolutely pulled the first lieutenant's hand from her dé-
colletage, placed it on his black trousers as if returning a borrowed
object, and rose to her feet, mighty and imperious. She put out the
chandelier. Only the small lamps were burning in the niches.

In the wan reddish twilight, the powdered white bodies
shone, the gold stars glinted, the silver sabers shimmered. One
couple after another stood up and vanished. Prohaska, having
long since reached the brandy stage, approached the regimental
surgeon and said, "You guys don't really need them, I'll take
them along!" And he took both women and, between them,
staggered off toward the stairs.

And so suddenly they were alone, Carl Joseph and the doctor.
Pollak the pianist was now merely tickling the ivories in the

opposite corner of the parlor. A soulful waltz came wafting through the room, timid and wispy. Otherwise the house was silent, almost cozy, and the clock on the mantelpiece was ticking away.

"I don't believe we two have anything to do here, do we?" asked the doctor. He stood up.

Carl Joseph checked the clock on the mantel and likewise rose to his feet. Unable to tell the time in the dark, he went over to the clock and then stepped back. In a bronze flyblown frame stood the Supreme Commander in Chief, a reduced version of the well-known ubiquitous portrait of His Majesty, in the sparkling white garb, with the blood-red sash and the Golden Fleece. Something has to be done, thought the lieutenant swiftly and childishly. Something has to be done! He sensed he had turned pale; his heart was pounding. He reached for the frame, opened the black paper backing, and removed the picture. He folded it, twice, once more, and slipped it into his pocket. He turned around. Behind him stood the regimental surgeon.

The doctor pointed his finger at the pocket where Carl Joseph had concealed the Emperor's portrait. The grandfather rescued him too, thought Dr. Demant.

Carl Joseph reddened. "Disgusting!" he said. "What do you think?"

"I don't know," replied the doctor. "I was only thinking of your grandfather."

"I am his grandson!" said Carl Joseph. "I have no chance to save his life—unfortunately!"

They placed four silver coins on the table and left the house of Frau Resi Horwath.

Chapter 6

MAX DEMANT, THE regimental surgeon, had been with the regiment for three years now. He lived outside the town, at its southern edge, where the highway led to the two graveyards, the "old" one and the "new" one. Both cemetery keepers were well acquainted with the physician. He came by several times a week to visit the dead, both the long gone and the still unforgotten. He sometimes lingered on and on among their graves, and now and then his saber could be heard jangling softly as it struck against a headstone. He was undoubtedly a strange man: a good doctor, people said, and thus in every respect an oddity among army medics. He avoided any social contact. It was purely his official duties that compelled him to show his face among his fellow officers—only sporadically, but still more often than he would have liked. By age and seniority he should have made captain of a medical corps long since. No one knew why he had not. He may not have known why himself. "Some careers have snags." That was one of the homilies of Rittmaster Taittinger, who always supplied the regiment with choice adages.

"A career with snags," the doctor himself would often muse. "A life with snags," he said to Lieutenant Trotta. "I have a life with snags. If fate had been kind to me, I could have become assistant to a great Viennese surgeon and then probably a professor."

Early on, the great name of the Viennese surgeon had cast its glamour on the dark confines of Demant's childhood. While still a boy, Max Demant had already made up his mind to be a physician. He came from one of the eastern border towns of the monarchy. His grandfather had been an orthodox Jewish tavern keeper, and his father, after twelve years in the militia, had

become a mid-level official at the post office of the nearest little
border town. Demant could still remember his grandfather
clearly. The old man used to sit at the huge arched entrance to
his border tavern at all hours of the day. His enormous beard of
crinkly silver concealed his chest and reached down to his knees.
The smell of dung and milk and hay and horses floated about
him. He sat outside, an old king among the tavern keepers.
When the farmers, heading home from the weekly pig market,
drew up at the tavern, the old man massively rose to his feet, like
a mountain in human guise. Since he was hard of hearing by
now, the small peasants had to cup their mouths and yell their
orders at him. He merely nodded. He understood. He granted
the wishes of his customers as if conferring favors rather than
being paid in good hard coin. With powerful hands, he unhar-
nessed their horses himself and led them to the stalls. And while
his daughters served brandy and dry salted peas to the patrons in
the wide, low taproom, he would fodder the horses with soothing words. On Saturdays he sat hunched over huge pious tomes.
His silvery beard covered the lower half of the black-printed
page. Had he known that his grandson would some day stroll
through the world murderously armed and in an officer's uniform, the old man would have cursed his old age and the fruit of
his loins. His own son, Dr. Demant's father, the mid-level postal
official, was already an abomination to the old man, though he
lovingly tolerated him. The tavern, handed down from their
forefathers, had to be left to his daughters and sons-in-law, while
his male descendants were destined to remain officials, intellec-
tuals, clerks, and muttonheads until the end of time. Until the
end of time: but that did not fit! For the regimental surgeon had
no children. Nor did he want any. You see, his wife—

At this point, Dr. Demant usually broke off his reminis-
cences. He thought about his mother: her life was one long
frantic search for some kind of extra income. His father sits in the
small coffeehouse after office hours. He plays tarot and loses and
has to pay the check. He would like his son to complete four
middle-school years and then work for the government—at the
post office, of course. "You always aim high!" he says to the
mother. However disorderly his life outside of work, he always

maintains a ludicrous order in all the props he has brought along from his army days. His uniform, the uniform of a full-term assistant paymaster, with the gold chevrons on the sleeves, the black trousers, and the infantry shako, hangs in the closet like a still surviving triparte person, with glistening buttons freshly polished once a week. Likewise cleaned once a week, the black, curving saber with the fluted hilt lies horizontal, held up by two nails, on the wall over the unused desk, a gold-yellow tassel dangling loosely, recalling a somewhat dusty sunflower in bud.

"If you hadn't come along," the father said to the mother, "I would have taken the exam and today I'd be a paymaster sergeant."

On the Kaiser's birthday, Postal Official Demant dons his government uniform with a crimson hat and a sword. On this day, he does not play tarot. Every year on the Kaiser's birthday he resolves to get a new debt-free lease on life. So he gets drunk. And he comes home late at night, draws his sword in the kitchen, and bosses a whole regiment around. The pots are platoons, the teacups troops, and the plates companies. Simon Demant is a colonel, a colonel in the service of Franz Joseph I. The mother, in a lace nightcap, a voluminously pleated nightgown, and a small fluttering jacket, gets out of bed to calm her husband.

One day, a day after the Kaiser's birthday, his father had a stroke in bed. He had a gentle death and a dazzling funeral. All the mailmen followed the coffin. And his image was lodged in the widow's faithful memory: a model husband, who had died in the service of the Emperor and the Imperial and Royal Postal Service. The uniforms—Assistant Paymaster Demant's and Postal Official Demant's—still hung side by side in the closet, maintained in their constant radiance by his widow with the help of brush, camphor, and brass polish. The uniforms looked like mummies, and whenever the closet was opened, the son felt as if he were seeing two corpses of his departed father.

He wanted to be a doctor at any price. He gave lessons for a wretched six crowns a month. He wore ragged boots. Whenever it rained he left huge wet footprints on the fine waxed floors of the well-to-do. His footprints were bigger when the boot soles were ragged. He finally obtained his secondary-school diploma. And he became a physician. But poverty still loomed before him, a black wall on which he shattered. He literally sank into the arms of the military. Seven years of food, seven years of drink, seven years of clothing, seven years of shelter: seven, seven long years! He became an army doctor. And he remained one. Life seemed to flow along more swiftly than thoughts. And before he even made a decision he was an old man.

And he had married Fräulein Eva Knopfmacher.

Here Regimental Surgeon Dr. Demant once again stemmed the flow of his memories. He headed home.

The evening had already begun; an unusually festive illumination poured from all the rooms. "The old gentleman is here," the orderly announced. The "old gentleman": that was his father-in-law, Herr Knopfmacher.

At that moment, he emerged from the bathroom in a long, downy, flowery dressing gown, holding a razor and sporting cheerfully reddened, freshly shaved, and fragrant cheeks that lay far apart. His face seemed to fall into two halves. It was held together only by the gray goatee.

"My dear Max!" said Herr Knopfmacher, gingerly placing his razor on a small table, spreading out his arms, and letting the dressing gown gape open. They embraced with two casual kisses and entered the study together. "I'd like a drink!" said Herr Knopfmacher.

Dr. Demant unlocked the cabinet, peered at several bottles for a while, then turned around. "I don't know anything about liquor," he said. "I don't know what you drink." He had arranged for a selection of alcohol, sort of like an uneducated man ordering a library.

"You still don't drink?" said Herr Knopfmacher. "Do you have slivovitz, arrack, rum, brandy, gentian cordial, vodka?" he asked quickly, in a manner thoroughly inconsistent with his dignity. He rose. He walked over to the cabinet, the ends of his dressing gown flapping, and with a sure hand he pulled out a bottle from the lineup.

"I wanted to surprise Eva," Herr Knopfmacher began. "And I must tell you right off, my dear Max, you were away all afternoon. Instead of you . . ."—he paused, then repeated—"instead of you I found a lieutenant here. A dimwit."

"He is the only friend," Max Demant retorted, "that I have made since the start of my military service. He is Lieutenant Trotta, a fine man!"

"A fine man!" the father-in-law echoed. "Well, take me, I'm a fine man too! But I would not advise you to leave me alone with a pretty woman for an hour if you care for her even this much." Knopfmacher joined the tips of his thumb and index finger and then repeated, after a while, "Even this much!"

The regimental surgeon blanched. He took off his glasses and polished them for a long time. He thereby enveloped his surroundings in a pleasant fog, in which his father-in-law in his dressing gown became a hazy albeit immense white splotch. Nor did Demant put his glasses back on when they were polished; instead, he held them and spoke into the fog.

"I have no grounds, dear Papá, for distrusting Eva or my friend."

He said it falteringly, the regimental surgeon. Even to him it sounded like an utterly alien phrase, borrowed from some remote text, heard in some forgotten play.

He put on his glasses, and old Knopfmacher, now distinct in size and silhouette, promptly closed in on the doctor. Now even the phrase he had just used seemed very distant. It was certainly no longer true. The doctor was as well aware of that as his father-in-law.

"No grounds!" Herr Knopfmacher repeated. "But *I* have grounds! I know my daughter! You don't know your wife! And I also know the lieutenants—and all men, for that matter. I'm not saying anything against the army. Let's stick to the matter at hand. When my wife—your mother-in-law—was young, I had lots of opportunities to get to know young men—in mufti and in uniform. Yes, you're a strange bunch, you . . . you . . . you . . ."

He cast about for a generic term for some vague category that would include his son-in-law and other dimwits. He would have preferred to say "you academics!" For Herr Knopfmacher had become smart, prosperous, and respected without attending a university. Indeed, he was about to receive the title of commercial councilor any day now. He spun out a delightful dream of the future, a dream of his charitable donations, huge donations. Their immediate consequence would be a title. And if, say, you acquired Hungarian citizenship, you could become a nobleman all the sooner. In Budapest, they didn't make life so hard on you. Incidentally, it was also academics who made life hard on you with all their abstract notions—those dimwits! His own son-in-law made things hard on him. If some minor scandal now erupted with the children, he could kiss the title goodbye. You always have to look after things yourself, personally! You also have to watch out for the virtue of other men's wives!

"My dear Max, I would like to put my cards on the table before it's too late."

The regimental surgeon did not care for that expression; he did not care for truth at any price. Ah, he knew his wife just as well as Herr Knopfmacher knew his daughter. But he loved her, he couldn't help it. He loved her. In Olomouc there had been District Commissioner Herdall, in Graz, District Judge Lederer. So long as they weren't fellow officers, the regimental surgeon thanked God and also his wife. If only he could leave the army. His life was in constant danger. How often had he geared himself up to suggest to his father-in-law . . . ? He tried once again.

"I know," he said, "that Eva's in danger. Always. For years now. She's frivolous, alas. She doesn't go to extremes. . . . " He paused and then stressed, "Not to extremes!" Those words killed all his own doubts, which had been eating at him for years. He wiped out his uncertainty; he was now convinced that his wife was not unfaithful. "By no means!" he said loudly. He was very sure. "Eva is a decent person, despite everything."

"Quite definitely," the father-in-law confirmed.

"But neither of us," the regimental surgeon went on, "can put up with this life much longer. I'm not at all happy with my profession, as you know. Where would I be today if I weren't in the military? I would have a major position in society, and Eva's ambition would be fulfilled. For she *is* ambitious, alas."

"She gets that from me," said Herr Knopfmacher, not without pleasure.

"She's dissatisfied," the regimental surgeon went on, while his father-in-law poured himself a refill. "She's dissatisfied and keeps looking for distractions. I can't blame her."

"You should distract her yourself!" the father-in-law broke in.

"I'm . . ." Dr. Demant was tongue-tied. He lapsed into silence and glanced at the alcohol.

"Come on, have a drink!" Herr Knopfmacher encouraged him. And he stood up, got a glass, and filled it. His dressing gown gaped again, revealing his hairy chest and his cheery belly, which was as rosy as his cheeks. He held the filled glass in front of his son-in-law's lips. Max Demant finally had a drink.

"And there's something else that may force me to leave the military. When I joined, my eyes were quite sound. Well, they're getting worse every year. I now have—I now can—it's impossible for me to see clearly without glasses. Actually, I'm duty-bound to report it and resign."

"Yes?" asked Herr Knopfmacher.

"And what should—"

"What should you live on?" His father-in-law crossed his legs; he was suddenly shivering. He shrouded himself in the dressing gown and held the collar together with his hands. "Yes," he said. "Do you think I can come up with the money? Ever since you got married, I've been helping you out with—I happen to know the exact amount—three hundred crowns a month. Oh, I know, I know! Eva needs a lot. And if you start a new life, she'll need just as much. And so will you, my son." He became affectionate. "Yes, my dear, dear Max! Things aren't going as well as they were years ago!"

Max held his tongue. Herr Knopfmacher felt he had warded off the assault and let his dressing gown fall open again. He had another drink. His mind would stay clear. He knew his limits. These fools! But this kind of son-in-law was still better than the other—that Hermann, Elisabeth's husband. His two daughters cost him six hundred crowns a month. He knew the exact amount by heart. If the physician were ever to go blind—he gazed at the sparkling glasses. He ought to keep an eye on his wife. That shouldn't be hard even for a nearsighted man!

"What time is it?" Herr Knopfmacher asked, very friendly and very innocent.

"Almost seven," said the doctor.

"I'm getting dressed," the father-in-law decided. He stood up, nodded, and swept through the door, slow and dignified.

The regimental surgeon remained. After the intimate solitude of the graveyard, the solitude in his own home seemed gigantic, unfamiliar, almost hostile. For the first time in his life he poured himself a drink. Indeed, he felt as if he were drinking a liquid for the first time in his life. Make order, he thought, I have to make order. He was determined to speak to his wife. He stepped into the corridor.

"Where is my wife?"

"In the bedroom," said the orderly.

Should I knock? the doctor wondered. No! his resolute heart commanded.

He opened the door.

There, at the closet mirror, his wife stood in blue panties, holding a large rosy powder puff.

"Ohh!" she cried, putting her hand across her bosom. The regimental surgeon remained in the doorway. "It's you?" said his wife. It was a question that sounded like a yawn.

"It's me!" replied the physician in a firm voice. It felt as if someone else were speaking. He had his glasses on, but he spoke into a fog. "Your father," he began, "told me that Lieutenant Trotta was here today."

She turned around. She stood in the blue panties, her right hand brandishing the puff like a weapon against her husband, and she said in a twittering voice, "Your friend, Trotta, was here. Papá came over. Have you see him already?"

"That's precisely why," said the regimental surgeon, instantly realizing he had made a false move.

He paused for a while.

"Why didn't you knock?" she asked.

"I wanted to do something nice for you."

"You're scaring me!"

"I—" the regimental surgeon began. He wanted to say, I'm your husband.

But he said, "I love you!"

He really did love her. There she stood, in blue panties, holding the rosy powder puff. And he loved her.

Why, I'm jealous! he thought. He said, "I don't like it when people come into the house without my knowing about it."

"He's a charming boy!" said his wife and began to powder herself in front of the mirror, slowly and lavishly.

The doctor stepped up close to his wife and clasped her shoulders. He peered into the mirror. He saw his brown, hairy hands on her white shoulders. She smiled. He saw it in the mirror—the glassy echo of her smile. "Be honest," he pleaded. It was as if his hands were kneeling on her shoulders. He instantly knew she would not be honest, and he repeated, "Be honest, please!" He saw her swift, pale hands fluffing the blond hair on her temples. A superfluous movement: it excited him. From her mirror, her glance struck him, a gray, cool, dry, rapid glance, like a steel bullet. I love her, the doctor thought. She hurts me, and I love her. He asked, "Are you annoyed that I was away all afternoon?"

She half turned. Now, her upper body twisting at the hips, she sat, a lifeless being, a mannequin made of wax and silk lingerie. From under the curtain of her long black lashes, her bright eyes emerged, false, simulated, icy lightning. Her slender hands lay on the panties like white birds embroidered on the blue silk background. And in a deep voice that he believed he had never heard from her and that sounded as if produced by a mechanism in her chest, she said very slowly, "I never miss you."

He began pacing up and down without looking at her. He pushed two chairs out of his way. He felt he had to clear a lot of things out of his way, perhaps shove back the walls, smash his head through the ceiling, kick the floorboards into the earth. His spurs jingled softly in his ears, from far away, as if worn by someone else. A single word galvanized his mind, it roared back and forth, it flew through his brain, incessantly: *over, over, over!* A small word. Swift, light as a feather yet weighing a ton, it flew through his head. His steps grew quicker and quicker; his feet kept time to the bouncy stroke of the word pendulating in his brain. Suddenly he halted.

"So you don't love me?" he asked.

He was certain she would not answer. She'll keep silent, he thought.

She answered, "No!" She raised the black curtain of her lashes and sized him up from head to foot with naked, dreadfully naked eyes, adding, "Why, you're drunk!"

It dawned on him that he had drunk too much. He thought contentedly, I'm drunk and I want to be drunk. And he said in an alien voice, as if it were now his duty to be drunk and not be himself, "Aha, I see!" By his muddled lights, it was those words and that sound that a drunken man had to sing at such moments. So he sang. And he did something else. "I'm going to kill you!" he said, very slowly.

"Kill me!" she twittered in her clear, usual, familiar voice.

She rose. She rose, lithe and nimble, the powder puff in her right hand. The full, slender curves of her silky legs vaguely reminded him of limbs in the windows of fashion salons; the entire woman was put together, pieced together. He no longer loved her, no longer loved her. He was filled with a hatred that he himself hated, an anger that had come to him like an unknown enemy from distant regions and now lived in his heart. He said aloud what he had been thinking an hour ago. "Make order! I'm going to make order!"

She guffawed in an uproarious voice that he was unfamiliar with. A theatrical voice, he thought.

An irrepressible urge to show her that he could make order gave his muscles power, gave his weak eyes an unwonted strength. He said, "I'll leave you to your father! I'm going to find Trotta."

"Go ahead, go ahead!" said the woman.

He left. Before going out, he returned to the study for another drink. He returned to the liquor as to a close friend—for the first time in his life. He poured himself a small snifter, then another, and a third. He left the house with jingly steps. He went to the officers' club. He asked the orderly, "Where is Herr Lieutenant Trotta?"

Lieutenant Trotta was not at the club.

The regimental surgeon turned into the dead-straight high-way leading to the barracks. The moon was already waning, but it still shone strong and silvery, almost a full moon. Not a breath was stirring on the silent highway. The scraggy shadows of the bare chestnut trees on both sides drew a tangled net on the slightly bulging center of the roadway. Dr. Demant's steps rang out hard and frozen. He was going to find Lieutenant Trotta. From far away he spotted, in bluish white, the tremendous wall of the barracks; he charged toward it, toward the enemy strong-hold. Toward him came the cold brassy call of taps. Dr. Demant marched straight toward the frozen metallic sounds; he trampled them to bits. Soon, at any moment, Lieutenant Trotta was bound to appear. He detached himself, a black stroke, from the tremendous white of the barracks and approached the physician. Three more minutes. Now they stood face-to-face. The lieu-tenant saluted. Dr. Demant heard himself as if from an infinite distance. "You visited my wife this afternoon, Herr Lieutenant?"

The question echoed from the blue glassy vault of the sky. For a long time now, for weeks, they had been on familiar terms. They used the familiar form with one another. But now they stood face-to-face like enemies.

"I visited your wife this afternoon, Herr Regimental Sur-geon," said the lieutenant.

Dr. Demant stepped up close to the lieutenant. "What is going on between my wife and you, Herr Lieutenant?" The physician's thick glasses were sparkling. The regimental surgeon had no eyes left, only glasses.

Carl Joseph kept silent. It was as if there were no answer to Dr. Demant's question in the whole big wide world. One could have wasted years searching for an answer, as if human speech were exhausted and dried up for all eternity. His heart pounded against his ribs with swift, dry, hard strokes. Dry and hard, the tongue stuck to the palate. A huge cruel emptiness roared through his brain. It was as if he were standing right in front of a nameless danger that had already wolfed him down. He stood on the brink of a gigantic black abyss and was already overwhelmed by its darkness. Dr. Demant's words resounded from an icy, glassy distance—dead words, corpses of words.

"Answer me, Herr Lieutenant!"

Nothingness. Silence. The stars twinkle and the moon shimmers.

"Answer me, Herr Lieutenant!"

That means Carl Joseph, he has to answer. He musters the woeful remnants of his strength. From the roaring void in his head, a thin, worthless sentence winds out. The lieutenant clicks his heels (out of military instinct and also to hear some kind of noise), and the jingle of his spurs calms him. And he murmurs very softly, "Herr Regimental Surgeon, there is nothing whatsoever going on between your wife and me."

Nothingness. Silence. The stars twinkle and the moon shimmers. Dr. Demant says nothing. Through dead glasses he peers at Carl Joseph.

The lieutenant repeats very softly, "Nothing whatsoever, Herr Regimental Surgeon."

He's gone crazy, the lieutenant thinks. And: It is shattered! Something is shattered. He feels as if he has heard a dry, splintery shattering. "Broken faith" crosses his mind—he once read that phrase somewhere. Shattered friendship. Yes, it is a shattered friendship.

All at once he knows that the regimental surgeon has been his friend for weeks: a friend! They have gotten together daily. Once he and the regimental surgeon went strolling through the cemetery, among the graves.

"There are so many graves," said the regimental surgeon. "Don't you feel as I do the way we live off the dead?"

"I live off my grandfather," said Trotta. He saw the portrait of the Hero of Solferino blurring under the ceiling of his father's house. Yes, something brotherly came from the regimental surgeon, brotherliness rushed like a small flame from Dr. Demant's heart.

"My grandfather," the regimental surgeon said, "was an old, tall Jew with a silver beard."

Carl Joseph saw the old, tall Jew with the silver beard. They were grandsons, they were both grandsons. When the regimental surgeon mounts his horse, he looks a bit silly, smaller, tinier than on foot; the horse carries him on its back like a small sack of oats. Carl Joseph rides just as wretchedly. He knows exactly what he looks like. He sees himself as in a mirror. In the entire regiment there are two officers behind whose backs the others have something to whisper about: Dr. Demant and the grandson of the Hero of Solferino. The only two in the entire regiment. Two friends.

"Your word of honor, Herr Lieutenant?" the physician asks. Without answering, Trotta holds out his hand. The physician says "Thank you!" and shakes it. Together they walk back along the highway, ten paces, twenty paces, not saying a word.

All at once, the regimental surgeon begins. "Please don't hold it against me. I've been drinking. My father-in-law came by today. He saw you. She doesn't love me. She doesn't love me. Can you understand?

"You're young!" says the regimental surgeon after a while, as if to say that he has spoken in vain. "You're young!"

"I understand," says Carl Joseph.

They march in lockstep, their spurs jingling, their sabers rattling. Yellowish and cozy, the lights of the town beckon to them. Both men wish that the road would never end. They would like to march side by side like that for a long, long time. Each of them has something to say, yet both keep silent. A word, a word so easily spoken: it is not spoken. This is the last time, the lieutenant thinks, this is the last time we'll be walking side by side.

Now they reach the edge of town. The regimental surgeon has to say something else before they enter the town. "It's not because of my wife," he says. "That's no longer important. I'm over that. It's for your sake."

He waits for an answer, knowing that none will come.

"It's all right, thank you!" he blurts out. "I'm going to the club. Are you coming along?"

No. Lieutenant Trotta is not going to the officers' club today. He is going back. "Good night," he says and wheels around. He goes to the barracks.

Chapter 7

THE WINTER CAME. In the morning, when the regiment marched
out, the world was still dark. The delicate film of ice on the streets
splintered under the hooves of the horses. Gray breath streamed
from the nostrils of the animals and the mouths of the riders. The
matte breath of the frost beaded on the sheaths of the heavy sabers
and on the barrels of the light carbines. The small town grew even
smaller. The muted, frozen bugle calls lured none of the usual
spectators to the curbs. Only the coachmen at their usual station
raised their bearded faces every morning. They drove sleighs
whenever a lot of snow had fallen. The little bells on the harnesses
of their horses jingled softly, incessantly moved by the restlessness
of the shivering animals. The days resembled one another like
snowflakes. The officers of the lancer regiment were waiting for
some extraordinary event to break the monotony of their days.
No one knew what kind of event it might be. But this winter
seemed to be concealing some kind of dreadful surprise in its
jingling bosom. And one day it erupted from the winter like red
lightning from white snow. . . .

That day, Rittmaster Taittinger was not sitting as usual behind
the huge mirror pane at the door of the pastry shop. Since early
afternoon the captain, surrounded by younger officers, had kept
to the small back room. He struck them as paler and more
haggard than normal. Mind you, all of them were pale. They
drank many liqueurs, but their faces did not redden. They did
not eat. Yet today, as always, a mountain of pastries loomed in
front of the captain. Indeed, he may have been indulging his
sweet tooth even more than on other days. For grief was
gnawing at his innards; it was hollowing him out, and he had to
keep alive. And as his haggard fingers shoved one pastry after

another into his gaping mouth, he reiterated his story, for the
fifth time already, to his ever-eager audience.

"Well, the main thing, gentlemen, is absolute discretion in
regard to the civilian populace. When I was in the Ninth
Dragoons, we had a chatterbox—in the reserves, of course, and
filthy rich, by the way—and just as he joined, the incident took
place. Naturally, by the time we buried poor Baron Seidl, the
whole town knew why he had died so suddenly. I hope, gentlemen, that this time we can have a more discreet—" he wanted
to say "funeral" but paused, mulled and mulled, failed to hit on a
word, and peered at the ceiling, while a dreadful silence roared
around his head and the heads of the listeners. Finally the
rittmaster concluded, "Can have a more discreet procedure."
He heaved a momentary sigh, swallowed a small pastry, and
gulped down his water.

They all felt that he had summoned Death. Death hovered
over them, and they were completely unfamiliar with the
feeling. They had been born in peacetime and become officers
in peaceful drills and maneuvers. They had no idea that several
years later every last one of them, with no exception, would
encounter death. Their ears were not sharp enough to catch the
whirring gears of the great hidden mills that were already
grinding out the Great War. A white winterly peace reigned in
the small garrison. And black and red, death fluttered over them
in the twilight of the small back room.

I can't understand it!" said one of the boys. They had all said
similar things.

"But I've already told you umpteen times!" replied Taittinger. "The touring players, that's how it began! I don't know
what got into me, going to that very operetta, that—what was
the title? Now I've even forgotten the title. What was it now?"

"*The Wandering Tinker*," someone said.

"Right! Well, it all began with *The Wandering Tinker*. Just as
I'm coming out of the theater, there's Trotta standing lonesome
and godforsaken in the snow on the square. You see, I ducked out
before the end; I always do that, gentlemen. I can never stand
waiting till the final curtain. If it's got a happy ending, you can
tell right away at the start of the third act, and then I know

everything, so I simply tiptoe out, as quiet as possible. Besides, I'd already seen the thing three times! Well, anyway, poor Trotta is standing there all by his lonesome in the snow. I say, 'The play was nice.' And then I tell him about how strange Demant's been acting. He barely glanced at me; he left his wife alone during the second act and just simply walked out and didn't come back! He could have asked me to look after her, you know—but just up and leaving like that, it's scandalous, and I tell Trotta all about it.

" 'Yes,' he says, 'I haven't talked to Demant for a long time.' "

"Trotta and Demant were seen together for weeks on end!" someone cried.

"I know, I know, and that's why I told Trotta about how strangely Demant was acting. But I don't butt into other people's business, so I ask Trotta if he wants to stop off at the pastry shop with me. 'No,' he says, 'I have an appointment.' So I leave. And tonight of all nights, the pastry shop closed early. Fate, gentlemen! So I'm off to the club, of course. And I innocently tell Tattenbach and whoever else was there about Demant and about Trotta having an appointment in the middle of the theater square. I can still hear Tattenbach whistling. 'What are you whistling about?' I ask. 'Doesn't mean a thing,' he says. 'Watch out! All I can say is, Watch out! Trotta and Eva, Trotta and Eva,' he sings twice, like a cabaret ditty, and I don't know who Eva is, I figure it's Eve from the Garden of Eden—sort of symbolic and generally speaking, you know, gentlemen! Understand?"

They all understood, which they confirmed with nods and shouts. They not only understood the captain's story, they knew it intimately, from start to finish. But nevertheless, they wanted to hear about the events over and over, for in their most foolish heart of hearts they hoped that the rittmaster's story would eventually change and allow some meager prospect of a happier end. They kept asking Taittinger over and over. But his story was always the same. There was no change in even the least of the sad details.

"What now?" someone asked.

"You already know the rest," the rittmaster replied. "Just as we're leaving the club—Tattenbach, Kindermann, and I—Trotta and Frau Demant practically walk right into us. 'Watch out!' says Tattenbach. 'Didn't Trotta say he had an appointment?' 'It could be a coincidence,' I say to Tattenbach. And it *was* a coincidence, as I know now. Frau Demant came out of the theater alone. Trotta felt obligated to see her home. He had to miss his appointment. Nothing would have happened if Demant had entrusted his wife to me during intermission. Nothing!"

"Nothing!" everyone confirmed.

"The next evening, at the club, Tattenbach is drunk as usual. And when Demant shows up, Tattenbach instantly gets up and says, 'Oy, hello, Izzy-whizzy!' That's how it began."

"Shoddy!" said two men in unison.

"Shoddy, of course, but he was drunk! What should we do? I say correctly, 'Good evening, Herr Regimental Surgeon!' And Demant, in a voice I would never have expected from him, says to Tattenbach, 'Captain, you know that I am the regimental surgeon!'

" 'Then you oughta stay home and watch out,' says Tattenbach, sticking to his chair. Incidentally, it was his birthday. Did I tell you?"

"No!" they all chorused.

"Well, now you know: it happened to be his birthday," Taittinger repeated.

They all slurped up the news greedily. It was as if the fact that it had been Tattenbach's birthday would provide a brand-new positive solution to the dismal affair. Each man privately wondered what benefit could be drawn from Tattenbach's birthday. And little Count Sternberg, through whose brain thoughts would shoot one at a time like lone birds through empty clouds, without brethren and leaving no trace, instantly stated, with premature jubilation in his voice, "Why, then, everything's fine! That changes everything! It was his birthday!"

They eyed little Count Sternberg, puzzled and cheerless and yet ready to grasp at that nonsensical straw. Sternberg's comment was utterly silly, but if you thought about it carefully, couldn't you cling to it, didn't it contain some hope, didn't some solace beckon?

The hollow laugh instantly emitted by Taittinger overwhelmed them with new horror. Their lips parted, with helpless sounds on their mute tongues; their eyes gaping and empty, they kept still—dumbstruck and blinded men who, for an instant, had believed they had heard a comforting sound, had sighted a comforting glint. Deaf and dark was the world around them. In the huge, mute, snowed-in winterly world there was nothing but Taittinger's eternally unchanging story, which he had already repeated five times. He continued.

" 'Then you oughta stay home and watch out,' says Tattenbach. And the doctor, you know—as if he were examining Tattenbach for being too sick to march, sticks his head out toward him and says, 'Herr Rittmaster, you are drunk!'

" 'You oughta stay home and watch out!' Tattenbach babbles again. 'Our kind don't let a wife go strollin' at midnight with lootenants!'

" 'You're drunk and you're a scoundrel!' says Demant. And just as I'm about to stand up and before I can even move, Tattenbach starts yelling like crazy, 'Yid, Yid, Yid!' He says it eight times in a row—I had enough presence of mind to count precisely."

"Bravo!" said little Sternberg, and Taittinger nodded at him.

"However," the rittmaster went on, "I had enough presence of mind to issue a command: 'Orderlies, leave!' For why should the orderlies be present?"

"Bravo!" little Sternberg shouted once again. And all of them nodded in approval.

They fell silent again. From the nearby kitchen of the pastry shop came the hard clattering of dishes and from the street the bright jingling of a sleigh. Taittinger stuffed another pastry into his mouth.

"Now the fat's in the fire!" shouted little Sternberg.

Taittinger swallowed the last remnant of his delicacy and only said, "Tomorrow morning, seven-twenty!"

Tomorrow morning, seventy-twenty! They knew the conditions: simultaneous exchange of bullets at ten paces. There was no way for Dr. Demant to use a sword. He couldn't fence.

Tomorrow morning at seven, the regiment will be marching to the water meadow for a drill. The so-called Green Square behind the old castle, where the duel is to take place, is barely two hundred feet from the water meadow.

Every officer knew that tomorrow, during the drilling, he would hear two shots. Everyone could hear them already—the two shots. With black and red wings, Death rustled over their heads.

"Check!" cried Taittinger. And they left the pastry shop.

It was snowing again. A mute dark-blue pack, they walked through the mute white snow, straggling off in twos or alone. Each was afraid to stay by himself, yet it was not possible for them to be together. They tried to lose themselves in the small streets of the tiny town—and were forced to run into one another within a few seconds. The crooked streets drove them together. They were trapped in the small town and in their great confusion. And whenever any of them came toward another, both were startled, each by the other's fear. They waited for dinnertime—and they simultaneously feared the imminent evening at the club, where today, already today, not all would be present.

And indeed, they were not all present. Tattenbach was missing, so were Major Prohaska, the doctor, First Lieutenant Zander, and Lieutenant Christ, and indeed all the seconds. Taittinger did not eat. He sat at a chessboard, playing against himself. No one spoke. The orderlies stood, silent and stony, at the doors; everyone heard the slow, hard ticking of the big grandfather clock; to its left, the Supreme Commander in Chief stared with cold china-blue eyes at his taciturn officers. No one had the nerve to leave by himself or to take his neighbor along. And so they lingered, each at his place. If two or three men sat together, their words dripped in single heavy drops from their mouths, and a huge leaden hush weighed between question and answer. Everyone felt the hush on his back.

They thought about the men who were not there, as if the absent were already corpses. They all remembered Dr. Demant's arrival several weeks ago, after a long medical furlough. They could see his faltering steps and his sparkling glasses. They could see Count Tattenbach, his short rotund body on bandy equestrian legs, the eternally red skull with the close-shorn clear-blond hair parted down the middle and his pale, beady, red-rimmed little eyes. They could hear the physician's gentle voice and the rittmaster's thunderous voice. And even though the words "honor" and "dying," "shooting" and "fighting," "death" and "grave" had been at home in their hearts and minds ever since they could think and feel, it struck them today as incomprehensible that they might be separated forever from the rittmaster's thunderous voice and the physician's gentle one. Whenever the doleful chimes of the large wall clock rang out, the men believed that their own final hour had struck. Unwilling to trust their ears, they looked at the wall. No doubt about it: time had not paused. Seven-twenty, seven-twenty, seven-twenty: it hammered in all brains.

They stood up, one by one, hesitant and shamefaced; as they went their separate ways, they felt they were betraying one another. Their steps were almost soundless. Their spurs did not jingle, their swords did not clatter, their soles numbly struck a numb floor. By midnight the club was empty. And at a quarter to midnight, First Lieutenant Schlegel and Lieutenant Kindermann reached the barracks where they lived. One flight up, where the officers' rooms were located, a single bright window cast a yellow rectangle into the square darkness of the parade ground. Both men looked up at the window together.

"That's Trotta!" said Kindermann.

"That's Trotta!" Schlegel echoed.

"We ought to look in on him."

"He won't like it!"

They jingled through the corridor, halted at Lieutenant Trotta's door, and listened. Nothing stirred. First Lieutenant Schlegel reached for the knob but did not turn it. He withdrew his hand, and the two men walked off. They exchanged nods and entered their rooms.

Lieutenant Trotta had indeed not heard them. For the past four hours, he had been struggling to write his father a detailed letter. He could not get beyond the opening lines.

Dear Father, he began, *I have innocently and unintentionally been the cause of a tragic affair of honor.* His hand was heavy. A dead, useless tool, it hovered with the trembling pen over the paper. This was the first difficult letter in his life. The lieutenant felt he could not possibly wait for the outcome of the affair before writing to the district captain. Ever since the disastrous quarrel between Tattenbach and Demant, Trotta had been putting off the letter from one day to the next. But there was no possibility of not sending it today. Today, before the duel. What would the Hero of Solferino have done in his place? Carl Joseph felt his grandfather's imperious gaze on the back of his neck. The Hero of Solferino dictated terse resoluteness to the timid grandson. He must write, instantly, on the spot. Why, he should have gone straight to his father. Between the dead Hero of Solferino and the wavering grandson stood the father, the district captain, the guardian of honor, the custodian of the legacy. The blood of the Hero of Solferino rolled alive and red in the district captain's veins. By not telling his father in time, Carl Joseph would appear to be hiding something from his grandfather as well.

But in order to write this letter, he had to be as strong as his grandfather, as simple, as resolute, as close to the peasants of Sipolje. Trotta was only the grandson! This letter was a dreadful interruption in the leisurely routine of weekly reports that all sounded alike and that the sons in the Trotta family had always written to their fathers. A gory letter; it had to be written.

The lieutenant went on:

> *I had gone on a harmless stroll—albeit around midnight—with the wife of our regimental surgeon. The circumstances left me no choice. We were seen by other officers. Captain Tattenbach, who, unfortunately, is often drunk, made a shoddy insinuation aimed at the physician. Tomorrow morning at seven-twenty, the two men are shooting it out. I will probably be forced to challenge Tattenbach if he survives, as I hope he does. The conditions are stringent.*
>
> > *Your dutiful son,*
> > *Carl Joseph Trotta, Lieutenant*
>
> *P.S. I may even have to leave the regiment.*

Now the lieutenant felt the worst was over. But when his eyes wandered across the shadowy ceiling, he suddenly saw his grandfather's admonishing face. Next to the Hero of Solferino he believed he also saw the white-bearded face of the Jewish tavern keeper, whose grandson was Regimental Surgeon Dr.

Demant. The dead seemed to be calling the living, and it was as if he himself would be reporting for the duel by tomorrow morning, at seven-twenty. Reporting for the duel and falling. Falling! Falling and dying!

On those long-vanished Sundays when Carl Joseph had stood on his father's balcony while Herr Nechwal's military band had intoned "The Radetzky March," it would have been a bagatelle to fall and die. The cadet at the Imperial and Royal Military Academy had been intimate with the notion of death, but it had been a very remote death. Tomorrow morning, seven-twenty, Death was waiting for his friend, Dr. Demant; the day after tomorrow, or in a few days, for Lieutenant Carl Joseph von Trotta. Oh, horror and darkness! To be the cause of Death's black arrival and finally to be his victim! And should he not become his victim, how many corpses still lined the roadway? Like milestones on other men's roads, the gravestones lay along Trotta's road. He was certain he would never see his friend again, just as he had never seen Katharina again. Never again! In front of Carl Joseph's eyes, this word stretched out without shore or limit, a dead sea of numb eternity. The little lieutenant clenched his white weak fist against the grand black law, which rolled up the headstones but set no dam against the relentlessness of *never* and refused to illuminate the everlasting darkness. He clenched his fist; he stepped over to the window to raise his fist against heaven. But he raised only his eyes. He saw the cold twinkling of the winter stars. He remembered the night, the last time he had walked with Dr. Demant, from the barracks to the town. The last time, he had known then.

Suddenly he felt a longing for his friend and also the hope that it was still possible to save the doctor. It was one-twenty. Dr. Demant had six more hours to live, six big hours. Now this time span seemed almost as mighty to the lieutenant as the shoreless eternity had seemed. He dashed over to the clothes hook, strapped on his saber and yanked on his coat, hurried along the corridor and practically soared down the stairs, raced across the nocturnal rectangle of the parade ground, out the gates, past the sentry, ran through the silent landscape, reached the little town in ten minutes and, a while later, the only sleigh that was on lonely night duty; and he glided amid the comforting jingling toward the southern edge of the town, toward the physician's house. Behind the gate the small house slept with sightless windows. Trotta rang the bell. The hush continued. He shouted Dr. Demant's name. Nothing stirred. He waited. He told the coachmen to crack his whip. No one responded.

Had he been looking for Count Tattenbach, it would have been easy The night before his duel he was probably at Frau Resi's, drinking his own health. But there was no guessing where Dr. Demant might be. Perhaps he was walking the streets of the town. Perhaps he was strolling among the familiar graves, already seeking his own.

"The cemetery!" the lieutenant ordered the startled coachman.

Not far from here the cemeteries lay side by side. The sleigh halted at the old wall and the locked gate. Trotta got out. He walked over to the gate. Heeding the crazy whim that had driven him here, he cupped his hands on his mouth and in an alien voice, which came like a wailing from his heart, he called Dr. Demant's name to the graves. He himself believed, while shouting, that he was already calling the dead man and no longer the living man; and he took fright and began trembling like one of the naked shrubs between the graves, over which the winter night storm was now whistling; and the saber rattled on the lieutenant's hip.

The coachman, on the box of the sleigh, was terrified of his passenger. He thought, simple as he was, that the officer was either a ghost or a madman. But he was too scared to whip his horse and drive off. His teeth chattered; his heart raced wildly against the thick coat of cat fur.

"Please get in, Herr Officer," he said.

The lieutenant obeyed. "Back to town!" he said. In the town, he got out and trudged conscientiously through the narrow winding alleys and across the small squares. The tinny strains of a pianola blaring somewhere through the nocturnal hush gave him a momentary goal; he hurried toward the metallic rattle. It resounded through the dimly lit glass door of a tavern near Frau Resi's establishment, a tavern patronized by the troops but off limits to officers. The lieutenant stepped up to the brightly glowing window and peered over the reddish curtain into the taproom. He could see the counter and the haggard proprietor in shirtsleeves. At one table, three men, likewise in shirtsleeves, were playing cards; at another table, a corporal was sitting, with a girl at his side and beer glasses in front of them. In the corner, a man sat alone, holding a pencil, hunched over a sheet of paper. He wrote something, broke off, sipped a drink, and stared into space. All at once his glasses focused on the window. Carl Joseph recognized him: it was Dr. Demant in mufti.

Carl Joseph knocked on the glass door; the tavern keeper came over; Carl Joseph asked him to send out the gentleman sitting alone. The regimental surgeon stepped into the street.

"It's me, Trotta!" said the lieutenant, holding out his hand.

"So you've found me," said the doctor. He spoke softly, as was his wont, but more distinctly than usual—or so it appeared to the lieutenant—for in some enigmatic way his quiet words drowned out the blaring pianola. This was the first time Trotta had ever seen him in civilian attire. The familiar voice emerging from the physician's altered appearance came toward the lieutenant like a warm greeting from home. Indeed, the voice sounded all the more familiar because Demant looked so alien. All the terrors that had confused the lieutenant during this night dissolved under his friend's voice, which Carl Joseph had not heard for many long weeks and which he had missed. Yes, he had missed it; now he knew. The pianola stopped blaring. They could hear the night wind howl from time to time, and their faces felt the snowy powder that it whirled up.

The lieutenant took one step closer to the doctor—he could not get close enough. You are not to die! he wanted to say. He realized that Demant was standing in front of him without a coat, in the snow, in the wind. If you're in civvies, it's not so obvious, he thought. And in a tender voice he said, "You're going to catch cold."

Dr. Demant's face promptly lit up with the old familiar smile, which gathered up his lips somewhat, raised his black moustache slightly. Carl Joseph reddened. Why, he won't be able to catch cold, the lieutenant thought. At the same time, he heard Dr.

Demant's gentle voice. "I have no time left to get sick, my dear friend." He spoke while smiling. The doctor's words went right through the old smile, and yet it remained whole all the same; a small sad white veil, it hung before his lips. "But let's go inside," the physician continued.

He stood, a black, immobile shadow, outside the dimly lit door, casting a second, paler shadow on the snowy street. The silvery snow powdered his black hair, which was lit by the dim glow from the tavern. The heavenly world already shimmered over his head, and Trotta was almost ready to turn back. Good night! he wanted to say and hurry off.

"Let's go inside," the doctor repeated. "I'll ask whether you can slip in unnoticed."

He entered, leaving Trotta outside. Then he returned with the proprietor. After cutting through a hallway and across a yard, they reached the tavern kitchen.

"Do people know you here?" asked Trotta.

"I sometimes come here," replied the physician. "That is, I used to come here a lot."

Carl Joseph stared at the doctor.

"You're surprised? Well, I had my particular habits."

Why does he say "had"? thought the lieutenant and remembered from his schooldays that this was called the past tense. "Had"! Why did the regimental surgeon say "had"?

The tavern keeper brought a small table and two chairs to the kitchen and lit a greenish gas lamp. In the taproom, the pianola blared away again—a potpourri of familiar marches, among which the opening drumbeats of "The Radetzky March," distorted by hoarse crackling but still recognizable, boomed at specific intervals. In the greenish shadows that the lampshade drew across the whitewashed kitchen walls, the familiar portrait of the Supreme Commander in Chief in the sparkling white uniform surfaced between two gigantic pans of reddish copper. The Kaiser's white uniform was densely flyblown as if riddled by minute grapeshot, and Franz Joseph's eyes, undoubtedly painted china blue as a matter of course, were snuffed in the shadow of the lampshade. The doctor stretched his finger toward the imperial image.

"Just a year ago it was hanging in the taproom," he said. "Now the tavern keeper no longer feels like proving that he is a loyal subject."

The pianola hushed up. That same instant, a wall clock struck two hard strokes.

"Two o'clock already!" said the lieutenant.

"Five more hours," replied the regimental surgeon.

The proprietor brought some slivovitz. "Seven-twenty" hammered in the lieutenant's brain.

He reached for the glass, raised it, and said in the strong voice trained for snapping orders, "To your health! You have to live!"

"To an easy death!" replied the regimental surgeon and drained his glass while Carl Joseph put his back on the table.

"This death is senseless," the doctor went on. "As senseless as my life was."

"I don't want you to die!" shouted the lieutenant, stamping on the tiles of the kitchen floor. "And I don't want to die either! And my life is senseless too!"

"Be quiet," Dr. Demant replied. "You are the grandson of the Hero of Solferino. He almost died as senselessly. Though it does makes a difference whether you go to your death with his deep faith or as faintheartedly as we two." He fell silent. "As we two," he began after a while. "Our grandfathers did not bequeath us great strength—little strength for life, it's just barely enough to die senselessly. Ahh!" The doctor pushed his glass aside, and it was as if he were shoving the entire world far away, including his friend. "Ahh," he repeated, "I'm tired, I've been tired for years. Tomorrow I'm going to die like a hero, a so-called hero, completely against my grain, and against the grain of my forebears and my tribe and against my grandfather's will. One of the huge old tomes he used to read says, 'He who raiseth his hand against his neighbor is a murderer.' Tomorrow someone is going to raise a pistol against me, and I'm going to raise a pistol against him. And I will be a murderer. But I'm nearsighted. I'm not going to take aim. I'll have my little revenge. Without my glasses, I can see nothing at all, nothing at all, and I will shoot without seeing. That will be more natural, more honest, and altogether fitting."

Lieutenant Trotta did not fully grasp what the doctor was saying. The doctor's voice was familiar to him, and once he got accustomed to his friend's mufti, his face and shape likewise grew familiar. But Dr. Demant's thoughts came from an utterly immense distance, that immensely faraway region where Demant's grandfather, the white-bearded king of Jewish tavern keepers, might have lived. Trotta cudgeled his brain, as he had once done in trigonometry at military school, but he understood less and less. He only felt that his new faith in the possibility of saving everything was gradually weakening, just as his hope slowly smoldered out into white, flimsy ashes, as frail as the threads glowing out over the small singing gas flame. His heart pounded as loudly as the tinny, hollow strokes of the wall clock. He did not understand his friend. Perhaps he had come too late. He had a lot more to say. But his tongue lay heavy in his mouth, burdened by weights. His lips parted. They were pale, trembling vaguely; he could barely close them.

"You must be running a temperature," said the regimental surgeon in the exact same tone he used with patients. He rapped on the table, and the tavern keeper came over with refills. "And you haven't even finished your first glass!"

Trotta obediently gulped down the first glass.

"I discovered drink too late—a pity!" said the doctor. "You won't believe me, but I'm sorry I never drank."

The lieutenant made a tremendous effort, looked up, and stared into the doctor's face for a couple of seconds. He raised his second glass. It was heavy; his hand shook, spilling a few drops. He drained it at one gulp. Anger flared inside him, rose to his head, reddened his face.

"Well, I'm going!" he said. "I can't stand your jokes. I was glad to find you. I tried your home. I rang. I drove to the cemetery. I shouted your name through the gate like a madman. I—" He broke off. Soundless words formed between his quivering lips, numb words, numb shadows of numb sounds. Suddenly his eyes filled with warm water, and a loud moaning came from his chest. He wanted to stand up and run away for he was terribly ashamed. Why, I'm crying! he thought. I'm crying! He felt powerless, immeasurably powerless against the incomprehensible power that forced him to weep. He willingly succumbed. He surrendered to the rapture of his powerlessness. He heard his own moaning and reveled in it; he was ashamed and he even enjoyed his shame. He threw himself into the arms of the sweet grief and kept repeating senselessly, amid constant sobs, "I don't want you to die, I don't want you to die, I don't want you to! I don't want you to!"

Dr. Demant rose, walked up and down the kitchen a few times, halted at the portrait of the Supreme Commander in Chief, began counting the black flyspecks on the Kaiser's tunic, interrupted his absurd occupation, walked over to Carl Joseph, and gently placed his hands on his heaving shoulders. His sparkling glasses approached the lieutenant's light-brown hair. He, the wise Dr. Demant, had already settled accounts with the world; he had sent his wife to her father in Vienna, given his orderly leave, closed down his house. He had been staying at the Golden Bear Hotel ever since the eruption of this disastrous affair. He was ready. Once he had started drinking liquor contrary to his habit, he had actually managed to find some sense in this senseless duel, to wish for death as the lawful end of a path bristling with errors—indeed, he managed to glean a shimmer of the next world, which he had always believed in. After all, long before the danger toward which he was now heading, he had been familiar with graves and dead friends. Gone was his childish love for his wife. Jealousy, painfully burning in his heart just weeks ago, was now a small pile of cold ashes. His will, just written, addressed to the colonel, was in his coat pocket. He had nothing to bequeath, few people to re-member, and thus had forgotten nothing. The alcohol gave him a light head; only the waiting made him impatient. Seven-twenty, the moment that for days now had been hammering dreadfully in the brains of all his comrades, pealed in his brain like a silvery chime. For the first time since he had donned his uniform, he felt strong, brave, and lighthearted. He enjoyed the nearness of death the way a convalescent enjoys the nearness of life. He had settled accounts, he was ready!

Now he stood again, nearsighted and helpless as ever, in front of his young friend. Yes, there were still such things as youth and friendship and tears shed for him. All at once he again longed for the dreariness of his life, the disgusting garrison, the hated uniform, the dullness of routine examinations, the stench of a throng of undressed troops, the drab vaccinations, the carbolic smell of the hospital, his wife's ugly moods, the safe confines of his house, the ash-gray workdays, the yawning Sundays, the torturous hours on horseback, the stupid maneuvers, and his own sorrow at all this emptiness. Through the lieutenant's sobbing and moaning, the shattering call of this living earth broke violently, and while the doctor cast about for words to calm Trotta, compassion flooded his heart and love flickered in him with a thousand tongues of flame. Far behind him lay his apathy of the past few days.

Now the wall clock struck three hard strokes. Trotta suddenly fell silent. They heard the echo of the three strokes drowning slowly in the humming of the gas lamp. The lieutenant began in a steady voice.

"Don't you see how stupid this whole business is? Taittinger was boring me the way he bores everyone else. So I told him I had an appointment in front of the theater that evening. Then your wife showed up alone. I had to see her home. And just as we were passing the club, they all came out into the street."

The doctor removed his hands from Trotta's shoulders and started wandering again. He walked almost soundlessly, with soft, attentive steps.

"I have to tell you," the lieutenant continued, "I instantly sensed that something bad would happen. And I could barely say a civil word to your wife. And then when I was outside your garden, at your house, the streetlight was burning. I remember I could distinctly make out your footprints in the snow between the garden gate and your front door, and then I had a strange idea, a crazy idea. . . ."

"Yes?" said the doctor, halting.

"A funny idea: for an instant I thought that your footprints were something like sentries—I can't put it into words, I simply thought they were looking up from the snow at your wife and me."

Dr. Demant sat down again, scrutinized Trotta, and said slowly, "Maybe you're in love with my wife and just don't realize it yourself?"

"None of this whole business is my fault in any way!" said Trotta.

"No, it's not your fault," the regimental surgeon confirmed.

"But I keep *feeling* that it's my fault!" said Carl Joseph. "You know, I told you all about Frau Slama." He fell silent. Then he whispered, "I'm scared, I'm scared everywhere."

The regimental surgeon spread out his arms, shrugged, and said, "You too are a grandson."

At that moment, he was not thinking about the lieutenant's fears. It struck him as highly possible that he could still escape all the danger. Disappear! he thought. Be dishonored, degraded, serve as a private for three years or flee abroad. Avoid getting shot!

Lieutenant Trotta, grandson of the Hero of Solverino, a man from another world, was already utterly alien to him. And he said loudly and with scoffing delight, "That stupidity! That honor that hangs in the silly tassel here on the saber. One cannot escort a woman home! You see how stupid that is? Didn't you rescue him"—he pointed at the Kaiser's picture—"from the brothel? Idiocy!" he suddenly shouted. "Shameful idiocy!"

Someone knocked; the tavern keeper came, bringing two full glasses. The regimental surgeon drank.

"Drink!" he said.

Carl Joseph drank. He did not quite grasp what the doctor was saying, but he sensed that Demant was no longer willing to die. The clock ticked its tinny seconds. Time did not stop. Seven-twenty, seven-twenty! It would take a miracle to keep Demant from dying. Miracles did not occur, that much the lieutenant knew. He himself—a preposterous thought—would show up tomorrow morning at seven-twenty and say, "Gentlemen, Demant went crazy last night. I'm dueling in his place." Drivel, ridiculous, impossible! He looked helplessly at the doctor again. Time did not stop; the clock kept endlessly stitching its seconds. Soon it would be 4 A.M. Three more hours!

"Well!" the regimental surgeon finally said. He sounded as if he had already made up his mind, as if he knew precisely what was to be done. But he knew nothing precisely. His thoughts drifted, blind and incoherent, along confused trails through the blind fog. He knew nothing. A contemptible, shameful, stupid, powerful iron-clad law was fettering him, sending him fettered to a stupid death. He caught the late-night sounds from the taproom. Clearly no one was left there. The tavern keeper was plunging the clinking beer glasses into the plashing water, shoving the chairs together, pushing tables aright, jingling his keys. They had to go. The street, the winter, the nightly sky, its stars, its snow might offer counsel and comfort. The physician went to the tavern keeper, paid, came back in his overcoat; black, in a broad soft hat, he stood, muffled up and transformed once more, in front of the lieutenant. He looked armed, far better armed than he had ever been in his uniform with saber and cap.

They walked across the courtyard, back through the corridor, into the night. The doctor looked up at the sky. The silent stars offered no counsel; they were colder than the snow all around. The houses were dark, the streets deaf and dumb, the night wind blasted the snow into powder, Trotta's spurs jingled softly, the doctor's boot soles crunched next to them. They hurried as if toward a specific goal. Shreds of ideas, of thoughts, of images raced through their minds. Their hearts pounded like swift, heavy hammers. Unwittingly the regimental surgeon set the direction; unwittingly the lieutenant followed him. They approached the Golden Bear Hotel. They stood in its arched doorway. In Carl Joseph's imagination, the image of Grandfather Demant awoke, the silver-bearded king of the Jewish tavern keepers. All his life, he had sat at such a gateway—a much bigger one, probably. He would rise to his feet when the farmers drew up. Since he could no longer hear, the little farmers would cup their hands on their mouths and yell out their orders. Seven-twenty, seven-twenty: it came again. At seven-twenty the grandson of that grandfather would be dead.

"Dead!" the lieutenant said aloud. Oh, he was wise no longer, that wise Dr. Demant. For a couple of days he had been free and brave for nothing; it was now obvious that he had not settled accounts. It was not easy settling things. His wise mind, inherited from a long long line of wise forebears, was as helpless as the simple mind of the lieutenant, whose ancestors had been the simple peasants of Sipolje. An obtuse iron-clad law had no loophole.

"I'm a fool, my dear friend," said the doctor. "I should have left Eva long ago. I don't have the strength to avoid this stupid duel. I'm going to be a hero out of stupidity, according to the code of honor and military regulations. A hero!" He laughed. His mirth rang through the night. "A hero!" he repeated, trudging up and down in front of the hotel entrance.

A childish hope whizzed through the lieutenant's youthful mind, which was ready to grab at any straw: they won't shoot at each other, they'll reconcile! Everything will work out! They'll be transferred to other regiments! So will I! Stupid, ridiculous, impossible, he instantly thought. And, lost, desperate, with a numb brain, dry palate, leaden limbs, he stood motionless before the doctor, who was walking to and fro.

What time was it? He did not dare look at his watch. The tower clock would be striking soon anyway. He would wait. "If we don't meet again—" the doctor broke off and then said, a few moments later, "I advise you to leave the army." Then he held out his hand. "Farewell! Go home! I'll manage by myself. So long!"

He tugged the bell wire. The buzzing resounded from the interior. Footsteps were already approaching. The door opened. Lieutenant Trotta took hold of the doctor's hand. In a normal voice that amazed him, too, he articulated a normal "So long." He had not even slipped off his glove. The door was already shut. There was already no Dr. Demant. As if drawn by an invisible hand, Lieutenant Trotta followed the usual route to the barracks. He did not hear a window being unlatched two stories overhead. The doctor leaned out once again, saw his friend vanish round the corner, closed the window, switched on all the lights in the room, walked over to the washstand, stropped his razor, tested it on his thumbnail, and soaped his face calmly, as on any other morning. He washed. He took the uniform from the closet. He dressed, buckled on the saber, and waited. He nodded off. He slept a calm, dreamless sleep in the wide armchair at the window.

When he awoke, the sky over the roofs was already bright; a dainty shimmer was turning blue across the snow. Soon someone would knock. He could already hear the distant jingling of a sleigh. It drew closer it halted. Now the doorbell rang. Now the stairs creaked. Now the spurs jingled. Now someone knocked.

Now they stood in the room, First Lieutenant Christ and Captain Wangert of the garrison infantry. They remained near the door, the lieutenant half a pace behind the captain. The regimental surgeon glanced at the sky. A distant echo from a distant childhood, his grandfather's faded voice reverberated. *Hear, O Israel*, said the voice, *the Lord our God, the Lord is One.*

"I'm ready, gentlemen!" said the regimental surgeon.

They sat, a bit crowded, in small sleighs; the bells jingled bravely, the brown horses raised their cropped tails and dropped big, round, yellow steaming turds on the snow. The regimental surgeon, who had been indifferent to all animals throughout his life, suddenly felt homesick for his horse. He will survive me! he thought. His face betrayed nothing. His companions were silent.

They halted some hundred paces from the glade. They reached the Green Square on foot. It was already morning, but the sun had not yet risen. The firs stood hushed; slender and upright, they proudly bore the snow on their branches. Far away, roosters crowed and crowed back. Tattenbach spoke loudly to his seconds. The head surgeon, Dr. Mangel, walked to and fro between the groups.

"Gentlemen!" a voice said. At that instant, Regimental Surgeon Dr. Demant took off his glasses as fussily as ever and placed them carefully upon a wide tree stump. Oddly enough, he could still clearly see his path, the designated place, the distance between himself and Count Tattenbach, and he saw the count himself. He waited. Until the final moment, he waited for the fog. But everything remained clear, as if the regimental surgeon had never been nearsighted. A voice counted, "One!" The regimental surgeon raised the pistol. He felt free and brave again, indeed, cocky—for the first time in his life he felt cocky. He aimed as the one-year volunteer had once aimed during target practice, even though he had already been a miserable shot back then. Why, I'm not nearsighted, he thought, I'll never need glasses again. From a medical standpoint, it was inexplicable. The regimental surgeon decided to check with ophthalmologists. At the very instant that the name of a certain specialist flashed through his mind, the voice counted, "Two!" The doctor could still see clearly. A shy bird of an unknown species began chirping, and from far away came the blaring of the bugles. It was at this time that the lancer regiment normally reached its drilling ground.

Lieutenant Trotta rode in the second squadron as on any other day. The matte breath of the frost beaded on the sheaths of the heavy sabers and on the barrels of the light carbines. The frozen bugles awoke the sleeping town. The coachmen in their thick furs, at their usual station, raised their bearded heads. When the regiment reached the water meadow and dismounted, and the troops as usual formed a double line for early morning exercises, Lieutenant Kindermann stepped over to Carl Joseph and said, "Are you sick? Do you have any idea what you look like?" He pulled out a coquettish pocket mirror and held it up to Trotta's eyes. In the small shimmering rectangle, Lieutenant Trotta spotted an ancient face that he was very familiar with: small black glowing eyes, the sharp bony ridge of a large nose, hollow ashen cheeks, and long thin clenched bloodless lips, which, like an old saber scar, isolated the chin from the moustache. Only that small brown moustache seemed alien to Carl Joseph. At home, under the ceiling of his father's study, his grandfather's blurring face had been stark naked.

"Thank you for asking," said the lieutenant. "I didn't sleep last night." He walked off the drill grounds.

He veered left, between the trunks, where a path branched off to the wide highway. It was seven-forty. No shots had been heard. Everything's fine, everything's fine, he told himself; a miracle has occurred! Within ten minutes at the latest, Major Prohaska is sure to come riding along; then I'll know everything. He could hear the hesitant noises of the small town awakening and the long shriek of a locomotive at the station.

When the lieutenant reached the spot where the path joined the highway, the major appeared on his chestnut; Lieutenant Trotta saluted.

"Good morning!" said the major, and nothing more. The narrow path was not wide enough for both horseman and pedestrian. So Lieutenant Trotta followed the riding major. Some two minutes from the water meadow—the commands of the junior officers could already be heard—the major pulled up, half turned in his saddle, and said only, "Both!" Then, riding on, he added, more to himself than to the lieutenant, "There was simply no way out."

That day the regiment returned to the barracks a good hour earlier than usual. The bugles blared as on all other days. In the afternoon, the junior officers on duty read Colonel Kovacs's announcement to the troops: Captain Count Tattenbach and Regimental Surgeon Dr. Demant had each died a soldier's death for the honor of the regiment.

Chapter 8

BACK THEN, BEFORE the Great War, when the incidents reported on these pages took place, it was not yet a matter of indifference whether a person lived or died. If a life was snuffed out from the host of the living, another life did not instantly replace it and make people forget the deceased. Instead, a gap remained where he had been, and both the near and distant witnesses of his demise fell silent whenever they saw this gap. If a fire devoured a house in a row of houses in a street, the charred site remained empty for a long time. For the bricklayers worked slowly and leisurely, and when the closest neighbors as well as casual passersby looked at the empty lot, they remembered the shape and the walls of the vanished house. That was how things were back then. Anything that grew took its time growing, and anything that perished took a long time to be forgotten. But everything that had once existed left its traces, and people lived on memories just as they now live on the ability to forget quickly and emphatically.

For a long time, the deaths of the regimental surgeon and Count Tattenbach stirred the emotions of the officers and troops of the lancer regiment and also the civilian populace. The deceased were buried according to the prescribed military and religious rites. Beyond their own ranks none of the officers had breathed a word about the manner of the deaths, but somehow the news had traveled through the small garrison that both men had fallen victim to their strict code of honor. And it was as if the forehead of every surviving officer now bore the mark of a close, violent death, and for the shopkeepers and craftsmen in the small town the foreign gentlemen had become even more foreign. The officers went about like incomprehensible worshipers of some remote and pitiless deity, but also like its gaudily clad and splendidly adorned sacrificial animals. People stared after them, shaking their heads. They even felt sorry for them. They have lots of privileges, the people told one another. They can strut around with sabers and attract women, and the Kaiser takes care of them personally as if they were his own sons. And yet before you can even bat an eyelash, one of them insults another, and the offense has to be washed away with blood!

So the men they were talking about were truly not to be envied. Even Captain Taittinger, who was rumored to have participated in several fatal duels in other regiments, altered his normal behavior. While the loud-mouthed and flippant were now silent and subdued, a strange uneasiness took hold of the usually soft-spoken, sweet-toothed, and haggard rittmaster. He could no longer spend hours sitting alone behind the glass door of the little pastry shop, devouring pastries or else wordlessly playing chess or dominoes with himself or with the colonel. Taittinger was now afraid of solitude. He literally clung to the other men. If no fellow officer was nearby, he would enter a shop to buy something he did not need. He would stand there for a long time, chatting with the storekeeper about useless and silly things, unable to make up his mind to leave—unless he spotted some casual acquaintance passing outside, whereupon Taittinger would instantly pounce on him. That was how greatly the world had changed. The officers' club remained empty. They stopped their convivial outings to Frau Resi's establishment. The orderlies had little to do. If an officer ordered a drink, he would look at the glass and muse that it was the very one from which Tattenbach had drunk just a couple of days ago. They still told the old jokes, but they no longer guffawed loudly; at most, they smiled. Lieutenant Trotta was seen only on duty.

It was as if a swift magical hand had washed the tinge of youth from Carl Joseph's face. No similar lieutenant could have been found in the entire Imperial and Royal Army. He felt he had to do something extraordinary now, but nothing extraordinary could be found far and wide. Needless to say, he was to leave the regiment and join another. But he looked about for some difficult task. He was really looking for a self-imposed penance. He could never have put it into words, but we may say that he was unspeakably afflicted by the thought of having been a tool in the hands of misfortune.

It was in this state of mind that he informed his father about the outcome of the duel and announced his unavoidable transfer to a different regiment. Although entitled to a brief furlough on this occasion, he concealed this from his father, for he was afraid to face him. But as it turned out, he underestimated the old man. For the district captain, that model of a civil servant, was well aware of military customs. And strangely enough, as could be read between the lines, he also seemed to know how to deal with his son's sorrow and confusion. For the district captain's answer went as follows:

Dear Son,

Thank you for your precise account and for your confidence. The fate your comrades met with touches me deeply. They died a death that befits men of honor.

In my day, duels were more frequent and honor far more precious than life. In my day, officers, it seems to me, were also made of sterner stuff. You are an officer, my son, and the grandson of the Hero of Solferino. You will know how to cope with your innocent and involuntary involvement in this tragic affair. Naturally you are sorry to leave the regiment, but you will still be serving our Kaiser in any regiment, anywhere in the army.

Your father,
Franz von Trotta

P.S. As for your two-week furlough, to which you are entitled with your transfer, you may spend it as you wish, either in my home or, even better, in your new garrison town, so that you may more easily familiarize yourself with your new situation.

F.v.T.

Lieutenant Trotta read the letter not without a sense of shame. His father had guessed everything. In the lieutenant's eyes, the district captain's image grew to an almost fearful magnitude. Indeed, it soon equaled his grandfather's. And if the lieutenant had previously been afraid of facing the old man, it was now impossible for him to spend his furlough at home. Later, later, when I get my regular furlough, thought the lieutenant, who was made of less stern stuff than the lieutenants of the district captain's youth.

Naturally you are sorry to leave the regiment, his father had written. Had he written it because he sensed that the opposite was true? What would Carl Joseph have been sorry to leave? This window, perhaps, the view of the troop rooms, the troops themselves perching on their cots, the mournful sounds of their harmonicas and the singing, the distant songs that sounded like uncomprehended echoes of similar songs crooned by the peasants in Sipolje. Perhaps he should go to Sipolje, the lieutenant wondered. He went over to the strategic map, the only wall decoration in this room. He could have found Sipolje in his sleep. It lay in the extreme south of the monarchy—the good, quiet village. The tiny hair-thin black letters spelling out the name of Sipolje were in the midst of a lightly cross-hatched pale brown. Nearby were: a draw well, a water mill, the small station of a monorail, a church and a mosque, a young broad-leafed wood, narrow forest trails, dirt roads, and lonesome cottages. It is evening in Sipolje. At the well, the women stand in particolored kerchiefs tinted golden by the glowing sunset. The Muslims lie in prayer on the old rugs in the mosque. The tiny engine of the forest train clangs through the dense dark green of the firs. The water mill clatters, the brook murmurs.

It was the intimate game he had played as a cadet. The familiar images emerged instantly. His grandfather's enigmatic gaze shone over everything else. There was probably no cavalry garrison nearby, so he would have to transfer to the infantry. It was not without pity that the mounted comrades looked down at the foot soldiers; it was not without pity that they would look down at the transferred lieutenant. His grandfather had likewise been a simple infantry captain. Marching across his native soil would almost mean coming home to his peasant forebears. They trudged across the hard clods with heavy feet, they plunged the plow into the rich flesh of the fields, they scattered the fruitful seeds with gestures of blessing. No! The lieutenant was not the least bit sorry to leave this regiment—perhaps to leave the

cavalry. His father would have to give his consent. The lieutenant would have to pass an infantry training course, a bit tedious
perhaps.

He had to make his farewells. A small soiree at the officers'
club. A round of drinks. A brief speech by the colonel. A bottle
of wine. Cordial handshakes with his comrades. They were
already whispering behind his back. A bottle of champagne.
Perhaps—who knows?—they would end the evening with a
full-strength march to Frau Resi's place. Another round of
drinks. Ah, if only these farewells were done with! He would
take his orderly Onufrij to the new post. He could not struggle
with a new name. He could avoid visiting his father. On the
whole, he would try to escape all tedious and difficult aspects of
transferring. Of course, he still had the hard, hard task of calling
on Dr. Demant's widow.

What a task! Lieutenant Trotta tried to convince himself that
after her husband's funeral Frau Eva Demant had gone back to
her father in Vienna. So Trotta thought to stand outside the
house, ringing and ringing in vain, find out her Viennese
address, and write her a terse and extremely sympathetic letter. It
is very pleasant to think that you have only one letter to write.
You are anything but brave, the lieutenant thought simultaneously. Didn't he constantly feel his grandfather's dark, enigmatic gaze on the back of his neck? Who could say how
woefully he would stagger through this arduous life? He was
brave only when he thought about the Hero of Solferino. He
had to keep returning to his grandfather for a bit of strength.

The lieutenant slowly set out to perform his hard chore. It was
three in the afternoon. The small storekeepers, wretched and
frozen, stood outside their doors, waiting for their rare customers. From the workshops of the craftsmen came familiar
productive noises. A cheerful hammering resounded from the
smithy, a hollow metallic thunder rattled from the plumber's
shop, a swift clattering rose from the cobbler's basement, and
saws ground in the cabinetmaker's workshop. The lieutenant
knew all the faces and all the noises of these workshops. He rode
past them twice a day. From his saddle he could see over the old
blue-and-white signs, his head looming above them. Every day

he saw the morning interiors of the upstairs rooms, the beds, the coffeepots, the men in shirtsleeves, the women with their hair down, the flowerpots on the windowsills, pickles and dried fruit behind ornamental ironwork.

Now he stood outside Dr. Demant's house. The gate creaked. He entered. The orderly opened the front door. The lieutenant waited. Frau Demant came. He trembled slightly. He remembered the condolence visit he had paid Sergeant Slama. He felt the sergeant's heavy, clammy, loose handshake. He saw the dark vestibule and the reddish parlor. His palate had the stale aftertaste of the raspberry drink. So she's not in Vienna, the lieutenant thought, the instant he spied the widow. He was surprised by her black dress. It was as if this were his first inkling that Frau Demant was the wife of the regimental surgeon. Nor was the room he now entered the same one he had sat in when his friend had been alive. On the wall hung a large crape-lined portrait of the dead man. It kept shifting farther away, like the Kaiser at the officers' club, as if it were not close to the eyes and within reach of the hands but unattainably far behind the wall, as if seen through a window.

"Thank you for coming," said Frau Demant.

"I wanted to say goodbye," replied Trotta.

Frau Demant raised her wan face. The lieutenant saw the lovely bright-gray shine of her large eyes. They were focused straight on his face, two round lights of glittering ice. In the twilight of the winter afternoon, all that shone was the woman's gaze. The lieutenant's eyes darted to her narrow white forehead and then to the wall, to the remote portrait of her dead husband. These preliminaries were dragging on far too long. It was time Frau Demant asked him to sit. But she said nothing. Yet one could feel the darkness of the nearby evening falling through the window, and he childishly feared that no light would ever be switched on in this house. No suitable words came to the lieutenant's rescue. He could hear the woman's quiet breathing.

"We're just standing around," she finally said. "Let's sit down."

They sat on opposite sides of the table. As once in Sergeant Slama's parlor, Carl Joseph had his back to the door. Once more he felt the door as something ominous. From time to time and for no reason, it seemed to open soundlessly and close soundlessly. The twilight deepened. Frau Eva Demant's black frock dissolved in it. Now she was dressed in the twilight itself. Her white face floated naked, exposed, on the dark surface of the evening. Gone was the portrait of her dead husband on the opposite wall.

"My husband," said Frau Demant's voice through the darkness.

The lieutenant could see her teeth shimmering; they were whiter than her face. Gradually he could again distinguish the shiny glow of her eyes.

"You were his only friend. He often said so. How often did he talk about you! If only you knew! It won't sink in that he's dead. And," she whispered, "that it's my fault."

"It's *my* fault!" said the lieutenant. His voice was very loud, hard and alien to his own ears. It was no comfort for the widow. "It's my fault!" he repeated. "I should have been more careful in seeing you home. I shouldn't have gone past the club."

The woman began to sob. He saw the wan face bending deeper and deeper over the table, like a huge white oval flower sinking slowly. All at once, the white hands emerged right and left, receiving the sinking face, cushioning it. And now, nothing could be heard but the woman's sobs for a while, for a minute, for another minute. An eternity for the lieutenant. Get up and let her cry and leave, he thought. He actually rose. Her hands promptly dropped on the table. In a calm voice that virtually came from a different throat than the weeping, she asked, "Where are you going?"

"To turn on the light," said Trotta.

She stood up and walked around the table, grazing him as she passed. He smelled a tender wave of perfume; then it was past him and already gone. The light was harsh; Trotta forced himself to look straight into the lamp. Frau Demant held one hand over her eyes.

"Turn on the light over the bracket," she ordered.

The lieutenant obeyed. She waited by the door, her hand over her eyes. When the tiny lamp under the soft gold-yellow shade was burning, she put out the ceiling light. She took her hand

from her eyes as if removing a visor. She looked very bold in the
black dress, with her wan face stretching toward Trotta. She was
angry and courageous. Faint trails of dry tears could be seen on
her cheeks. Her eyes were as shiny as ever.

"Sit over there, on the sofa!" Frau Demant ordered. Carl
Joseph sat down. The comfortable cushions slid from all sides,
from the back, from the corners, slyly and cautiously, toward the
lieutenant. He felt it was dangerous sitting here and he shifted
resolutely toward the edge, placing his hands on the hilt of the
upright saber as he saw Frau Eva coming over. She looked like
the dangerous commander of all the pillows and cushions. On
the wall to the right of the sofa hung the picture of his dead
friend. Frau Eva sat down. A small soft pillow lay between them.
Trotta did not stir. As always when he could see no way out of
the countless agonizing predicaments he stumbled into, he
imagined himself able to leave.

"So you're being transferred?" asked Frau Demant.

"I'm transferring voluntarily," he said, gazing down at the
rug, his chin in his hands and his hands on the saber hilt.

"Do you have to?"

"Yes, I have to!"

"I'm sorry. Very sorry."

Frau Demant sat like him, her elbows propped on her lap, her
chin in her hands, and her eyes on the rug. She was probably
waiting for a comforting word, a bit of charity. He was silent. He
relished the blissful feeling that his callous silence was a dreadful
revenge for his friend's death. He thought of the dangerous
pretty little husband-killing women who often recurred in the
conversations of officers. She most likely belonged to the dangerous tribe of weak murderesses. He had to do his best to
escape her power immediately. He girded himself to leave. At
that moment, Frau Demant's changed her position. She took
her hands from her chin. Her left hand began gently and
conscientiously smoothing the silk braid along the sofa's edge.
Her fingers moved along the narrow glossy path leading from
her to Lieutenant Trotta, to and fro, regular and gradual. Those
fingers stole into his field of vision; he longed for blinders. The
white fingers entangled him in a mute conversation that could

not possibly be broken off. Smoke a cigarette: a wonderful idea! He pulled out his cigarette case, his matches.

"Give me one!" said Frau Demant.

He was forced to look into her face when he gave her a light. He felt it was inappropriate of her to smoke—as if nicotine were not permissible during mourning. And there was something exuberant and vicious about the way she took the first puff, the way her lips rounded into a small red ring from which the dainty blue cloud emerged.

"Do you have any idea where you're being transferred to?"

"No," said the lieutenant, "but I'm making every effort to get very far away."

"Very far? Where, for instance?"

"Perhaps Bosnia!"

"Do you believe you can be happy there?"

"I don't believe I can be happy anywhere."

"I hope you do find happiness!" she said quickly—very quickly, it seemed to Trotta.

She stood up, came back with an ashtray, placed it on the floor between them, and said, "So we'll probably never meet again."

Never again! The words, the feared, shoreless, dead sea of numb eternity! Never again could he see Katharina, or Dr. Demant, or this woman! Carl Joseph said, "Probably not. Unfortunately!" He wanted to add, And I will never again see Max Demant. The lieutenant also thought of one of Taittinger's bold adages: "Widows should be burned!"

They heard the doorbell, then movement out in the hall.

"That's my father," said Frau Demant. Herr Knopfmacher was already entering.

"Ah, there you are, there you are!" he said, bringing a pungent whiff of snow into the room. He unfolded a large dazzling-white handkerchief, loudly blew his nose, and cautiously buried the handkerchief in his breast pocket as if secreting a precious object. He reached toward the door molding, switched on the ceiling lamp, stepped closer to Trotta, and shook his hand. Trotta, who had already gotten up at Herr Knopfmacher's entrance, had been standing for a while. Through this handshake Herr Knopfmacher announced all the grief that could be expressed for the physician's death. Pointing to the ceiling lamp, Knopfmacher was already saying to his daughter, "Forgive me, but I can't stand such a sad moody light!" It was as if he had hurled a stone at the crape-lined portrait of the dead man.

"My, you look awful!" said Knopfmacher a moment later, in a jubilant voice. "It's been pretty hard on you, hasn't it—this misfortune, huh?"

"He was my only friend."

"You know," said Knopfmacher, sitting down at the table and adding with a smile, "Please don't get up!" He went on when the lieutenant was sitting on the sofa again: "He said the very same thing about you when he was alive. What a calamity!" And he shook his head a few times, and his full, reddened cheeks quivered slightly.

Frau Demant drew a wispy handkerchief from her sleeve, dabbed her eyes, stood up, and left the room.

"Who knows how she'll get over it?" said Knopfmacher. "Well, I coaxed her long enough, before. She wouldn't listen! You know, dear Herr Lieutenant, every profession has its dangers. But an officer! An officer—do forgive me—should not really marry. Just between you and me—but he must have told you too—he wanted to resign and devote himself exclusively to science. And I can't tell you how delighted I was to hear it. He would certainly have made a great physician. Dear, good Max!" Herr Knopfmacher looked up at the portrait, let his eyes linger on it, and concluded his obituary: "An authority!"

Frau Demant brought the slivovitz that her father loved. "You'll join me, won't you?" asked Knopfmacher, filling some small glasses. He himself gingerly carried them over to the sofa. The lieutenant got to his feet. He had a stale taste in his mouth like after the raspberry drink. He gulped down the alcohol.

"When did you last see him?" asked Knopfmacher.

"The day before," said the lieutenant.

"He asked Eva to go to Vienna but he didn't even drop a hint. And she left totally unaware. And then his farewell letter arrived. And I knew instantly that nothing could be done."

"No, nothing could be done."

"It's so out of date—do forgive me—that code of honor! This *is* the twentieth century, after all, just imagine! We've got the gramophone, you can telephone someone hundreds of miles away, and Blériot and others are already flying through the air! And—I don't know if you read the newspapers and keep up with politics, but they say the constitution is going to be thoroughly amended. Ever since they introduced universal suffrage and the secret ballot—one per person—all sorts of things have been happening, in our country and all over the world. Our Kaiser, God bless him and keep him, is not so old-fashioned as some people think. Of course, the so-called conservative forces aren't all that wrong either. You have to proceed slowly, take your time, think it through. Just don't rush things!"

"I don't know anything about politics," said Trotta.

Knopfmacher was very annoyed. He resented that stupid army and its hare-brained institutions. His child was now a widow, his son-in-law dead, a new one had to be found—a civilian this time—and the title of commercial councilor might likewise have been postponed. It was high time they did away with such nonsense. Young good-for-nothings like the lieutenant should control their exuberance in the twentieth century. The nations were insisting on their rights, a citizen is a citizen, no more privileges for the nobility. The Social Democrats *were* dangerous, but they provided a good balance. People kept talking about war constantly, but it was certain not to come. We'd show them. These times were enlightened. In England, for instance, the king had no say.

"Naturally!" he said. "After all, politics has no place in the army. Although he"—Knopfmacher pointed at the portrait—"did know a thing or two about politics."

"He was very wise," Trotta murmured.

"Nothing could be done!" Knopfmacher repeated.

"He may have been," said the lieutenant—and he himself felt as if an alien wisdom were speaking out of him, a wisdom from the big ancient tomes of the silver-bearded king of the tavern keepers—"he may have been very wise and quite alone."

He paled. He felt Frau Demant's shiny glances. He had to leave. The room grew very still. There was nothing more to say.

"We won't be seeing Baron Trotta anymore either, Papá!" said Frau Demant. "He's being transferred."

"But you'll stay in touch?" asked Knopfmacher.

"You'll write me," said Frau Demant.

The lieutenant got up. "Best of luck!" said Knopfmacher. His hand was big and soft, like warm velvet.

Frau Demant led the way. The orderly came, held the coat. Frau Demant stood at their side. Trotta clicked his heels. She said very quickly, "Write me! I'll want to know where you are." It was a swift puff of warm air, immediately gone. The orderly was already opening the door. There lay the steps. Now the gate was opened, like when he had left the sergeant.

He walked to town rapidly, entered the first café along the road, stood at the counter, drank a brandy, then another. "We always drink Hennessy!" he heard the district captain say. He hurried to the barracks.

At the door to his room, Onufrij, a blue stroke against bare white, was waiting. The officer's orderly had brought the lieutenant a package from the colonel. Narrow, in brown paper, it was leaning in the corner. A letter lay on the table. The lieutenant read:

My dear friend, I leave you my saber and my watch.
Max Demant

Trotta unwrapped the saber. Dr. Demant's smooth silver watch dangled from the hilt. The watch had stopped. It showed ten minutes to twelve. The lieutenant wound it and held it to his ear. Its frail, swift voice ticked comfortingly. He pried the cap open with his penknife, curious and eager to play—a boy. Inside were the initials *M.D.* He pulled the saber from its sheath. Right beneath the hilt, Dr. Demant had used a knife to carve a few clumsy, sprawling letters into the steel. *Live well and free!* said the inscription. The lieutenant hung the saber in the closet. He held the sword hanger in his hand. Its wired silk glided through his fingers—a cool, golden rain. Trotta shut the closet; he shut a coffin.

He turned off the light and stretched out fully dressed on the bed. The yellow shimmer from the troop rooms floated in the white enamel of the door and was mirrored in the glittering knob. The accordion over there sighed hoarsely and nostalgically amid the roar of the deep voices of the men. They were singing the Ukrainian song about the Emperor and the Empress:

> Oh, our Emperor is a good fine man,
> And our lady is his wife, the Empress.
> He rides ahead of all his lancers brave,
> And she remains alone in the castle,
> And she waits for him. . . .
> She waits for the Emperor—our Empress.

The Empress had died long ago. But the Ruthenian peasants believed she was still alive.

PART TWO

Chapter 9

THE RAYS OF the Hapsburg sun reached eastward all the way to the border of the Russian czar's territory. It was the same sun under which the Trotta dynasty had gained its titles of nobility and its prestige. Franz Joseph's gratitude had a long memory, and his benevolence had a long arm. If one of his favorite children was about to do something foolish, the Emperor's ministers and servants intervened in time, making the foolish person act cautious and sensible. It would scarcely have been appropriate for the sole offspring of the newly ennobled dynasty of Trotta und Sipolje to serve in the province that had given birth to the Hero of Solferino, the grandson of illiterate Slovenian peasants, the son of a constabulary sergeant. The descendant might, of course, exchange service with the lancers for a modest commission in the infantry: he would thereby remain loyal to the memory of his grandfather, the plain infantry lieutenant who had saved the Kaiser's life. However, the Imperial and Royal Ministry of War was prudent enough not to send the bearer of a title of nobility to the area of a Slovenian village if his name was exactly that of the very village from which the dynastic progenitor came. This view was fully shared by the district captain, the son of the Hero of Solferino. Granted—though certainly not with a light heart—he did permit his son to transfer to the infantry. But he utterly disapproved of Carl Joseph's desire to be stationed in the Slovenian province. He himself, the district captain, had never wished to see his father's homeland. He was an Austrian, a servant and official of the Hapsburgs, and his homeland was the Imperial Palace in Vienna. Had he entertained any political ideas about a useful reshaping of the great and multifarious empire, it would have suited him for all the crown lands to be merely large variegated forecourts of the Imperial Palace and all the nations in the monarchy to be servants of the Hapsburgs. He was a district captain. In his bailiwick he represented the Apostolic Majesty. He wore the gold collar, the cocked hat, and the sword. He did not wish to push a plow across the fertile Slovenian soil. The decisive letter to his son contained the words: *Fate has turned our family of frontier peasants into an Austrian dynasty. That is what we shall remain.*

Thus it was that the southern borderland remained closed to the son, Carl Joseph, Baron von Trotta und Sipolje, and he was limited to the choice of serving either in the interior of the empire or on its eastern border. He opted for the rifle battalion, which was stationed only a few miles from the Russian border. Nearby lay Burdlaki, Onufrij's native village. This area was the related homeland of the Ukrainian peasants, their mournful accordions, and their haunting songs; it was the northern sister of Slovenia.

Lieutenant Trotta sat in the train for seventeen hours. During the eighteenth hour, the monarchy's final eastern railroad station emerged. Here he got out. He was accompanied by Onufrij, his orderly. The rifle barracks lay in the middle of the small town. Before they entered the courtyard of the barracks, Onufrij crossed himself three times. It was morning. The spring, long since at home in the interior of the empire, had come this far only recently. The forsythia was already glowing on the slopes of the railroad embankment. The violets were already blossoming in the damp woods. The frogs were already croaking in the endless swamps. The storks were already circling over the low thatched roofs of the rustic huts, seeking the old wheels, the foundations of their summer homes.

At this time, the border between Austria and Russia, in the northeast of the dual monarchy, was one of the strangest areas. Carl Joseph's rifle battalion was stationed in a town of ten thousand inhabitants. The town had a spacious ring square, with two large thoroughfares crossing at the center. One ran from east to west, the other from north to south. One led from the train depot to the graveyard, the other from the castle ruins to the steam mill. Of the ten thousand inhabitants of the town, roughly one third worked at some kind of craft. Another third lived wretchedly on their tiny farms. And the rest were involved in some sort of commerce.

We say "some sort of commerce." For neither the wares nor the business practices corresponded to the civilized world's notion of commerce. The tradesmen in those parts lived far more on happenstance than prospects, far more on unpredictable providence than any commercial planning, and any tradesman was willing at any time to seize the goods that destiny had put his way or to invent goods if God had blessed him with none. Indeed, the livelihoods of these tradesmen were a riddle. They had no shops. They had no names. They had no credit. But they did possess a finely whetted, miraculous instinct for any and all secret and mysterious sources of money. They lived off other people's work, but they also created work for others. They were frugal. They lived as squalidly as if subsisting on manual labor, but it was other people's labor. Always on the move, always on the alert, with glib tongues and quick minds, they might have had the stuff to conquer half the world—had they known what the world was all about. But they did not know. For they lived far from the world, between East and West, squeezed in between night and day—virtually as living ghosts spawned by the night and haunting the day.

Did we say they lived "squeezed in"? Nature in their homeland prevented them from feeling squeezed in. Nature forged an unending horizon around the borderland people and surrounded them with a noble ring of green forests and blue hills. When they walked through the darkness of the firs, they could actually have believed that they were favored by God—if the daily anxiety about bread for wife and children had left them time to recognize God's goodness. But they walked through the fir forests to purchase wood for city buyers as soon as winter drew near. For they also dealt in wood. Incidentally, they also dealt in corals for the peasant women in the encircling villages and also for the peasant women who lived on the other side of the border, on Russian soil. They dealt in feathers for feather beds, in horsehair, in tobacco, in silver ingots, in jewels, in Chinese tea, in southern fruit, in horses and cattle, in poultry and eggs, in fish and vegetables, in jute and wool, in cheese and butter, in fields and woodlands, in Italian marble, in human hair from China for the manufacture of wigs, in raw silk and finished silk, in textiles from Manchester, in Brussels lace and Moscow galoshes, in linen from Vienna and lead from Bohemia. None of the wonderful and none of the cheap goods in which the world is so rich remained unknown to the dealers and agents in this region. If they could not acquire or sell something in accordance with the current laws, they would get hold of it unlawfully through cunning and calculation, through boldness and deceit. Some of them even dealt in human beings, live human beings. They sent deserters from the Russian army to the United States and young peasant girls to Brazil and Argentina. They ran shipping offices and also agencies for foreign brothels. And yet their profits were paltry, and they had no inkling of the vast and splendid affluence a man can live in. Their senses, so polished and skilled in finding money, their hands, so gifted in striking gold from gravel like sparks from flint, were incapable of gaining joy for their hearts or health for their bodies.

The people in this area were the spawn of the swamps. For the swamps lay incredibly widespread across the entire face of the land, on both sides of the highway, with frogs, fever germs, and treacherous grass that could be a horrible lure into a horrible death for innocent wanderers unfamiliar with the terrain. Many died, and their final cries for help went unheard. But all the people who were born there knew the treachery of the swamps and had something of that treachery themselves. In spring and summer, the air was thick with an intense and incessant croaking of frogs. An equally intense trilling of larks exulted under the skies. And a tireless dialogue took place between sky and swamp.

Among the dealers we have spoken of were many Jews. A whim of nature, perhaps the mysterious law of an unknown descent from the legendary tribe of the Khazars, gave many of the borderland Jews red hair. The hair blazed on their heads. Their beards were aflame. On the backs of their deft hands, hard, red bristles stood rigid like tiny spears. And their ears were rank with soft reddish wool like the haze of the red fires that might be glowing inside their heads.

Any stranger coming into this region was doomed to gradual decay. No one was as strong as the swamp. No one could hold out against the borderland. By this time, the high-placed gentlemen in Vienna and St. Petersburg were already starting to prepare for the Great War. The borderlanders felt it coming earlier than the others, not only because they were used to sensing future things but also because they could see the omens of doom every day with their own eyes. They profited even from these preparations. Any number of them lived from spying and counterspying; they received Austrian guldens from the Austrian police and Russian rubles from the Russian police. And in the isolated swampy bleakness of the garrison, one or another officer fell prey to despair, gambling, debts, and sinister men. The graveyards of border garrisons held many young corpses of weak men.

But here too the soldiers drilled, as in any other garrison of the empire. Every day the rifle battalion, splattered with springtime mire, gray mud on their boots, marched back to the barracks. Major Zoglauer rode at their head. The second platoon of the first company was led by Lieutenant Trotta. The beat to which the riflemen marched was set by the bugler's long, sober signal, not the haughty fanfare that marshaled, interrupted, and blared at the clattering hooves of the lancer horses. Carl Joseph trudged along, pretending to himself that he felt better on foot. All around him the riflemen's hobnailed boots crunched over the sharp-edged gravel that, at the behest of the military authorities, was sacrificed constantly—in spring, weekly—to the swampy roads. All the stones, millions of stones, were swallowed up by the insatiable ground. And more and more victorious, shimmering, silvery-gray layers of mud welled up from the depths, ate stone and gravel, and slapped together over the stamping boots of the soldiers.

The barracks lay behind the town park. To the left of the barracks stood the District Court, faced by the district captain's office, behind whose festive and ramshackle wall stood two churches, a Roman Catholic and a Greek Orthodox; and to the right of the barracks loomed the high school. The town was so tiny that one could walk across it in twenty minutes. Its important buildings crowded together as irksome neighbors. Every evening the strollers, like convicts in a prison yard, did their regular round of the park. It took a good half hour to walk to the train depot.

The rifle officers' mess hall was located in two small rooms of a private home. Most of the officers ate at the station restaurant. So did Carl Joseph. He liked to march through the slapping mire just to see the station. It was the last of all the monarchy's stations; nevertheless, it too displayed two pairs of glittering rails ribboning uninterruptedly into the core of the empire. This station too had not only bright, glassy, cheerful signals jingling with soft echoes of calls from home but also an incessantly ticking Morse apparatus on which the lovely, confused voices of a lost and distant world were diligently hammered out, stitched out as if on a bustling sewing machine. This station too had a stationmaster, and this master swung a jangling bell, and the bell signified, All aboard! All aboard! Once a day, at the stroke of noon, the stationmaster swung his bell at the train heading west, toward Crakow, Bogumin, Vienna. A good, dear train! It lingered almost until the end of lunch, outside the windows of the first-class dining room where the officers sat. The engine did not whistle until the coffee arrived. The gray steam billowed against the panes. By the time the damp beads began streaking the glass, the train was gone. The bleak group of diners drank their coffee and slowly straggled back through the silvery-gray mud. Not even generals on tours of inspection cared to come this far. They did not come. Nobody came. At the small town's only hotel, where most of the officers resided as permanent tenants, the rich hops dealers from Nuremberg and Prague and Zatec would stay only twice a year. Once they completed their inscrutable deals, they would send for musicians and play cards at the only café, which belonged to the hotel.

Carl Joseph could take in the entire small town from the third floor of the Hotel Brodnitzer. He could see the gabled roof of the District Court, the white turret of the district captain's office, the black-and-yellow flag over the barracks, the twofold cross of the Greek church, the weathercock on the town hall, and all the dark-gray shingle roofs of the small one-story houses.

The Hotel Brodnitzer was the highest building in town. It was as much a landmark as the church, the town hall, or any other municipal structures. The streets had no names and the cottages no numbers, and if anyone asked how to reach a specific place, he would have to go by the vague directions he was offered. So-and-so lived behind the church, so-and-so opposite the town jail, someone else to the right of the District Court. People lived as if in a hamlet.

And the secrets of the people in these low cottages, under the dark-gray shingle roofs, behind the small square windowpanes and the wooden doors, oozed through chinks and rafters into the miry streets and even into the large, eternally remote barracks yard. One man had been cuckolded, another had sold his daughter to the Russian captain; someone was vending rotten eggs, someone else was regularly living off contraband; one man was an ex-convict, another had just barely avoided prison; this one lent money to officers, and his neighbor pocketed one third of the profits. The officers, nonaristocrats mostly and from a German-speaking background, had been stationed in this garrison for years and years; it had become both their home and their fate. Cut off from their homeland customs, from their German mother tongue (which had become an officialese here), at the mercy of the unending bleakness of the swamps, they fell prey to gambling and to the sharp schnapps distilled in this area and sold under the label 180 Proof. From the harmless mediocrity in which military school and traditional drilling had trained them, they skittered into the corruption of this land, with the vast breath of the huge hostile czarist empire blowing across it. Less than nine miles separated them from Russia. The Russian officers of the border regiment often came across in their long sandy-yellow and dove-gray coats, with heavy gold-and-silver epaulets on their broad shoulders and with reflective galoshes on their glossy top boots in all weathers. The two garrisons even maintained a certain camaraderie with each other. Sometimes the Austrian officers would ride small canvas-covered baggage vans across the border to watch the Cossacks showing off their riding feats and to drink the Russian liquor. Over there, in the Russian garrison, the liquor kegs stood on the curbs of the

wooden sidewalks, guarded by privates with rifles and long
fixed triple-edged bayonets. When evening set in, the kegs,
kicked along by Cossack boots, trundled and rumbled over the
bumpy streets toward the Russian officers' club, and a soft
splashing and gurgling revealed the contents of the kegs to the
populace. The czar's officers showed His Apostolic Majesty's
officers the meaning of Russian hospitality. And not one of the
czar's officers and not one of His Apostolic Majesty's officers
knew that Death was already crossing his haggard, invisible
hands over the glass beakers from which the men drank.

In the vast plain between the two border forests, the Austrian
and the Russian, the sotnias of the borderland Cossacks, uniformed winds in military formations, raced around on the
mercuric ponies of their homeland steppes, swinging their
lances over their tall fur caps like lightning streaks on long
wooden poles—coquettish lightning with dainty pennons. On
the soft, springy, swampy ground, the clatter of hooves could
barely be heard. A damp, quiet sigh was the wet soil's only
response to the flying thuds. The dark-green grasses scarcely
yielded. It was as if the Cossacks were soaring over the
meadows. And when they galloped along the sandy-yellow
highway, a huge, bright, golden column of fine-grained dust
rose up, flickering in the sun, shredding widely, dissolving,
sinking in a thousand tiny cloudlets. The invited guests sat on
rough wooden stands. The riders' movements were almost
swifter than the spectators' eyes. With their strong yellow horse
teeth, the saddled Cossacks, in mid-gallop, lifted their red-and-
blue handkerchiefs from the ground, their bodies, suddenly
felled, ducked under the horses' bellies, while the legs in the
reflective boots still squeezed the animals' flanks. Other riders
flung their lances high into the air, and the weapons whirled and
obediently dropped back into the horsemen's raised fists—they
returned like living falcons into their masters' hands. Still other
riders, with torsos crouching horizontal along the horses' backs,
human mouths fraternally pressing against animal mouths,
leaped through wondrously small rounds of iron hoops that
could have girded a small keg. The horses splayed all four legs.
Their manes rose like wings, their tails stood as upright as

rudders, their narrow heads resembled the slender bows of skidding canoes. Further riders vaulted across a line of twenty beer kegs placed bottom to bottom. The horse always neighed as it prepared to jump. The rider came bounding from infinitely far away; at first a tiny gray dot, he grew at breakneck speed into a stroke, a body, a rider, became a gigantic mythical bird, half man, half horse, a winged centaur who then, after a successful leap, halted, stock-still, a hundred yards beyond the kegs—a statue, a monument of lifeless matter. Others in turn, whizzing like arrows (and, as shooters, looking like gunshots), fired at flying targets that racing riders held at their sides on large round white disks: the shooters galloped, shot, and hit. An occasional horseman sank from his mount. The comrades following him whooshed across his body—no hoof struck him. There were riders who galloped alongside another horse and, while galloping, sprang from one saddle to the other, then back to the first, then suddenly fell upon the accompanying horse, and finally, one hand propped on each saddle, legs dangling between the horses' bodies, they jerked the animals to a halt at the indicated destination and held both mounts tight so that they stood there immobile like bronze steeds.

These festivals of Cossack horsemanship were not the only ones in the borderland between the monarchy and Russia. A dragoon regiment was also stationed in the garrison. Intimate ties between rifle officers, dragoon officers, and gentlemen of the Russian border regiments were established by Count Chojnicki, one of the richest Polish landowners in the area. Count Wojciech Chojnicki—kin to the Ledochowskis and the Potockis, related by marriage to the Sternbergs, friendly with the Thuns, a man of the world, forty years old but of no discernible age, a cavalry captain in the reserve, a bachelor, both happy-go-lucky and melancholy at once—loved horses, liquor, society, frivolity, and also seriousness. He always wintered in big cities and in the gambling casinos of the Riviera. But once the forsythia started blossoming on the railroad embankments, the count, like a migrant bird, would return to his ancestral homeland, bringing along a faintly perfumed whiff of high society and tales of gallantry and adventure. He was the sort of man who could have no foes, but also no friends, only comrades, companions, or indifferent acquaintances. With his bright, smart, slightly bulging eyes, his smooth, bald, glossy head, his wispy blond moustache, his narrow shoulders, his exceedingly lanky legs, Chojnicki was liked by all the people whom he accidentally or deliberately encountered.

He alternated between two homes, which the populace knew and respected as the Old Castle and the New Castle. The so-called Old Castle was a huge ramshackle hunting lodge that the count, for unfathomable reasons, refused to fix up. The New Castle was a spacious two-story villa whose upper landing was constantly occupied by odd and at times even sinister strangers. These were the count's "poor relations." Even had he carried out the most painstaking genealogical investigation, he could not possibly have tracked down their degrees of kinship. It had gradually become customary for Chojnicki's relatives to move into the New Castle and stay all summer. But as soon as the first flocks of starlings could be heard in the nights and the season for corn on the cob was over, these visitors, sated, relaxed, and sometimes even supplied with new clothes from the count's local tailor, headed back to the unknown regions where they apparently were at home. The host noticed neither the arrivals nor the sojourns nor the departures of his guests. His Jewish steward had standing orders to check the visitors' family credentials, regulate their food and drink, and make sure they left at the approach of winter. The house had two entrances. While the count and the nonrelated guests used the front door, his kinfolk had to take the wide detour through the orchard and go in and out through a small gate in the garden wall. Otherwise these uninvited boarders could do as they pleased.

Twice a week, on Mondays and Thursdays, Count Chojnicki gave his so-called small soirees and once a month his so-called parties. For the small soirees, only six rooms were lit and open to the guests, but for the parties there were twelve rooms. At the small soirees the footmen served without gloves and in dark-yellow liveries, but at the parties they wore white gloves and brick-brown coats with black velvet collars and silver buttons. The evening always began with vermouth and dry Spanish wines. These gave way to burgundy and bordeaux. Next came the champagne. It was followed by cognac. And, paying the tribute due their homeland, they ended with the fruit of the local soil, the 180 Proof.

At these functions, the officers of the ultrafeudal dragoon regiment and the mostly nonaristocratic officers of the rifle battalion swore tearful oaths of lifelong friendship. The summer dawns peering through the broad arched windows of the castle witnessed a gaudy chaos of infantry and cavalry uniforms. The sleepers snored toward the golden sun. At around 5 A.M., a throng of despairing orderlies dashed over to the castle to awaken their masters. For at six the regiments began their drills. The host, who was never worn out by liquor, had long since returned to his small hunting lodge. There he fiddled around with peculiar test tubes, tiny flames, laboratory apparatuses. Rumor had it that the count was trying to make gold. He certainly appeared to be engaged in foolish alchemical experiments. But while he may not have succeeded in producing gold, he did know how to win at roulette. He occasionally let on that he had inherited an infallible "system" from a mysterious long-deceased gambler.

For years now, he had been a deputy to the Imperial Council, routinely reelected by his district, beating all other candidates with the help of money, violence, and surprise attacks; a minion of the government, he despised the parliamentary body to which he belonged. He had never given a speech and never heckled. Impious, derisive, fearless, and without qualms, Chojnicki used to say that the Kaiser was mindless and senile, the government a gang of nincompoops, the Imperial Council a gathering of gullible and grandiloquent idiots, and the national authorities venal, cowardly, and lazy. The German Austrians were waltzers and boozy crooners, the Hungarians stank, the Czechs were born bootlickers, the Ruthenians were treacherous Russians in disguise, the Croats and Slovenes, whom he called Cravats and Slobbers, were brushmakers and chestnut roasters, and the Poles, of whom he himself was one after all, were skirt chasers, hairdressers, and fashion photographers. Every time he came home from Vienna or another haunt of high society where he romped about so familiarly, he would deliver a gloomy lecture, which went more or less:

"This empire is doomed. The instant the Kaiser shuts his eyes, we'll crumble into a hundred pieces. The Balkans will be more powerful than we. All the nations will set up their own filthy little states, and even the Jews are going to proclaim a king in Palestine. Vienna already stinks of the sweat of the Democrats; I can't stand being on Ringstrasse anymore. The workers wave red flags and don't care to work. The mayor of Vienna is a pious janitor. The padres are already going with the people; their sermons are in Czech. The Burgtheater is playing Jewish smut, and every week a Hungarian toilet manufacturer becomes a baron. I tell you, gentlemen, if we don't start shooting now, we're doomed. We'll live to see it for ourselves!"

The men listening to the count laughed and drank another round. They did not understand him. People fired bullets occasionally, especially around election time, in order to, say, assure Count Chojnicki's mandate, thereby showing that the world could not go under without a fight. The Kaiser was still alive. He would be followed by his successor. The army drilled and shone in all the regulation colors. The nations in the empire loved the imperial dynasty and paid homage to it in the most disparate ethnic costumes. Chojnicki was a jokester.

But Lieutenant Trotta, more sensitive than his comrades, sadder than they, his soul constantly echoing with the dark, roaring wings of Death, which he had already encountered twice—the lieutenant sometimes felt the dark weight of these prophecies.

Chapter 10

EVERY WEEK WHEN he was on barracks duty, Lieutenant Trotta would pen his monotonous accounts to the district captain. The barracks had no electric light. In the guardrooms they still burned the regulation government candles, as in the days of the old Hero of Solferino. Now they had "Apollo candles" made of spongier snow-white stearin, with well-plaited wicks and steady flames. The lieutenant's letters revealed nothing about his changed way of life and the unusual conditions at the border. The district captain avoided asking any questions. His replies, routinely dispatched to his son every fourth Sunday, were as monotonous as the lieutenant's letters.

Every morning old Jacques brought the mail into the room where the district captain had been breakfasting for many years. It was a somewhat out-of-the-way room that was never used during the day. The window, facing east, willingly let in all the mornings—the cloudy, the warm, the cool, and the rainy ones; it was open during breakfast in both summer and winter. In the winter, the district captain wrapped his legs in a warm shawl and the table was moved close to the wide stove, which crackled with a fire lit by old Jacques half an hour earlier. Every fifteenth of April, Jacques stopped lighting the stove. Every fifteenth of April, the district captain, regardless of the weather, resumed his summer-morning constitutionals.

The barber's assistant, groggy and himself unshaven, came to Trotta's bedroom at 6 A.M. By six-fifteen the district captain's chin lay smooth and powdered between the slightly silver pinions of his whiskers. His bald skull had already been massaged and slightly reddened by a few drops of cologne that had been rubbed in, and all superfluous hair—some sprouting from the nostrils, some from the ear conches or even on the back of the neck, welling over the high stand-up collar—had been removed without a trace. Then the district captain reached for the light-colored cane and the gray silk hat and headed toward the municipal park. He wore a white high-necked waistcoat with gray buttons and a dove-gray morning coat. The narrow creaseless trousers were fastened by dark-gray straps to the narrow pointed boots, untipped and seamless and made of the softest kidskin.

The streets were still empty. The sprinkler wagon, pulled by two lumbering brown horses, came rattling over the bumpy cobblestones. Upon spotting the district captain, the driver on his high seat lowered his whip, looped the reins over the brake handle, and swung his hat so low that it grazed his knees. He was the only person in the town—nay, the district—whom Herr von Trotta greeted with a cheerful, almost exuberant wave of his hand. At the entrance to the park, the policeman saluted. Without moving his hand, the district captain wished him a hearty "Good day!" Then he strolled on toward the blond owner of the soda-water stand. Here he tipped his silk hat, drank a glass of tonic, drew a coin from his waistcoat pocket without removing his gray gloves, and continued his stroll. Bakers, chimney sweeps, grocers, butchers came his way. Each one greeted him. The district captain responded by gently placing his forefinger on his hat brim.

He did not doff his hat until he encountered Kronauer, the pharmacist, who likewise enjoyed morning constitutionals and was also, incidentally, the borough councilor. Sometimes Herr von Trotta would also say, "Good morning, Herr Pharmacist," stand still, and ask, "How are you?"

"Excellent!" said the pharmacist.

"Glad to hear it!" remarked the district captain, doffing his hat once more and resuming his stroll.

He never came back before 8 A.M. Sometimes he ran into the postman in the vestibule or out on the steps. Next he would spend some time in his office. For he liked finding the letters next to his breakfast tray. It was impossible for him to see, much less speak to, anyone during breakfast. Old Jacques might happen to walk in on winter days to check the stove or on summer days to shut the window if it was raining all too hard. But Fräulein Hirschwitz was out of the question. The sight of her before 1 P.M. was anathema to the district captain.

One morning in May, Herr von Trotta returned from his constitutional at five minutes after eight. The mailman must have come long since. Herr von Trotta sat down at the table in the breakfast room. The egg, soft-boiled as usual, was in its silver cup. The honey shimmered golden, the fresh kaiser rolls smelled of fire and yeast, the butter shone yellow, embedded in a gigantic dark-green leaf, the coffee steamed in the gold-rimmed porcelain. Nothing was missing. Or at least it seemed to Herr von Trotta at first glance that nothing was missing. But then he promptly stood up, put down his napkin, and scrutinized the table again. The letters were missing from their usual place. For as long as the district captain could remember, no day had ever passed without official mail. First Herr von Trotta went to the open window as if to convince himself that the world still existed outside. Yes, the old chestnut trees in the city park still wore their dense green crowns. The invisible birds were making their usual morning racket in the foliage. The milk wagon, which normally drew up at his residence around this time, stood there today, nonchalant, as if this were a day like any other. So nothing has changed outside, the district captain determined. Was it possible that there had been no mail? Was it possible that Jacques had forgotten it? Herr von Trotta shook the handbell. Its silvery peal scurried through the silent house. No one came. The district captain did not touch his breakfast for now. He shook the bell once more. Finally there was a knock. He was amazed, startled, and offended upon seeing his housekeeper, Fräulein Hirschwitz, enter.

She wore a kind of morning armor in which he had never viewed her before. A huge apron of dark-blue oilcloth covered her from throat to foot and a white coif perched rigidly on her head, displaying her big ears with their soft, broad, fleshy lobes. It made her extraordinarily repulsive to Herr von Trotta—he could not stand the smell of oilcloth.

"Highly annoying!" he said without returning her greeting. "Where is Jacques?"

"Jacques has been stricken with an indisposition today."

"Stricken?" the district captain repeated, not understanding immediately. "Is he sick?" he then asked.

"He has a fever," said Fräulein Hirschwitz.

"Thank you!" said Herr von Trotta, waving his hand.

He sat back down at the table. He only drank the coffee. The egg, the honey, the butter, and the kaiser rolls were left on the tray. He now understood that Jacques was sick and therefore unable to bring the letters. But why was Jacques sick? He had always been as sound as the postal service, for instance. If it had suddenly stopped delivering mail, that would have come as no greater surprise. The district captain himself was never sick. Getting sick meant dying. Sickness was merely nature's way of getting people accustomed to death. Epidemics—cholera had still been feared in Herr von Trotta's youth—could be overcome by some people. But when other diseases simply came sneaking along, striking only one person, he was bound to succumb—no matter how many different names were applied to those complaints. The doctors, whom the district captain called medics, pretended they could heal patients—but only to avoid starving. Even if there *were* exceptions and people did survive an illness, Herr von Trotta, so far as he could remember, had never noticed such a case among people he knew personally or heard about.

He rang again. "I would like the mail," he said to Fräulein Hirschwitz. "Please have someone, anyone, bring it to me! . . . Incidentally, what's wrong with Jacques?"

"He has a fever," said Fräulein Hirschwitz. "He must have caught a chill."

"A chill?! In May?"

"He is no longer young!"

"Send for Dr. Sribny!"

This was the district medical officer. He was on duty every morning from nine to twelve at the district captain's headquarters. He was bound to arrive soon. In the district captain's opinion, the doctor was a "decent sort."

Meanwhile the office assistant brought the mail. The district captain glanced at the envelopes, handed them back, and ordered his assistant to leave them in his office. He stood at the window and could not get over the fact that the world outside seemed to know nothing as yet about the changes in his house. Today he had neither breakfasted nor read the mail. Jacques was in bed with a mysterious disease. And yet life was taking its usual course.

Very slowly, his mind occupied with several unclear thoughts, Herr von Trotta walked to his office; twenty minutes later than normal he sat down at his desk. The assistant district commissioner came and delivered his report. Yesterday there had been another meeting of Czech workers. A Sokol gymnasts' celebration had been announced; delegates from "Slavic countries"— Serbia and Russia were meant but never named in officialese— were due tomorrow. The German-language Social Democrats were likewise drawing attention. A worker at the spinning plant had been beaten up by other workers, supposedly—and this was confirmed by reports from agents—for refusing to join the red party. All these things worried the district captain, they pained him, they upset him, they wounded him. Anything the disobedient segments of the populace undertook to weaken the state, insult His Majesty the Kaiser directly or indirectly, make the law even more powerless than it already was, disturb the peace, offend decency, scoff at official dignity, set up Czech schools, elect opposition deputies—all those actions were aimed at him personally, the district captain. At first he had merely belittled the nations that demanded autonomy and the "working people" who demanded "more rights." But gradually he was getting to hate them—the carpenters, the arsonists, the electioneers. He gave his assistant stringent orders to instantly break up any meeting that dared to pass a resolution. Of all the words that had lately become modern, he hated this one most of all—perhaps because it needed to change just a single tiny letter to turn into the most disgraceful word of all: revolution. That word he had utterly exterminated. It did not exist in his vocabulary, not even in his official usage, and if an agent's report employed, say, the term "revolutionary agitator" for one of the active Social Democrats, von Trotta crossed out those words, changing them in red ink to "suspicious individual." Perhaps there were revolutionaries elsewhere in the monarchy, but they did not exist in Herr von Trotta's bailiwick.

"Tell Sergeant Slama to see me this afternoon," Herr von Trotta told his assistant. "Request constable reinforcements for those Sokols. Write a brief report for the governor's office and get it to me by tomorrow. We may have to contact the military authorities. In any case, the constabulary is to be on alert as of tomorrow. I would like a short outline of the latest ministerial edict regarding military alertness."

"Yessir, Herr District Captain!"

"Good. Has Dr. Sribny shown up yet?"

"He was immediately sent in to Jacques."

"I'd like to see him."

The district captain touched no other document that day. Long ago, in the quiet years, when he had started getting his bearings in his office, there had been no autonomists, no Socialists, and relatively few "suspicious individuals." And as the years wore by, he scarcely noticed that those groups were growing, spreading, and becoming dangerous. But now the district captain felt as if Jacques's illness were suddenly making him aware of the dreadful changes in the world, as if Death, perhaps already perching on the edge of the old footman's bed, were menacing not just him. If Jacques dies, it occurred to the district captain, then in a sense the Hero of Solferino will die once again and perhaps—and here Herr von Trotta's heart skipped a beat— the man whom the Hero of Solferino had rescued from death. Oh! It was not only Jacques who had fallen ill today! The letters lay unopened on the desk, in front of the district captain; who knew what they might contain? The Sokols were gathering in the interior of the empire, before the very eyes of the authorities and the constabulary. These Sokols—whom the district captain privately nicknamed "Sokolists," as if to turn this one large group among the Slavic peoples into a sort of minor political party—only pretended to be athletes strengthening their muscles. In reality they were spies or rebels, paid by the czar. Yesterday's *Foreign News* had said that German students in Prague occasionally sang "The Watch on the Rhine", that anthem of the Prussians, Austria's archenemies and allies. Who could still be trusted? The district captain shuddered. And for the first time since he had begun working in this office, he went over to the window and shut it on an undeniably warm spring day.

At that instant, the district physician walked in, and Herr von Trotta inquired how old Jacques was doing.

Dr. Sribny said, "If it turns into pneumonia, he won't make it. He's very old. His temperature's up to one hundred four. He's been asking for the priest."

The district captain leaned over his desk. He was afraid that Dr. Sribny would catch some change in his face, and he felt that something in his face was indeed beginning to change. He pulled out the drawer, removed the cigars, and offered one to the doctor. He pointed mutely to the armchair. Now both were smoking.

"So you don't have much hope?" Herr von Trotta finally asked.

"Really very little, to tell the truth," the doctor replied. "At his age . . ." He did not complete the sentence, and he peered at the district captain as if trying to determine whether the master was a lot younger than the servant.

"He's never been sick!" said the district captain, as though it were an extenuating circumstance and the doctor were the supreme judge ruling on life and death.

"Yes, yes," was all the doctor said. "It happens. How old is he actually?"

The district captain pondered and said, "Oh, seventy-eight or eighty."

"Yes," said Dr. Sribny, "that's what I figured. That is: only today. As long as someone is up and about, you think he's going to live forever."

Whereupon the district physician rose and went to his office.

Herr von Trotta wrote on a slip, *I am at Jacques's cottage,"* put the note under a paperweight, and walked into the courtyard.

He had never been in Jacques's cottage before. The tiny home with an oversized chimney on its tiny roof was built against the back wall of the courtyard. The cottage had three yellow-brick walls with a brown door in the middle. You stepped first into the kitchen and then, through a glass door, into the parlor. Jacques's tame canary stood on the top knob of its domed cage, next to the window with the white curtain, which, being somewhat short, made the pane seem overly large. The smooth-planed table was pushed up against the wall. Above it hung a blue oil lamp with a round reflector. On the table, the Holy Mother of God stood in a large frame, leaning against the wall, like a portrait of a relative. In the bed, with his head against the window wall, Jacques lay under a white mountain of sheets and pillows. Thinking the priest had come, he heaved a deep sigh of relief as if grace were already approaching him.

"Ah, Herr Baron!" he then said.

The district captain stepped over to the old man. The district captain's grandfather, the constable sergeant, had lain in state in a similar room, in the pensioners' quarters of Laxenburg Castle. The district captain could still see the yellow glow of the large white candles in the twilight of the curtained room, and the gigantic boot soles of the festively garbed corpse thrust themselves into his face. Was Jacques's turn coming up? The old man propped himself on his elbows. He wore an embroidered dark-blue woolen nightcap, his silver hair shimmering through the dense stitches. His clean-shaven face, bony and reddened by fever, looked like colored ivory.

The district captain sat on a bedside chair and said, "Well, the doctor's just told me it's not so bad. Probably a cold in the head."

"Yessir, Herr Baron!" replied Jacques, making a feeble attempt to click his heels under the blanket. He sat up. "Please forgive me," he added. "It'll be over by tomorrow, I think."

"Within a couple of days, I'm sure of it!"

"I'm waiting for the priest, Herr Baron."

"Yes, yes," said Herr von Trotta, "he'll be coming. There's more than enough time!"

"He's already on the way," replied Jacques, as if with his own eyes he could see the priest approaching. "He's coming," he went on, and suddenly he no longer seemed aware that the district captain was sitting next to him. "When the late Herr Baron passed away," he continued, "none of us realized anything. That morning, or maybe it was the previous day, he came into the courtyard and he said, 'Jacques, where are the boots?' Yes, that was the day before. And the next morning, he didn't need them anymore. The winter then set in right away, it was a very cold winter. I think I'll make it to winter. Winter isn't all that far away, I just need a little patience. It's July now, so July, June, May, April, August, November, and by Christmas I think I'll be able to go out, march off—company, march!'' He paused and his large, shiny blue eyes peered through the district captain as if through glass.

Herr von Trotta tried to press the old man gently into the pillows, but Jacques's upper body was stiff and unyielding. Only his head trembled, and his dark-blue nightcap likewise trembled incessantly. Tiny beads of sweat glittered on his high, bony, yellow forehead. From time to time, the district captain dried them with a handkerchief, but new ones kept forming. He took old Jacques's hand and gazed at the scaly, brittle, reddish skin on its wide back and the powerful, prominent thumb. Then he placed the hand carefully upon the blanket, returned to his office, told the orderly to get the priest and a Sister of Mercy, while Fräulein Hirschwitz was to sit with Jacques. The district captain asked for his hat, cane, and gloves and went to the park at this unwonted hour—to the surprise of all the people who happened to be there.

But he soon felt compelled to leave the deep shade of the chestnut trees and return to the house. Upon nearing his door, he caught the silvery tinkling of the priest administering the Blessed Sacrament. Herr von Trotta doffed his hat and bowed his head and lingered at the entrance. Some of the passersby likewise halted. Now the priest emerged from the cottage. A few people waited until the district captain had vanished in the hallway; following him curiously, they learned from the orderly that Jacques was dying. He was well known in the small town. And so they devoted a few minutes of reverential silence to the old man who was about to pass away.

The district captain strode right across the courtyard and entered the dying man's room. In the dark kitchen he cautiously looked for a place to leave his hat, cane, and gloves, finally storing them among pots and plates on the shelves of the étagère. He sent

Fräulein Hirschwitz away and sat down by the bed. The sun was so high in the heavens now that it filled the whole broad court-yard of the district captain's residence, and its rays fell through the window into Jacques's room. The short white curtain now hung like a small, cheery, sunny apron in front of the panes. The canary twittered merrily and without stopping, the bare shiny floor-boards shimmered yellow in the glow of the sun, a wide silvery band of sunlight lay across the foot of the bed, the lower part of the white bedcover was now a more intense, virtually celestial white, and the band of sunlight was also visibly climbing the wall by the bed. From time to time a soft wind wafted through the few old trees that stood along the courtyard walls and might have been as old as Jacques, or even older, and whose shade had sheltered him every day. The wind blew, and their crowns rustled, and Jacques seemed to know it, for he sat up and said, "Please, Herr Baron, the window!" The district captain unlatched the window, and instantly the cheery May-like noises of the court-yard penetrated the small room. They could hear the rustling of the branches, the soft puffing of the breeze, the exuberant buzz-ing of the sparkling Spanish flies, and the warbling of the larks from infinite blue heights. The canary darted out, but only to show that it could still fly. For it came back several moments later, perched on the windowsill, and began singing twice as intensely as before. The world was cheerful, indoors and out.

And Jacques leaned out of the bed, listening immobile, the tiny beads of sweat glittered on his hard forehead, and his thin lips slowly parted. First he just smiled mutely. Then he closed his eyes tight, his gaunt, reddened cheeks creased at the cheekbones. Now he looked like an old rogue, and a thin giggling emerged from his throat. He laughed. He laughed nonstop. The pillows trembled softly, and the bedstead even creaked a bit. The district captain likewise smirked. Yes, Death was coming to old Jacques like a vivacious girl in spring, and Jacques opened his old mouth and showed Death his sparse yellow teeth. He lifted his hand, pointed to the window, and, still giggling, shook his head.

"Nice day today," the district captain observed.

"Here he comes, here he comes!" said Jacques. "On a white horse, dressed all in white—why is he riding so slowly? Look,

look, how slowly he's riding! Good day! Good day! Won't you come closer? Come on! Come on over! Nice day today, isn't it?''

He withdrew his hand, focused his eyes on the district captain, and said, "How slowly he's riding! It's because he's from over there. He's been dead for a long time and he's no longer used to riding around on the stones here. Yes, way back when! Do you remember what he looked like? I'd love to see the picture. Has he really changed? Bring it over, the picture; please, bring it over. Please, Herr Baron!''

The district captain instantly realized that Jacques was asking for the portrait of the Hero of Solferino. He obediently went out. He even took the steps two at a time, hurried into his study, climbed on a chair, and removed the picture of the Hero of Solferino from its hook. It was a bit dusty; he blew on it and rubbed it with the handkerchief that he had used to wipe the dying man's forehead. The district captain was still grinning nonstop. He was cheerful. He had not been cheerful for a long time. With the large portrait under his arm, he dashed across the courtyard. He walked over to Jacques's bed. Jacques stared at the portrait for a long time, stretched out his forefinger, poked around the face of the Hero of Solferino, and finally said, "Hold it in the sun!" The district captain obeyed. He held the portrait in the sunny strip at the end of the bed. Jacques sat up and said, "Yes, that's exactly what he looked like!" and lay back again on the pillows.

The district captain placed the picture on the table, next to the Mother of God, and returned to the bed.

"Soon we'll be going up!" said Jacques with a smile and pointed at the ceiling.

"You've got plenty of time," the district captain replied.

"No, no!" said Jacques and let out a ringing laugh. "I've had time long enough. Now we'll be going up! Check on how old I am. I've forgotten."

"Where should I check?"

"Down there!" said Jacques, pointing at the bedstead. It contained a drawer. The district captain pulled it out. He saw a small, neatly tied package in brown wrapping paper, next to a round tin box with a colorful but faded picture on the lid, a shepherdess in a white wig, and he remembered that it was one of those candy boxes that had lain under the Christmas trees of some of his childhood friends.

"That's the book!" said Jacques. It was his army paybook.

The district captain put on his pince-nez and read, "*Franz Xaver Joseph Kromichl*. Is that your book?" asked Herr von Trotta.

"Of course!" said Jacques.

"Your name is Franz Xaver Joseph?"

"Must be!"

"Then why do you call yourself Jacques?"

"Those were his orders!"

"I see," said Herr von Trotta and read the birth year. "You'll be turning eighty-two in August."

"What's today?"

"May nineteenth."

"How long is it till August?"

"Three months."

"Fine, I won't live that long," said Jacques very softly.

He leaned back again.

"Open the box!" said Jacques, and the district captain opened the box. "Saint Anthony and Saint George are inside," Jacques went on. "You can keep them. There's also a piece of root, for fever. Give that to your son, Carl Joseph. My best regards to him. He can use the root, that area's swampy! And now close the window. I'd like to sleep."

It was noon already. The bed was now basking fully in the brightest sunshine. Big Spanish flies stuck motionless to the window, and the canary had stopped twittering and was pecking on some sugar. Twelve strokes boomed from the tower of the town hall, their golden echoes fading in the courtyard. Jacques was breathing silently. The district captain went into the dining room

"I'm not eating," he told Fräulein Hirschwitz. He scanned the dining room. Here, in this place, Jacques had always stood with the platter; he had stepped up to the table and had held out the platter. Herr von Trotta could not eat today. He walked down into the courtyard, sat on a bench at the wall under the brown timberwork of the wooden balcony, and waited for the Sister of Mercy.

"He's asleep now," the baron said when she came. The soft wind fanned through from time to time. The shadow of the timberwork slowly grew broader and longer. The flies buzzed around the district captain's whiskers. Now and then he slapped at the flies, and his cuff rattled. For the first time since he had entered his Kaiser's service he remained idle in broad daylight on a weekday. He had never felt any need to take a furlough. This was his very first day off. He kept thinking about old Jacques but was cheerful all the same. Old Jacques was dying, but it was as if he were celebrating a grand event and as if the district captain were taking his first day off for that occasion.

All at once he heard the Sister of Mercy step out of the door. She explained that Jacques, apparently with a clear mind and without fever, had gotten out of bed and was getting dressed. And indeed the district captain promptly spotted the old man at the window. He had placed his brush, soap, and razor on the sill, as he did every morning on normal days, and he had hung the small mirror from the window handle and was about to shave. Jacques opened the window and in his healthy, familiar voice he called, "I'm fine, Herr Baron, I'm as fit as a fiddle. Do forgive me, please, and please don't inconvenience yourself!"

"Well, then, everything's fine! I'm delighted, absolutely delighted. Now you can start a new life as Franz Xaver Joseph!"

"I'd rather stick with Jacques!"

Herr von Trotta, thrilled by this miraculous event but also a bit perplexed, returned to his bench, told the Sister of Mercy to stay on just in case, and asked her whether she knew of similar rapid recoveries among people this old. The nun, her eyes lowered to her rosary and her fingers picking out the answer from among the beads, replied that recovery and illness, fast or slow, were in God's hands, and His will had often swiftly turned the dying into the living. The district captain would have preferred a more scientific answer, and he resolved to ask the district physician the next day. Meanwhile he went to his office, freed of a great worry but also filled with an even greater and inexplicable anxiety. He was unable to work. Sergeant Slama had been waiting for a long time, and Herr von Trotta gave him instructions for the Sokol celebration, but without severity or emphasis. Suddenly, all the dangers looming for the district of W and the monarchy seemed less threatening than in the morning. He dismissed the sergeant but immediately called him back and said, "Listen, Slama, have you ever heard anything of the sort? This morning old Jacques was on the verge of death, and now he's completely chipper!"

No, Sergeant Slama had never heard anything of the sort. And when the district captain asked him whether he wanted to see the old man, Slama said of course he would. And the two men stepped into the courtyard.

Jacques was sitting on his stool, a military line of boot pairs in front of him, the brush in his hand, and he was spitting vigorously into the wooden box of shoe polish. He wanted to rise when the district captain stood before him, but he could not manage quickly enough and he already felt Herr von Trotta's hands on his shoulders. Jacques cheerfully saluted the sergeant with his brush. The district captain sat down on the bench; the sergeant leaned his rifle against the wall and likewise sat down at an appropriate distance. Jacques remained on his stool, polishing the boots, albeit slower and more gently than usual. Meanwhile the Sister of Mercy sat praying in Jacques's room.

"It just hit me," said Jacques, "that I used the familiar form with the Herr Baron. I remembered all at once."

"It doesn't matter." said Herr von Trotta. "It was the fever."

"Yes, my corpse was talking. And you ought to lock me up for fraud, Sergeant. You see, my name is Franz Xaver Joseph! But I'd like my gravestone to say 'Jacques.' And my bankbook is under my army book—there's something for my funeral and a mass, and my name's Jacques there too!"

"All in good time," said the district captain. "We can wait!"

The sergeant guffawed and wiped his forehead.

Jacques had polished all the boots until they shone. A slight shiver ran through him; he went indoors, came back wrapped in his winter fur, which he also wore in summer when it rained, and sat down on the stool. The canary followed him, fluttering over his silvery head, seeking a perch for a while, then settling on the bar from which a few rugs were hanging. The bird began to carol. Its song awoke hundreds of sparrow voices in the crowns of the few trees, and for several minutes the air was filled with a merry, twittering, whistling chaos. Jacques raised his head and listened, not without pride, to his canary's victorious voice, which outsang all the others. The district captain smiled. The sergeant laughed, holding his handkerchief to his face, and Jacques giggled. The nun even stopped praying and smiled through the window. The golden afternoon sunshine already lay on the wooden timberwork and was flashing high up in the green foliage. The evening gnats capered wearily in soft round swarms, and now and then a maybug buzzed heavily past the seated people, straight into the leaves and to its doom, probably into the open bills of the sparrows. The wind blew harder. Now the birds hushed. The segment of sky turned deep blue and the white cloudlets rosy.

"Now you're going to bed!" said Herr von Trotta to Jacques.

"I have to take the picture upstairs," the old man murmured; he went over to get the portrait of the Hero of Solferino and disappeared in the darkness of the stairs.

The sergeant peered after him and said, "Strange!"

"Yes, quite strange!" replied Herr von Trotta.

Jacques came back and walked over to the bench. Without a word he sat down—surprisingly between the district captain and the sergeant—opened his mouth, took a deep breath, and before the other two men could even turn to him, his old neck sank upon the back of the bench, his hands fell upon the seat, his fur coat opened, his legs stiffened, and the curving tips of his slippers loomed in the air. The wind gusted briefly through the courtyard. Gently the reddish cloudlets scudded along. The sun had vanished behind the wall. The district captain bedded his servant's silvery head in his left hand while his right hand groped for the unconscious man's heart. The sergeant stood there, alarmed, his black cap on the ground. The Sister of Mercy came over with broad, hurried steps. She took the old man's hand, held it in her fingers for a while, placed it gently on the fur, and made the sign of the cross. She gazed silently at the sergeant. He understood and thrust his hands under Jacques's arms. She took hold of the legs. They carried him into the small room, laid him out on the bed, folded his hands, twisted the rosary around them, and put the effigy of the Mother of God at his head. They knelt at his bedside, and the district captain prayed. He had not prayed in a long time. From the buried depths of his childhood a prayer returned to him, a prayer for the salvation of dead relatives, and that prayer was what he whispered. He rose, glanced at his trousers, brushed the dust from his knees, and strode out, followed by the sergeant.

"That's how I would like to die some day, my dear Slama," he said instead of his usual "Goodbye!" and walked into the study.

On a large sheet of official stationery, he wrote instructions for the laying out and burial of his servant, itemizing deliberately, point by point, section and subsection. The next morning he drove to the cemetery to choose a grave, purchased a headstone, and provided the inscription—*Here rests in God Franz Xaver Joseph Kromichl, known as Jacques, an old servant and a true friend*—and ordered a first-class funeral, with four black horses and eight liveried footmen.

Three days later he walked behind the coffin as the sole mourner, followed at a respectful distance by Sergeant Slama and a number of other people, who joined the cortège because they had known Jacques and especially because they saw Herr von Trotta on foot. Thus it was that a stately group accompanied old Franz Xaver Joseph Kromichl, known as Jacques, to his grave.

Now the district captain felt that his house was changed: empty and no longer homey. He no longer found his mail next to his breakfast tray, and he also hesitated to give his orderly new instructions. He no longer touched a single one of the small silver bells on his desk; if he sometimes absently reached for one, he merely caressed it. Now and then in the afternoon, he pricked up his ears, thinking he could hear old Jacques's ghostly footfalls in the staircase. Sometimes he entered the small cottage where Jacques had lived, and he reached through the cage bars to hand the canary a morsel of sugar.

One day, just before the Sokol celebration, when his presence in his office was not without importance, he made a surprising decision.

We will report on it in the next chapter.

Chapter 11

THE DISTRICT CAPTAIN decided to visit his son in the remote border garrison. For a man like Herr von Trotta, this was no easy undertaking. He had unusual notions about the eastern border of the monarchy. Because of embarrassing lapses in duty, two of his schoolmates had been transferred to that distant crownland, at whose edges the Siberian wind could probably be heard howling. The civilized Austrian was menaced there by bears and wolves and even more dreadful monsters, such as lice and bedbugs. The Ruthenian peasants made sacrifices to pagan gods, and the Jews raged cruelly against other people's property. Herr von Trotta took along his old revolver. He was not the least bit terrified of adventure; indeed, he experienced that intoxication he had felt in his long-buried boyhood—the excitement that had driven him and his friend Moser to go hunting in the mysterious wooded depths of his father's estate and to visit the graveyard at midnight.

Herr von Trotta took a terse and cheery leave of Fräulein Hirschwitz, vaguely and boldly hoping he would never see her again. He drove to the station alone. The ticket clerk said, "Oh, a long trip at last. Bon voyage!"

The stationmaster hurried to the platform. "Is this an official trip?" he asked.

And the district captain, in that expansive mood in which one occasionally likes to appear enigmatic, replied, "In a manner of speaking, Herr Stationmaster. It is sort of 'official.' "

"Will you be gone a long time?"

"I'm not sure."

"So you'll probably be visiting your son?"

"If I can manage it!"

The district captain stood at the window, waving his hand. He cheerfully said goodbye to his district. He did not think about his return. He checked through all the stations in the timetable. "Change trains in Bogumin!" he repeated to himself. He compared the scheduled times of arrival and departure with the actual times and his watch with all the station clocks that the train passed. His heart was delighted—indeed, refreshed—by every irregularity. In Bogumin he let one train go by. Inquisitive, peering every which way, he walked across the platforms, through the waiting rooms, and briefly along the road to town. Returning to the station, he pretended he was late through no fault of his own and explicitly told the porter, "I've missed my train!" He was disappointed that the porter was not surprised. He had to change again in Crakow. He welcomed it. If he had not informed Carl Joseph of his arrival time and if that "dangerous nest" had been serviced by two trains a day, Herr von Trotta would gladly have stopped off to take a look at the world. Nevertheless, it could be viewed through the compartment window. Springtime greeted him all along the trip. He arrived in the afternoon.

Unruffled and sprightly, he got off the footboard with that "elastic step" that the newspapers always ascribed to the old Kaiser and that many elderly government officials had gradually mastered. For in those days people in the monarchy had a very distinctive and now completely forgotten way of leaving trains and carriages, entering restaurants, mounting perrons, stepping into houses, and approaching friends and relatives: it was a way of walking that may have been partly dictated by the snug trousers of the elderly gentlemen and by the rubber straps with which many of them fastened their trousers to their boots.

And so Herr von Trotta left the train with that distinctive step. He embraced his son, who had stationed himself in front of the footboard. That day Herr von Trotta was the only stranger leaving the first-or second-class coach. A few soldiers returning from furlough, some railroad workers, and some Jews in long black fluttering robes emerged from the third-class car. They looked at the father and the son. The district captain hurried to the waiting room. Here he kissed Carl Joseph on the forehead. At the buffet he ordered two brandies. The mirror hung on the wall behind the shelves of bottles. While drinking, father and son each gazed at the other's reflected face.

"Is the mirror wretched," asked Herr von Trotta, "or do you really look so awful?"

Have you really turned so gray? Carl Joseph would have liked to ask. For he saw a lot of silver shimmering in his father's dark whiskers and on his temples.

"Let me have a look at you!" the district captain went on. "It's certainly not the mirror. Could it be the conditions out here perhaps? Is it bad?" The district captain ascertained that his son did not look like what a young lieutenant should look like. Maybe he's sick, the father thought. Aside from the illnesses one died of, there were only those terrible illnesses that, according to hearsay, struck no small number of officers.

"Are you allowed to drink brandy?" he asked, to clear up the matter circuitously.

"Of course, Papá," said the lieutenant. He could still hear that voice which had tested him years ago on silent Sunday mornings, that nasal government-official voice, the strict, slightly amazed, and questioning voice that made every lie perish on your tongue.

"Do you like the infantry?"

"Very much, Papá!"

"What about your horse?"

"I took it along, Papá!"

"Do you ride a lot?"

"Seldom, Papá!"

"You don't like to?"

"No, I never liked it, Papá!"

"Stop calling me Papá," Herr von Trotta suddenly said. "You're big enough. And I'm on vacation!"

They drove into town.

"Well, it's not all that wild," said the district captain. "Can people have a good time here?"

"Very much so!" said Carl Joseph. "At Count Chojnicki's home. Everybody comes. You'll meet him. I like him a lot."

"So he'd be the first friend you've ever had?"

"Dr. Max Demant was also my friend," replied Carl Joseph.

"Here's your room, Papá!" said the lieutenant. "The other officers live here and sometimes they get noisy at night. But there's no other hotel. They'll hold back as long as you're here."

"It's all right, it's all right!" said the district captain.

He unpacked a round tin box from the suitcase, opened the lid, and showed the box to Carl Joseph. "It's a kind of root—it's supposed to be good for swamp fever. It's from Jacques."

"How is he?"

"He's up there!" The district captain pointed at the ceiling.

"He's up there!" the lieutenant repeated.

To the district captain he sounded like an old man. His son must have a lot of secrets. The father did not know them. One said "father and son," but many years lay between them, huge mountains. He knew little more about Carl Joseph than about any other lieutenant. He had joined the cavalry and had transferred to the infantry. He wore the green lapels of the riflemen instead of the red ones of the dragoons. Oh, well. That was all the father knew. He was obviously growing old. He no longer belonged to his office and to his duties. He belonged to Jacques and to Carl Joseph. He had brought the stone-hard weathered root from one to the other.

The district captain, still leaning over the valise, opened his mouth. He spoke into the valise as into an open grave. But he did not say, I love you, my son, as he meant to; he said, "He died an easy death. It was a true May evening, and all the birds were chirping. Do you remember his canary? It twittered the loudest. Jacques polished all the boots. Then he died, in the courtyard, on the bench. Slama was also there. He was running a fever just that morning. He sent you his best."

Then the district captain glanced up from the valise and looked into his son's face. "That's exactly how I would like to die some day."

The lieutenant went to his room, opened the wardrobe, and put the bit of root, the remedy for fever, in the top drawer, next to Katharina's letters and Max Demant's saber. He pulled out the doctor's watch. He thought he saw the thin second hand circling faster than any other along the tiny round and thought he heard the jingly ticking more intensely. Soon I'll also be hearing Papá's watch; he's going to leave it to me. The portrait of the the Hero of Solferino will hang in my room and Max Demant's saber and an heirloom from Papá. With me everything will be buried. I am the last Trotta.

He was young enough to draw sweet delight from his grief and a painful dignity from the certainty that he was the last. From the nearby swamps came the broad, blaring croaking of the frogs. The setting sun reddened the walls and furniture in the room. He heard a lightweight carriage rolling up, the soft clatter of hooves on the dusty street. The carriage halted, a straw-yellow britska, Count Chojnicki's summer vehicle. Three times, his snapping whip interrupted the chant of the frogs.

He was curious, that Count Chojnicki. No other passion than curiosity sent him traveling into the wide world, fettered him to the tables of the great gambling casinos, locked him behind the doors of his old hunting lodge, sat him on the bench of the parliamentarians, ordered him home every spring, made him hold his usual festivities, and blocked the path to suicide. Curiosity was all that kept him alive. He was insatiably curious. Lieutenant Trotta had told him that he was expecting his father, the district captain, and although Count Chojnicki was acquainted with a good dozen Austrian district captains and countless fathers of lieutenants, he was still eager to meet District Captain Trotta.

"I am your son's friend," said Chojnicki. "You are my guest. Your son must have told you. Incidentally, we've met before. Aren't you acquainted with Dr. Swoboda in the Ministry of Commerce?"

"We were schoolmates."

"There you are!" cried Chojnicki. "Swoboda is my good friend. He's getting a little odd in the course of time, but a fine man! May I be completely honest with you? You remind me of Franz Joseph."

A momentary hush ensued. The district captain had never spoken the Kaiser's name. On solemn occasions one said "His Majesty." In everyday life one said "the Kaiser." But this Chojnicki said "Franz Joseph," just as he had said "Swoboda."

"Yes, you remind me of Franz Joseph," Chojnicki repeated.

They were driving along. On both sides the unending choruses of the frogs were clamoring, the unending blue-green swamps were stretching out. The evening floated toward them, violet and golden. They heard the soft rolling of the wheels in the soft sand of the dirt road and the clear crunching of the axles. Chojnicki halted at the small hunting lodge.

The back wall leaned against the dark edge of the fir forest. It was separated from the narrow road by a small garden and a stone fence. The hedges lining both sides of the short path from the garden gate to the front door had not been trimmed in a long time, and they proliferated wildly and randomly here and there across the path, bending their branches toward one another and allowing only one person at a time to pass through. So the three men walked in single file; obediently the horse followed them, pulling the small carriage; the horse appeared to be familiar with this path, and it seemed to live in the lodge like a human being. Behind the hedges vast areas stretched out, dotted with blossoming thistles, guarded by the broad dark-green faces of the coltsfoot. To the right loomed a broken stone pillar, perhaps the vestige of a tower. Like a mighty broken tooth, the stone grew from the bosom of the front garden against the sky, with many dark-green moss spots and soft black cracks. The heavy wooden front door bore the Chojnickis' coat of arms, a tripartite blue shield with three gilt stags, their antlers inextricably entangled. Chojnicki turned on the light. They stood in a vast low room. The final twilight of the day was still falling through the narrow cracks of the green blinds. The set table under the lamp bore plates, bottles, pitchers, silver cutlery, and tureens.

"I took the liberty of preparing a little snack for you," said Chojnicki. He poured the 180 Proof, clear as water, into three small glasses, handed two of them to the guests, and raised the third one himself. They all drank. The district captain was somewhat confused when he put the glass back on the table. However, the reality of the food contradicted the mysterious character of the lodge, and the district captain's appetite was greater than his confusion. The brown liver pâté, studded with pitch-black truffles, lay in a glittering wreath of fresh ice crystals. The tender breast of pheasant loomed lonesome on the snowy platter, surrounded by a gaudy retinue of green, red, white, and yellow vegetables, each in a bowl with a blue-gold rim and a coat of arms. In a spacious crystal vase, millions of pearls of black-gray caviar teemed within a circle of golden lemon slices. And the round pink wheels of ham, guarded by a large three-pronged silver form, lined up obediently in an oval bowl, surrounded by red-cheeked radishes that reminded one of small crisp country girls. Boiled, roasted, and marinated with sweet-and-sour onions, the fat broad pieces of carp and the narrow slippery pike lay on glass, silver, and porcelain. Round loaves of bread, brown and white, rested in simple, rustically pleated straw baskets, like babies in cradles, almost invisibly sliced, and with the slices so artfully rejoined that the bread looked hale and undivided. Among the dishes stood fat-bellied bottles and tall narrow crystal carafes with four or six sides and smooth round ones, some with long and others with short necks, with or without labels; and all followed by a regiment of glasses in various shapes and sizes.

They began to eat.

For the district captain, this unusual manner of having a "snack" at an unwonted time was an extremely pleasant sign of the unusual customs at the border. In the old Imperial and Royal Monarchy, even people with Spartan natures, like Herr von Trotta, were thoroughgoing hedonists. A long time had passed since the district captain had had an extraordinary meal. The occasion had been the going-away party for the governor, Prince M, who had left with an honorable commission for the freshly occupied territories of Bosnia and Herzegovina, thanks to his renowned linguistic abilities and his alleged knack for "taming wild nations." Yes, at that time the district captain had eaten and drunk unwontedly. And that day, along with other days of drinking and banqueting, had lodged in his memory as sharply as the special days when he had received praise from the governor's office and, later on, been named district captain. As was his habit, he tasted the exquisiteness of food with his eyes as others did with their palates. His eyes swept across the rich table a few times, enjoying and lingering here and there in enjoyment. He had forgotten the mysterious, indeed sinister surroundings. They ate. They drank from various bottles. And the district captain praised everything by saying "delicious" or "excellent" whenever he went on from one dish to another. His face slowly reddened. And his sideburns kept moving.

"I have invited you gentlemen here because we would have been disturbed in the New Castle. There my door is always open, so to speak, and my friends can all drop in whenever they like. Otherwise I usually work here."

"You work?" asked the district captain.

"Yes," said Chojnicki, "I work. I work for the fun of it, so to speak. I am merely continuing the tradition of my fore-bears. Frankly, I am not always so earnest about it as my grand-father was. The peasants in this region regarded him as a powerful sorcerer, and perhaps he *was*. They regard me as one too, but I'm not. So far I haven't succeeded in producing even a speck."

"A speck?" asked the district captain. "What sort of speck?"

"Gold, of course!" said Chojnicki as if it were the most natural thing in the world. "I know something about chemis-try," he went on. "It's an old talent in our family. As you can see, I have the oldest and the most modern equipment." He pointed to the walls. The district captain saw six rows of wooden shelves on each wall. On the shelves stood mortars, small and large paper bags, glass containers as in old-fashioned apothecaries, bizarre glass spheres filled with gaudy liquids, tiny lamps, gas burners, and test tubes.

"Very strange, strange, strange!" said Herr von Trotta.

"And I myself can't really say whether I'm earnest or not. Yes, sometimes I'm overwhelmed with passion when I come here in the morning, and I read through my grandfather's formulas and I go and test and laugh at myself and leave. And I keep coming again and keep testing again."

"Strange, strange!" the district captain repeated.

"No stranger," said the count, "than anything else I might do. Should I become Minister of Culture? It's been suggested to me. Should I become section head in the Ministry of the Interior? That's been suggested to me too. Should I go to court, become Comptroller of the Royal Household? I could do that too; Franz Joseph knows me."

The district captain shifted his chair back two inches. He felt a pang whenever Chojnicki used the Kaiser's name as intimately as if he were one of those ridiculous deputies who had been sitting in Parliament since the introduction of universal suffrage with a secret vote, one per person, or as if he were, at best, already dead and a figure in the Fatherland's history.

Chojnicki corrected himself. "His Majesty knows me."

The district captain shifted closer to the table and asked, "And why—if you'll forgive me—would it be just as super-fluous serving the Fatherland as making gold?"

"Because the Fatherland no longer exists."

"I don't understand!" said Herr von Trotta.

"I assumed you wouldn't understand," said Chojnicki. "We are all no longer alive!"

It was very still. The final glint of twilight had long since vanished. Through the narrow gaps of the green blinds they could have seen a few stars in the sky. The broad and blaring chant of the frogs had been replaced by the quiet metallic chant of the nightly field crickets. From time to time they heard the harsh cry of the cuckoo.

The district captain, put in an unfamiliar, almost enchanted state by the alcohol, the bizarre surroundings, and the count's unusual words, stole a glance at his son, merely to see a close and familiar person. But Carl Joseph too seemed neither close nor familiar to him. Perhaps Chojnicki was correct and they all really no longer existed: not the Fatherland nor the district captain nor his son! Straining greatly, Herr von Trotta managed to ask, "I don't understand. How can you say the monarchy no longer exists?"

"Naturally!" replied Chojnicki. "In literal terms, it still exists. We still have an army"—the count pointed at the lieutenant—"and officials"—the count pointed at the district captain—"but the monarchy is disintegrating while still alive; it is doomed! An old man, with one foot in the grave, endangered whenever his nose runs, keeps the old throne through the sheer miracle that he can still sit on it. How much longer, how much longer? This era no longer wants us! This era wants to create independent nation-states! People no longer believe in God. The new religion is nationalism. Nations no longer go to church. They go to national associations. Monarchy, our monarchy, is founded on piety, on the faith that God chose the Hapsburgs to rule over so and so many Christian nations. Our Kaiser is a secular brother of the Pope, he is His Imperial and Royal Apostolic Majesty; no other is as apostolic, no other majesty in Europe is as dependent on the grace of God and on the faith of the nations in the grace of God. The German Kaiser still rules even when God abandons him; perhaps by the grace of the nation. The Emperor of Austria-Hungary must not be abandoned by God. But God *has* abandoned him!"

The district captain rose to his feet. He would never have believed there could exist a person in this world who could say that God had abandoned the Kaiser. All his life he had left matters of heaven to the theologians and regarded the church, the mass, the Corpus Christi ceremony, the clergy, and the Good Lord as institutions of the monarchy; but now all at once, the count's statement seemed to explain all the confusion he had been feeling for the past few weeks, especially since old Jacques's death. That was it: God had abandoned the old Kaiser! The district captain took a few steps, the old boards creaking under his feet. He went over to the window, and through the gaps in the blinds he saw the narrow stripes of the dark-blue night. All processes in nature and all events of everyday life suddenly achieved an ominous and incomprehensible meaning. Incomprehensible was the whispering chorus of crickets, incomprehensible the twinkling of the stars, incomprehensible the velvety blue of the night, incomprehensible the district captain's trip to the border and his visit with this count. He returned to the table and ran his hand over one sideburn, as he would do whenever he felt a bit perplexed. A bit perplexed? Never had he been as perplexed as he was now!

In front of him stood a full glass. He swiftly drained it. "So," he said, "you believe, you believe that we—"

"Are doomed," Chojnicki completed. "We are doomed, you and your son and I. We are, I tell you, the last members of a world in which God sheds his grace on majesties, and lunatics like myself make gold. Listen! Look!" And Chojnicki stood up, went to the door, turned a switch, and the lights on the large chandelier shone. "Look!" said Chojnicki again. "This is the age of electricity, not alchemy. Chemistry too, you know! Do you know what this thing is called? Nitroglycerine." The count articulated each syllable. "Nitroglycerine!" he repeated. "No more gold! In Franz Joseph's palace they still often burn candles. Do you understand? Nitroglycerine and electricity will be the death of us! It won't last much longer, not much longer!"

The glow spread by the electric lamps aroused green, red, and blue reflections trembling narrow and broad in the test tubes on the wall shelves. Carl Joseph sat there, pale and silent. He had been drinking all this time. The district captain looked at the lieutenant. He thought of his friend Moser, the painter. And since he himself had already been drinking, old Herr von Trotta, he spotted, as if in a very remote mirror, the wan image of his drunken son under the green trees of the park, with a slouch hat on his head and a large portfolio under his arm, and it was as if the count's prophetic gift for seeing the historical future had also been granted to the district captain, enabling him to know his offspring's future. The plates, glasses, bottles, and tureens were half empty and dismal; the lights in the pipes all around the walls shone magically. Two old footmen with sideburns, both of them resembling Kaiser Franz Joseph and the district captain like brothers, started clearing the table. From time to time the harsh cry of the cuckoo fell like a hammer on the chirping of the crickets. Chojnicki held up a bottle. "You have to drink the local" (that was what he called the liquor). "There's only a bit left!" And they drank the last of the "local."

The district captain drew out his watch but could not precisely recognize the position of the hands. It was as if they were rotating so swiftly along the white circle of the face that there were a hundred hands instead of the regulation two. And instead of twelve numbers there were twelve times twelve, for they crowded into each other like the strokes indicating minutes. It could be nine in the evening or already midnight.

"Ten o'clock!" said Chojnicki.

The footmen with sideburns gently took the arms of the guests and led them out. Chojnicki's large barouche was waiting. The sky was very close; a good familiar shell made of a familiar blue glass, it lay within reach, over the earth. Earthly hands had pinned the stars into the nearby sky like tiny flags into a map. At times the entire blue night whirled around the district captain, rocking softly and then standing still. The frogs croaked in the unending swamps. The air smelled of rain and grass. The horses were ghostly white in front of the black carriage, and over them loomed the coachman in a black overcoat. The horses whinnied, and as soft as cat paws their hoofs scratched the damp, sandy ground.

The coachman clicked his tongue, and off they went.

They drove back along the route they had taken; they turned into the broad, macadamized, birch-lined avenue and reached the lanterns heralding the New Castle. The silver birch trunks shimmered more brightly than the lanterns. The strong rubber wheels of the barouche rolled smoothly and with a dull murmur over the macadam; only the hard thuds of the swift horse hooves could be heard. The barouche was wide and comfortable. They leaned back in it as on a sofa. Lieutenant Trotta was asleep. He sat next to his father. His pale face lay almost horizontal on the upholstered back; through the open window the wind wafted across it. From time to time a lantern illuminated his face. And then Chojnicki, sitting opposite his guests, could see the lieutenant's bloodless parted lips and his hard, jutting, bony nose. "He's sound asleep!" said Chojnicki to the district captain. They felt like two fathers of the lieutenant. The district captain was sobered by the night wind, but a vague fear nestled in his heart. He saw the world going under, and it was his world. Chojnicki sat across from him, to all appearance a live man, whose knees sometimes even bumped into Herr von Trotta's shin, and yet sinister. The old revolver that Herr von Trotta had taken along pressed in his back pocket. What good was a revolver? They saw no bears and no wolves in the borderland. All they saw was the collapse of the world!

The carriage halted in front of the arched wooden gate. The coachman snapped his whip. The two wings of the gate opened, and the white horses gravely strode up the gentle rise. Along the full length of the window facade, yellow light fell upon the gravel and the grassy areas on both sides of the driveway. Voices could be heard, and a piano. It was without a doubt a "party."

The partygoers had already eaten. The footmen were dashing about with large glasses of gaudy liquors. The guests were dancing, drinking, playing tarot or whist; someone was giving a speech to people who weren't listening. A few were reeling through the rooms, others were sleeping in the corners. Only men were dancing with one another. The black dress shirts of the dragoons pressed against the blue ones of the riflemen. Chojnicki had candles burning in the rooms of the New Castle. The thick snow-white or wax-yellow candles loomed from huge silver candelabras that stood on stone plate rails and ledges or were held by footmen, who changed every half hour. The tiny flames sometimes trembled in the night breeze drawing in through the open windows. Whenever the piano fell silent for a few moments, one could hear the nightingales warbling and the crickets whispering and, from time to time, the wax tears dripping softly on the silver.

The district captain looked for his son. A nameless fear drove the old man through the rooms. His son—where was he? Neither among the dancers, nor among the reeling drunks, nor among the gamblers, nor among the older, well-bred men who were conversing in nooks here and there. The lieutenant was sitting alone in a secluded room. The huge bulging bottle stood at his feet, loyal and half drained. Next to the thin collapsed drinker it looked tremendous, almost as if it could devour him. The district captain stood in front of the lieutenant. The tips of his narrow boots touched the bottle.

The son noticed two and more fathers; they multiplied by the second. He felt harried by them. It made no sense getting up in front of all of them and paying all of them the respect due to only one. It made no sense, so the lieutenant remained in his strange position—that is, he sat, lay, and crouched simultaneously.

The district captain did not stir. His brain was working very rapidly; it birthed a thousand memories at once. He saw, for instance, Carl Joseph the cadet on the summer Sundays when he had sat in the study, the snow-white gloves and the black cap on his lap, answering every question in a ringing voice and with obedient childlike eyes. The district captain saw the freshly promoted cavalry lieutenant, blue, gold, and blood-red, entering the same room. But now this young man was very remote from the old Herr von Trotta. Why did it hurt so badly, seeing an alien, drunken rifle lieutenant? Why did it hurt so badly?

Lieutenant Trotta did not stir. He was able to remember that his father had just arrived, and he was able to register that it was not this one father but several fathers standing before him. But he failed to understand why his father had happened to come precisely today or why he was multiplying so intensely or why he himself, the lieutenant, was incapable of rising.

Several weeks ago Lieutenant Trotta had gotten accustomed to the 180 Proof. It never went to your head, it went, as the connoisseurs liked phrasing it, "only to your feet." First it created an agreeable warmth in your chest. The blood started rolling faster through your veins; appetite replaced queasiness and the desire to vomit. Then you drank another 180 Proof. No matter how cool or dismal the morning, you stepped into it boldly and in the best possible mood, as if it were a sun-drenched, happy morning. During halts, you had a snack with fellow officers in the border tavern, near the border forest, where the riflemen drilled, and you drank another 180 Proof. It ran down your throat like a swift fire that snuffs itself. You barely felt that you had eaten. You returned to the barracks, changed, and went to the railroad station for lunch. Even though you had walked a long way, you weren't at all hungry. And so you drank another 180 Proof. You ate and were promptly sleepy. So you had a black coffee and then another 180 Proof. In short, in the course of the boring day there was never an opportunity not to have a drink. On the contrary: there were any number of afternoons and any number of evenings on which a drink was called for.

For life became easy as soon as you drank. Oh, miracle of this borderland! It made life hard for a sober man, but whom did it leave sober? Whenever he drank, Lieutenant Trotta saw his comrades, superiors, and subalterns as old and good friends. He was as intimate with the little town as if he had been born and bred here. He could step into the tiny shops, which were dark, narrow, convoluted, crammed with all kinds of goods, and dug like hamster holes into the thick walls of the bazaar, and there he could haggle over useless things: false corals, cheap mirrors, a miserable soap, aspen combs, and plaited dog leashes; he was just cheerfully heeding the calls of the red-haired vendors. He smiled at all the people—the peasant women in their gaudy kerchiefs and with the large bast baskets under their arms, the decked-out daughters of the Jews, the officials of the district administration, and the high school teachers. A broad torrent of kindness and friendliness surged through this small world. Cheerful greetings poured toward the lieutenant from all people. Nor was there anything embarrassing anymore. Nothing embarrassing in his service or outside his service. He implemented everything smoothly and quickly. People understood Onufrij's language. Occasionally the lieutenant came to one of the surrounding villages; he asked the peasants for directions, and they replied in a foreign tongue. He understood them. He never rode his horse. He lent it to one or another fellow officer: good horsemen, who could appreciate a horse. In a word, he was content. Only Lieutenant Trotta didn't realize that his gait was unsteady, his blouse had stains, his trousers had no pleat, buttons were missing from his shirt, his skin was yellow in the evening and ashen in the morning, and his gaze had no goal. He never gambled—that in itself calmed Major Zoglauer. There were times in every man's life when he had to drink. It didn't matter, it was just a phase! Liquor was cheap. Most of the men were destroyed only by their debts. Trotta was no less neglectful in his work than anyone else. He never made a ruckus like any number of other men. On the contrary, he grew gentler the more he drank. Some day he'll get married and sober up, thought the major. He has friends in the highest places. He'll advance quickly. He'll get into the general staff if he wants to.

Herr von Trotta cautiously settled next to his son on the edge of the sofa and cast about for an appropriate word. He wasn't used to speaking to drunks. "You should," he said after a long consideration, "be careful with liquor. Me, for instance, I only do social drinking."

The lieutenant made a tremendous effort to change from his disrespectful crouching to a sitting position. His attempt was useless. He gazed at the old man: now, thank goodness, there was only one, making do with the narrow edge of the sofa, propping himself with his hands on his knees. The lieutenant asked, "What did you say, Papá?"

"You should be careful with liquor!" the district captain repeated.

"Why?" asked the lieutenant.

"What are you asking?" said Herr von Trotta, a bit comforted because his son at least seemed clearheaded enough to grasp his father's words. "Liquor will destroy you. Do you remember Moser?"

"Moser, Moser," said Carl Joseph. "Of course! But he's right. I remember him. He painted Grandfather's portrait."

"You forgot?" murmured Herr von Trotta.

"I haven't forgotten him," replied the lieutenant. "I've never stopped thinking about the portrait. I'm not strong enough for that portrait. The dead! I can't forget the dead! Father, I can't forget anything! Father!"

Herr von Trotta sat helpless next to his son. He didn't quite understand what Carl Joseph was saying, but he sensed that it was not drunkeness alone speaking. He felt that cries for help were coming out of the boy, and he could not help! He had come to the borderland to find a little help himself. For he was all alone in this world. And this world too was going under. Jacques lay under the ground, Herr von Trotta was alone, he wanted to see his son again, and his son was likewise alone and perhaps, being younger, was closer to the collapse of the world. How simple the world had always looked! the district captain mused. There was a specific attitude for every situation. When your son came home for vacation, you tested him. When he became a lieutenant, you congratulated him. When he wrote his obedient letters, which said so little, you replied with a few measured lines. But how should you behave if your son was drunk, if he cried "Father!" if the cry "Father!" came out of him?

Herr von Trotta saw Chojnicki entering and stood up more intensely than was his wont. "There's a telegram for you," said Chojnicki. "The bellboy brought it over." It was an official telegram. It summoned Herr von Trotta home. "Unfortunately they're ordering you home already," said Chojnicki. "It must have something to do with the Sokols."

"Yes, that's probably it," said Herr von Trotta. "There must be disturbances." He now knew that he was too weak to do anything about disturbances. He was very tired. Only a few years were left until his retirement! But at that moment he had a sudden whim to retire soon. He could take care of Carl Joseph, a fitting task for an old father.

Chojnicki said, "It's not easy to do something about disturbances if your hands are tied as in this damn monarchy. You just arrest a couple of ringleaders, and the Freemasons, the deputies, the national leaders, the newspapers pounce on you, and they're all released. Break up the Sokol Association, and you'll be rebuked by the governor's office. Autonomy! Yeah, just wait! Here in my district every disturbance ends with bullets. So long as I live here, I'm the government candidate and I get elected. Luckily, this area is sufficiently remote from all the modern ideas that they spawn in their filthy editors' offices!"

He went over to Carl Joseph and said with the emphasis and knowledge of a man used to dealing with drunks, "Your Papá has to go home!"

Carl Joseph instantly understood. He could even get to his feet. His glassy eyes searched for his father. "I'm sorry, Father!"

"I'm a little worried about him," the district captain told Chojnicki.

"Rightfully so!" the count replied. "He has to get away from this area. When he's on furlough, I'll try to show him a little of the world. Then he won't have any desire to come back. Maybe he'll fall in love."

"I don't fall in love," said Carl Joseph very slowly.

They drove back to the hotel.

During the entire ride only one word was spoken, one single word: "Father!" said Carl Joseph, and that was all.

The next day the district captain woke up very late; he could already hear the bugles of the returning battalion. The train was leaving in two hours. Carl Joseph arrived. Chojnicki's whip signal was already snapping below. The district captain ate at the riflemen's table in the station restaurant.

Since his departure from W district, a tremendous amount of time had worn by. He barely remembered boarding the train just two days ago. The only civilian aside from Count Cho-jnicki, he sat, dark and gaunt, at the long horseshoe-shaped table of the particolored officers, under the wall portrait of Franz Joseph I, the familiar omnipresent portrait of the Supreme Commander in Chief in the sparkling-white field marshal's tunic with the blood-red sash. Right under and almost parallel to the Kaiser's white sideburns, twenty inches below, loomed the black, slightly silvered sides of the Trotta whiskers. The youngest officers, sitting at the ends of the horseshoe, could see the resemblance between His Apostolic Majesty and his servant. From his seat Lieutenant Trotta could likewise compare the Kaiser's face with his father's. And for a few seconds it seemed to the lieutenant as if his aged father's portrait were hanging up on the wall and the Kaiser, in the flesh, slightly rejuvenated, and in mufti, were sitting below at the table. And far and foreign were both his Kaiser and his father.

Meanwhile the district captain sent a hopeless, scrutinizing look around the table, at the downy, almost beardless faces of the young officers and the moustachioed faces of the older ones. Next to him sat Major Zoglauer. Ah, Herr von Trotta und Sipolje would have liked to exchange a few anxious words with him about Carl Joseph! There was no time left. Outside the window the train was already being marshaled.

The district captain was quite despondent. They all drank his health, a bon voyage, and success in his official tasks. He smiled in all directions, rose, clinked glasses, and his mind was heavy with worries and his heart besieged by dark inklings. After all, a tremendous amount of time had gone by since his departure from his district. Yes indeed, the district captain had been cheerful and exuberant when he had ridden into an adventuresome region and to his dear son. Now he was returning home, alone, from a lonesome son and from this borderland, where the collapse of the world could already be seen as clearly as one sees a thunderstorm on the edge of a city, whose streets lie still unaware and blissful under a blue sky. The doorman's cheery bell was already ringing. The locomotive was already whistling. The wet steam of the train was already banging against the restaurant windows in fine gray beads. The meal was already over, and they all stood up. The whole battalion escorted Herr von Trotta to the platform. Herr von Trotta wanted to say something special, but nothing suitable occurred to him. He glanced tenderly at his son. But then he instantly feared that someone would notice that glance, and he lowered his eyes. He shook Major Zoglauer's hand. He thanked Chojnicki. He tipped his dignified gray silk hat, which he always wore when traveling. He held the hat in his left hand and threw his right arm around Carl Joseph's back. He kissed his son on both cheeks. And always he wanted to say, Don't cause me any grief, I love you, my son! All he said was, "Stay well!" For the Trottas were shy people.

He was already boarding, the district captain. He was already at the window. His hand in the dark-gray kid glove lay on the open window. His bald skull shone. Once again his worried eyes looked for Carl Joseph's face.

"The next time you visit, Herr District Captain," said Captain Wagner, who was always in a good mood, "you'll find a little Monte Carlo here!"

"What do you mean?" asked the district captain.

"They're going to open a gambling casino!" replied Wagner. And before Herr von Trotta und Sipolje could call over his son to urgently warn him about the announced Monte Carlo, the locomotive whistled, the buffers smashed and boomed into one another, and the train glided away. The district captain waved with his gray glove, and all the officers saluted. Carl Joseph did not stir.

He walked back alongside Captain Wagner. "It's going to be fabulous," said the captain. "A real casino! Oh, God, how long has it been since I saw a roulette wheel? You know, I love the way it rolls, and that noise! I'm so delighted!"

Captain Wagner was not the only one looking forward to the opening of the casino. They were all waiting. So far as we know, the border garrison had spent years waiting for the casino that Kapturak was supposed to open.

One week after the district captain's departure, Kapturak arrived. And he probably would have caused a greater stir if, by a strange coincidence, the woman on whom they all focused their attention had not arrived at the same time.

Chapter 12

IN THOSE DAYS there were a lot of men like Kapturak on the borders of the Austro-Hungarian monarchy. They began to circle around the old empire like those black cowardly birds that ogle a dying man from infinitely far away. Dark and impatient, beating their wings, they wait for his end. Their slanting beaks jab into their prey. No one knows where they come from or where they fly off to. They are the feathered brethren of enigmatic Death; they are his harbingers, his escorts, and his successors.

Kapturak is a short man with a nondescript face. Rumors flit around him, fly ahead of him on his twisty paths, and follow the barely perceptible footprints he leaves behind. He lives at the border inn. He associates with the agents of the South American shipping companies whose steamers carry thousands of Russian deserters to a new and cruel homeland year after year. He gambles a lot and drinks little. Nor does he lack a certain careworn affability. He says that for years he used to do his smuggling of Russian deserters on the other side of the border and that he left a home, a wife, and children there for fear of being packed off to Siberia after several officials and officers had been caught and sentenced. And when asked what he plans to do here, Kapturak tersely replies with a smile, "Business."

The hotel where the officers resided was owned by a certain Herr Brodnitzer, of a Silesian background; no one knew how he had ended up in the borderland. It was he who opened the casino. He hung a large notice in the window of the café. It announced that he had all sorts of games of chance, that a band would be "concertizing" every evening until morning, and that he had hired "renowned chanteuses." The renewal of the premises began with concerts by the band—eight musicians hastily scraped together. Later on, the so-called Mariahilf Nightingale arrived, a blond girl from Bogumin. She sang waltzes by Lehár, plus the naughty ditty "When I wander through the gray dawn of a night of love," as well as the encore: "Underneath my frock I wear pink and pleated undies." Thus did Brodnitzer heighten the expectations of his clientele.

It turned out that along with the countless short and long card tables Brodnitzer had also set up a small roulette table in a shadowy curtained alcove. Captain Wagner told everyone about it, stoking enthusiasm. To these men, who had been serving on the border for many years (and many had never seen a roulette wheel), the tiny ball was one of those magical objects of the great world, something that helped a man to suddenly win beautiful women, expensive horses, splendid castles. Who could not be helped by the ball? They had all spent a wretched boyhood in parochial school, a harsh adolescence in military school, and cruel years in borderland service. They were waiting for the war. But instead, the army had partially mobilized against Serbia, then returned ingloriously to the usual expectation of routine promotions. Maneuvers, service, officers' club, officers' club, service, maneuvers! The first time they heard the clickety-click of the little ball they knew that fortune itself was turning among them, smiling on this man today and that man tomorrow. Sitting there were strange, pale, rich, mute gentlemen such as they had never seen before. One day Captain Wagner won five hundred crowns. The next day his debts were settled. This was the first month in a long time that he received his pay intact, a whole three thirds. Then again, Lieutenant Schnable and Lieutenant Gründler had each lost a hundred crowns. Tomorrow they could win a thousand!

When the white ball began to scurry, looking for all the world like a milky circle drawn along the periphery of black and red squares, when the black and red squares similarly blended into a single blurring round of indefinable colors, then the hearts of the officers trembled and a strange roar swept through their heads, as if a separate ball were rotating in each brain, and they saw only black and red, black and red. Their knees buckled even though they were seated. Their eyes desperately chased the ball they could not grab. Obeying its own laws, it finally began to reel, drunk from its dash, and, exhausted, collapsed in a numbered niche. They all moaned. Even the losers felt relieved. The next morning each man told another, and a great delirium overwhelmed them all. More and more officers flocked to the casino. Foreign civilians likewise came from inscrutable areas. It was they who heated up the game, filled the coffers, drew huge bills from wallets, gold ducats, watches, and chains from vest pockets, and rings from fingers. The hotel was booked solid. The sleepy droshkies, which had always waited at their stand, like mock-up vehicles in a waxworks, with the yawning drivers on the boxes and the scrawny jades in front—they too awoke, and lo and behold: the wheels were able to roll, the scrawny jades galloped with clattering hooves from the train depot to the hotel, from the hotel to the border, and back again to the little town. The morose shopkeepers smiled. The murky stores seemed to grow brighter, the displayed wares gaudier. Night after night, the Mariahilf Nightingale sang. And as if her warbling had wakened other sisters, new, made-up girls, never seen before, came to the café. The tables were pushed apart, and people danced to Lehár's waltzes. The whole world had changed. . . .

Yes, the whole world! In other places, men put up strange posters such as had never been seen here before. In all languages they exhorted the bristle workers to stop working. Bristle manufacturing is the only wretched industry in this region. The workers are poor peasants. Some of them survive by chopping wood in winter, by harvesting in autumn. In summer, they all have to go to the bristle factory. Others come from the Jewish lower classes. These Jews cannot do arithmetic and cannot do business, nor have they learned any trade. Far and wide, within a radius of some twenty leagues, there is no other factory.

The manufacture of bristles was governed by inconvenient and expensive regulations; the manufacturers did not like observing them. The workers had to be provided with masks against dust and germs, the workrooms had to be large and bright, the refuse had to be burned twice a day, and any workers who started coughing had to be replaced. For everyone whose job was to clean the bristles began spitting blood after a short time. The factory was an ancient tumbledown ruin with small windows and a defective slate roof; fenced in by a wildly rampant willow hedge, it stood in the middle of a broad, desolate square, where garbage had been dumped since time immemorial: dead cats and rats decomposed, metal utensils rusted away, smashed earthen pots lay next to tattered shoes. All around, fields stretched out, alive with the golden bounty of grain, athrob with the incessant chirping of crickets, and dark-green swamps constantly echoed with the cheery croaking of frogs. At the small gray factory windows, the workers sat, tirelessly combing the dense shrubs of the bristle clusters with large iron rakes and swallowing the dry cloudlets of dust to which every new cluster gave birth, and the iridescent summer flies danced outside the windows, white and colored butterflies flitted about, and through the big skylight came the victorious blaring of the larks. The workers, who had come from their free villages just a few short months ago, the villages where they had been born and bred in the sweet scent of hay, in the cold breath of snow, in the pungent smell of dung, in the shattering din of the birds, in the whole mercurial wealth of nature—these workers peered through the gray cloudlets of dust and saw swallows, butterflies, and dancing gnats and felt homesick. When the larks trilled, the workers grew dissatisfied. Earlier they had not known that the manufacturers were required by law to protect the workers' health, that there was a parliament in the monarchy, that this parliament included deputies who were workers themselves. Strange men came, put up posters, held meetings, explained the constitution and the gaps in the constitution, read newspaper articles to them, and spoke in all tongues. They were louder than the larks and the frogs: the workers went on strike.

This was the first strike in this region. It frightened the civil authorities. For decades they had been accustomed to taking leisurely censuses, celebrating the Kaiser's birthday, assisting with the annual military recruitments, and sending the same old reports to the governor's office. Now and then they arrested russophile Ukrainians, an Orthodox priest, Jews caught smuggling tobacco, and spies. For centuries this region had cleaned bristles, sent them to the brush factories in Moravia, Bohemia, and Silesia, and received finished brushes in return. For years the workers had coughed, spit blood, fallen ill, and died in the hospitals. But they never went on strike. Now the constabularies from miles around had to be called in and a report dispatched to the governor's office. The governor's office contacted the Army High Command. And the Army High Command notified the garrison commanders.

The junior officers imagined that "the people"—the lowest stratum of civilians, that is—wanted equality with officials, aristocrats, and industrialists. On no account should equality be granted if a revolution was to be averted. And they wanted no revolution; and so they had to shoot before it was too late. Major Zoglauer gave a short speech clarifying all these points: Of course, a war is much more pleasant. We're not constabulary or police officers. But there is no war for now. Orders are orders. We might advance with lowered bayonets and command, "Fire!" Orders are orders! Meanwhile no one is prevented from visiting Brodnitzer's casino and winning a lot of money.

One day Captain Wagner lost a lot of money. A foreign gentleman with a resonant name, formerly an active lancer and now a landowner in Silesia, won two evenings in a row, loaned some money to the captain, and was summoned home by telegram on the third day. The debt totaled two thousand crowns, a bagatelle for a cavalry officer; no bagatelle for a rifle captain! He could have approached Chojnicki if he had not already owed him three hundred.

Brodnitzer said, "Herr Captain, by all means use my name."

"Yes," said the captain. "Who'd loan me that much on your name?"

Brodnitzer mulled for a while. "Herr Kapturak."

Kapturak appeared and said, "So it's a sum of two thousand crowns. Till when?"

"Who knows?"

"A lot of money, Herr Captain!"

"I'll pay it back," replied Wagner.

"How, in what installments? You know that only one third of your pay can be garnisheed. And all the officers' salaries are already committed. I see no possibility."

"Herr Brodnitzer—" the captain began.

"Herr Brodnitzer," Kapturak began, as if Brodnitzer were not present, "owes me a lot of money too. I could advance the desired sum if one of your fellow officers whose salary is not garnisheed could step in—for example, Lieutenant Trotta. He used to be in the cavalry; he owns a horse!"

"Fine," said the captain. "I'll talk to him." And he woke up Lieutenant Trotta.

They stood in the long, dark, narrow corridor of the hotel. "Sign, quick!" whispered the captain. "They're waiting over there. They can tell you don't want to!"

Trotta signed.

"Come right down," said Wagner. "I'll wait for you."

Carl Joseph halted at the small back door, where the permanent tenants of the hotel entered the café. This was his first look at Brodnitzer's newly opened casino. This was his first look at *any* casino. A dark-green rib curtain surrounded the roulette table. Captain Wagner lifted the curtain and glided across into a different world. Carl Joseph heard the soft velvety hum of the ball. He did not have the nerve to raise the curtain any farther. At the other end of the café, by the street entrance, lay the platform, and on the platform stood the indefatigable Mariahilf Nightingale, warbling away. People gambled at the tables. The cards slapped down on the faux marble. The gamblers emitted unintelligible cries. They looked uniformed: all of them in white shirtsleeves, a sitting regiment of gamblers. Their jackets dangled from the backs of their chairs. Gently and ghostly, the empty jacket sleeves swayed at every movement of the gamblers. A dense thundercloud of smoke hovered over their heads. The tiny tips of cigarettes glowed reddish and silvery in the gray haze, constantly sending up new bluish fog to nourish the dense thundercloud. And under the visible cloud of smoke a second cloud seemed to be gathering, made up of noise, a roaring, tumbling, rumbling cloud. If you shut your eyes, you could believe that an enormous mob of dreadfully singing locusts had been released over the sitting people.

Captain Wagner, utterly transformed, came stepping through the curtain into the café. His eyes lay in violet caverns. Over his mouth the brown moustache hung bristly, its one half looking strangely shortened, and reddish stubble stood on his chin, a small lavish field of tiny lances.

"Where are you, Trotta?" cried the captain, although they were standing chest to chest. "I lost two hundred!" he bellowed. "That goddamn red! My luck's run out on me at roulette. I'll have to try something else!" And he dragged Trotta to the card table.

Kapturak and Brodnitzer got to their feet. "Did you win?" asked Kapturak, for he saw that the captain had lost.

"Lost, lost!" yelled the captain.

"Too bad, too bad," said Kapturak. "Now just take me, for instance: how often have I won and lost! Listen, at times I'd already lost everything! And I won everything back. Don't stick to the same game all the time. Just don't stick to the same game all the time. That's the main thing!"

Captain Wagner unhooked his tunic collar. The usual brownish red returned to his face. His moustache virtually adjusted itself. He slapped Trotta on the back. "You've never touched a card!"

Trotta watches Kapturak pull a virgin deck of glossy cards from his pocket and place it on the table gingerly, as if to avoid hurting the colorful face of the bottom card. He caresses the small pack with his deft fingers. The backs of the cards shine like small, smooth, dark-green mirrors. The ceiling lights float in the curving backs of the cards. A few cards rise on their own, stand vertical on their sharp edges, lie down alternately on their backs or bellies, gather into a small pile, which strips down with a gentle clatter, lets the black and red faces rush by like a brief, gaudy storm, closes again, falls on the table, divides into smaller heaps. Individual cards glide from these piles, shift gently into one another, each card covering half the back of the next, round themselves into a circle, recall a flat, strangely inverted artichoke, fly back into a row, and finally collect into the small pack. All cards heed the noiseless calls of the fingers. Captain Wagner follows this prelude with hungry eyes.

Ah, he loved the cards! Sometimes the ones he had called came to him and sometimes they fled him. He loved seeing his wild wishes galloping after the fleeing cards, eventually forcing them to double back. Sometimes, of course, the fleeing ones were faster, and the captain's wishes had to turn back, worn out. Over the years the captain had devised a murky, utterly tangled war plan that ignored no method of forcing his luck: neither persuasion nor violence, neither surprise attack nor fervent begging nor love-crazy beckoning. Once, the poor captain, wishing for a heart, had to act desperate and secretly assure the evasive card that if it did not come soon, he would commit suicide that very night. Another time, he felt his prospects would improve if he remained aloof, feigning utter indifference to the ardently desired card. A third time, in order to win, he had to shuffle the cards himself, with his left hand—a skill he had finally mastered by dint of iron willpower and long practice. And a fourth time he found it more useful to sit on the right side of the croupier. In most cases, though, he had to combine all methods or switch them very quickly, so quickly that none of the other players might catch on. For that was crucial.

"Let's change places," the captain might, for example, say, quite innocuously. And if he believed he had spotted a smile of recognition in someone's face, he would add with a laugh, "You're wrong! I'm not superstitious! The light's bothering me here!" You see, if the other players learned anything about the captain's strategic ploys, their hands would betray his intentions to the cards. The cards would, so to speak, get wind of his guile and have time to flee. And so no sooner did the captain sit down at the table than he began working as zealously as an entire general staff. And while his brain pulled off this superhuman achievement, his heart was consumed by heat and frost, hope and pain, jubilation and bitterness. He fought, he battled, he agonized. He had gone to work on cunning war plans against the wiles of the ball within the first few days of the roulette game here. (But he knew very well that the ball was harder to defeat than the playing card.)

He nearly always played baccarat, though it was not only prohibited, it was also severely chastised. Yet what did he care about games in which you had to reflect and calculate—reflect and calculate in a rational manner—if his speculations already verged on the incalculable and inexplicable, exposing and often even overcoming them? No! He wanted to grapple hand-to-hand with the enigmas of fate and solve them! So he sat down to baccarat. And he did win. He had three nines and three eights in a row, while Trotta got nothing but knaves and kings, Kapturak fours and fives only twice. And now Captain Wagner forgot himself. Although one of his rules was never to so much as hint at his good luck, so that no one would be certain of it, he suddenly tripled his wager, for he hoped to wipe out his debt tonight. And now the disaster began. The captain lost, and Trotta did not stop losing. In the end, Kapturak won five hundred crowns. The captain had to sign a new IOU.

Wagner and Trotta stood up. They began mixing cognac with 180 Proof and then the latter with Okocim beer. Captain Wagner was ashamed of his defeat, just like a general retreating from a lost battle to which he has invited a friend to share his victory. But the lieutenant shared the captain's shame. And both knew they could not possibly look into one another's eyes without alcohol. They nursed their drinks, taking small, regular sips.

"Your health!" said the captain.

"Your health!" said Trotta.

Each time they repeated these toasts, they exchanged encouraging glances, proving to each other that they were indifferent to their disaster. But suddenly it seemed to the lieutenant that the captain, his best friend, was the unhappiest man on earth, and Trotta began weeping bitterly.

"Why are you crying?" asked the captain. His own lips were already quivering.

"About you, about you!" said Trotta. "My poor friend!" And they lost themselves in partly wordless, partly verbose laments.

Captain Wagner recalled an old plan. It concerned Trotta's horse, which the captain rode daily; having grown to love it, he had wanted to buy it for himself. It had then instantly occurred to him that if he had enough cash to buy the horse, he could, without a doubt, win a fortune at baccarat and own several horses. He then thought of getting the horse from the lieutenant, not paying for it, using it as collateral, gambling with the money, and then buying the horse back. Was that unfair? Whom would it hurt? How long would it take? Two hours of playing, and he would have everything! He was most certain to win if he sat down at the card table without fear, not calculating even slightly. Oh, if he could have gambled just once like a rich man of independent means! Just once! The captain cursed his pay. It was so paltry that it did not allow him to gamble "decently."

Now that they were sitting side by side, in such deep emotion, forgetting all the world around them but convinced they had been forgotten by all the world around them, the captain felt he could finally say, "Sell me your horse."

"It's yours as a gift," said Trotta with great tenderness.

You can't sell a present, even temporarily, the captain thought, and he said, "No, sell it to me."

"Take it," begged Trotta.

"I'm paying!" the captain insisted. They argued for several minutes. Finally the captain lurched to his feet, reeling slightly, and shouted, "I order you to sell it to me!"

"Yessir, Herr Captain," said Trotta mechanically.

"But I don't have any money," the captain slurred, sitting back down and turning kind again.

"It doesn't matter! I'm giving it to you."

"No, absolutely not! And I don' wanna buy it anymore. If only I had the money!"

"I can sell it to someone else!" said Trotta. He beamed joyfully at this unique inspiration.

"Wonderful!" cried the captain. "But who?"

"Chojnicki, for instance!"

"Wonderful!" the captain repeated. "I owe him five hundred crowns."

"I'll take over your debt," said Trotta.

Because he was drunk, his heart was bursting with commiseration for the captain. This poor comrade had to be rescued. He was in great danger. Trotta was very close to him, very intimate with him—dear Captain Wagner. Besides, at this point the lieutenant felt it was necessary—indeed, unavoidable—to say a kind, comforting, perhaps even noble word and do some salutary deed. Friendship, magnanimity, and the need to appear very strong and helpful converged in his heart like three warm currents.

Trotta stands up. Day is dawning. Only a few lamps are still on, already dimming in the pale grayness of the day, which floods through the blinds. Aside from Herr Brodnitzer and his only waiter, no one is left in the place. Bleak and betrayed, the tables and chairs stand on the platform where the Mariahilf Nightingale hopped about during the night. All the surrounding desolation arouses terrible images of an abrupt departure that may have taken place here, as if the patrons, surprised by some danger, had abruptly stampeded out of the café. The floor is covered with short cigar stubs and heaps of long cardboard cigarette tips. Those are the remains of Russian papirossi, and they reveal that foreign guests have drunk and gambled with natives.

"Check!" shouts the captain. He embraces the lieutenant. He squeezes him long and poignantly. "God bless you!" he says, his eyes brimming with tears.

The full morning was already in the streets, the morning of a small East European town, redolent with chestnut candles, newly blossoming lilac, and the fresh, sourish black bread that the bakers carried out in large baskets. The birds made a racket; it was an unending sea of chirping, a noisy sea in the air. A transparent pale-blue heaven stretched low and smooth over the gray, crooked shingle roofs of the small houses. The tiny sluggish carts of the peasants trundled gently and drowsily along the dusty road, scattering straw, chaff, and dry wisps of last year's hay on all sides. On the clear eastern horizon, the sun rose very swiftly. Lieutenant Trotta walked toward the sun, a bit sobered by the soft breeze heralding the day; he was filled with the proud intention of rescuing his comrade. It was not easy selling his horse without first asking the district captain's permission. Still, he was doing it for his friend! Nor was it so easy—and what *would* have been easy for Lieutenant Trotta?—to offer the horse to Chojnicki. But the more difficult the enterprise sounded, the more vigorously and decisively Trotta marched toward it. The church tower was already striking. Trotta reached the entrance to the New Castle just as Chojnicki, booted and holding his riding crop, was about to step into his summer carriage. The count noticed the sham reddish freshness in the lieutenant's unshaven, haggard face: it was a drinker's makeup. It lay over his real pallor like the reflection of a red lamp on a white table. He's going to the dogs! thought Chojnicki.

"I wanted to make you a proposition," said Trotta. "Would you like my horse?" He was terrified by his own question. Suddenly he was tongue-tied.

"You don't enjoy riding, I know," said the count. "And you did leave the cavalry. Oh, well, you simply don't like tending the animal since you don't care to use it. Oh, well, but you might regret it."

"No," said Trotta. He would lay his cards on the table. "I need money!"

The lieutenant felt ashamed. There was nothing dubious, dishonorable, disreputable about borrowing money from Chojnicki. And yet Carl Joseph felt that this first loan would be launching a new phase in his life and that he virtually needed his father's permission. The lieutenant was ashamed. He said, "To come straight out with it: I co-signed a comrade's IOU. A large sum. Then he lost a smaller sum last night. I don't want him to be in debt to that café owner. But there is no way I can loan him that much. No," the lieutenant repeated, "there is no way. The officer in question already owes you money."

"But he's no concern of yours!" said Chojnicki. "In this matter he's no concern of yours. You'll pay me back soon. It's a trifle! Look, I'm rich, I'm what people call rich. I can't relate to money. If you ask me for a drink, it's exactly the same thing. Look at all this! Look!" And Chojnicki stretched his hand toward the horizon, marking a semicircle. "All these forests belong to me. It's quite unimportant—simply to spare you pangs of conscience. I'm grateful to anyone who takes something off my hands. No, ridiculous, it doesn't matter—too bad we're wasting so many words. Let me make a suggestion: I'll buy your horse and leave it with you for a year. After a year, it belongs to me."

Chojnicki was clearly losing patience. Besides, the battalion would soon have to march out. The sun was relentlessly climbing higher. The full day was here.

Trotta hurried toward the barracks. In half an hour the battalion would turn out. He had no time to shave. Major

Zoglauer was due around eleven hundred hours. (The major did not care for unshaven platoon leaders. All he had learned to heed over his years of serving on the border were "cleanliness and service dress while on duty.") Well, it was too late! Trotta dashed toward the barracks. At least he had sobered up. He met Captain Wagner in front of the assembled company. "Yes, it's settled," Trotta said hastily and stood in front of his platoon. And he ordered, "Double file, right face! Forward march!" The sabers glittered. The bugles blared. The battalion marched out.

Today Captain Wagner paid for the so-called "refreshment" at the border tavern. They had thirty minutes to drink two or three 180 Proofs. Captain Wagner knew quite well that he was gaining mastery over his luck. He was solely in charge of it. This afternoon, two thousand five hundred crowns! He would give back fifteen hundred immediately and sit down at the baccarat table, quite calmly, quite carefree, quite like a rich man! He would take over the bank! He would shuffle the cards himself! And with his left hand! Perhaps he would pay back only a thousand for now and sit down at the game with all of fifteen hundred, quite calmly, quite carefree, quite like a rich man: five hundred for the roulette and a thousand for the baccarat. That would be even better. "Put it on Captain Wagner's tab!" he called over to the bar. And they stood up. The halt was over, and the "field exercises" were to start.

Fortunately Major Zoglauer left today after half an hour. Captain Wagner handed over his command to First Lieutenant Zander and rode as fast as he could to the Hotel Brodnitzer. He inquired whether he might count on other players that afternoon, toward four. Yes indeed, without a doubt! Everything was off to a marvelous start. Even the "house spirits," those invisible familiars that Captain Wagner could sense wherever people gambled, that he sometimes inaudibly conversed with—and even then in a gobbledygook he had concocted over the years—today those ghosts were chock-full of sheer benevolence for Wagner. To improve their mood even further or at least prevent them from changing their minds, Wagner decided to lunch at the Café Brodnitzer for a change and not stir from his seat until Trotta arrived. He remained. Around 3 P.M., the first players showed up. Captain Wagner began to tremble. What if Trotta stood him up and didn't bring the money until tomorrow? By then his luck could desert him. A man might never again have such a good day! The gods were in a fine mood, and it was a Thursday. But Friday! Appealing to luck on a Friday was like expecting a medical officer to drill a company. The more time passed, the more grimly Captain Wagner thought about the tardy Lieutenant Trotta. He wasn't coming, the young scoundrel! And yet Captain Wagner had gone to so much trouble, cutting the drill short, skipping his normal lunch at the train station, arduously haggling with the house spirits, and, as it were, stretching out the favorable Thursday! And now he was being stood up. The hands on the wall clock inched on tirelessly, but Trotta did not come, did not come, did not come!

Wrong! He's coming! The door opens, and Wagner's eyes light up. He doesn't even shake Trotta's hand. His fingers tremble. His fingers all resemble jittery highwaymen. A moment later, they are already squeezing a splendid crackling envelope.

"Sit!" the captain ordered. "You'll see me again within half an hour at the latest!" And he vanished behind the green curtain.

The half hour wore by, then another hour and another. It was already evening, the lights were burning. Captain Wagner slowly approached. He could be recognized at most by his uniform, and even it had changed. It was unbuttoned, the black rubber neckband stuck out, the saber hilt was under the tunic, the pockets gaped, and cigar ashes were strewn on the blouse. The hairs along the demolished brown part curled on the captain's head, and his lips were open under the disheveled moustache. The captain wheezed, "Everything!" and sat down.

They had nothing more to say to each other. A couple of times, Trotta attempted to ask a question. With an outstretched hand and virtually outstretched eyes, Wagner requested silence. Then he stood up. He adjusted his uniform. He realized his life was pointless. He now went to put an end to it. "Farewell," he said solemnly—and left.

But outside he was fanned by a gentle summery evening with a hundred thousand stars and a hundred fragrances. After all, it was easier to stop gambling than stop living. And he swore to himself that he would never gamble again. He would rather die than touch another card. Never again! Never was a long time; it was shortened. He told himself, Until August 31, no gambling! Then we'll see. So, word of honor, Captain Wagner!

And with a squeaky-clean conscience, proud of his steadfastness, and cheery about the life he has just saved, Captain Wagner goes to Chojnicki. The count is standing in the doorway. He has known the captain long enough to see at first glance that he has lost a huge sum and has once more resolved never to gamble again. And the count calls out, "Where did you leave Trotta?"

"Haven't seen him."

"Everything?"

The captain's head sinks; he peers at the tips of his boots and says, "I've given my word of honor."

"Excellent!" says Chojnicki. "It's about time!"

He is determined to rescue Lieutenant Trotta from his friendship with the insane captain. Send him away! thinks Chojnicki. For now, give him a few days' furlough—with Vally! And he drives to town.

"Yes," says Trotta without hesitating. He is afraid of Vienna and of traveling with a woman. But he has to go. He now feels that very specific anguish that has regularly assailed him before every change in his life. He senses that a new danger is threatening him, the greatest danger of all—namely, one that he himself has yearned for. He doesn't have the nerve to ask who the woman is. Many faces of unknown women—blue, brown, and black eyes, blond hair, black hair, hips, breasts, and legs, women he may once have brushed up against, as a boy, as an adolescent—they all sweep past him, all of them at once: a marvelous, tender storm of women. He smells the fragrance of these strangers; he feels the cool, hard tenderness of their knees; the sweet yoke of naked arms is already around his throat and the bolt of intertwined arms lies in back of his neck.

There is a fear of voluptuousness that is itself voluptuous, just as a certain fear of death can itself be deadly. Lieutenant Trotta is now filled with that fear of voluptuousness.

Chapter 13

FRAU VON TAUSSIG was beautiful and no longer young. The daughter of a stationmaster, the widow of a rittmaster named Eichberg who had died young, she had married the freshly ennobled Herr von Taussig several years ago. A rich and sick manufacturer, he had a light case of so-called circular insanity. His attacks recurred every six months. For weeks ahead of time, he would feel one coming. And so he went to that institution on Lake Constance where spoiled, wealthy madmen underwent careful and expensive treatments, and the attendants were as nurturing as midwives. Shortly before an attack and at the advice of one of those mundane and feather-brained physicians who prescribe "spiritual emotions" just as frivolously as old-fashioned family doctors prescribed rhubarb and castor oil, Herr von Taussig had married the widow of his friend Eichberg. Taussig did experience a "spiritual emotion," but his attacks also came faster and more violently.

During her brief marriage to Herr von Eichberg, his wife had made many friends, and after his death she had rejected a few ardent marriage proposals. Out of pure esteem, people ignored her adulteries. That was a stern time, as we know. But it recognized exceptions and even liked them. It was one of the rare aristocratic principles, such as that mere commoners were second-class human beings yet certain middle-class officers became personal adjutants to the Kaiser; that Jews could claim no higher distinctions yet certain Jews were knighted and became friends with archdukes; that women had to observe a traditional morality yet certain women could philander like a cavalry officer. (Those were principles that would be labeled "hypocritical" today because we are so much more relentless: relentless, honest, and humorless.)

The only intimate friend who did not propose to the widow was Chojnicki. The world worth living in was doomed. The world that would follow it deserved no decent inhabitants. So it made no sense loving for keeps, marrying, perhaps having off-spring. Chojnicki looked at the widow with his sad, pale-blue, somewhat bulging eyes and said, "Forgive me for not wanting to marry you." With these words he ended his condolence visit.

So the widow married the insane Herr von Taussig. She needed money and he was more manageable than a child. Once he got over an attack, he would send for her. She came, allowed him one kiss, and took him home.

"Till we meet again, I hope," said Herr von Taussig to the physician, who walked him to the gate of the closed section. "See you very soon!" said the wife. (She loved the periods when her husband was ill.) And they went home.

She had last visited Chojnicki ten years ago, when she had not yet married Taussig, had been no less beautiful than today and a whole ten years younger. Nor had she gone back alone that time either. A lieutenant, as sad and young as this one, had escorted her. His name was Ewald and he was a lancer. (In those days there had been lancers along the border.) It would have been the first real pain of her life to go back without an escort and a disappointment to be escorted by, say, a first lieutenant. She felt nowhere near old enough for senior ranks. Ten years from now—perhaps.

But old age was approaching with cruel, hushed steps and sometimes in crafty disguises. She counted the days slipping past her and, every morning, the fine wrinkles, delicate webs that old age had spun at night around her innocently sleeping eyes. Yet her heart was that of a sixteen-year-old girl. Blessed with constant youth, it dwelled in the middle of the aging body, a lovely secret in a ruinous castle. Every young man whom Frau von Taussig took in her arms was the guest she had so long been yearning for. Unfortunately he lingered in the vestibule. After all, she wasn't living; she was only waiting. She saw one man after another leave with anxious, unslaked, embittered eyes. Gradually she got used to seeing men come and go: a race of childish giants, resembling clumsy mammoth insects, fleeting and yet weighty; an army of awkward fools who tried to flutter

with leaden wings; warriors who believed that they had con-
quered when they were despised, that they possessed when they
were ridiculed, that they had enjoyed when they had barely
tasted; a barbaric horde, for whom she nevertheless waited
lifelong. Perhaps, perhaps some day a single one would arise
from their dark, chaotic midst, an airy, shimmering prince with
blessed hands. He did not come! She waited; he did not come!
She grew old; he did not come! Frau von Taussig put up young
men as dams against the approach of old age. Fearing their
discerning gazes, she entered into every so-called adventure
with closed eyes. And with her desires she bewitched the foolish
men, using them to her own ends. Unfortunately they never
noticed. And so they did not change in the slightest.

She assessed Lieutenant Trotta. He looks old for his age, she
thought, he's experienced sad things, but he hasn't grown any
wiser. He does not love passionately, but perhaps not casually
either. He is already so unhappy that all you can really do is
make him happy.

The next morning Trotta was given three days' leave "to
attend to family matters." At 1 P.M., he said goodbye to his
comrades in the officers' mess. Envied and cheered, he escorted
Frau von Taussig into a first-class compartment, for which,
however, he had paid extra.

When night came, he felt scared of the darkness like a child
and left the compartment in order to smoke—under the pretext,
that is, of having to smoke. He stood in the corridor, filled with
garbled images, and peered through the nocturnal window at
the flying serpents instantly formed by the white-hot sparks
from the locomotive and instantly fading, and he peered at the
thick blackness of the forests and the peaceful stars in the vault of
the sky. Gently he pushed back the door and tiptoed into the
compartment.

"Perhaps we should have taken sleeping cars!" the woman said,
surprising him—indeed, frightening him—from the darkness.
"You're a chain smoker. You can smoke in here, you know."

So she still wasn't asleep. His match illuminated her face,
which lay, white, framed by black tangled hair, on the crimson
upholstery. Yes, perhaps they should have taken sleeping cars. The

tiny head of the cigarette glowed reddish through the darkness. They lumbered over a bridge; the wheels clattered more noisily.

"The bridges!" she said. "I'm scared they'll collapse."

Yes, thought the lieutenant, let them collapse!

His only choice was between a sudden disaster and one that crept up very slowly. He sat opposite the woman, motionless, saw the lights of each whizzing station brighten the compartment for an instant, saw Frau Taussig's pale face grow even paler. He was tongue-tied. He imagined he ought to kiss her rather than talk. He kept putting off the expected kiss more and more. After the next station, he told himself. All at once, the woman stretched out her hand, groped for the bolt on the compartment door, found it, and snapped it shut. And Trotta bent over her hand.

Frau Taussig made love with the lieutenant as intensely as she had made love with Lieutenant Ewald ten years earlier, on the same route and—who knows?—in the same compartment. But for now that lancer was snuffed out, like the earlier men, like the later men. Pleasure roared over memory, washing away all traces. Frau von Taussig's first name was Valerie, shortened to the usual Vally. Her nickname, whispered to her in all tender moments, sounded brand-new each time. This young man was rebaptizing her; she was a child—and as fresh as her name. Nevertheless, out of habit, she wistfully noted that he was "much older" than she: a remark she often dared make to young men—in some degree, a foolhardy precaution. Besides, her remark always inspired a new series of caresses. She now pulled forth all the tender words that she spoke so glibly, using them with one man or another. Next— how well, alas, she knew this sequence—would come the man's always identical plea not to talk about age or time. She knew how meaningless these pleas were—and she believed them. She waited. But Lieutenant Trotta kept silent, an obstinate young man. She was afraid his silence was a verdict, and so she cautiously began. "How much older do you think I am?"

He was at a loss. One did not respond to such a remark, nor did it really concern him. He felt the swift alternation of smooth coolness and equally smooth heat on her skin, the abrupt climatic changes that are among the enchanting manifestations of love. (Within a single hour they accumulate all the features of all the seasons on a single female shoulder. They truly suspend the laws of time.)

"I'm old enough to be your mother!" the woman whispered. "Guess my age."

"I don't know!" said the unhappy man.

"Forty-one!" said Frau Vally. She had turned forty-two just one month ago. But some women are prohibited by nature itself from telling the truth—the nature that prevents them from aging. Frau von Taussig may have been too proud to cover up three whole years. But stealing a single wretched year from truth was no theft.

"You're lying!" he eventually said, very gruffly, out of politeness. And she gratefully embraced him in a new, roaring surge. The white lights of stations dashed by the window, illuminating the compartment, brightening up her white face, and appearing to bare her shoulders once again. The lieutenant lay with his head at her breast like a child. She felt a blissful, beneficial, a motherly pain. A motherly love poured into her arms, filling her with new strength. She wanted to do something good for her lover as if for her own child: as if her womb had birthed him, the same womb that now received him.

"My child, my child!" she repeated. She no longer feared old age. Indeed, for the first time she blessed the years that separated her from the lieutenant. And when morning, a radiant early-summer morning, broke through the flying windows, she fearlessly showed the lieutenant her face, which was not yet equipped for the day. Of course, she was reckoning a little with the dawn. For the window she sat at happened to be facing east.

To Lieutenant Trotta the world looked different. As a result, he fancied that this was love—the materialization, that is, of his notions about love. In reality he was merely thankful, a sated child.

"We'll stay together in Vienna, won't we?"

Dear child, dear child! she kept thinking. She gazed at him, filled with maternal pride as if she could take credit for the virtues that he did not possess and that she ascribed to him like a mother.

She imagined an endless series of small parties. Luckily they happened to be arriving at Corpus Christi. She would obtain two seats on the grandstand. Together they would enjoy the colorful procession that she loved, just like all Austrian women of all classes.

She got seats on the grandstand. The cheerful and solemn pomp gave her a warm, rejuvenating glow. Since her youth she had been familiar—and probably no less precisely than the Controller of the Royal Household—with all phases, portions, and rules of the Corpus Christi procession, the way the old spectators in hereditary boxes are familiar with each and every scene in their favorite operas. Their pleasure in looking is not reduced; on the contrary, it is nourished by this intimate familiarity.

Inside Carl Joseph the old childish and heroic dreams surfaced, the ones that had filled him and made him happy during vacations at home, on his father's balcony, when he had heard the strains of "The Radetzky March." The full majestic might of the old empire passed before his eyes. The lieutenant thought about his grandfather, the Hero of Solferino, and the unshakable patriotism of a father who was like a small but strong rock amid the towering mountains of Hapsburg power. He thought about his own holy mission to die for the Kaiser at any moment, on water or on land, or also in the air—in short, any place. The oath he had perfunctorily sworn a few times came alive. It rose up, word for word, each word a banner. The porcelain-blue eyes of the Supreme Commander in Chief—eyes grown cold in so many portraits on so many walls in the empire and now filled with a new fatherly solicitude and benevolence—gazed like a whole blue sky at the grandson of the Hero of Solferino. The light-blue breeches of the infantry were radiant. Like the serious embodiment of ballistic science, the coffee-brown artillerists marched past. The blood-red fezzes on the heads of the azure Bosnians burned in the sun like tiny bonfires lit by Islam in honor of His Apostolic Majesty. In black lacquered carriages sat the gold-decked Knights of the Golden Fleece and the black-clad red-cheeked municipal councilors. After them, sweeping like the majestic tempests that rein in their passion near the Kaiser, came the horsehair busbies of the bodyguard infantry. Finally, heralded by the blare of the beating to arms, came the Imperial and Royal anthem of the earthly but nevertheless Apostolic Army cherubs—

"God preserve him, God protect him"—over the standing crowd, the marching soldiers, the gently trotting chargers, and the soundlessly rolling vehicles. It floated over all heads, a sky of melody, a baldachin of black-and-yellow notes. And the lieutenant's heart stood still yet pounded fiercely—a challenge to all medical science. Over the slow strains of the anthem, the cheers fluttered like small white flags amid huge banners painted with coats of arms. The white Lipizzaner steed capered along with the majestic coquettishness of the famous Lipizzaner horses trained at the Imperial and Royal Stud Farm. The steed was followed by the trotting hooves of a half squadron of dragoons—a delicate parade thunder. The black-and-gold helmets flashed in the sun. The loud fanfares resounded, the voices of cheerful heralds: Clear the way! Clear the way! The old Kaiser's coming!

And the Kaiser came; eight radiant-white horses drew his carriage. And on the white horses rode the footmen in black gold-embroidered coats and white periwigs. They looked like gods and yet they were merely servants of demigods. On each side of the carriage stood two Hungarian bodyguards with a black-and-yellow panther skin over one shoulder. They recalled the sentries on the walls of Jerusalem, the holy city, and Kaiser Franz Joseph was its king. The Emperor wore the snow-white tunic well known from all the portraits in the monarchy, and an enormous crest of green parrot feathers on his hat. The feathers swayed gently in the wind. The Kaiser smiled in all directions. The smile hovered on his old face like a small sun that he himself had created. The bells tolled from St. Stephen's Cathedral, the salutes of the Roman Church, presented to the ruler of the Holy Roman Empire of the German Nation. The old Kaiser stepped from the carriage, showing the elastic gait praised by all newspapers, and entered the church like any normal man; he walked into the church, the Holy Roman Emperor of the German Nation, immersed in the tolling of bells.

No lieutenant in the Imperial and Royal Army could have watched this ceremony apathetically. And Carl Joseph was one of the most impressionable. He saw the golden radiance streaming from the procession and he did not hear the dark beating of the vultures' wings. For they were already circling over the two-headed eagle of the Hapsburgs—vultures, the eagle's brotherly foes.

No, the world was not going under, as Chojnicki had said; you could see with your own eyes that it was very much alive. The inhabitants of this city surged across the broad Ring Street, cheerful subjects of His Apostolic Majesty, all of them members of his court retinue. The entire city was simply a gigantic outer court of his palace. Mighty in the entrance arches of the ancient palaces stood the liveried doorkeepers clutching their staffs— the gods among the footmen. Black coaches on high noble wheels with rubber tires and thin spokes drew up at the gates. The horses caressed the asphalt with solicitous hooves. Government officials with black cocked hats, gold-embroidered collars, and slender swords came from the procession, dignified and sweaty. White-clad schoolgirls, blossoms in their hair and candles in their hands, returned home, wedged between their solemn parents as if their somewhat bewildered and perhaps slightly beaten souls had become flesh. The delicate canopies of parasols vaulted over the bright hats of the bright women, who were leading their beaux along like dogs on leashes. Blue, brown, and black uniforms decorated with gold and silver moved like bizarre plants and saplings that had escaped from a southern garden and were striving back to their distant homeland. The black fire of the top hats glowed over red, zealous faces. Particolored sashes, the rainbows of the burghers, slanted across wide chests, waistcoats, and bellies. Now, along Ring Street, the bodyguardists came floating in two broad files, sporting white angelic pelerines with red lapels and white panaches and gripping shimmery halberds, and trolleys, fiacres, and even automobiles pulled over as though for familiar ghosts from history. At the corners and crossings, the obese flower women in tenfold petticoats—urban sisters of the fairies—held dark-green cans to water their radiant bouquets and tied lilies of the valley together; their old tongues wagged freely and their smiling glances blessed the loving couples who strolled past. The gold helmets of the firemen, who were marching toward the uproar, sparkled, cheerfully evoking danger and disaster. Everything was redolent of lilac and hawthorn. The hubbub of the city was not loud enough to drown out the whistling blackbirds in the gardens and the trilling larks in the air. The world lavished all these things on Lieutenant Trotta. He sat next to his mistress in the carriage, he loved her, and he was riding through what seemed like the first good day of his life.

And he really felt his life was beginning. He learned how to drink wine, just as he had drunk the 180 Proof in the borderland. He and the woman dined in that renowned restaurant whose proprietress was as dignified as an empress, her establishment as serene and pious as a temple, as elegant as a castle, and as peaceful as a cottage. Here the Excellencies ate at hereditary tables, and the waiters who served them looked almost like their peers, so that diners and waiters appeared to be spelling one another at scheduled intervals. The patrons were on a first-name basis like brothers, yet they greeted one another like princes. They knew the young and the old, the good horsemen and the bad, the gallants and the gamblers, the fops, the strivers, the favorites; the heirs to a time-blessed, proverbial, and ubiquitously honored stupidity; and also the smart ones who would gain power tomorrow. One heard only the delicate tinkles of well-bred forks and spoons and, at each table, that smiling whisper caught only by the companion and guessed all the same by the knowledgeable neighbor. A peaceful glow came from the white tablecloths, a discreet daylight poured in through the high curtained windows, the wine gurgled tenderly from the bottles, and anyone who wished to summon a waiter had only to raise his eyes. For in this well-mannered hush the twitch of an eyelid was like a call anywhere else.

Yes, thus began what he called "life" and what may have been life at that time: driving in a smooth carriage amid the dense perfumes of mellow spring, next to a woman who loved you. Each of her tender glances seemed to justify his youthful conviction that he was an outstanding man of many virtues and even a "swell officer," in the sense that this term had inside the army. He remembered that most of his life he had been sad, shy, one could say bitter. Yet now, thinking he knew himself, he could not understand why he had been sad, shy, and bitter. The nearness of death had terrified him, but he still drew pleasure from his rueful thoughts about Katharina and Max Demant. He had, in his opinion, endured harsh things. He deserved the tender glances of a beautiful woman. Yet from time to time, he eyed her a bit anxiously. Wasn't it just a whim for her, taking him along like a boy and giving him a few good days? That was something he could not stand for. He was, as was already established, a really swell guy, and any woman who loved him had to love him completely, honestly, and unto death, like poor Katharina. And who knew how many men this beautiful woman thought of while she believed she loved only him or pretended to? Was he jealous? Of course he was jealous! And also powerless, as he promptly realized. Jealous and with no way of remaining here or riding farther with the woman, holding on to her as long as he wished, and fathoming her and winning her. Yes, he was a poor little lieutenant with fifty crowns a month from his father, and he had debts. . . .

"Do you men gamble in your garrison?" Frau von Taussig suddenly asked.

"The other officers do," he said. "Captain Wagner, for instance. He loses tremendous amounts!"

"And you?"

"Not at all!" said the lieutenant. At that moment, he knew how a man could become powerful. He rebelled against his mediocre fate. He wanted a glorious destiny. Had he become a government official, he might have gotten the chance to apply some of his intellectual virtues, which he certainly possessed; he could have had a career. What was an officer in peacetime? What had the Hero of Solferino gained even in war and by his deed?

"Just don't gamble!" said Frau von Taussig. "You don't look like a man who's lucky at cards."

He was offended. He instantly wanted to prove that he was lucky—everywhere! He began hatching secret plans, for today, now, for tonight. His embraces were virtually provisional, the foretaste of a love he wanted to give tomorrow, as a man who was not only outstanding but also powerful. He wondered what time it was, looked at his watch, and was already thinking up an excuse to avoid getting away too late. Frau Vally sent him off herself.

"It's getting late, you have to go."

"Tomorrow morning!"
"Tomorrow morning!"
The hotel clerk gave him the name of a nearby casino. The lieutenant was greeted with bustling cordiality. Spotting a few high-ranking officers, he halted in front of them in the regulation rigidity. They casually waved, staring blankly at him as if unable to grasp that he was observing military rules, as if they had left the army long ago and were merely wearing its uniforms sloppily, and as if this innocent newcomer were stirring their very distant memory of a very distant time when they had been officers. They were now in a different, perhaps a more secret phase of their lives, and only their clothes and stars recalled their normal everyday life, which would recommence tomorrow with the dawning day.

The lieutenant counted his cash: he had one hundred fifty crowns. Imitating Captain Wagner, he put fifty crowns in his pocket, the rest in his cigarette case. For a while, he sat at one of the two roulette tables without betting—he was too unfamiliar with cards and did not dare approach them. He was very calm and astonished at his calm. He saw the red, white, and blue piles of chips grow smaller, grow bigger, shift to and fro. But it never occurred to him that he had come here to see them all wandering in his direction. He finally decided to bet, but merely out of a sense of duty. He won. He staked half his winnings and won again. He did not check the colors or the numbers. He put his chips down anywhere, indifferently. He won. He bet all his winnings. He won a fourth time. A major beckoned to him. Trotta stood up.

The major: "This is your first time here. You've won a thousand crowns. You'd be better off leaving right away."

"Yessir, Herr Major!" said Trotta and left obediently. But when he cashed in his chips, he was sorry he had obeyed. He was angry at himself for being obedient to just about anyone. Why did he let himself be sent away? And why did he not have the courage to return? He left, dissatisfied with himself and unhappy about his first winnings.

It was late and so still that one could hear the footsteps of individual pedestrians in remote streets. In the strip of sky over the narrow street, which was lined with high buildings, the stars twinkled, alien and peaceful. A dark shape turned the corner and staggered toward the lieutenant. It reeled—a drunkard, no doubt. The lieutenant recognized him immediately: it was Moser the painter, making his usual rounds, with his portfolio and slouch hat, through the nocturnal streets of the inner city. He saluted with one finger and began offering his pictures: "Girl, girls, in all kinds of positions!"

Carl Joseph halted. He felt that destiny itself had sent Moser his way. He had no inkling that for years now he could have run into the professor at the same time on any street in the inner city. He drew out the fifty crowns he had stowed away in his pocket and handed the cash to the old man. He did it as if following soundless orders, the way one carries out a command. Just like him, just like him, he thought, he is quite happy, he is quite right! He was frightened by this thought. He wondered why Moser the painter should be right; he found no reason, was even more frightened, and already felt a thirst for alcohol, the drinker's thirst, which is a thirst of soul and body. Suddenly you see dimly like a person who's nearsighted, you hear poorly like a person who's hard of hearing. You have to have a drink right away, on the spot. The lieutenant turned, stopped Moser the painter, and asked, "Where can we get a drink?"

There was an all-night café not far from Wollzeile. There you could get slivovitz; unfortunately it was twenty-five percent weaker than the 180 Proof. The lieutenant and the painter sat down and drank. Gradually it dawned on Trotta that he had long since stopped being the master of his fate, long since stopped being an outstanding man with all kinds of virtues. He was actually poor and wretched and utterly rueful about his obedience to the major, who had prevented him from winning hundreds of thousands of crowns. No! He was not meant to be lucky or happy! Frau von Taussig and the major in the casino and indeed everyone: they all made fun of him. This man, Moser the painter—one could already call him a friend—was the only person who was honest, loyal, and sincere. The lieutenant should identify himself. This outstanding man was his father's oldest friend, his only friend. Why should Carl Joseph be embarrassed about him? He had painted Grandfather!

The lieutenant took a deep breath to draw courage from the air and said, "Do you realize we met a long time ago?"

Moser the painter pulled back his head, his eyes flashed under his bushy brows, and he asked, "Long—time—ago? Personally? Of course you know me as a painter. I'm known widely as a painter. I'm sorry, I'm sorry, I'm afraid you're mistaken! Or"— Moser was distressed—"perhaps you're confusing me with someone else?"

"My name is Trotta!" said the lieutenant.

Moser the painter gazed at the lieutenant with sightless, glassy eyes and held out his hand. Then a joyous shout thundered out of him. He yanked the lieutenant halfway across the table, bent toward him, and, in the middle of the table, they exchanged a lengthy brotherly kiss.

"And what is your father up to?" asked the professor. "Is he still in office? Is he governor already? I haven't heard from him! Some time ago I ran into him here, in the park; he gave me some money, he wasn't alone, he was with his son, that little boy— wait a moment, that was you."

"Yes, that was me," said the lieutenant. "It was a long time ago, it was a very, very long time ago."

He recalled the terror he had felt at the sight of the red, clammy hand on his father's thigh.

"I must beg your forgiveness, yes, forgiveness!" said the lieutenant. "I treated you miserably back then, I treated you miserably! Please forgive me, dear friend!"

"Yes, miserably," Moser confirmed. "I forgive you. Not another word about it! Where do you live? I'll see you home."

The café was closing. Arm in arm they staggered through the silent streets. "I'm getting off here," the painter murmured. "This is my address. Visit me tomorrow, my boy!" And he gave the lieutenant one of his overdone business cards, which he was in the habit of distributing in cafés.

Chapter 14

THE DAY ON which the lieutenant had to return to his garrison was a saddening day and also a sad day. He once more walked along the streets where the pageant had drawn by two days earlier. For a brief hour, the lieutenant thought, he had been proud of himself and his profession. But today the thought of his return strode alongside him like a guard next to a prisoner.

For once, Lieutenant Trotta was rebelling against the military laws that ruled his life. He had obeyed since earliest boyhood. And he wanted to stop obeying. He had no idea what freedom meant, but he sensed that it was as different from a furlough as a war is from maneuvers. This comparison flashed into his mind because he was a soldier—and because war is the soldier's freedom. It struck him that the ammunition you need for freedom is money. But the cash in his pockets somewhat resembled the blank cartridges fired on maneuvers. Did he even own anything? Could he afford freedom? Had his grandfather, the Hero of Solferino, left a fortune? Would he inherit it from his father some day? Never before had he had such thoughts! Now they flew to him like a flock of exotic birds, nesting in his brain and fluttering around him nervously. Now he heard all the confusing calls of the great world. He had learned yesterday that this year Chojnicki would be leaving his homeland earlier than usual, heading south with his lady friend this very week. And Trotta got to know envy, envy of his friend, and he felt doubly ashamed.

He was going to the northeastern border. But the woman and the friend were going south. And the "south," hitherto a geographic term, now shone in all the bewitching colors of an unknown paradise. The south lay in a foreign country! And lo: there were foreign countries that were not subject to Kaiser

Franz Joseph I, countries with their own armies, with many thousands of lieutenants in small and large garrisons. In those other lands, the name of the Hero of Solferino meant nothing. They too had monarchs. And these monarchs had their own rescuers. Following such trains of thought was highly confusing; for a lieutenant in the monarchy it was as confusing as when people like us imagine that the world is only one heavenly body among millions upon millions, that there are countless suns in the Milky Way, each one with its own planets, and that you yourself are a very worthless individual—if not, to put it quite grossly, a pile of crap.

The lieutenant still had seven hundred crowns left over from his winnings. He had not dared visit another casino. Not only did he fear that unknown major, who may have been sent by city headquarters to keep an eye on young officers; he was also afraid of remembering his woeful flight. Ahh! He knew he would promptly leave any casino another hundred times, at any superior's beck and call. And like a sick child he lost himself with a certain relish in the painful realization that he was powerless to force his luck. He felt extraordinarily sorry for himself, and at this moment it did him good to feel sorry for himself. He had a few drinks and instantly felt at home in his powerlessness. And like someone entering a prison or a monastery, the lieutenant felt that the money he had on him was oppressive and superfluous. He decided to spend it all at once.

Stepping into the boutique where his father had gotten the silver cigarette case, he bought a string of pearls for his girlfriend. With flowers in his hand, the necklace in his trouser pocket, and a woebegone face, he appeared before Frau von Taussig. "I've brought you something," he confessed, as if to say, I've stolen something for you!

He felt he was illegitimately playing a strange role—that of a man of the world. And the moment he held his present, it occurred to him that he was ridiculously overdoing it, that it degraded him and perhaps offended the rich woman.

"Please excuse me!" he said. "I wanted to buy you a little something, but . . ." And he was tongue-tied. And he turned crimson. And he lowered his eyes.

Ah! Lieutenant Trotta did not understand women who see old age approaching. He did not know that she welcomed every present like a magic gift to make her younger, and that her intelligent and yearning eyes had a very different standard for assessing things! Frau von Taussig loved his helplessness, and the more evident his youth, the younger she herself became. And so, wise and impetuous, she threw her arms around him, kissed him like a child of her own, wept because she was about to lose him, laughed because she still held him, and also a little because the pearls were beautiful, and she said, through an intense and splendid flood of tears, "You're sweet, very sweet, my boy!" She promptly regretted those words, especially "My boy." For they made her older than she actually was at that instant. Luckily she noticed right away that he was as proud as if he had been decorated by the Supreme Commander in Chief himself. He's too young, she thought, to know how old I am!

But to wipe out, root out her real age, scuttle it in the sea of her passion, she grabbed the shoulders of the young man whose warm, tender bones were confusing her hands and drew him to the sofa. She pounced on him with her stupendous yearning to be young. Passion erupted from her in violent sweeps of flame, chaining the lieutenant and subjugating him. Her eyes, blissful and grateful, blinked at the young man's face above her face. Looking at him made her young again. And her lust to remain eternally young was as great as her lust to love. For a while she thought she could never let go of this lieutenant. But then a moment later she said, "Too bad you're leaving today."

"Won't I ever see you again?" he asked, reverent, a young lover.

"Wait for me, I'll be back!" And: "Don't cheat on me!" she quickly added, with an aging woman's dread of infidelity and another woman's youth.

"You're the only one I love!" answered the honest voice of a young man to whom nothing seems as important as fidelity.

That was how they said goodbye.

Lieutenant Trotta went to the train, arrived too early, and had to wait a long time. But he felt he was already traveling. Every additional minute spent in the city would have been painful, perhaps even humiliating. He struggled against his obsession by pretending to leave a bit earlier than he had to. At last he could get into the train. He fell into a happy, mostly unbroken sleep and only woke up right before the border.

His orderly, Onufrij, who was waiting for him, reported that the town was in ferment. The bristle workers were demonstrating, and the garrison was on alert.

Now it hit Lieutenant Trotta why Chojnicki had left the area so early. So he was going "south" with Frau von Taussig! And Trotta was a helpless prisoner who could not immediately turn around, hop the train, and go back!

Today no cabs were waiting at the station. So Trotta went on foot. Onufrij walked behind him, clutching the lieutenant's bag. The small shops of the little town were shut. Iron poles barricaded the wooden doors and shutters of the low houses. Constables patrolled with fixed bayonets. No sound was heard apart from the familiar croaking of the frogs in the swamps. The dust produced indefatigably by this sandy earth had been lavishly poured by the wind over roofs, walls, picket fences, wooden pavements, and scattered willow trees. Centuries of dust seemed to be coating this forgotten world. No inhabitant could be seen in the streets—as if they had all been struck dead behind their bolted doors and windows. Double sentries were posted outside the barracks. All the officers had moved here since yesterday, and Brodnitzer's hotel stood empty.

Lieutenant Trotta reported to Major Zoglauer. From his superior he learned that the trip had done him good. By the lights of this man, who had been serving at the border for over a decade, a trip could not help doing good. And as if it were a perfectly routine matter, the major told the lieutenant that a platoon of riflemen would march out at dawn, station themselves on the highway opposite the bristle factory, and, if necessary, take armed action against "seditious disturbances" by the striking workers. This platoon was to be commanded by Lieutenant Trotta. It was a minor affair, said the major, and there was reason to assume that the constabulary was strong enough to keep the strikers duly respectful; we only had to maintain cool heads and not move prematurely; in the end, however, the civil authorities would have to decide whether or not the riflemen had to proceed; this was certainly not very pleasant for an officer, for how could they be bossed around by a district commissioner? But ultimately this delicate task was a kind of distinction for the youngest lieutenant in the battalion; and besides, the other officers hadn't had any furlough, and the simplest rule of solidarity would demand . . . and so on and so forth.

"Yessir, Herr Major!" said the lieutenant and left.

One could not fault Major Zoglauer for anything. He had practically asked the grandson of the Hero of Solferino instead of ordering him. And after all, the grandson of the Hero of Solferino had had an unexpected and marvelous furlough. Now he cut across the grounds to the officers' mess. Fate had prepared this political demonstration for him. That was why he had wound up at the border. He was certain now that a scheming, treacherous fate had granted him his furlough in order to destroy him upon his return.

The others sat in the officers' mess and greeted him with an exaggerated jubilation that sprang more from their curiosity to find out something than from any deep feelings at having him back. And they also asked, in unison, how "it" had been. But Captain Wagner said, "When everything's done tomorrow, he can tell us!" And they all hushed.

"What if I'm killed tomorrow?" Lieutenant Trotta said to Captain Wagner.

"Goddammit!" replied the captain. "A disgusting death. The whole thing's disgusting! But they're poor devils. And maybe they're right after all."

It had not yet occurred to the lieutenant that the workers were poor wretches who could be right. Now the captain's remark struck Trotta as excellent, and he no longer doubted that they were poor devils. So he drank two 180 Proofs and said, "Then I simply won't order the men to shoot! Or to advance with fixed bayonets! The constabulary should fend for itself."

"You'll do what you have to, you know you will."

No! Carl Joseph did not know it at this moment. He drank. And he very quickly got into a state in which he felt capable of just about anything: insubordination, resigning from the army, winning a fortune. No more corpses should lie on his path. "Leave the army!" Dr. Max Demant had said. The lieutenant had been a weakling long enough. Instead of leaving the army, he had gotten himself transferred to the border. Now everything was to have an end. He would not be degraded tomorrow to a kind of high-level policeman. The day after, he might have to walk a beat and give tourists directions! Ridiculous, playing the soldier in peacetime! There will never be a war! They'll rot in the officers' mess! But as for him, Lieutenant Trotta, who knows? By next week at this time he might be sitting in the south!

He said all this to Captain Wagner in a loud, eager voice. A few comrades surrounded him, listening. Several were certainly in no mood for war. Most of them would have been content with anything so long as they got somewhat higher pay, somewhat more comfortable garrisons, and somewhat faster promotions. Several found Lieutenant Trotta strange and also a bit unsettling. He enjoyed special protection. He had just returned from a wonderful trip. What? And he didn't feel like marching out tomorrow?

Lieutenant Trotta sensed a hostile stillness around him. For the first time since joining the army, he decided to provoke his fellow officers. And knowing what was bound to offend them the most, he said, "Maybe I'll apply to staff school!"

Sure, why not? the officers said. He had come from the cavalry, why not go to staff school? He would certainly pass the exams and even make general without seniority, at an age when their kind were just making captain and putting on their first spurs. So it couldn't hurt him to march off to the huggermugger tomorrow!

The next day he had to march off at the crack of dawn. For it was the army that regulated the sequence of the hours. It grabbed time and put it wherever the military found appropriate. Even though the "seditious disturbances" were not expected until noon, Lieutenant Trotta marched out by eight hundred hours, along the wide dusty highway. Behind the neat, systematic rifle stacks, which looked both peaceful and dangerous, the soldiers lay, stood, and wandered. The larks blared, the crickets chirped, the mosquitoes hummed. In the remote fields, they could see the colorful, radiant kerchiefs of the peasant women. They were singing. And sometimes the soldiers who were natives of this area responded with the same songs. They would have known what to do in those fields, but they did not understand what they were waiting for here. Had the war begun already? Were they going to die this afternoon?

There was a small village tavern nearby. And that was where Lieutenant Trotta went to drink a 180 Proof. The low taproom was crowded. The lieutenant realized that these were the workers who were supposed to assemble outside the factory at noon. They all fell silent when he entered, jingling and fearsomely girded. He halted at the counter. Slowly, all too slowly, the tavern keeper fiddled around with bottle and glasses. Behind Trotta's back the hush towered, a massif of silence. He drained his glass at one gulp. He sensed that they were all waiting for him to leave. He would have liked to tell them that it wasn't his fault. But he was incapable of speaking to them or leaving immediately. He did not want to appear timorous, so he had several more drinks in a row. The men were still hushed. Perhaps they were making signs behind his back. He did not turn around. At last he left the tavern, squeezing past the hard rock of silence, and hundreds of gazes bristled on the back of his neck like dark lances.

Upon reaching his platoon again, he felt he should order the men to fall in even though it was only ten hundred hours. He was bored, and he had also learned that troops are demoralized by boredom, while rifle drills boost their morale. In a flash his platoon stood before him in the regulation two lines, and suddenly, and no doubt for the first time in his soldierly life, it seemed to him as if the precise limbs of the men were dead components of dead machines that produced nothing. The entire platoon stood motionless, all the men with bated breath. But after feeling that dark, weighty hush on his back at the tavern, Lieutenant Trotta suddenly realized that there are two kinds of silence. And perhaps, he thought further, there are several kinds of silence just as there are several kinds of noises? No one had ordered the workers to fall in when he had entered the tavern. Nevertheless they had hushed all at once. And their silence had poured out a dark, dumb hatred, the way pregnant and infinitely silent clouds sometimes pour out the mute electric sultriness of an unspent thunderstorm.

Lieutenant Trotta listened. But from the dead silence of his motionless platoon nothing came pouring. One stony face waited next to another. Most of them vaguely resembled his orderly, Onufrij. They had broad mouths, and heavy lips that could barely close, and blank, bright, narrow eyes. And as he stood there in front of his platoon, poor Lieutenant Trotta, overarched by the blue radiance of the early-summer day, surrounded by blaring larks, chirping crickets, and humming mosquitoes, and yet believing he could hear the dead hush of his soldiers more strongly than all the voices of the day, was overwhelmed by the certainty that he did not belong here. But then where did he belong? he wondered, while the platoon awaited his further orders. Where *do* I belong? Not among the men in the tavern. In Sipolje, perhaps? Among the fathers of my father? Does the plow belong in my hand and not the sword? And the lieutenant kept his platoon at rigid attention.

"At ease!" he finally commanded. "Rifles on the ground! Platoon dismissed!"

And things were as before. The soldiers lay behind the rifle stacks. The singing of the peasant women came from the distant fields. And the soldiers responded with the same songs.

The constabulary marched over from the town, three reinforced files of sentinels, accompanied by District Commissioner Horak. Lieutenant Trotta knew him. He was a good dancer, a Silesian Pole, both dashing and upright at once, and though none of the men had known Horak's father, Horak nevertheless reminded them of him. His father had been a mailman. Today, as prescribed on duty, he wore the uniform, black and green with violet lapels, and the sword. His short blond moustache shone as golden as wheat, and the scent of the powder on his full, rosy cheeks could be smelled far away. He was as cheerful as a Sunday and a parade.

"My orders," he told Lieutenant Trotta, "are to break up the meeting at once. Presumably you are ready, Herr Lieutenant."

He arranged his constables around the desolate factory square, where the meeting was to be held.

Lieutenant Trotta said "Yes!" and wheeled around.

He waited. He would have liked another 180 Proof, but he couldn't return to the tavern. He saw the corporal, the platoon leader, and the lance corporal vanish inside the tavern and reemerge. He stretched out on the roadside grass and waited. The day grew fuller and fuller, the sun rose higher, and the songs of the peasant women in the distant fields died out. Lieutenant Trotta felt as if an endless stretch of time had passed since his return from Vienna. From those remote days he saw only the woman, who could be in the south by now, who had left him— betrayed him, he thought. Now he lay on the roadside in the border garrison and waited, not for the enemy but for the demonstrators.

They came. They came from the direction of the tavern. Ahead of them wafted their singing, a song the lieutenant had never heard before. It had scarcely been heard in this region. It was "The Internationale," sung in three languages. District Commissioner Horak knew it, for professional reasons. Lieutenant Trotta couldn't make out a word. But the melody seemed to be a musical translation of the hush he had felt in back of him. A solemn excitement overcame the dashing district commissioner. He ran from one constable to the next, clutching a notebook and a pencil. Once again Trotta commanded, "Fall in!" And like a cloud that had dropped to the earth, the dense group of strikers marched past the twofold fence of gaping riflemen. The lieutenant had a dark foreboding of the end of the world. He remembered the rainbow splendor of the Corpus Christi pageant, and for a brief instant he felt as if the murky cloud of rebels were rolling toward that imperial procession. For all of a single rapid moment the lieutenant had the sublime ability to see in images, and he saw the times rolling toward one another like two rocks, and he himself, the lieutenant, was smashed between them.

His men shouldered their rifles while opposite them, lifted by invisible hands, a male head and torso appeared above the dense, black, incessantly moving circle of the throng. Soon the floating body was almost the exact midpoint of the circle. Its hands rose aloft. From its mouth came incomprehensible sounds. The throng yelled. Next to the lieutenant stood Commissioner Horak, notebook and pencil in hand. All at once, he shut his book and slowly walked between two sparkling constables toward the throng on the other side of the road.

"In the name of the law!" he cried. His clear voice drowned out the speaker. The demonstrators were ordered to disperse.

There was an instant of silence. Then a single shriek broke from all the strikers. Next, the white fists emerged, flanking each face. The constables formed a cordon. The next moment, the semicircle of demonstrators began moving. They surged shrieking toward the constables.

"Bayonets at the charge!" Trotta commanded.

He drew his sword. He could not see that his weapon flashed in the sun, casting a fleeting, playful, provocative reflection upon the shady side of the highway, where the throng had gathered. The pommels of the constables' helmets and their bayonet points had abruptly submerged in the throng.

"Toward the factory!" Trotta commanded. "Forward march!"

The riflemen advanced, and toward them flew dark wooden objects, brown laths, and white stones, whizzing and whistling, snuffing and snorting. Nimble as a weasel Horak ran alongside the lieutenant, whispering, "Shoot, Lieutenant, for God's sake!"

"Platoon halt!" Trotta commanded. "Fire!"

In accordance with Major Zoglauer's instructions, the riflemen fired their first round into the air. Next came utter silence. For a second they could hear all the peaceable voices of the summer afternoon. And they felt the benevolent brooding of the sun through the dust whirled up by the soldiers and by the crowd and through the faint burning smell produced by the cartridges and now wafting away. All at once, a woman's sharp, howling voice sliced through the afternoon. And since a few in the throng evidently believed she had been hit by a bullet, they again began to hurl their haphazard missiles at the soldiers. And the few hurlers were instantly followed by several more and finally the whole throng. And several riflemen in the front line were already sinking to the ground, and while Lieutenant Trotta stood there rather perplexed, his sword in his right hand, his left hand groping for his pistol holster, he caught Horak's whispering voice at his side. "Shoot! For God's sake shoot them!"

In one second a hundred fragmented thoughts and images churned through Lieutenant Trotta's agitated brain, a few simultaneously, and tangled voices in his heart enjoined him to show now pity, now cruelty, reminded him of what his grandfather would have done in this situation, predicted that he himself would die the next moment, and also presented his own death as the only possible and desirable outcome of this battle. Someone, he believed, raised his hand, someone else's voice coming out of him repeated the order—"Fire!"—and he managed to see that this time the rifles pointed at the demonstrators. A second later he knew nothing more. For in the throng a portion that had seemed to have fled or pretended to flee was merely circling around and rushing in behind the riflemen, so that Trotta's platoon was hemmed in between the two groups.

While the riflemen fired the second round, stones and nailed slats plummeted upon their backs and necks. Struck on the head by one of those missiles, Lieutenant Trotta sank to the ground, unconscious. The workers banged away at the fallen man with all kinds of objects. The riflemen now shot without orders, helter-skelter, firing at their attackers and forcing them to flee. The whole thing lasted barely three minutes. When the riflemen fell in, forming two lines under the command of the junior officer, wounded soldiers and workers lay in the dust of the highway, and it took a long time for the ambulances to arrive.

Lieutenant Trotta was taken to the small garrison hospital, where he was diagnosed as having a fractured skull and a broken left clavicle and possibly encephalitis. Chance, clearly senseless, had left the grandson of the Hero of Solferino with an injured clavicle, but none of the living, except for the Kaiser, perhaps, could have known that the Trottas owed their rise to the wounded collarbone of the Hero of Solferino.

Three days later the lieutenant did have encephalitis. And the district captain would have been notified if the lieutenant, waking up from his blackout on the very day he was delivered to the garrison hospital, had not begged the major under no circumstances to inform the father about the incident. While the lieutenant was now unconscious again, and there was ample reason to fear for his life, the major nevertheless preferred to wait. So two weeks passed before the district captain learned about the borderland rebellion and the unfortunate role his son had played. He first read about it in the newspapers, which mentioned it because of the opposition's politicians. For the opposition was determined that the army, the rifle battalion, and especially Lieutenant Trotta, who had given the order to fire, were all to be held responsible for the casualties and for the widows and orphans. And the lieutenant was actually threatened with an investigation of sorts—that is, a formal investigation, undertaken to calm the politicians, conducted by military authorities, and used to rehabilitate the defendant and perhaps even distinguish him in some fashion.But this did not put the district captain's mind at ease. He sent two telegrams to his son and one to Major Zoglauer. By then, the lieutenant was improving. He could not yet move in bed, but he was out of danger. He wrote a brief account to his father. And he was not worried about his health.

He mused that corpses were lying in his path again, and he was resolved to finally leave the army. Occupied with such thoughts he could not possibly see or speak to his father, even though he missed him. He felt something like homesickness for his father, but he also knew that his home was no longer with his father. The army was no longer his profession. And however much he shuddered at what had brought him to the hospital, he welcomed his illness because it put off the necessity of acting on decisions. He surrendered to the dismal smell of carbolic acid, the snowy bleakness of walls and bed, the pain, the changes of bandages, the strict nurturing of the attendants, and the boring visits by eternally jocular comrades. He had read nothing since military school, but he now reread a few of the books that his father had once assigned him to peruse on his own, and every line reminded him of his father and the quiet Sunday mornings in summer, and Jacques, Bandmaster Nechwal, and "The Radetzky March."

One day, Captain Wagner came to visit and he sat on the bed for a long time, emitting a word or two every so often, standing up and sitting down again. Finally with a sigh he pulled an IOU from his pocket and asked Trotta to co-sign it. Trotta signed. It was for fifteen hundred crowns. Kapturak had expressly asked for Trotta's guarantee. Captain Wagner grew very animated, told a detailed story about a racehorse he was planning to buy for a song, hoping to race it in Baden; he added a few jokes and suddenly took off.

Two days later the head physician appeared at Trotta's bedside, pale and anxious, and explained that Captain Wagner was dead. He had shot himself in the border forest. He had left a farewell letter to all his fellow officers and best wishes for Lieutenant Trotta.

The lieutenant did not think about the IOUs or the consequences of his signature. He became feverish. He dreamed—and also said—that the dead were calling him and that it was time for him to leave this world. Old Jacques, Max Demant, Captain Wagner, and the unknown workers who had been shot were standing in a line and calling him. Between him and the dead stood a deserted roulette table, on which the ball, spun by no hand, kept rotating endlessly.

His fever dragged on for two weeks, a welcome pretext for the military authorities to postpone the inquiry and inform several political offices that the army likewise had victims to mourn, that the civil authorities in the border town bore the responsibility, and that the constabulary should have been reinforced in time. Immense files swelled around the Trotta case, and the files grew, and every department in every agency splattered a little more ink on them, the way one waters flowers, to make them grow. The entire matter was finally submitted to the Kaiser's military cabinet, because an especially circumspect senior assessor had discovered that the lieutenant was a grandson of that vanished Hero of Solferino, who had had a now thoroughly forgotten but in any case intimate connection with the Supreme Commander in Chief, and this lieutenant was bound to be of interest to supreme figures, and it would be better to wait before starting an investigation.

So one morning at seven, the Kaiser, just back from Ischl, had to deal with a certain Carl Joseph, Baron von Trotta und Sipolje.

And since the Kaiser was old, though refreshed by his sojourn in Ischl, he could not figure out why that name evoked the Battle of Solferino, and he left his desk and with the short steps of an old man he shuffled up and down his humble study, up and down, surprising his old valet, who, starting to worry, knocked on the door.

"Come in!" said the Kaiser, and, upon spotting his servant, "When is Montenuovo coming?"

"At eight A.M., Your Majesty!"

Eight A.M. was still half an hour away. The Kaiser felt he couldn't stand this uncertainty any longer. Now just why, oh, why did Trotta's name remind him of Solferino? And why couldn't he remember the link between them? Was he that old already? Since returning from Ischl, he had been haunted by the question of how old he really was, for it suddenly struck him as odd that you could tell your age by subtracting the year of your birth from the current calender year, but that each year began in January, while his birthday was the eighteenth of August! Now if the year began in August! And if, say, he had been born on the eighteenth of January, then it wouldn't have made much difference. But this way, you couldn't possibly know whether you were eighty-two and in your eighty-third year or eighty-three and in your eighty-fourth year. Nor did the Kaiser care to ask. People had a lot to do anyhow, and it didn't matter at all whether you were one year younger or older, and ultimately, even if you'd been younger, you still wouldn't have remembered why that damn Trotta reminded you of Solferino. The Comptroller of the Royal Household knew. But he wasn't due until eight o'clock. Maybe the valet knew?

And the Kaiser paused in his shuffling and asked the valet, "Listen, does the name Trotta ring a bell?"

Actually the Kaiser had meant to use the familiar form with his valet, as he often did, but he was dealing with an historic issue and he respected even the people whom he asked about historic events.

"Trotta?" said the Kaiser's valet. "Trotta!"

The valet too was old and he very vaguely remembered a schoolbook piece entitled "The Battle of Solferino." And all at once the memory radiated from his face like a sun. "Trotta!" he cried. "Trotta! He saved Your Majesty's life!"

The Kaiser went over to the desk. The jubilance of the morning birds of Schönbrunn came through the open window of the study. The Kaiser felt young again, and he heard the rattling of the rifles, and he felt someone grabbing his shoulders and yanking him to the ground. And suddenly he was very familiar with the name Trotta, just as he was with the name Solferino.

"Yes, yes," said the Kaiser, waving his hand, and on the edge of the Trotta dossier he wrote, *Settle favorably.*

Then he stood up again and shuffled over to the window. The birds were jubilating, and the old man smiled at them as if he could see them.

Chapter 15

THE KAISER WAS an old man. He was the oldest emperor in the world. All around him Death was circling, circling and mowing. The entire field was already cleared, and only the Kaiser, like a forgotten silver stalk, was still standing and waiting. For many years his bright hard eyes had been peering, lost, into a lost distance. His skull was bare like a vaulted wasteland. His whiskers were white like a pair of wings made of snow. The wrinkles in his face were a tangled thicket dwelt in by the decades. His body was thin, his back slightly bowed. At home he shuffled about. But upon going outdoors, he tried to make his thighs hard, his knees elastic, his feet light, his back straight. He filled his eyes with sham kindness, with the true characteristic of imperial eyes: they seemed to look at everyone who looked at the Kaiser, and they greeted everyone who greeted him. But actually, the faces merely swirled and floated past his eyes, which gazed straight at that soft fine line that is the frontier between life and death—gazed at the edge of the horizon, which is always seen by the eyes of the old even when it is blocked by houses, forests, or mountains.

People thought Franz Joseph knew less than they because he was so much older than they. But he may have known more than some. He saw the sun going down on his empire, but he said nothing. He knew he would die before it set. At times he feigned ignorance and was delighted when someone gave him a long-winded explanation about things he knew thoroughly. For with the slyness of children and oldsters he liked leading people down the garden path. And he was delighted at their vanity in proving to themselves that they were smarter than he. The Kaiser disguised his wisdom as simplicity: for it does not behoove an emperor to be as smart as his advisers. Far better to appear simple than wise. If he went hunting, he knew quite well that the game was placed in front of his rifle, and though he could have felled some other prey, he nevertheless shot only the prey that had been driven before his barrel. For it does not behoove an old emperor to show that he sees through a trick and can shoot better than a gamekeeper. If he was told a fairy tale, he pretended to believe it. For it does not behoove an emperor to catch someone in a falsehood. If people smirked behind his back, he pretended not to know about it. For it does not behoove an emperor to know he is being smirked at, and this smirk is foolish so long as he refuses to notice it. If he ran a fever, and people trembled all around him, and the court physician lied to him, telling him he had no fever, the emperor said, "Well, then, everything's fine," although he knew he had a fever. For an emperor does not accuse a medical man of lying. Besides, he knew that the hour of his death had not yet come. He also experienced many nights of being plagued by fever unbeknownst to his physicians. For sometimes he was ill, and no one realized it. And at other times he was well, and they said he was ill, and he pretended to be ill. When he was considered kind, he was indifferent. And when they said he was cold, his heart bled. He had lived long enough to know that it is foolish to tell the truth. So he allowed people their errors, and he believed less in the permanence of the world than did the wags who told jokes about him in his vast empire. But it does not behoove an emperor to compete with wags and sophisticates. So the Emperor held his tongue.

Even though he was well rested, and his physician was satisfied with his pulse, lungs, and respiration, he had had the sniffles since yesterday. He wouldn't dream of letting anyone notice. They might prevent him from attending autumn maneuvers on the eastern border, and he wanted to watch maneuvers again, at least for a day. The file on that man who'd saved his life, whose name had slipped his mind again, had conjured up Solferino. He didn't like wars (for he knew that one loses them), but he loved the military, the war games, the uniforms, the rifle drills, the parades, the reviews, and the company drills. He was sometimes vexed that the officers wore higher hats than he himself, sharp creases in their trousers, patent-leather shoes, and overly high collars on their tunics. Many were even clean-shaven. Just recently he had spotted a clean-shaven militia officer in the street, and his heart had been heavy the rest of the day. But when he went over to the people themselves, they again knew the difference between rules and mere swagger. He could snap at certain ones more grossly. For in the army everything behooved the emperor, in the army even the emperor was a soldier. Ah! He loved the blaring of the trumpets, though he always feigned interest in the operational plans. And while he knew that God Himself had placed him on his throne, he felt upset in weak moments that he was not a front-line officer, and he bore a grudge against the staff officers. He remembered how undisciplined the retreating troops had been after the Battle of Solferino, and he had chewed them out like a sergeant and gotten them back in line. He was convinced—but whom could he tell?—that ten good sergeants are a lot more useful than twenty general-staff officers. He yearned for maneuvers!

So he decided to conceal his sniffles and pull out his handkerchief just as little as possible. Nor was anyone to be forewarned; he wanted to surprise the maneuvers and all the people around him with his decision to attend. He looked forward to the despair of the civil authorities, who would not have provided enough police protection. He wasn't scared. He knew very well that the hour of his death had not yet come. He alarmed everyone. They tried to dissuade him. He dug in his heels. One day he stepped into the imperial train and rolled toward the east.

In the village of Z, not ten miles from the Russian border, they had prepared his quarters in an old castle. The Emperor would have rather been billeted in one of the huts assigned to the officers. For years now he had not been allowed to enjoy an authentically military life. Just once, during that unfortunate Italian campaign, he had, for example, seen a real-live flea in his bed but had told no one. For he was an emperor, and an emperor does not talk about insects. That had already been his opinion.

They closed the windows in his bedroom. At night, when he couldn't sleep, but all around him everyone who was supposed to guard him was asleep, the Emperor, in his long pleated nightshirt, crept quietly out of bed and softly, to avoid waking anyone, unlatched the narrow wings of the high window. He stood there for a while, breathing the coolness of the autumn night and gazing at the stars in the deep-blue sky and the reddish campfires of the soldiers.

Once he had read a book about his life, which said, "Franz Joseph I is no romantic." They write, the old man mused, that I'm no romantic. But I love campfires. He would have liked to be an ordinary lieutenant, to be young. I may not be the least bit romantic, he mused, but I wish I were young! If I'm not mistaken, he went on thinking, I was eighteen when I mounted the throne. When I mounted the throne: that sentence struck the Kaiser as very bold; at this moment it was hard for him to believe that he was the Kaiser. Certainly! It was written in the book that had been presented to him with the usual devout dedications. There was no doubt that he was Franz Joseph I! The infinite, deep-blue, starry night arched outside his window. The countryside was flat and vast. He had been told that these windows faced northeast. So you could see all the way to Russia. But the border, needless to say, was invisible. And at this moment Kaiser Franz Joseph would have liked to see the border of his empire. His empire! He smiled.

The night was blue and round and vast and full of stars. The Kaiser stood at the window, thin and old in a white nightshirt, and felt very tiny in the face of the immense night. The least of his soldiers, who could patrol in front of the tents, was more powerful than he. The least of his soldiers! And he was the Supreme Commander in Chief! Every soldier, swearing by God the Almighty, pledged his allegiance to Kaiser Franz Joseph I. He was a majesty by the grace of God, and he believed in God the Almighty, who hid behind the gold-starred blue of the heavens, the Almighty—inconceivable! It was His stars that shone up there in the sky, and it was His sky that arched over the earth, and He had allocated a portion of the earth, namely the Austro-Hungarian monarchy, to Franz Joseph I. And Franz Joseph I was a thin old man, standing at the open window and fearing that his guards might surprise him at any moment.

The crickets chirped. Their chant, as infinite as the night, aroused the same awe in the Kaiser as the stars. At times it sounded as if the stars themselves were singing. He shivered slightly. But he was afraid of closing the window; he might not manage as smoothly as before. His hands trembled. He remembered that he must have already attended maneuvers in these parts long ago. This bedroom likewise resurfaced from forgotten times. But he didn't know whether ten, twenty, or more years had elapsed since then. He felt as if he were drifting on the sea of time—not toward any goal but erratically, on the surface, often pushed back to the reefs, which looked familiar. Someday, somewhere, he would go under. He had to sneeze. Yes, his sniffles! No one stirred in the antechamber. Cautiously he latched the window, and his thin, naked feet fumbled their way back to bed. He took along the image of the blue starry round of the heavens. It was preserved in his closed eyes. And so he fell asleep, under the vault of night, as if lying outdoors.

He awoke punctually at oh-four-hundred hours, as he always did "in the field" (and that was what he called the maneuvers). His valet was already standing in the room. And the equerries, he knew, were already waiting outside the door. Yes, he had to start his day. He would scarcely have a moment to himself all day long. To make up for it, he had outwitted all of them that night by standing at the open window for a good quarter hour. He thought about that slyly filched pleasure and smiled. He smirked at the valet and also at the boy who now entered and froze lifeless, terrified by the Kaiser's smirk; by His Majesty's suspenders, which he saw for the first time in his life; by the tousled, slightly tangled whiskers, between which the smirk fluttered to and fro like an old, quiet, weary bird; by the Kaiser's sallow complexion; and by his bald, scaling scalp. They didn't know whether to smile with the old man or wait mutely. All at once the Kaiser began to whistle. He actually pursed his lips, his whiskers parted slightly, and he whistled a well-known melody, though slightly off key. It sounded like a shepherd's reedy piping. And the Kaiser said, "Hojos is always whistling this song! I'd like to know what it is!" But neither the valet nor the boy could tell him, and by the time the Kaiser was washing, a bit later, he had already forgotten about the song.

It was a heavy day. Franz Joseph looked at the slip outlining his agenda hour by hour. The only church in the village was Greek Orthodox. Mass would be celebrated first by a Roman Catholic priest, then by a Greek Orthodox priest. The most strenuous duties of all were the church ceremonies. He felt he had to pull himself together before God as if facing a superior. And he was old already. He could spare me any number of things! the Kaiser mused. But God is even older than I, and His decisions seem as unfathomable to me as mine seem to the soldiers in the army. And where would we be if every subordinate could criticize his superior?

Through the lofty arched windows the Kaiser saw God's sun rising. He crossed himself and genuflected. Since time immemorial he had seen the sun come up every morning. Most of his life he had gotten up first, just as a soldier gets up earlier than his superior. He knew all sunrises, the fiery and cheery ones in summer and the late, dreary, foggy ones in winter. And while he no longer recalled the dates, or the names of the days, the months, the years when disaster or good fortune had overtaken him, he did remember every morning that had ushered in an important day in his life. And he knew that a certain morning had been dismal and another cheerful. And every morning, he had crossed himself and genuflected, the way some trees open their leaves to the sun every morning, whether on a day of storm or a felling ax or deadly frost in spring or else days of peace and warmth and life.

The Kaiser stood up. His barber came. Every morning he regularly held out his chin, and his whiskers were trimmed and neatly brushed. The cold metal of the scissors tickled his nostrils and earlobes. At times the Kaiser had to sneeze. Today he sat before a small oval mirror, serenely and eagerly following the movements of the barber's thin hands. After every little hair that dropped, after every scrape of the razor and every tug of the comb or brush, the barber sprang back and breathed "Your Majesty!" with quivering lips. The Kaiser didn't hear those whispered words. He only saw the barber's lips in perpetual motion, didn't dare ask, and finally concluded that the man was a bit nervous.

"What's your name?" asked the Kaiser.

The barber—he had the rank of corporal, although he had been with the militia for just six months, but he served his colonel impeccably, enjoying the goodwill of his superiors—the barber sprang over to the door, his bearing elegant, as demanded by his craft, but also military: it was both a leap, a bow, and a stiffening at once, and the Kaiser nodded benignly.

"Hartenstein!" cried the barber.

"Why are you jumping like that?" asked Franz Joseph. But he received no answer.

The corporal timidly reapproached the Kaiser and completed his work with hasty hands. He wished he were far away and back at the camp.

"Hold on!" said the Kaiser. "Ah, you're a corporal! Have you been serving for a long time?"

"Six months, Your Majesty!" the barber breathed.

"I see, I see! Corporal already? In my day," said the Kaiser, as a veteran might have said, "it never went that fast. But then you're a very smart-looking soldier. Do you plan to stay in the military?"

Hartenstein the barber had a wife and child and a prosperous shop in Olomouc and had already tried feigning rheumatism several times in order to get out fairly soon. But he couldn't say no to the Kaiser. "Yes, Your Majesty," he said, knowing he had just messed up his entire life.

"Fine. Now you're a sergeant. But don't be so nervous!"

So. The Kaiser had made someone happy. He was glad. He was glad. He was glad. He had done something wonderful for that Hartenstein. Now the day could begin. His carriage was waiting. They slowly drove uphill to the Greek Orthodox church on the peak. Its golden double cross sparkled in the morning sun. The military bands were playing the imperial anthem, "God Save." The Kaiser stepped down and entered the church. He knelt at the altar, moving his lips but not praying. He kept thinking about the barber. The Almighty could not show the Kaiser such sudden favors as the Kaiser could show a corporal, and that was too bad. King of Jerusalem: that was the highest rank God could award a majesty. And Franz Joseph was already King of Jerusalem. Too bad, the Kaiser mused. Someone whispered to him that the Jews were waiting for him outside in the village. They had forgotten all about the Jews. Ah, now those Jews too! the Kaiser thought, distressed. Fine! Let them come. But they had to step on it! Otherwise they'd be late for the fighting.

The Greek Orthodox priest hurried through the mass. The bands launched again into the imperial anthem. The Kaiser emerged from the church. It was oh-nine-hundred hours. The fighting was to start at oh-nine-twenty. Franz Joseph decided to mount a horse instead of climbing back into the carriage. Those Jews could just as well be received on horseback. He sent off the carriage and rode out toward the Jews. At the end of the village, by the start of the wide highway leading to his quarters and also to the battle site, they billowed toward him, a dark cloud. Like a field of strange black stalks in the wind, the congregation of Jews bowed to the Kaiser. He could see their bent backs from his saddle. Then, riding closer, he could make out their long, flowing, silvery-white, coal-black, and fiery-red beards, which stirred in the gentle autumn breeze, and the long bony noses, which seemed to be hunting for something on the ground. The Kaiser sat, in his blue coat, on his white horse. His whiskers shimmered in the silvery autumn sun. White mists rose from the fields all around.

The leader of the Jews, a patriarch with a wafting beard in a white prayer shawl with black stripes, flowed toward the Kaiser. The Kaiser paced his horse. The old Jew trudged slower and slower. Eventually he seemed to both pause in one spot yet keep moving. Franz Joseph shivered slightly. He suddenly halted, and his white horse reared. The emperor dismounted. So did his retinue. He walked. His glossy boots became covered with highway dust, and their narrow edges were coated with heavy gray mire. The black throng of Jews billowed toward him. Their backs rose and sank. Their coal-black, fiery-red, and silvery-white beards wafted in the soft breeze. The patriarch stopped three paces from the Kaiser. In his arms he carried a huge purple Torah scroll topped by a gold crown with tiny, softly jingling bells. The Jew then lifted the Torah scroll toward the Emperor. And in an incomprehensible language his toothless, wildly overgrown mouth babbled the blessing that Jews must recite upon seeing an emperor. Franz Joseph lowered his head. Fine silvery gossamer floated over his black cap, the wild ducks shrieked in the air, a rooster hollered in a distant farmyard. Otherwise there was silence. A dark muttering rose from the throng of Jews. Their backs bowed even deeper. The silver-blue sky stretched cloudless and infinite over the earth.

"Blessed art thou," the Jew said to the Kaiser. "Thou shalt not live to see the end of the world."

I know! thought Franz Joseph. He shook the old man's hand. He turned around. He mounted his white horse.

He trotted to the left over the hard clods of the autumnal fields, his suite behind him. The wind brought him the words that Captain Kaunitz said to the friend riding at his side: "I didn't understand a thing the Jew said."

The Kaiser turned in his saddle and said, "He was speaking only to me, my dear Kaunitz," and rode on.

Franz Joseph could make no sense of the maneuvers. All he knew was that the Blues were fighting the Reds. He had everything explained to him. "I see, I see," he kept saying. He was delighted that the others believed he wanted to understand but couldn't. Idiots! he thought. He shook his head. But they thought his head was waggling because he was an old man. "I see, I see," the Kaiser kept saying. The operations were fairly advanced by now. For the past two days, the left wing of the Blues, stationed a few miles outside the village of Z, had been constantly retreating from the cavalry of the Reds, who kept thrusting forward. The center held the terrain around P, a hilly area, hard to attack, easy to defend, but also vulnerable to being surrounded if the Reds— and this was what they were now concentrating on—succeeded in cutting the two wings of the Blues off from their center. Though the left wing was in retreat, the right wing never flinched; indeed, it gradually pushed ahead, showing a tendency to fan out, as if intent on circling the enemy's flank. To the Kaiser's mind, the situation was quite banal. Had *he* been leading the Reds, he would have kept retreating farther and farther, enticing the impetuous wing of the Blues to focus its combat strength on the outermost lines until he eventually found an exposed position between that wing and the center.

But the Kaiser said nothing. He was distressed by the monstrous fact that Colonel Lugatti, a Triestino, vain as, in Franz Joseph's unshakable opinion, only an Italian could be, was wearing a high overcoat collar, even higher than was permitted for a tunic; nevertheless he displayed his rank by leaving that dreadfully high collar coquettishly open.

"Tell me, Herr Colonel," asked the Kaiser, "where do you have your overcoats made, in Milan? Unfortunately, I've totally forgotten the names of the Milanese tailors."

Staff Colonel Lugatti clicked his heels and buttoned his overcoat collar.

"Now people could mistake you for a lieutenant," said Franz Joseph. "You look young, you know!"

And he put spurs to his white horse and galloped up the hill, where, quite in keeping with older battles, the generals were stationed. The Kaiser was determined to stop the "fighting" if it lasted too long, since he yearned to see the march-past. Franz Ferdinand would certainly take a different approach. He would favor one army, side with it, start ordering it around, and always win, of course. Where was there a general who would have beaten the successor to the throne? The Kaiser's old pale-blue eyes swept over the faces. Vain sorts, all of them! he mused. A few short years ago he would have been annoyed. But no more, no more! He wasn't quite sure how old he was, but when the others surrounded him he felt he must be very old. Sometimes he felt he was actually floating away from people and from the earth. They all kept shrinking the longer he gazed at them, and their words reached his ears as if from a remote distance and fell away, indifferent clangs. And if someone met with some disaster, the Kaiser saw that they went to great lengths to inform him gingerly. Ah, they didn't realize he could endure anything! The great sorrows were already at home in his soul, and the new sorrows merely joined the old ones like long-awaited brothers. He no longer got annoyed so dreadfully. He no longer rejoiced so intensely. He no longer suffered so painfully. Now he did in fact "stop the fighting," and the march-past was to begin.

They fell in on the boundless fields, the regiments of all branches, unfortunately in field gray (another newfangled innovation that was not to the Kaiser's liking). Nevertheless, the bloody red of the cavalry trousers still blazed over the parched yellow of the stubble fields, erupting from the gray of the infantrists like fire from clouds. The matte, narrow glints of the swords flashed before the marching columns and double columns; the red crosses on white backgrounds shone behind the machine-gun divisions. The artillerists rolled along like ancient war gods on their heavy chariots, and the beautiful dun and chestnut steeds reared in strong, proud compliance.

Through his binoculars Franz Joseph watched the movements of each individual platoon; for several minutes he felt proud of his army and for several minutes he also felt sorry to lose it. For he already saw it smashed and scattered, split up among the many nations of his vast empire. The huge golden sun of the Hapsburgs was setting for him, shattered on the ultimate bottom of the universe, splintering into several tiny solar balls that had to shine as independent stars on independent nations.

They just don't want to be ruled by me anymore! thought the old man. What can you do? he added to himself. For he was an Austrian.

So to the dismay of all the chiefs he descended from his hill and began inspecting the motionless regiments, almost platoon by platoon. And occasionally he walked between the lines, viewing the new kit bags and the bread pouches, now and then pulling out a tin can and asking what was in it, now and then spotting a blank face and asking it about its homeland, family, and occupation, barely hearing the replies, and sometimes stretching out an old hand and clapping a lieutenant on the back. In this way he reached the rifle battalion in which Trotta served.

Four weeks had passed since Trotta had left the hospital. He stood in front of his platoon, pale, gaunt, and apathetic. But as the Kaiser drew nearer, Trotta began to notice his apathy and regret it. He felt he was shirking a duty. The army had become alien to him. The Supreme Commander in Chief was alien to him. Lieutenant Trotta resembled a man who has lost not only his homeland but also his homesickness for his homeland. He pitied the white-bearded oldster who drew nearer and nearer, curiously fingering kit bags, bread pouches, tin cans. The lieutenant wished for the intoxication that had overcome him in all festive moments of his military career: at home, during the summer Sundays, on his father's balcony, at every parade, when he had received his commission, and just a few months ago at the Corpus Christi pageant in Vienna. Nothing stirred in Lieutenant Trotta as he stood five paces in front of his Kaiser, nothing stirred in his thrust-out chest except pity for an old man. Major Zoglauer rattled out the regulation formula. For some reason the Kaiser didn't like him. Franz Joseph suspected that things weren't quite as they should be in the battalion commanded by this man, and he decided to have a closer look. He gazed hard at the unstirring faces, pointed to Carl Joseph, and asked, "Is he sick?"

Major Zoglauer reported what had happened to Lieutenant Trotta. The name rang a bell in Franz Joseph, something familiar yet irksome, and he recalled the incident as described in the files, and behind the incident that long-slumbering incident at the Battle of Solferino. He could still plainly see the captain who, in a ridiculous audience, had so insistently pleaded for the removal of a patriotic selection from a reader. Selection No. 15. The Kaiser remembered the number with the pleasure aroused by minor evidence of his "good memory." His mood improved visibly. Major Zoglauer seemed less unpleasant.

"I remember your father very well," the Kaiser said to Trotta. "He was very modest, the Hero of Solferino!"

"Your Majesty," the lieutenant replied, "that was my grandfather."

The Kaiser took a step back as if shoved away by the vast thrust of time that had suddenly loomed up between him and the boy. Yes, yes! He could still recall the selection number but not the legion of years that he had already lived through.

"Ah!" he said. "So that was your grandfather! I see, I see! And your father is a colonel, isn't he?"

"District commissioner of W."

"I see, I see!" Franz Joseph repeated. "I'll make a note of it," he added, as if vaguely apologizing for the mistake he had just made.

He stood in front of the lieutenant for a while, but he saw neither Trotta nor the others. He no longer felt like striding along the lines, but he had to go on lest people realized he was frightened by his own age. His eyes, as usual, peered into the distance, where the edges of eternity were already surfacing. But he failed to notice that a glassy drop appeared on his nose, and that everyone was staring, spellbound, at that drop, which finally fell into his thick, silvery moustache, invisibly embedding itself.

And everyone felt relieved. And the march-past could begin.

PART THREE

Chapter 16

VARIOUS MAJOR CHANGES were occurring in the district captain's home and life. He noted them, astonished and a bit grim. Minor signs—which, however, he regarded as tremendous—convinced him that the world was changing all around him, and he thought about its doom and about Chojnicki's prophecies. He was looking for a new butler. Much younger and clearly respectable men with impeccable references had been recommended to him, men who had served in the army for three years and had even made sergeant. The district captain took one or another into his home on a trial basis. He kept none, however. Their names were Karl, Franz, Alexander, Joseph, Alois, or Christoph, or whatever. But he tried to call each one "Jacques." After all, the real Jacques had originally been christened something else and only adopted this name and proudly borne it his entire long life, the way a famous poet bears his nom de plume, under which he writes immortal songs and poems. Within a few days, however, it turned out that the Aloises, the Alexanders, the Josephs, and the others refused to respond to the illustrious name of Jacques, and the district captain regarded this unruliness not only as insubordination toward him and toward the order of the world but also as an insult to the irrevocable dead. What? They minded being called Jacques? These good-for-nothings without experience or caliber, intelligence or discipline?

The dead Jacques lived on in the district captain's memory as a servant of exemplary qualities, as the very model of a human being. And surprised as Herr von Trotta was at the unruliness of the successors, he was even more amazed at the carelessness of the employers and authorities who had written favorable references for such miserable wretches. Take a certain individual named Alexander Cak, a man whose name he would never forget, a name spoken with a certain malice, so that if the district captain pronounced that name, it sounded as if Cak had been shot. Now if it was at all possible that this Cak belonged to the Social Democratic Party, yet had made sergeant in his regiment, then one had to despair not only of this regiment but of the entire army. And the army, in the district captain's opinion, was the only force that you could still rely on in the monarchy.

The district captain felt as if the whole world were suddenly made up of Czechs—a people he viewed as unruly, hardheaded, and stupid and as the inventors of the very concept of "nation." A lot of peoples might exist, but no nations. And besides, the governor's office kept sending him various barely comprehensible decrees and orders detailing a gentler treatment of "national minorities"—one of the terms that Herr von Trotta hated most, for by his lights "national minorities" were nothing but large communities of "revolutionary individuals." He was totally surrounded by revolutionary individuals. He even thought he noticed that they were multiplying unnaturally, in a way that was not suitable for human beings. It had become quite clear to the district captain that the "loyal elements" were growing less and less fertile and bearing fewer and fewer children, as proved by the census statistics, which he sometimes leafed through. He could no longer squelch the dreadful thought that providence itself was displeased with the monarchy; and although he was, in the usual sense, a practicing but not very devout Christian, he nevertheless tended to assume that God Himself was punishing the Kaiser.

Indeed, he was having all kinds of strange thoughts. The dignity he had borne since the first day on which he had become district captain of W had instantly aged him. Granted, even when his whiskers had still been black, nobody would have ever dreamt of regarding Herr von Trotta as a young man. Yet it was only now that the people in his small town were starting to say that the district captain was growing old. He had been forced to discard all sorts of long-ingrained habits. Thus, since old Jacques's death and his son's return from the border garrison, Herr von Trotta had stopped taking his pre-breakfast constitutional, lest any of the suspect and so frequently changing wretches who served him forgot to place the mail on the breakfast table or open the window. He despised his house-keeper. He had always despised her but had addressed her now and then. Ever since old Jacques had stopped serving, the district captain refused to speak at the table. For in reality his nasty comments had always been for Jacques's benefit and were, to some extent, meant to court his approval. Only now that the old man was dead did Herr von Trotta realize that he had spoken only for Jacques, like an actor who knows that a seasoned admirer of his art is sitting in the orchestra. And if the district captain had always eaten hastily, he now strove to leave the table after a few nibbles. For he felt it was blasphemous enjoying the garnished roast while the worms were devouring old Jacques in the grave. And if he glanced upward now and then, hoping with an innate piety that the dead man was in heaven and could see him, the district captain saw only the familiar ceiling of his room, for he had abandoned his simple faith, and his senses no longer obeyed the dictates of his heart. Oh, it was dreadful!

Now and then the district captain even forgot to go to the office on normal days. And on some mornings, say, on a Thursday, he would actually slip into his black Sunday coat in order to go to church. It was not until he was outdoors that all sorts of indubitable weekday signs convinced him it was not Sunday, so that he turned around and changed into his everyday suit. Then again he forgot to go to church on some Sundays, while remaining in bed longer than usual and remembering that it was Sunday only when Kapellmeister Nechwal appeared down below with his musicians. Roast garnished with vegeta-bles was served, as on all Sundays. And Herr Nechwal came for coffee. They sat in the study. They smoked Virginia cigars. Herr Nechwal had likewise gotten older. He was due to retire soon. He did not travel to Vienna so often now, and when he told jokes, even the district captain felt he had known them verbatim for years. He still did not understand them, but he recognized them, like certain people he kept running into without knowing their names.

"How is your family?" asked Herr von Trotta.

"Thank you, they're doing just fine," said the kapellmeister.
"How is Frau Nechwal?"

"Very well!"

"And the children?"—for the district captain still did not
know whether Herr Nechwal had sons or daughters, which was
why for twenty years now he had been cautiously asking about
the "children."

"My eldest boy has made lieutenant!" replied Nechwal.

"Infantry, naturally?" Herr von Trotta asked out of habit,
then promptly remembered that his own son was now serving
with the riflemen and not the cavalry.

"Yessir, infantry!" said Nechwal. "He'll be visiting us soon. I
hope you will permit me to present him to you."

"Please, by all means, I'd be delighted!" said the district
captain.

One day young Nechwal called on him. He was serving with
the German Masters (an infantry regiment), had received his
commission a year earlier, and looked, in Herr von Trotta's
opinion, like a "fiddler."

"You take after your father," said the district captain, "his spit
'n' image," although young Nechwal actually resembled his
mother more than the kapellmeister. "Like a fiddler": the district
captain was referring to a very specific carefree dash in the lieutenant's face, the tiny, blond, twirled-up moustache that lay like a
curling horizontal bracket under the short broad nose, and the
well-shaped, symmetrical, doll-like little ears that seemed made
of porcelain, and the neat sunny hair parted down the middle.

"A jolly-looking boy!" said Herr von Trotta to Herr Nechwal. "Are you content?" he then asked the boy.

"Frankly, Herr District Captain," the kapellmeister's son
replied, "it's a little boring."

"Boring?" asked Herr von Trotta. "In Vienna?"

"Yes," said young Nechwal, "boring! You know, Herr District Captain, if you're stationed in a small garrison, you never
even realize you don't have money!"

The district captain was offended. He felt it was not proper to
talk about money, and he was afraid that young Nechwal was
alluding to Carl Joseph's better financial position.

"My son *is* serving on the border," said Herr von Trotta, "but he has always managed well. Even in the cavalry." He stressed that last word. This was the first time he felt embarrassed that Carl Joseph had left the lancers. People like Nechwal certainly did not turn up in the cavalry! And the sheer thought that this bandmaster's son imagined he resembled young Trotta in any way caused the district captain almost physical pain. He decided to nail this "fiddler." He downright smelled treason in this boy, whose nose looked Czech.

"Do you like serving in the army?" asked the district captain.

"Frankly," said Lieutenant Nechwal, "I could imagine a better profession."

"What do you mean, a better one?"

"A more practical one," said young Nechwal.

"Isn't it practical to fight for your country?" asked Herr von Trotta. "Assuming, of course, that a man has a practical mind."

It was clear that he put an ironical stress on the word "practical."

"But we don't fight," retorted the lieutenant. "And if ever we *did* fight, it might not be all that practical."

"Why not?" asked the district captain.

"Because we're sure to lose the war," said Nechwal the lieutenant. "This is a different era," he added—and not without malice, or so it sounded to Herr von Trotta. The lieutenant narrowed his small eyes so they vanished almost entirely, and in a way that seemed quite unendurable to the district captain, his upper lip bared his gum, his moustache touched his nose, which, in Herr von Trotta's opinion resembled the broad nostrils of some animal. A thoroughly repulsive fellow, the district captain thought.

"A new era," young Nechwal repeated. "All these ethnic groups won't be hanging together for long!"

"I see," said the district captain. "And how do you know all this, Herr Lieutenant?" And the district captain simultaneously knew that his scorn was pointless, and he felt like an old soldier flashing his harmless, powerless sword against a foe.

"Everyone knows," said the boy, "and they say so too!"

"Say so?" Herr von Trotta repeated. "Do your comrades say so?"

"Yes, they say so!"

The district captain lapsed into silence. All at once he felt he was standing on a high mountain facing Lieutenant Nechwal, who was down in a deep valley. Lieutenant Nechwal was very tiny! But even though he was tiny and far below, he was right all the same. And the world was no longer the old world. It was about to end. And it was quite in order that an hour before its end the valleys should prove the mountains wrong, the young the old, the stupid the sensible. The district captain remained silent. It was a Sunday afternoon in summer. The yellow blinds filtered golden sunlight into the study. The clock ticked. The flies buzzed. The district captain remembered that summer day when his son, Carl Joseph, had arrived in the uniform of a cavalry lieutenant. How much time had passed since that day? A few years. But during those years, the district captain felt, events had been piling up fast and thick. It was as if the sun had risen twice a day and set twice a day; as if every week had had two Sundays and every month sixty days and the years had been double years. And yet Herr von Trotta felt cheated by time even though it had given him twice as much; it was as if eternity had offered him double pseudo-years instead of single genuine ones. And while he despised the lieutenant who stood opposite him, deep down in his vale of tears, he distrusted the mountain on which he himself stood. Oh! It was all so unjust! Unjust, unjust! For the first time in his life the district captain felt like a victim of injustice.

He yearned for Dr. Skowronnek, the man he had been playing chess with every afternoon for several months now. For even the regular chess game was one of the changes in the district captain's life. He had known Dr. Skowronnek a long time, just as he knew the other café patrons, no more and no less. One afternoon they were sitting across from one another, each half-covered by an unfolded, outspread newspaper. As if at a command, they both put down their newspapers, and their eyes met. Instantly and simultaneously they realized they had been reading the same item. It was a report on a summer festival in Hietzing, where a butcher named Alois Schinagl had won the rib-eating competition by dint of his preternatural gluttony and been awarded the Gold Medal of the Food Contest Association of Hietzing. And the eyes of the two men said in unison: We like meat too, but awarding a gold medal for this kind of thing is really a newfangled crackpot notion! Whether there is love at first sight is rightfully questioned by experts. But there is no question about friendship at first sight, a friendship between elderly men. Dr. Skowronnek peered at the district captain over the rimless oval lenses of his spectacles, and at the same moment the district captain took off his pince-nez. He raised it. And Dr. Skowronnek stepped over to the district captain's table.

"Do you play chess?" asked Dr. Skowronnek.

"Gladly!" said the district captain.

They did not have to make appointments. They met every afternoon at the same time. They arrived simultaneously. Their daily habits seemed governed by a harmonious accord. While playing they barely exchanged a word. Nor did they need to converse. On the small chessboard their gaunt fingers sometimes bumped into one another like people in a small square, jerked back, and returned home. But however casual these touches, their fingers virtually had eyes and ears, perceiving everything about one another and about the men they belonged to. And after their hands had bumped into one another several times, both the district captain and Dr. Skowronnek felt as if they had known each other for years and had no secrets from each other. And so one day gentle conversation began to surround their games, and their remarks about weather and world, politics and people floated over their hands, which were long since intimate. An estimable man! the district captain thought about Dr. Skowronnek. An extraordinarily fine man! Dr. Skowronnek thought about the district captain.

Most of the year Dr. Skowronnek had nothing to do. He worked only four months out of the twelve as a spa physician in Frantiskovy Lazne, and his entire knowledge of the world was based on the confessions of his female patients. For these women told him everything that preyed on their minds, and there was nothing in the world that did not prey on their minds. Their health suffered from their husbands' professions as well as from their lack of attention, from the "overall agony of the times," from the rising cost of living, from the political crises, from the constant threat of war, from the newspapers their husbands subscribed to, from having nothing to do, from the unfaithfulness of lovers, the indifference of men, but also from their jealousy. In this way, Dr. Skowronnek got to know the various classes of people and their home life, their kitchens and bedrooms, their passions, propensities, and stupidities. And since he did not believe everything he heard from the women, accepting only three-fourths of what they told him, he eventually acquired an excellent knowledge of the world, a knowledge more valuable than his medical science. Even when he spoke with men, the skeptical yet obliging smile of a man who is ready to hear anything hovered on his lips. A sort of aloof kindness shone from his small puckered face. And, in fact, he liked people as much as he looked down on them.

Did Herr von Trotta's simple soul have any inkling of Dr. Skowronnek's warm slyness? In any case the physician was the first person for whom the district captain began to feel esteem and trust since his boyhood friend Moser.

"Have you been living in our town for a long time, Herr Doctor?" he asked.

"Since my birth," said Skowronnek.

"Too bad, too bad," said the district captain, "that we've met so belatedly."

"I've known you for a long time, Herr District Captain," said Skowronnek.

"I've occasionally seen you," replied Herr von Trotta.

"Your son was here once," said Skowronnek. "That was a few years ago."

"Yes, yes, I remember!" said the district captain.

He thought about the afternoon when Carl Joseph had come with the letters of Frau Slama, who was dead. It was summer. It had rained. The boy had ordered a bad cognac at the counter.

"He got himself transferred," said Herr von Trotta. "He's now serving with the riflemen on the border, in B."

"And he's a great source of pride for you?" asked Skowronnek. But he wanted to say "problems."

"Yes, he really is! Certainly! Yes!" the district captain replied. He stood up very swiftly and left Dr. Skowronnek.

He had long been toying with the idea of telling Dr. Skowronnek about all the problems. He was growing old; he needed a good listener. Every afternoon the district captain again resolved to talk to Dr. Skowronnek. But he did not come out with the right words for initiating an intimate conversation. Dr. Skowronnek looked forward to it daily. He sensed that the time had come for the district captain to open up.

For several weeks now the district captain had been carrying a letter from his son in his breast pocket. Herr von Trotta had to answer it, but he couldn't. Meanwhile the letter grew heavier and heavier, almost a burden. Soon the district captain felt as if he were carrying the letter on his old heart. For Carl Joseph had written that he was thinking of leaving the army. Indeed, the very first sentence of his letter read, *I am toying with the idea of quitting the military.* Upon reading that sentence, the district captain broke off and glanced at the signature to make certain that no one but Carl Joseph had written the letter. Then Herr von Trotta put away the pince-nez he used for reading, and the letter as well. He leaned back in his chair. He sat in his office. The official correspondence had not yet been opened. It might have contained important matters, issues to be addressed without delay, but things concerning his work seemed to have been taken care of in the most unsatisfactory way by Carl Joseph's words. For the first time in his life the district captain subordinated his official duties to his personal experiences. And however modest, nay, humble a state servant he may have been, his son's thoughts of leaving the army affected Herr von Trotta as profoundly as if he had been notified that the entire Imperial and Royal Army had made up its mind to disband. Everything, everything in the world seemed meaningless. The end of the world was nigh! And when the district captain nevertheless decided to read the official mail, he felt he was performing a futile and anonymous act of heroism, like, say, the radio operator on a sinking ship.

It was only more than an hour later that he went on reading his son's letter. Carl Joseph was requesting his approval. And the district captain replied as follows:

My Dear Son,
 Your letter has shaken me to the core. I must wait a bit before informing you of my final decision.

           Your Father

Carl Joseph did not respond to this letter. In fact, his regular series of standard reports broke off, so that the district captain did not hear from him for a long time. The old man waited every morning, knowing all the while that he was waiting in vain. And it was not that the expected letter failed to arrive every morning but that the expected and dreaded silence came every morning. The son kept silent. But the father heard his silence. It was as if the son were once again terminating his obedience to the old man every day. And the more time dragged by without Carl Joseph's reports, the harder it was for the district captain to write the promised letter. While he had at first taken it for granted that he would simply prohibit the boy from leaving the army, Herr von Trotta now gradually started believing that he no longer had a right to prohibit anything.

He was quite despondent, the Herr District Captain. His whiskers grew more and more silvery. His temples were already completely white. His head sometimes drooped to his chest, and his chin and his whiskers lay on his starched shirt. Thus he suddenly fell asleep in his chair, jumped up after a few minutes, and imagined he had slept an eternity. He had lost his meticulous sense of the passing of time ever since he had given up several old habits. For after all, the hours and the days were meant precisely to maintain those habits, and now the hours and the days resembled empty vessels that could no longer be filled and that need not be bothered with anymore. The only thing the district captain showed up for punctually was the afternoon chess game with Dr. Skowronnek.

One day he received a surprise visit. While hunched over some papers in his office, he heard the familiar blustery voice of his boyhood friend Moser and his clerk's useless efforts to repel the professor. The district captain rang his bell and had the visitor ushered in.

"Good day, Herr Governor!" said Moser. Given his slouch hat, his portfolio, and his lack of a coat, he did not look like someone who had taken a trip and had just gotten off the train; he seemed to be coming from the house across the way. And the district captain was terrified at the dreadful thought that Moser might be planning to settle permanently in W.

First the professor went back to the door, turned the key, and said, "Just so nobody walks in unexpectedly, my friend. It could hurt your career!"

Then he trudged back to the desk, embraced the district captain, and placed a resounding kiss on his bald head. Next he flopped down in the armchair by the desk, placed his hat and his portfolio on the floor in front of his feet, and fell silent.

Herr von Trotta likewise remained silent. He knew why Moser had come. He had sent the professor no money for three months. "I apologize!" said Herr von Trotta. "I'll pay you everything immediately! Please forgive me. I've had a lot of problems lately."

"I can imagine," replied Moser. "That son of yours is expensive! I see him in Vienna every other week. He looks like he's having a good time, the Herr Lieutenant."

The district captain stood up. He reached for his breast pocket. He felt Carl Joseph's letter there. He went over to the window. With his back toward Moser, his eyes fixed on the old chestnuts in the park, he asked, "Have you spoken to him?"

"We have a drink whenever we meet," said Moser. "He's certainly generous, your son!"

"So! He's generous!" Herr von Trotta repeated.

He hurried back to the desk, yanked out a drawer, counted through some banknotes, pulled out a few, and handed them to the painter. Moser inserted the money in his hat, between the felt and the threadbare lining, and stood up.

"One moment!" said the district captain. He went to the door, unlocked it, and told his assistant, "Take the Herr Professor to the station. He's going to Vienna. The train's leaving in one hour."

"Your devoted servant!" said Moser and bowed. The district captain waited a few minutes. Then he took his hat and cane and headed to the café.

He was a bit late. Dr. Skowronnek was already sitting at the table, with the figures already standing on the chessboard. Herr von Trotta sat down.

"Black or white, Herr District Captain?" asked Skowronnek.

"I'm not playing today," said the district captain. He ordered a cognac, drank it, and began. "I'd like to pick your brain, if you'd allow me."

"Please do!" said Skowronnek.

"It's about my son," the district captain went on. And in his slow, slightly nasal officialese, he described his problems as if talking about administrative matters to a government councilor. He classified his problems into main problems and subproblems, as it were. And item by item, in small paragraphs, he related his father's history, his own, and his son's. By the time he finished, all the patrons had vanished, and the greenish gas flames in the room had been lit and were hissing monotonously over the empty tables.

"Well, that's it!" the district captain concluded.

A long silence ensued between the two men. The district captain did not dare look at Dr. Skowronnek. And Dr. Skowronnek did not dare look at the district captain. They cast down their eyes as if they had caught each other in an embarrassing moment. At last Skowronnek said, "Could some woman be involved? What reason would your son have to be in Vienna so often?"

The district captain would certainly never have thought of a woman. But now he was at a loss as to why something that obvious had not instantly occurred to him. For everything— and it was certainly not much—that he had ever heard about the nefarious influence that women can exert on young men suddenly crashed into his brain, simultaneously liberating his heart. If it had been merely a woman who had triggered Carl Joseph's decision to leave the army, then, while nothing might be repaired as yet, they could at least see the cause of the disaster, and the end of the world was no longer the fault of dark, secret, unidentifiable forces that could not be warded off. A woman! he thought. No, he knew nothing about a woman. And he said in his officialese, "I have heard nothing about any female!"

"Female!" Dr. Skowronnek repeated with a smile. "It might possibly be a lady."

"So you believe," said the district captain, "that my son is seriously weighing marriage."

"Not even that," said Skowronnek. "One doesn't have to *marry* a lady."

He realized that the district captain was one of those simple souls who virtually have to be sent back to school, so he decided to treat him like a child that has to learn its native tongue. "Let's forget about the ladies, Herr District Captain. That's not the issue. For some reason or other, your son does not care to remain in the army. And I can understand that."

"You can understand?"

"Certainly, Herr District Captain! A young officer in our army cannot be satisfied with his career if he gives it any thought. He has to yearn for war, but he knows that war will spell the end of the monarchy."

"The end of the monarchy?"

"The end, Herr District Captain! I'm sorry. Let your son do as he wishes. Perhaps he'd be better suited for some other profession."

"Some other profession!" Herr von Trotta repeated. "Some other profession!" he said once again. There was a long pause. Then the district captain said for the third time, "Some other profession!"

He strove to familiarize himself with these words, but they remained as alien as, say, the words "revolutionary" or "national minorities." And the district captain felt he would not have to wait very long for the end of the world. He banged his gaunt fist on the table, his round cuff rattled, and the greenish lamp wobbled slightly above the small table. "What sort of profession, Herr Doctor?" He asked.

"He could," said Dr. Skowronnek, "perhaps get a job with the railroad."

An instant later the district captain saw his son in a conductor's uniform, holding a clipper to punch tickets. The word "job" sent a shudder through his old heart. He froze.

"Oh! You really think so?"

"I can't think of anything else," said Dr. Skowronnek. And since the district captain now got to his feet, Dr. Skowronnek likewise stood up, saying, "I'll walk you back."

They marched through the park. It was raining. The district captain did not open his umbrella. Here and there, heavy drops from the dense crowns of trees fell on his shoulders and his stiff hat. It was dark and still. Whenever they passed one of the meager streetlights, which concealed their silver tops in the dark foliage, the two men lowered their heads. And when they stood at the exit of the park, they hesitated for an instant. And Dr. Skowronnek abruptly said, "*Auf Wiedersehen*, Herr District Captain!" And Herr von Trotta crossed the street alone, toward the broadly arched entrance of his official residence.

He ran into his housekeeper on the stairs, said, "I'm not dining tonight, madam!" and hurried on. He wanted to take two steps at a time but, embarrassed, walked straight to his office with his usual dignity. This was the first evening since assuming his rank of district captain that he sat in his office. He lit the green table lamp, which burned in the afternoon only during winter. The windows were open. The rain beat vehemently against the metal windowsills. Herr von Trotta drew a sheet of official stationery from the drawer and wrote:

"Dear Son,
> *Upon careful deliberation, I have decided to leave the responsibility for your future to you. All I ask is that you inform me of your decisions.*
> > *Your Father*

Herr von Trotta sat in front of his letter for a long while. Several times he reread the two sentences he had penned. They sounded like his will. Earlier he would never have dreamt of taking his paternal role more seriously than his official role. But now that he was relinquishing his paternal authority with this letter, he felt that his life had lost all meaning and that he simultaneously had to stop being an official. What he was doing was not dishonorable, but he felt he was disgracing himself. He left his office, letter in hand, and went to the study. Here he lit all the lamps, the floor lamp in the corner and the lamp hanging from the ceiling, and stood in front of the portrait of the Hero of Solferino. He could not see his father's face sharply. The painting splintered into a hundred tiny, oily dabs and highlights, the mouth was a pale-red stroke, and the eyes were two black splinters of coal.

The district captain, who hadn't stood on a chair since boyhood, climbed up on one, stretched, stood on tiptoe, and, holding the pince-nez to his eyes, just barely made out Moser's signature in the portrait's lower right-hand corner. He clambered down somewhat arduously, stifled a sigh, backed up toward the wall, banged violently and painfully into a corner of the table, and began studying the picture from a distance. He extinguished the ceiling light, and in the deep dusk he thought that his father's face shimmered lifelike. It kept approaching and withdrawing, appeared to slip behind the wall and gaze into the room through an open window as if from immensely far away. Herr von Trotta felt a huge fatigue. He sat down in the armchair, adjusted it so that he was directly facing the portrait, and opened his vest. He heard the less and less frequent drops of the slackening rain, pattering hard and irregular against the windows, and from time to time he heard the wind soughing in the old chestnut trees opposite. He closed his eyes. And he nodded off, the letter in an envelope in his hand, which hung motionless over the arm of the chair.

When he awoke, full morning was streaming through the three big arched windows. The district captain first looked at the portrait of the Hero of Solferino, then he felt the letter in his hand, saw the address, read his son's name, and got up, sighing. His shirtfront was crumpled, his broad dark-red tie with white dots was twisted to the left, and for the first time since wearing long pants Herr von Trotta noticed dreadful horizontal creases in his striped trousers. He studied himself in the mirror for a while. He saw that his whiskers were tousled and that a few wretched gray hairs were curling on his bald head and that his prickly eyebrows were as straggly as if a small storm had swept across them. The district captain checked his watch. And since the barber was due any minute, Herr von Trotta tore off his clothes and slipped into bed, trying to feign a normal morning for the barber's benefit. But he kept the letter in his hand. And he held it while his face was lathered and shaved, and after that, when he was washing, the letter lay on the edge of the small table where the basin lay. It was only when the district captain sat down to breakfast that he handed the letter to his assistant, ordering him to dispatch it with the next government mail.

He went to work as on any other day. And no one would have been able to notice that Herr von Trotta had lost his faith, for he took care of his obligations no less meticulously than on other days. Except that his meticulousness was very, very different. Herr von Trotta resembled a virtuoso in whom the fire has died, whose soul has become empty and hollow, and whose fingers strike the right notes only with cold, seasoned precision thanks to their own dead memory. But, as we have said, no one noticed. And in the afternoon, Sergeant Slama came as usual. And Herr von Trotta asked him, "Tell me, Slama, have you ever remarried?"

He himself did not know why he asked this question today and why the constable's private life suddenly concerned him.

"No, Herr Baron," said Slama. "And I won't ever remarry!"

"You're doing the right thing!" said Herr von Trotta. But he did not know why the constable was doing the right thing by resolving not to remarry.

This was his normal time for appearing at the café, so that was where he went. The chessboard was already on the table. Dr. Skowronnek arrived at the same time, and they sat down.

"Black or white, Herr District Captain?" the doctor asked, as on any other day.

"Whatever you like," said the district captain.

And they began to play. Herr von Trotta played carefully today, almost reverently, and won.

"You're gradually turning into a real chess champion," said Skowronnek.

The district captain felt truly flattered. "Maybe I could have become one!" he replied. And he mused that it would have been better, that everything would have been better. "By the way, I've written to my son," he began after a while. "He can do as he likes."

"That sounds right to me," said Dr. Skowronnek. "One cannot bear responsibility. No man can bear responsibility for another."

"My father bore responsibility for me, and my grandfather for my father."

"Things were different back then," Skowronnek replied. "Now not even the Kaiser bears responsibility for his monarchy. Why, it even looks as if God Himself no longer wishes to bear responsibility for the world. It was easier in those days! Everything was so secure. Every stone lay in its place. The streets of life were well-paved. Secure roofs rested on the walls of the houses. But today, Herr District Captain, the stones on the street lie askew and confused and in dangerous heaps, and the roofs have holes, and the rain falls into the houses, and everyone has to know on his own which street he is taking and what kind of house he is moving into. When your late father said you would become a public official rather than a farmer, he was right. You have become a model official. But when you told your son he had to be a soldier, you were wrong. He is not a model soldier."

"Yes, yes!" confirmed Herr von Trotta.

"And that's why we should let everyone do as he wishes, each on his own path. When my children refuse to obey me, all I do is try not to lose my dignity. That is all one can do. I sometimes look at them when they're asleep. Their faces then look very alien to me, almost unrecognizable, and I see that they are strangers, from a time that is yet to come and that I will not live to see. My children are still very young. One is eight, the other ten, and they have round, rosy faces when they sleep. Sometimes I feel it is the cruelty of their time, the future, that overcomes the children in their sleep. I would not care to live that long."

"Yes, yes!" said the district captain.

They played another round, but this time Herr von Trotta lost. "I won't be a champion," he said mildly, virtually reconciled to his defects. It was late by now, the greenish gas lamps, the voices of silence, were already hissing, and the café was empty. They again walked home across the park. Tonight the evening was cheerful, and cheerful strollers came their way. The two men talked about the frequent rainfall that summer and about the dryness of the previous summer and the foreseeable harshness of the coming winter. Skowronnek went as far as the door of the district captain's residence. "You did the right thing with your letter, Herr District Captain," the doctor said.

"Yes, yes!" Herr von Trotta confirmed.

He entered, went to the table, and wordlessly choked down his half chicken with salad. The housekeeper stole anxious glances at him. She served the meals now that Jacques was dead. She left the room before the district captain, curtsying awkwardly just as the little girl had curtsied to her school principal thirty years ago. The district captain waved at her as if shooing flies. Then he rose and went to bed. He felt tired and almost ill; the previous night lay as a very distant dream in his memory but as a very close terror in his limbs.

He calmly fell asleep, believing the worst was over. He did not know—old Herr Trotta—that fate was brewing bitter grief for him while he slept. He was old and tired, and death was already lurking, but life would not yet let him go. Like a cruel host it held him fast at the table because he had not yet tasted all the bitterness that had been prepared for him.

Chapter 17

No, THE DISTRICT captain had not yet tasted the full measure of bitterness! Carl Joseph received his father's letter too late—that is, long after deciding to open no more letters and write no more. As for Frau von Taussig, she sent him wires. Like swift small swallows, they summoned him every other week. And Carl Joseph dashed to his closet, pulled out his gray civilian suit, his better, more important, and secret life, and changed clothes. Instantly he felt at home in the world he was about to enter; he forgot his military existence.

Taking Captain Wagner's place, Captain Jedlicek had come to the battalion from the First Lancers: a "good guy" with enormous bodily dimensions, broad, merry, as gentle as any giant, and open to any persuasion. What a man! The moment he arrived, everyone knew he was equal to this swamp and was stronger than the borderland. You could rely on him! He flouted all military rules, but as if he were knocking them over. He looked like the sort of man who could have devised and introduced and put through a new set of regulations. He needed lots of money, but it came pouring in from all sides. His comrades loaned him cash, co-signed his IOUs, pawned their rings and watches for him, wrote to their fathers for his sake and to their aunts. Not that they actually loved him, for love would have brought them closer to him, and he did not seem to want anyone getting close to him. Indeed, it would not have been easy for sheer physical reasons: his size, his girth, his forceful personality kept everyone at bay, and so he had no problem being good-natured.

"Just go on your trip," he told Lieutenant Trotta. "I'll take responsibility." He took responsibility, and he could take it. And he needed money every week. Lieutenant Trotta got it from Kapturak. He needed money himself, Trotta did. He felt it was wretched to show up at Frau von Taussig's home without money. He'd be an unarmed man entering an armed camp. How foolhardy! His needs gradually increased, and he took along higher and higher sums, but all the same he returned from each excursion with his very last crown, and he always resolved to take along more the next time. Occasionally he tried to account for the lost money, but he never managed to recall the individual expenses, and often he couldn't even do simple additions. Arithmetic was beyond him.

His small memo books could have testified to his pathetic efforts to keep order. Endless columns of figures lined each page. But they were tangled and mixed up: they virtually slipped through his fingers, they added themselves up and deceived him with wrong totals, they galloped away before his gaping eyes, they returned a moment later, fully changed and unrecognizable. He didn't even succeed in adding up his debts. Nor did he understand the interest. His loans vanished behind his debts like a hill behind a mountain. Nor did he understand how Kapturak calculated. And while he distrusted Kapturak's honesty, he had even less faith in his own arithmetic. In the end, he was bored by every number. And once and for all he gave up calculating, abandoned his efforts with the courage born of despair and impotence.

He owed Kapturak and Brodnitzer six thousand crowns. When he compared this sum with his monthly pay, it was gigantic even for his hazy conception of numbers. (And a third of his pay was deducted regularly.) Nevertheless he had slowly gotten used to the figure six thousand as if it were an overpowering but very old enemy. Why, in good moments the sum might even appear to be shrinking and losing strength. But in bad moments it seemed to be growing and gaining strength.

He went to Frau von Taussig. For weeks now he had been taking these brief, furtive trips as if they were sinful pilgrimages. Like the naive believers for whom a pilgrimage is a kind of delight, a distraction, and sometimes even a sensation, Lieutenant Trotta associated the goal of his pilgrimage with a number of things: the environment he lived in, his eternal longing for what he pictured as a free life, the civvies he put on, and the lure of the forbidden. He loved his trips. He loved the drive in a closed carriage to the station—ten minutes of imagining that he was incognito. He loved the borrowed hundred-crown bills in his breast pocket—they were his alone today and tomorrow, and no one could tell that they were borrowed and that they were already starting to grow and fatten in Kapturak's notebooks. Trotta loved his civilian anonymity when he passed through Vienna's North Station. Nobody recognized him. Officers and privates walked by. He didn't salute, nor was he saluted. Sometimes his arm rose on its own. He then quickly remembered his mufti and dropped his arm. His vest, for instance, was a source of childish pleasure. He thrust his hands in all its pockets, not knowing how to use them. And his vain fingers fondled the knot of his tie above the vest: it was the only tie he owned, a present from Frau von Taussig, but he still didn't know how to knot it despite countless efforts. The most dim-witted police detective would have seen at first glance that Lieutenant Trotta was an officer in civvies.

Frau von Taussig stood on the platform in North Station. Twenty years ago—she imagined it was fifteen, for she had been denying her age for so long that she herself was convinced her years had ground to a halt and would not go till the end—twenty years ago she had likewise stood in North Station, waiting for another lieutenant, albeit a cavalry lieutenant. She climbed up to the platform as if it were a fountain of youth. She submerged in the caustic haze of coal dust, in the hissing and steaming of shunting locomotives, in the dense ringing of signal bells. She wore a short travel veil. She imagined it had been fashionable fifteen years ago. But it had been twenty-five years ago, not even twenty! She loved waiting on the platform. She loved the moment when the train rolled in, and she spotted Trotta's ridiculous little dark-green hat at the compartment window and his beloved, perplexed young face. For she made Carl Joseph younger, as she did herself, made him more naive and more perplexed, as she did herself. The instant the lieutenant left the lowest footboard, her arms opened as they had opened twenty or rather fifteen years ago. And from the face she wore today, that earlier one emerged, the rosy, uncreased face she had worn twenty or rather fifteen years ago, a girl's face, sweet and slightly flushed. Around her throat, where two parallel rills were already digging in, she had hung the thin childish gold necklace that had been her sole ornament twenty or rather fifteen years ago. And, as she had done twenty or rather fifteen years ago, she rode with the lieutenant to one of those small hotels where concealed love blossomed in squalid, squeaking, and delicious bed paradises that were rented by the hour.

The strolls began. The amorous quarter hours in the young greenery of the Vienna Woods, the small sudden squalls of the blood. The evenings in the reddish twilight of opera boxes, behind drawn curtains. The caresses, well-known and yet surprising, which the experienced and yet unsuspecting flesh looked forward to. Her ears knew the oft-heard music, but her eyes knew only fragments of scenes. For in her opera box Frau von Taussig had always drawn the curtain or kept her eyes shut. The caresses, spawned by the music and virtually entrusted to the man's hands by the orchestra, were both cool and hot on her skin: long familiar and eternally youthful sisters, presents she thought she had often received but then forgotten and merely dreamt of some day receiving. The quiet restaurants opened up. The silent dinners began, in corners where the wine they drank seemed to have grown, ripened by the love that shone eternally here in the darkness. The parting came, a final embrace in the afternoon, harried by the ruthlessly ticking watch on the nightstand and already filled with the joyous prospect of their next meeting; and their haste in getting to the train; and the final kiss on the footboard; and the hope, abandoned in the last moment, of her traveling back with him.

Tired but imbued with all the sweetnesses of life and love, Lieutenant Trotta arrived back in his garrison. His orderly, Onufrij, had the uniform ready for him. Trotta changed in the back room of the restaurant and drove to the barracks. He went to the company office. Everything in order, nothing had happened. Captain Jedlicek was as cheery and merry, as healthy and massive as ever, Lieutenant Trotta felt both relieved and disappointed. In a secret nook of his heart he had hoped for a catastrophe that would make it impossible for him to remain in the army. He would then have gone straight back to Vienna. But nothing had happened. And so he had to wait for another twelve days, cooped up inside the four walls of the barrack square, within the tiny, desolate streets of this town. He glanced at the target dummies lining the walls of the barrack square. Small blue mannequins, riddled with bullets and then refurbished, they looked like wicked trolls, familiars of the barracks, threatening the barracks with the very weapons that they themselves were shot with—they were no longer targets but dangerous marksmen. As soon as Trotta reached the Hotel Brodnitzer, entered his bare room, and flopped down on the iron bed, he resolved not to return to the garrison after his next leave.

But he was incapable of acting on his decision, and he knew it. He was really waiting for some kind of strange fluke, something that would fall into his lap one day, forever liberating him from the military and from the necessity of leaving it of his own free will. The only thing he managed to do was to stop writing to his father and to leave a few letters from him unopened, intending to open them later on. Sometime later on. . . .

The next twelve days rolled by. He opened his closet, gazed at his civilian suit, and waited for the telegram. It always came at this time, at dusk, right before nightfall, like a bird coming home to its nest. But today it did not come, not even after nightfall. The lieutenant did not switch on a lamp, refusing to acknowledge the night. Fully dressed and with open eyes he lay on the bed. All the familiar voices of spring wafted in through the open window: the deep croaking of the frogs and, above it, the softer, clearer chirping of the crickets and in between the distant calls of the nocturnal jay and the songs of the boys and girls in the border village.

At last the telegram came. It informed the lieutenant that he could not visit this time. Frau von Taussig had gone to her husband. She wanted to get back soon but didn't know when. The text concluded with "a thousand kisses." Their number offended the lieutenant. She shouldn't have been so miserly, he thought. She could just as easily have wired a hundred thousand!

It hit him that he owed a debt of six thousand crowns. Compared with that a thousand kisses were a paltry number. He stood up to shut the closet door. There, clean and straight, a neatly pressed corpse, hung the free dark-gray civilian Trotta. The door shut upon him. A coffin: Buried! Buried!

The lieutenant opened the door to the corridor. Onufrij always sat there, silent or softly humming or with the harmonica at his lips, his hands cupped over it to muffle the notes. Sometimes Onufrij sat on a chair. Sometimes he squatted at the threshold. He should have left the military a year ago. He stayed on voluntarily. His village, Burdlaki, was located nearby. Whenever the lieutenant left town, Onufrij went to his village. He would take along a cherrywood stick and a white handkerchief with blue flowers, wrap enigmatic objects in this cloth, hang the bundle at the end of his stick, shoulder the stick, accompany the lieutenant to the station, wait until the departure of the train, stand in a rigid salute on the platform even if Trotta wasn't peering out the window, and then hike off to Burdlaki, between the swamps, along the safe narrow path lined with willows, the only path with no danger of sinking. Onufrij always came back in time to wait for Trotta. And he sat down outside Trotta's door, silent, humming, or playing the harmonica under his cupped hands.

The lieutenant opened the door to the corridor. "You can't go to Burdlaki today. I'm not leaving!"

"Yessir, Herr Lieutenant!" Onufrij stood in a rigid salute, a straight dark-blue line in the white corridor.

"You're to stay here!" Trotta repeated; he thought Onufrij hadn't understood.

But Onufrij only repeated, "Yessir!" And as if prove he understood more than he was told, he went downstairs and came back with a bottle of 180 Proof.

Trotta drank. The bare room grew homier. The naked electric bulb on its twisted wire, circled by whirring moths and swaying in the nocturnal wind, aroused fleeting cozy reflections on the brownish gloss of the table. Gradually Trotta's disappointment mellowed into a pleasurable pain. He formed a kind of alliance with his grief. Everything in the world was extremely sorrowful today, and he, the lieutenant, was the midpoint of this miserable world. It was for him that the frogs were croaking so dolefully; the rueful crickets were lamenting for him. It was for him that the spring night was imbued with such a sweet, gentle sorrow, that the stars were so unreachably high in the heavens; for him alone their light twinkled with unrequited yearning. The infinite sorrow of the world fitted in perfectly with Trotta's misery. He suffered in utter harmony with the suffering universe. From behind the deep-blue vault of the sky, God Himself gazed down at him in pity.

Trotta reopened his closet. There, forever dead, hung the free Trotta. At his side shone the saber that had belonged to Max Demant, his dead friend. In the trunk lay old Jacques's memento, the stone-hard root, next to the letters of Frau Slama, who was dead. And on the windowsill lay no less than three unopened letters from his father, who may likewise have died. Ohh! Lieutenant Trotta was not only sad and unhappy but also wicked, with a thoroughly wicked character! He returned to the table, poured himself another glass, and gulped it down.

In the corridor, outside the door, Onufrij was starting a new tune on his harmonica, the well-known song "Oh, Our Emperor." Trotta knew only the first few words in Ukrainian: "*Oh, nash tshizar, tshizareva.*" He hadn't managed to learn the local vernacular. Not only did he have a thoroughly wicked character, but his mind was tired and foolish. In short: he was an utter failure. His chest tightened. The tears were already welling up in his throat; soon they would reach his eyes. He drank another glass to ease their passage. Finally they gushed from his eyes. He put his arms on the table, bedded his head on his arms, and began sobbing wretchedly. He must have wept for some fifteen minutes. He didn't hear Onufrij breaking off his music, he didn't hear the knock on the door. It was only when the door closed that Trotta raised his head. And he saw Kapturak.

Trotta managed to hold back his tears and ask in a sharp voice, "What are you doing here?"

Kapturak, cap in hand, stood right by the door; he barely loomed above the knob. His yellowish-gray face was smiling. He was dressed in gray. He wore gray canvas shoes. Their edges were coated with the gray, fresh, shiny springtime mire of this land. A few small gray locks curled distinctly on his tiny skull. "Good evening!" he said with a slight bow. At the same time, his shadow flitted up the white door and instantly crumpled again.

"Where's my orderly?" asked Trotta. "And what do you want?"

"You haven't gone to Vienna this time," Kapturak began.

"I never go to Vienna," said Trotta.

"You don't need money this week," said Kapturak. "I was expecting you today. I wanted to inquire about you. I've just left Captain Jedlicek's room. He's not at home!"

"He's not at home," Trotta repeated apathetically.

"Right," said Kapturak. "He's not at home. Something's happened to him!"

Trotta did hear him say that something had happened to Captain Jedlicek. But he inquired no further. For one thing he wasn't curious. (He wasn't curious today.) Second, he felt that so terribly much had happened to him, too much, so he wasn't at all concerned about anyone else. Third, he had absolutely no interest in listening to anything Kapturak had to say. He was furious that Kapturak was here, but he didn't have the strength to do anything about the little man. A very vague memory of the six thousand crowns he owed his visitor kept resurfacing in him. An embarrassing memory; he wanted to suppress it. The money, he mentally tried to persuade himself, had nothing to do with his visit. They are two different persons: the one I owe money to is not here; the other, standing in this room, only wants to tell me something unimportant about Jedlicek. He stared at Kapturak. For a few seconds, his guest seemed to be melting and then piecing himself together out of gray, hazy splotches. The lieutenant waited until Kapturak was completely restored. It cost Trotta some effort to make quick use of that moment, for there was some danger that the small gray man might instantly melt and dissolve again. Kapturak came one step closer, as if aware that he was not distinctly visible to the lieutenant, and repeated somewhat louder, "Something has happened to the captain!"

"Well, just what has happened to him?" asked Trotta dreamily, as if asleep.

Kapturak took another step toward the table and whispered, cupping his hands over his mouth so that his whisper turned into a rustle, "He's been arrested and shipped off. On suspicion of espionage."

Upon hearing that word, the lieutenant rose. He now stood, propping both hands on the table. He barely sensed his legs. He felt he was standing on his hands. He almost buried them in the table. "I don't wish to hear anything about it from you," he said. "Get out!"

"Alas, impossible, impossible!" said Kapturak. He now stood close to the table, next to Trotta. Lowering his head as if confessing something shameful, he said, "I must insist on a partial repayment."

"Tomorrow!" said Trotta.

"Tomorrow!" repeated Kapturak. "Tomorrow may be impossible. You can see what surprises each day may bring. I've lost a fortune with the captain. Who knows whether we'll ever see him again? And you're his friend!"

"What did you say?" asked Trotta. He raised his hands from the table and suddenly stood firmly on his feet. It dawned on him that Kapturak had said something monstrous yet true, and it sounded monstrous only because he was telling the truth. At the same time, the lieutenant recalled the only moment in his life when he had been dangerous to other people. He wished he were as well armed now as then, with sword and pistol, and backed up by his platoon. This small gray man was a lot more dangerous than the hundreds of strikers had been. And to make up for his defenselessness, the lieutenant tried to fill his heart with an alien rage. He clenched his fists. He had never done this before, and he sensed that he could not be menacing, that he could at most only play a menacing person. A blue vein swelled on his forehead, his faced reddened, the blood rose to his eyes, and he glared. He succeeded in looking dangerous. Kapturak flinched.

"What did you say?" Trotta repeated.

"Nothing," said Kapturak.

"Repeat what you said!" Trotta commanded.

"Nothing," Kapturak replied.

For an instant he again dissolved into gray, hazy splotches. The lieutenant was overcome with a tremendous fear that the little man had the ghostly ability to crumble into bits and then piece himself back into a whole. The lieutenant was filled with an irresistible yearning to experience Kapturak's substance—a yearning similar to the indomitable passion of a scientist. In back of him, on the bedpost, hung the saber, his weapon, the defender of his military and private honor and oddly enough, at this moment, a magical instrument capable of exposing the law of governing sinister phantoms. He felt the glittering saber behind him and a magnetic force emanating from it. And virtually pulled by that force he jumped back, his eyes fixed on the endlessly disintegrating and reconstituting Kapturak. The lieutenant's left hand grabbed the scabbard, his right hand whipped out the blade. Kapturak jumped toward the door, and his cap slipped from his hands and landed at his gray canvas shoes; Trotta followed him, waving his saber. And without knowing what he was doing, the lieutenant held the point of his blade against the chest of the gray phantom, felt the resistance of cloth and body through the full length of steel, sighed in relief because he finally had proof that Kapturak was human—and yet the lieutenant was unable to drop the blade.

It was only for an instant. But in that instant Lieutenant Trotta heard, saw, and smelled everything that was alive in the world: the voices of the night, the stars in the sky, the light of the lamp, the objects in the room, his own shape—as if he were standing in front of it rather than carrying it—the dance of the mosquitoes around the light, the damp haze of the swamps, and the cool breath of the nocturnal wind. All at once Kapturak spread out his arms. His small thin hands dug into the right and the left doorpost. His bald head with its few gray curls sank to his shoulder. At the same time, he put one foot in front of the other, twisting his ludicrous gray shoes into a knot. And in back of him, on the white door, before Lieutenant Trotta's bulging eyes, there suddenly loomed the black, reeling shadow of a cross.

Trotta's hands trembled and he dropped the blade. It landed with a soft, jingly whimper. That same moment, Kapturak's arms sank. His head slid from his shoulder and slumped forward on his chest. His eyes were shut. His lips trembled. His whole body trembled. There was silence. They could hear the fluttering of the mosquitoes around the lamplight and, through the open window, the frogs, the crickets, and, intermittently, the nearby barking of a dog.

Lieutenant Trotta staggered. He turned around. "Sit down!" he said and pointed to the only chair in the room.

"Yes," said Kapturak, "I'll sit down."

As he stepped briskly toward the chair, briskly, as if—so it seemed to Trotta—nothing had happened, Kapturak's toes grazed the saber on the floor. He bent over and picked it up. As if assigned to make order in the room, he walked on, holding the naked steel between two fingers of a lifted hand, to the table where the scabbard lay. Without glancing at the lieutenant, Kapturak slipped in the saber and hung it back on the bedpost. Then he circled the table and sat down opposite Trotta, who remained standing. Only then did Kapturak look at him.

"I'm just staying for a moment," he said, "to recover."

The lieutenant held his tongue.

"Please have the entire sum for me a week from today, at this exact time," Kapturak went on. "I don't wish to haggle with you. It amounts to seven thousand two hundred fifty crowns in all. I must also inform you that Herr Brodnitzer is standing outside the door and has heard everything. This year, as you know, Count Chojnicki is returning later than normal, perhaps not at all. I would like to leave, Herr Lieutenant!"

He rose, walked to the door, bent down, picked up his cap, and took a last look around. The door shut behind him.

The lieutenant was now completely sober. Nevertheless, it all seemed like a dream. He opened the door. Onufrij sat on a chair as usual, even though it must have been very late. Trotta glanced at his watch. It was nine-thirty.

"Why aren't you in bed?" he asked.

"Because of visit!" replied Onufrij.

"Did you hear everything?"

"Everything!" said Onufrij.

"Was Brodnitzer here?"

"Yessir!" Onufrij confirmed.

There was no doubt about it, everything had happened just as Lieutenant Trotta had experienced it. So he had to report the whole matter the next morning. His fellow officers had not yet returned. He went from door to door; the rooms were empty. They must have been in the officers' mess, discussing Captain Jedlicek's case, the dreadful case of Captain Jedlicek. He would be court-martialed, dishonorably discharged, and shot.

Trotta buckled on his saber, grabbed his cap, and went downstairs. He had to wait for his comrades there. He marched to and fro outside the hotel. More important than the scene he had just gone through with Kapturak was, strangely enough, the Jedlicek affair. He believed he could detect the insidious machinations of some dark power; he felt it was an uncanny coincidence that Frau von Taussig had gone off to see her husband today of all days, and gradually the lieutenant saw all the somber events of his life fitting together in a somber mosaic as if manipulated by some powerful, hateful, invisible wire puller who was intent on destroying him. It was obvious—it was, as they say, clear as the nose on his face—that Lieutenant Trotta, the grandson of the Hero of Solferino, in part caused the doom of others and in part was drawn along by the doomed, and that in any case he was one of those ill-fated persons on whom an evil power had cast an evil eye.

He walked up and down the silent street, his footsteps echoing from the other side, from the illuminated and curtained windows of the café where music was playing, cards were pattering on tables, and a new entertainer, not the old Nightingale, was singing and dancing—the old songs and the old dances. Today none of the officers could be sitting there. In any case, he did not wish to check. For Captain Jedlicek's disgrace lay on Trotta even though he had long hated his service in the army. The captain's disgrace weighed on the entire battalion. Lieutenant Trotta's military upbringing was so thorough that he couldn't understand how after the news of the Jedlicek case the officers in this garrison dared to go out on the street in uniform.

Yes, that Jedlicek! He was big, strong, and cheerful, a good comrade, and he needed lots and lots of money. He took everything on his broad shoulders. Zoglauer loved him, the troops loved him. To all of them he had seemed more powerful than the swamp and the border. And he had been a spy!

Music tinkled from the café, tangled voices resounded and cups clattered, and all the sounds kept melting into the nocturnal chorus of the tireless frogs. Spring was here! But Chojnicki wouldn't be coming. The only man whose money could have helped him! Trotta's debt had long since grown beyond six thousand, it was now seven thousand two hundred fifty! Payment was due next week at exactly this time. If he didn't pay, some sort of link would be fabricated between him and Captain Jedlicek. He had been Jedlicek's friend! But then everyone had been his friend. Nevertheless, anything was possible for this ill-fated Lieutenant Trotta! Destiny, his destiny! Just two weeks ago at this time he had been a free and cheerful man in civvies. At this very time he had met Moser the painter and had had a drink with him! And today he envied Professor Moser.

He heard familiar steps from around the corner. The other officers were coming home. All who lived at the Hotel Brodnitzer were coming, they walked along, a mute pack. He headed toward them.

"Oh, you haven't left!" said Winter. "So you know! Awful! Horrible!"

They walked upstairs in single file, wordless, each striving to be as quiet as possible. They almost crept up the steps.

"Everybody to room nine!" First Lieutenant Hruba ordered. Number nine was his, the largest in the hotel. Heads drooping, they all entered Hruba's room.

"We have to do something," Hruba began. "You saw Zoglauer. He's at his wits' end! He's going to shoot himself! We have to do something!"

"Nonsense, Herr First Lieutenant," said Lieutenant Lippowitz. He had been late in joining the army, only after two semesters of law. He never managed to slough off the "civilian," and people showed him the somewhat timid and somewhat mocking respect paid to reserve officers. "There's nothing we can do here," said Lippowitz. "Keep quiet and keep serving! This isn't the first case. Nor will it, unfortunately, be the last in the army!"

No one responded. They realized that nothing could be done. And yet each of them had hoped that by gathering in a room they could hit on all sorts of solutions. But now it suddenly dawned on them that terror alone had driven them together because each man dreaded remaining alone with his terror inside his own four walls. However, they also realized that it did them no good to herd together and that every single one of them, although among comrades, was nevertheless alone with his terror. Their heads rose and they exchanged glances and their heads drooped again. They had already sat together like that once before, after Captain Wagner's suicide. Each of them thought of Captain Jedlicek's predecessor, Captain Wagner; each of them now wished that Jedlicek too had shot himself. And each of them now had a suspicion that their dead comrade Wagner may have likewise shot himself only to avoid arrest.

"I'll go to him, I'll force my way in," said Lieutenant Habermann, "and I'll shoot him down."

"First of all, you won't be able to force your way in," retorted Lippowitz. "Secondly, they're already making sure that he'll kill himself. As soon as they've gotten everything out of him, they'll hand him a pistol and lock him up."

"Yeah, right, that's it!" cried several. They sighed in relief. They began hoping that the captain had already killed himself. And they felt as if all of them, by dint of their own intelligence, had only just introduced this sensible practice of military justice.

"I came within inches of killing someone tonight," said Lieutenant Trotta.

"Who? How? Why?" they asked chaotically.

"It was Kapturak—you all know him," Trotta began. He spoke slowly, cast about for words, turned crimson, and when he was done found it impossible to explain why he hadn't thrust in his saber. He sensed they weren't following him. No, they didn't understand him.

"I would have killed him!" shouted one man.

"Me too," another joined in.

"Me too," said a third.

"It's not so easy," Lippowitz threw in.

"That bloodsucker, that Jew!" someone said—and they all froze upon remembering that Lippowitz's father was Jewish.

Trotta resumed. "Yes, I suddenly"—and he was extremely surprised that he spontaneously thought of the dead Max Demant and the doctor's grandfather, the white-bearded king of the innkeepers—"I suddenly saw a cross behind him!"

Someone laughed. Another said coldly, "You were drunk!"

"That's it!" Hruba finally ordered. "We'll report all this to Zoglauer tomorrow."

Trotta peered at each face in turn: limp, weary, agitated faces, yet provocatively cheerful in their weariness and agitation. If only Demant were alive now, Trotta thought. I could talk to him, to the grandson of the white-bearded king of the innkeepers! The lieutenant tried to steal out unnoticed. He went to his room.

The next morning he reported the incident. He narrated it in the army lingo in which he had reported and recounted since boyhood, the jargon that was his mother tongue. But he felt that he hadn't told everything, not even the gist, and that his experience and the report he was giving were separated by a vast, enigmatic gulf, virtually a whole strange country. Nor did he forget to tell about the shadow of the cross he believed he had seen.

And smiling just as Trotta had expected, the major asked, "How much did you have to drink?"

"Half a bottle," said Trotta.

"Well, there you are!" Zoglauer remarked.

He had smiled only for an instant, that harried Major Zoglauer. This was a serious issue. The serious issues were piling up, alas. An embarrassing matter—in any case, it had to be reported to a higher authority. But it could wait.

"Do you have the cash?" asked the major.

"No," said the lieutenant.

And they looked at each other helplessly, with blank, gaping eyes, the poor eyes of men who dared not even admit to themselves that they were helpless. Not everything was covered by army regulations. You could leaf through the rule books from front to back and then from back to front; not everything was covered! Had the lieutenant done the right thing? Had he reached for his saber prematurely? Had that man done the right thing— loaning a fortune and demanding it back? And if the major were to call all his officers together and confer with them, who could come up with a way out? Who could be wiser than the commander of the battalion? And just what was wrong with this ill-fated lieutenant? It had already cost some effort to hush up that strike business. Disaster after disaster was piling up on Major Zoglauer's head, disaster over Trotta, disaster over this battalion. He would have gladly wrung his hands, that Major Zoglauer, if only it had been possible to wring one's hands in the army. And if all the officers in the battalion were to chip in, they couldn't possibly raise the whole sum for Lieutenant Trotta! And the matter would only get more complicated if the loan were not repaid.

"Why did you need all that money?" asked Zoglauer, but then promptly recalled that he knew everything. He waved his hand. He wanted no details. "Write to your papá, you have to," said Zoglauer. He felt he had expressed a brilliant idea. And so the report was terminated.

And Lieutenant Trotta went home and sat down and began writing to his papá. He couldn't do it without liquor. And so he went down to the café, ordered a 180 Proof, plus ink, pen, and paper. He began. What a hard letter! What an impossible letter! Lieutenant Trotta took a few stabs at it, crumpled the paper up, started again. Nothing is more difficult for a lieutenant than describing events that involve him, even endanger him. It turned out on this occasion that Lieutenant Trotta, who had long hated serving in the military, still possessed enough soldierly ambition to avoid being drummed out of the army. And while trying to present the intricate facts to his father, he unexpectedly changed into Trotta the cadet, who, on the balcony of his father's house, had wished to die for Hapsburg and Austria while hearing "The Radetzky March." So strange, so mutable, and so confused is the human soul.

It took Trotta over two hours to set down the facts of the case. By now it was late afternoon. The cardplayers and roulette players were already gathering in the café. They were joined by the proprietor, Herr Brodnitzer. His cordiality was unusual and terrifying. He bowed low before the lieutenant, who instantly realized that Brodnitzer wanted to remind him of his scene with Kapturak and his own presence as a witness. Trotta went to look for Onufrij. He walked into the vestibule and shouted Onufrij's name up the stairs several times. But Onufrij did not respond. Brodnitzer, however, came over and reported, "Your orderly left early this morning."

So the lieutenant took off for the station himself in order to mail his letter. It was only en route that he realized Onufrij had left without permission. Trotta's military upbringing dictated anger toward the orderly. He himself, the lieutenant, had frequently slipped off to Vienna—AWOL and in mufti. Perhaps, he thought, the orderly had only been emulating his officer. I'm gonna lock him up and throw away the key! thought Lieutenant Trotta. But he also realized that this phrase was not of his own devising and he didn't mean it seriously. It was a mechanical formula, forever ready—one of the countless mechanical formulas that replace thoughts and anticipate decisions in military minds.

No, Onufrij had no girl in his village. He had four and a half acres, inherited from his father and looked after by his brother-in-law, and he had twenty gold ten-crown ducats buried in the ground, by the third willow left of the hut, on the path leading to his neighbor, Nikofor. Onufrij had gotten up before sunrise, polished the lieutenant's boots, brushed his uniform, placed the boots outside the door, and draped the uniform over the chair. He had then taken his cherrywood stick and marched off to Burdlaki.

He hiked along the narrow willow-lined path, the only path that revealed the dryness of the soil. For the willows used up all the wetness of the swamps. On both sides of the narrow path, the gray, ghostly morning fog rose in its many shapes, which billowed toward him, compelling him to cross himself. With quivering lips he kept incessantly murmuring the Lord's Prayer. Nevertheless he was in high spirits. Now, to his left, came the large railroad storehouses with their slate roofs, reassuring him somewhat because they stood where he had expected them to stand. He crossed himself once more, this time out of gratitude for God's goodness, which allowed the railroad storehouses to stand in their usual place.

He reached the village of Burdlaki an hour after sunrise. His sister and his brother-in-law were already out in the fields. He entered his father's hut, where they lived. The children were still asleep in the cradles, which hung from thick ropes winding around iron hooks attached to the ceiling. He got a spade and a rake from the small vegetable patch in the rear and went off in quest of the third willow to the left of the hut. First he stood with his back to the door and his eyes on the horizon. It took him awhile to convince himself that his right arm was his right, his left arm his left; then he headed left, toward his neighbor Nikofor, to the third willow. Here he began to dig. From time to time he glanced around to make sure no one was watching. No! Nobody saw what he was doing. He dug and dug. The sun rose so fast in the sky that he thought it was already noon. But it was only 9 A.M.

At last he heard the iron tongue of his spade hit something hard and resonant. He put down the spade, began gently caressing the loosened soil with his rake, then tossed the rake aside as well, lay down on the ground, and used all ten fingers to comb away the loose crumbs of damp earth. He touched a linen handkerchief, groped for the knot, and pulled out the cloth. There was his money: twenty gold ten-crown ducats.

He took no time to count them. He stowed the treasure in his trouser pocket and went to the Jewish innkeeper in the village of Burdlaki, a man named Hirsch Beniover, the only banker in the world whom he knew personally.

"I know you!" said Hirsch Beniover. "I knew your father, too. Do you need sugar, flour, Russian tobacco, or money?"

"Money!" said Onufrij.

"How much do you need?" asked Beniover.

"A lot!" said Onufrij—and spread out his arms as wide as he could to show how much he needed.

"Fine," said Beniover. "Let's see how much you've got."

And Beniover opened a huge book. This book indicated that Onufrij Kolohin owned four and a half acres of land. Beniover was prepared to lend him three hundred crowns on that.

"Let's go to the mayor," said Beniover. He called his wife, told her to mind the store, and he and Onufrij Kolohin went to the mayor.

Here he gave Onufrij three hundred crowns. Onufrij sat down at a brown worm-eaten table and began writing his name at the bottom of a document. He removed his hat. The sun was already high up in the sky. It managed to send its burning rays through the tiny windows of the peasant hut where the mayor of Burdlaki officiated. Onufrij was perspiring. The beads of sweat grew on his low brow like transparent crystal boils. Every letter that Onufrij wrote produced a crystal boil on his forehead. These boils ran, ran down like tears wept by Onufrij's brain. At last his name was at the bottom of the document. And with the twenty gold ten-crown ducats in his trouser pocket and the three hundred-crown bills in his blouse pocket, Onufrij Kolohin set out on his hike back.

He appeared at the hotel that afternoon. He went into the café, asked where his officer was, and had stationed himself amid the cardplayers when, as carefree as if he were standing in the barrack square, he spotted Trotta. The orderly's whole broad face beamed like a sun. Trotta glared and glared at him, with tenderness in his heart and severity in his eyes.

"I'm gonna lock you up and throw away the key!" said the lieutenant's lips, obeying the dictates of his military brain. "Come up to my room!" And Trotta got to his feet.

The lieutenant climbed the stairs. Onufrij followed precisely three steps behind him. They stood in the room.

Onufrij, his face still sunny, reported, "Herr Lieutenant, here is money!" and from his trouser pocket and tunic pocket he pulled out everything he owned; he came over and put the money on the table. Silvery gray bits of mud still stuck to the dark-red handkerchief that had so long concealed the twenty gold ten-crown ducats in the ground. Next to the handkerchief lay the blue banknotes. Trotta counted them. Then he undid the cloth. He counted the gold pieces. Then he added the bills to the gold pieces in the cloth, reknotted it, and handed Onufrij the bundle.

"I'm sorry, but I can't take any money from you, do you understand?" said Trotta. "It's against regulations, do you understand? If I take money from you, I'll be demoted and drummed out of the army, do you understand?"

Onufrij nodded.

The lieutenant stood there, holding the bundle in his raised hand. Onufrij kept nodding. He reached out and took the bundle. It swung in the air awhile.

"Dismissed!" said Trotta, and Onufrij left with the bundle.

The lieutenant remembered that autumn night in the cavalry garrison when he had heard Onufrij stamping behind him. And he recalled the military humoresques he had read in the slim green-bound booklets at the military hospital. They teemed with poignant orderlies, uncouth peasant boys with hearts of gold. Now Lieutenant Trotta had no literary taste, and whenever he heard the word *literature* he could think of nothing but Theodor Körner's drama *Zriny* and that was all, but he had always felt a dull resentment toward the melancholy gentleness of those booklets and their golden characters. Lieutenant Trotta wasn't experienced enough to know that uncouth peasant boys with noble hearts exist in real life and that a lot of truths about the living world are recorded in bad books; they are just badly written.

All in all, Lieutenant Trotta's experiences amounted to very little.

Chapter 18

ONE FRESH AND sunny spring morning the district captain received the lieutenant's unhappy letter. Herr von Trotta balanced the envelope on his palm before opening it. This letter felt heavier than any other he had ever received from his son. It had to be two pages long, a letter of exceptional length. Herr von Trotta's aged heart filled up with grief, paternal anger, joy, and anxious forebodings. When he opened the envelope, the hard cuff rattled slightly on his old hand. His left hand clutched the pince-nez, which had gotten somewhat shaky during the past few months, and his right hand brought the letter rather close to his face so that the edges of his whiskers rustled softly against the paper. Herr von Trotta was as terrified by the obvious haste of the handwriting as he was by the extraordinary contents. The district captain likewise searched between the lines for any other hidden terrors, for he suddenly felt that the letter did not hold enough and he had long been waiting for the worst news day after day, especially since his son had stopped writing. That was probably why he remained calm when he put the letter down.

He was an old man from an old era. The old men from the era before the Great War may have been more foolish than the young men of today. But in the moments that preceded those horrible ones and that in our time might be shrugged off with a casual joke, the old decent men maintained heroic equanimity. Nowadays the concepts of honor—professional, familial, and personal—that Herr von Trotta lived by seem like relics of implausible and juvenile legends. But in those days an Austrian district captain like Herr von Trotta would have been less shaken by the news of the sudden death of his only child than by the news of even a seemingly dishonorable action of that only child.

That lost era, which was virtually buried under the fresh grave mounds of the fallen, was ruled by very different notions. If someone offended the honor of an officer of the Imperial and Royal Army, and that officer failed to kill the man apparently because he owed him money, then that officer was a misfortune and worse than a misfortune: he was a disgrace to his progenitor, to the army, and to the monarchy.

At first it was to some extent Herr von Trotta's official heart that was stirred and not his paternal heart. And he said to himself, resign immediately. Take early retirement. You have no further business serving your Emperor! But a moment later the father's heart yelled, it's the fault of the times we live in! It's the fault of the border garrison! It's your own fault! Your son is honest and noble, but unfortunately he's weak and you have to help him.

He had to help him! He had to make sure that the Trotta name would not be sullied and dishonored. And on this point both of Herr von Trotta's hearts, the official one and the paternal one, were in agreement. So the most important thing was to get money—seven thousand two hundred fifty crowns. The five thousand florins with which the Kaiser had once gifted the son of the Hero of Solferino was long gone, as was the father's inheritance. The money had run through the district captain's fingers for one thing or another: for the household, for the military academy in Hranice, for Moser the painter, for the horse, for charitable purposes. Herr von Trotta had always made a point of appearing richer than he was. He had the instincts of a true gentleman. And in those days (and perhaps in our day too) no instincts were more expensive than those. People favored with such curses do not know how much they possess or how much they spend. They draw from an invisible source. They never keep accounts. They assume that their wealth cannot lag behind their generosity.

For the first time in his very long life, Herr von Trotta was confronted with the impossible task of coming up with a relatively large sum of money on the spot. He had no friends, aside from those old schoolmates and fellow students who now sat in government offices as he did but whom he hadn't seen in years. Most of them were poor. He was acquainted with the richest man in this district seat, old Herr von Winternigg. And the baron slowly began adjusting to the hideous thought of going to Herr von Winternigg, tomorrow, the day after, or even today, and asking for a loan. Herr von Trotta did not have much of an imagination. Nevertheless he managed to picture that terrible step in all its torturous clarity. And for the first time in his very long life he realized how hard it is to be helpless yet maintain one's dignity. This insight struck him like a lightning bolt, shattering the pride that he had so carefully nurtured and fostered for such a long time, that he had inherited and was determined to pass down. He already felt humiliated, like a man who has been petitioning people in vain for many years. Earlier, pride had been the staunch companion of his youth, then his support in middle age. Now he was robbed of all pride—the poor old district captain!

He decided to write to Herr von Winternigg immediately. But no sooner had he set pen to paper than he knew he was not even up to announcing a visit that should really be termed a plea. Old Trotta felt he would be committing a kind of fraud unless he stated the reason for his visit right off the bat, but he found it impossible to come up with any suitable wording for his intention. And so he sat there on and on, pen in hand, mulling and polishing and rejecting every sentence.

He could, of course, ring up Herr von Winternigg. But since the installation of a telephone in the district captain's headquarters—and that had been no longer than two years ago—he had used it only for official calls. He could not see himself stepping up to the large, brown, slightly eerie box, twisting the handle, and starting a conversation with Herr von Winternigg after hearing that dreadful "Hello!" which almost offended Herr von Trotta, sounding as it did like the childish watchword of an inappropriate bravura with which certain people tackle a discussion of serious matters.

Meanwhile the district captain remembered that his son was waiting for a response, perhaps a telegram. And what could the district captain wire? Perhaps "Will try everything. Details later"? Or "Wait patiently for news"? Or "Trying other means, impossible here"? Impossible! This word triggered a long and dreadful echo. What was impossible, saving the honor of the Trottas? It had to be possible. It could not be impossible! Up and down, up and down; the district captain paced up and down his office as on those Sunday mornings when he had tested little Carl Joseph. One hand was on his back, the cuff rattled on the other. Then he went down to the courtyard, driven by the insane notion that dead Jacques might be sitting there, in the shade of the beams. The courtyard was empty. The window of the tiny cottage where Jacques had lived was open, and the canary was still alive. It perched on the windowsill, chirping for all it was worth.

The district captain went back, took his hat and cane, and left the house. He had decided to do something extraordinary—namely, go and see Dr. Skowronnek at his home. He crossed the small marketplace, turned into Lenaugasse, and scrutinized the signs on the house doors, for he didn't know the doctor's number. Eventually he had to ask a storekeeper for Skowronnek's address, although he viewed it as indiscreet to bother a stranger for information. But Herr von Trotta got through this ordeal with self-confidence and strength of mind, and he entered the house that had been pointed out to him. Dr. Skowronnek, book in hand, was sitting under a gigantic sunshade in the small back garden.

"Good God!" cried Skowronnek. For he knew very well that something unusual must have occurred to make the district captain come to his home.

Herr von Trotta reeled off a whole set of involved apologies before he began. Then he told him the story, sitting on the bench in the small garden, his head drooping, his cane poking the colored gravel on the narrow path. He handed his son's letter to Skowronnek. Then he fell silent, quelling a sigh as he took a deep breath.

"My savings," said Skowronnek, "add up to two thousand crowns, and they are yours for the asking, Herr District Commissioner, if that's all right with you." He raced through that sentence as if afraid the district captain might break in. In his embarrassment, the doctor took hold of Herr von Trotta's cane and began poking around in the gravel himself, for he could not sit around with idle hands after uttering that sentence.

Herr von Trotta said, "Thank you, Herr Doctor, I'll take it. I'll give you an IOU. I'll pay you back in installments, if that's all right with you."

"That's out of the question," said Skowronnek.

"Good!" said the district captain. He suddenly found it impossible to say a lot of useless words, such as he had employed throughout his life out of politeness to strangers. All at once, time was breathing down his neck. The few days at his disposal suddenly melted, becoming nothing.

"As for the rest," Skowronnek went on, "you could get it only from Herr von Winternigg. Do you know him?"

"Casually."

"You have no choice, Herr District Captain! But I believe I know what sort of man he is. I once treated his daughter-in-law. He appears to be a monster, as they say. And it may be, it may be, Herr District Captain, that he will refuse your request."

Hereupon, Skowronnek fell silent. The district captain took back his cane. And there was a deep hush. The only sound was the scraping of the cane in the gravel.

"Refuse," whispered the district captain. "I'm not afraid," he said aloud. "But then what?"

"Then," said Skowronnek, "there is only one alternative, a very strange one. It keeps going through my mind, but it strikes even me as too fantastic. I mean, in your case it may not be so improbable. If I were you, I would go there straight, straight to the Old Man—I mean, the Emperor. For it's not just a question of money. There's always the danger, forgive me for speaking so bluntly, that your son may—"

Skowronnek wanted to say "be thrown out," but he said, "Your son may have to leave the army!"

Upon uttering those words, Skowronnek felt ashamed. And he added, "Perhaps it's just a childish idea. And even while saying it, I feel as if we were two schoolboys mulling over impossible things. Yes, that's how old we've gotten, and we're burdened with care, and yet there's some bravado in my idea. Forgive me!"

But to Herr von Trotta's simple soul Dr. Skowronnek's idea did not seem the least bit childish. With every document he drew up or signed, with the most trifling instruction he gave to his assistant or even just Constable Sergeant Slama, the baron was directly under the Kaiser's outstretched scepter. And there was nothing odd about the fact that the Kaiser had once spoken to Carl Joseph. The Hero of Solferino had shed his blood for the Emperor and so had Carl Joseph, in a sense, by fighting against the turbulent and suspicious "individuals" and "elements." In Herr von Trotta's simple terms, it was no abuse of the Kaiser's grace if His Majesty's servant approached Franz Joseph trustfully, the way a child in trouble approaches his father.

A startled Dr. Skowronnek began to doubt the district captain's sanity when the old man exclaimed, "An excellent idea, Herr Doctor—the simplest thing in the world!"

"It's not that simple," said Skowronnek. "You don't have much time. A private audience can't be whipped up on two days' notice."

The district captain agreed. And they decided he should first try Winternigg.

"Even at the risk of a refusal," said the district captain.

"Even at the risk of a refusal," repeated Dr. Skowronnek.

The district captain started out immediately. He took a fiacre. It was noontime. He hadn't eaten. He stopped at the café and drank a brandy.

He realized he was doing something highly inappropriate. He'd be barging in during old Winternigg's lunch. But he has no time. The matter must be settled by this afternoon. The day after tomorrow he'll see the Kaiser. And he tells the cabby to stop once again. He gets off at the post office and, in a firm hand, writes out a telegram to Carl Joseph: BEING TAKEN CARE OF. BEST, FATHER. He is quite certain that everything will work out. For while it may be impossible to dig up the money, it is even more impossible to jeopardize the Trotta honor. Yes indeed, the district captain imagines that the ghost of his father, the Hero of Solferino, is guarding and escorting him. And the brandy warms his old heart. It beats a little faster. But he is quite calm.

He pays the cabby at the entrance to Winternigg's villa and benevolently salutes him with one finger, just as he always salutes little people. He also smiles benevolently at the butler. Clutching his hat and his cane, he waits.

Herr von Winternigg emerged, tiny and yellow. He held his shriveled little hand out toward the district captain and sank into a wide armchair, almost vanishing in the green upholstery. His colorless eyes focused on the large windows. No gaze lived in his eyes, or else they concealed his gaze; they were old, dim, small mirrors, and all that the district captain saw in them was his own small image.

He began, more fluently than he would have expected, with well-spoken apologies, explaining why it had been impossible for him to give advance notice of his visit. Then he said, "Herr von Winternigg, I am an old man." He hadn't meant to say that. Winternigg's wrinkly, yellow lids blinked a few times, and the district captain felt he was talking to an old, shriveled bird that did not understand human speech.

"Highly regrettable!" Herr von Winternigg said all the same. He spoke very softly. His voice had no timbre, just as his eyes had no gaze. He breathed when he spoke, baring a set of surprisingly robust teeth—broad, yellowish, a powerful barrier guarding his words. "Highly regrettable!" Herr von Winternigg said once again. "But I have no ready cash."

The district captain instantly rose. Winternigg likewise bounced up. He stood, tiny and yellow, in front of the district captain, beardless in front of silvery whiskers, and Herr von Trotta seemed to grow and felt he was growing. Was his pride broken? Not at all! Was he humiliated? By no means! He had to save the honor of the Hero of Solferino, just as the Hero of Solferino had had to save the Kaiser's life. That's how easy it was to make a plea. For the first time, Herr von Trotta's heart was filled with contempt, with true contempt, and the contempt was almost as great as his pride. He took his leave. And he said in his old voice, the arrogantly nasal voice of an official, "Good day, Herr von Winternigg!" He went on foot, upright, slow, shimmering in his full silvery dignity, walking along the lengthy avenue that ran from Winternigg's villa to the town. The avenue was deserted, the sparrows hopped across it, and the blackbirds whistled, and the old green chestnut trees flanked the Herr District Captain's route.

At home, he waved the silver handbell for the first time in a long while. Its tinkly voice raced through the entire house. "Madam," said Herr von Trotta to Fräulein Hirschwitz, "I would like my trunk packed within thirty minutes. My uniform with my cocked hat and my sword, the tuxedo and the white tie, please! In thirty minutes." He drew out his watch, and the lid audibly clapped open. He sat down in the armchair and closed his eyes.

His dress uniform hung in the closet, on five hooks: coat, waistcoat, trousers, cocked hat, and sword. Piece by piece the uniform emerged from the closet as if on its own, not so much carried as merely accompanied by the housekeeper's cautious hands. The district captain's huge trunk in its protective envelope of brown linen opened its maw, lined with rustling tissue paper, and took in the uniform, piece by piece. The sword obediently entered its leather sheath. The white bow tie wrapped itself up in a tender paper veil. The white gloves bedded themselves in the lining of the waistcoat. Then the trunk closed. Fräulein Hirschwitz came and reported that everything was ready.

And so the Herr District Captain went to Vienna.

He arrived late in the evening. But he knew where to find the men he needed. He knew the houses they lived in, the restaurants they ate in. And Government Councilor Smekal and Privy Councilor Pollak and Chief Imperial Audit Councilor Pollitzer and Chief City Councilor Busch and District Councilor Leschnigg and Police Councilor Fuchs: all of them and several others as well saw the peculiar Herr von Trotta walk in that evening, and although he was just as old as they, each of them was nevertheless disturbed at seeing how old the district captain had grown. For he was much older than any of them. Why, he actually struck them as venerable, and they almost had qualms about addressing him by his first name. He was seen in many places that evening, popping up almost simultaneously in all of them, and he looked like a ghost, a ghost of the old times and the old Hapsburg monarchy: the shadow of history. And strange as his enterprise may have sounded—namely, to secure a private audience with the Kaiser in two days—he looked far stranger himself, Herr von Trotta did, prematurely old and virtually old since birth; and little by little they found his plan to be perfectly fair and natural.

In Court Comptroller Montenuovo's office sat that lucky stiff Gustl, whom they all envied, even though they knew his glory would come to a wretched end when the Old Man died and Franz Ferdinand mounted the throne. They were already waiting. Meanwhile, he had married—and married a Fugger at that: he, a commoner, whom they all knew, from the third row, left-hand corner, whom they had all prompted whenever he was tested, and whose "luck" had been accompanied by their bitter comments for thirty years now. Gustl had been knighted and given a place in the Office of the Court Comptroller. His name was no longer Hasselbrunner, it was now *von* Hasselbrunner. His job was simple, a sinecure, while all of them, the others, had to take care of unendurable and highly intricate matters. Hasselbrunner! He was the only one who could help.

And so by nine the next morning the district captain was stationed outside Hasselbrunner's door in the Office of the Court Comptroller. He learned that Hasselbrunner was out of town but might return that afternoon. By coincidence along came Smetana, whom the district captain had been unable to locate yesterday. And Smetana, swiftly clued in and quick-witted as ever, was full of ideas. Hasselbrunner might be out of town, but Lang was sitting next door. And Lang was a nice fellow. And so the indefatigable district captain began his odyssey from office to office.

He knew nothing of the secret laws governing the Imperial and Royal authorities in Vienna. But now he got to know them. Obeying these laws, the office receptionists were surly until he produced his card; whereupon, recognizing his rank, they bowed and scraped. Every last higher official greeted him with the tenderest respect. During the first quarter hour each of them, without exception, seemed more than willing to risk his career and even his life for the district captain. It was only during the next quarter hour that their eyes dimmed, their faces fell.

Infinite grief crept into their hearts, crippling their willingness, and each of them said, "Ah, if only things were different, I'd be delighted! But as things stand, dear, dear Baron Trotta—even for someone in my position; well, I don't have to tell you!" And in such and similar terms their apologies glanced off the unshakable Herr von Trotta.

He walked through cloisters and patios, up to the third floor, the fourth, back to the first, then the ground floor. And then he decided to wait for Hasselbrunner. He waited till afternoon, when he learned that Hasselbrunner was not really out of town; he had merely stayed home. And the undaunted champion of the honor of the Trottas forced his way into Hasselbrunner's presence. Here at last he found a faint glint of hope. They drove from person to person, Hasselbrunner and old Herr von Trotta. Their goal was to forge all the way to Montenuovo. And finally, around 6 P.M., they succeeding in tracking down a friend of Montenuovo's in that renowned patisserie where the empire's lighthearted, sweet-toothed dignitaries occasionally dropped by in the afternoon. For the fifteenth time that day the district captain was told that his plan was impossible. But he remained unshakable. And the silvery dignity of his years and the slightly bizarre and somewhat crazy determination with which he spoke about his son and the danger threatening his name, the solemnity with which he called his forgotten father "the Hero of Solferino" and nothing else, with which he called the Kaiser "His Majesty" and nothing else—all these things struck such deep chords in the listeners that they gradually found Herr von Trotta's plan to be perfectly fair and natural.

If all else failed, said this district captain from W, he, an old servant of His Majesty and the son of the Hero of Solferino, would throw himself like an ordinary market worker in front of the carriage that His Majesty rode every afternoon from Schönbrunn Castle to the palace. He, District Captain Franz von Trotta, had to settle the entire matter. And he was so enthusiastic about his plan to enlist the Kaiser's help in saving the honor of the Trottas that he felt as if his long life had finally been given proper meaning by his son's accident, as he privately called the whole affair. Yes, this alone had given it its meaning.

It was hard to flout protocol. They told him so fifteen times. He replied that his father, the Hero of Solferino, had also flouted protocol. "He grabbed His Majesty's shoulders like this, with his hands, and shoved him down!" said the district captain. He, who cringed slightly at anyone's vehement or superfluous movement, rose to his feet, clutched the shoulders of the man to whom he was describing the scene, and tried to reenact the historic rescue then and there. And no one smiled. And they cast about for a way of circumventing protocol.

He entered a stationery shop, bought a sheet of official foolscap, a vial of ink, and a steel pen with an Adler point, the only kind he could write with. And with a fleet hand but in his usual penmanship, which rigidly observed the finest laws of calligraphy, he indited the regulation petition to his Imperial and Royal Apostolic Majesty; and he did not doubt for even an instant—that is, allow himself to doubt for even an instant—that his petition would be dealt with "favorably." He was ready to wake up Montenuovo himself in the middle of the night. In the course of that day, Herr von Trotta had come to believe that his son's concern was now the Hero of Solferino's concern and thereby the Kaiser's—to some extent, the Fatherland's concern.

He had barely eaten since leaving W. He looked gaunter than usual, reminding his friend Hasselbrunner of the exotic birds at the Schönbrunn Zoo—creatures that constitute Nature's attempt to replicate the Hapsburg physiognomy within the animal kingdom. Indeed, the district captain reminded anyone who had seen the Kaiser of Franz Joseph himself. These gentlemen in Vienna were utterly unaccustomed to the degree of resoluteness demonstrated by the district captain. They were used to tackling far more difficult government matters with bubbly bon mots devised in the coffeehouses of the capital. And so Herr von Trotta seemed like some character from a province that was historically rather than geographically remote, like a ghost from the Fatherland's past, the embodied pang of a patriotic conscience.

Their eternally ready wit, which so assiduously greeted all signs of their own imminent doom, faded for the length of an hour, and the name "Solferino" aroused their dread and awe: the battle that had first heralded the end of the Imperial and

Royal monarchy. Indeed, the appearance and the words of this strange district captain made them shudder. Perhaps they already felt the breath of Death, who was to grab them all a few months later—grab them by the throat! And they felt Death breathing icily down their necks.

Altogether Herr von Trotta had three days. And within a single night of not sleeping, not eating, not drinking, he succeeded in smashing through the iron and golden law of court etiquette. Just as the name of the Hero of Solferino could no longer be found in the history books or the readers for Austrian elementary and high schools, so too was the name of the son of the Hero of Solferino missing from Montenuovo's archives. Aside from Montenuovo himself and Franz Joseph's recently deceased valet, no one in the world knows that District Captain Franz, Baron von Trotta, was received one morning by the Kaiser—in fact, just before the Emperor's departure for Ischl.

It was a wonderful morning. The district captain had been trying his dress uniform on all night long. He left the window open. It was a bright summer night. From time to time he went over to the window. He would then hear the sounds of the slumbering city and the crowing of roosters in distant farmyards. He smelled the breath of summer; he saw the stars in the patch of nocturnal sky, he heard the even footfalls of the policeman on his beat. He waited for morning. For the tenth time he stood at the mirror, adjusted the bow of his white tie over the corners of the stand-up collar, ran his white cambric handkerchief once again over the gold buttons on his coat, polished the gold pommel of his sword, brushed his shoes, combed out his whiskers, and forced down the few wisps on his bald pate even though they kept sticking up and curling, and he once again brushed the swallow tails of his coat. He took the cocked hat in his hand. He stood in front of the mirror and rehearsed: "Your Majesty, I beg for clemency for my son!" He saw his whiskers moving in the mirror and considered that inappropriate, and he began pronouncing the sentence in such a way that his whiskers did not stir even though the words were distinct and audible.

He did not feel the slightest fatigue. He stepped back to the window like a man on a far shore. And he yearned for morning the way that man looks forward to a ship that will carry him home. Yes, he was homesick for the Kaiser. He stood at the window until the gray shimmer of dawn brightened the sky, the morning star died, and the confused voices of birds announced the rising of the sun. Then he switched out the lights in the room. He rang the bell by the door. He sent for the barber. He slipped off his coat. He sat down. He had himself shaved. "Twice," he told the groggy young man, "and against the grain!" Now his chin glistened bluish between his silvery whiskers. The alum tingled, the powder cooled his throat. His audience was scheduled for eight-thirty. Once again he brushed his black-and-green coat. He repeated in front of the mirror, "Your Majesty, I beg for clemency for my son!" Then he closed the door behind him.

He walked down the stairs. The rest of the hotel was still asleep. He tugged at the white gloves, smoothed the fingers, stroked down the kid, and paused for a moment at the large staircase mirror between the second and first floors, trying to catch a glimpse of his profile. Then, with only his toes touching the red carpet on the steps, he cautiously descended, emanating silvery dignity, the fragrance of powder and cologne, and the pungent smell of shoe polish. The doorman bowed low. The two-horse carriage drew up at the revolving door. The district captain dusted the upholstered seat with his handkerchief and settled in. "Schönbrunn!" he ordered. And he sat bolt upright in the fiacre for the remainder of the drive. The horses' hooves cheerfully struck against the freshly sprayed streets, and the hurrying white bakery boys stopped and peered after the fiacre as if watching a parade. Herr von Trotta rolled toward the Kaiser like the pièce de résistance of a procession.

He ordered the cabby to halt at what seemed like a suitable distance. And with his dazzling gloves on both sides of his black-and-green coat, he walked up the straight road to Schönbrunn Castle, cautiously placing one foot before the other in order to protect his glossy boots against the dust of the tree-lined avenue. The morning birds exulted overhead. He was dazed by the scent of lilac and jasmine. Wafting over from the white chestnut candles, a petal or two alighted on his shoulders. He flicked them away with two fingers. Slowly he mounted the flat, radiant steps, which already lay white in the morning sun. The guard presented arms, District Captain von Trotta entered the palace.

He waited. He was inspected, in accordance with etiquette, by a Gentleman of the Household. His coat, his gloves, his trousers, his boots were impeccable. It would have been impossible to detect a flaw in Herr von Trotta. He waited. He waited in the large antechamber outside His Majesty's study; the six huge arched windows, still curtained against the morning sun but already open, admitted all the wealth of early summer, all the sweet scents, all the wild voices of the birds of Schönbrunn. But the district captain seemed to hear nothing. Nor did he seem to notice the gentleman whose discreet task it was to inspect the Kaiser's visitors and inform them of the rules of deportment. However, when faced with the district captain's unapproachable and silvery dignity, the gentleman fell silent, neglecting his duty.

The high white gilt-edged double door was flanked by two giant sentries, like dead statues. The brownish-yellow parquet floor, with only its center covered by a strip of red carpeting, hazily mirrored the lower part of Herr von Trotta's body: the black trousers, the gilt tip of the scabbard, and also the billowing shadow of the coattails. Herr von Trotta rose. He walked across the carpet with timid, soundless steps. His heart pounded. But his soul was tranquil. At this moment, five minutes before his audience with his Kaiser, Herr von Trotta felt as if he had been frequenting this place for years, as if he were accustomed to reporting to His Majesty Kaiser Franz Joseph I every morning and supplying his personal account of all the previous day's incidents in the Moravian district of W. The Herr District Captain felt thoroughly at home in his Kaiser's palace. At most he was bothered by the thought that he might need to run his fingers once more through his whiskers but had no time to pull off his white gloves. No minister of the Kaiser's, not even the Comptroller himself, could have felt more at home here than Herr von Trotta. From time to time the wind billowed the sunny yellow curtains on the high arched windows, and a touch of summery green stole into the district captain's field of vision.

The birds kept warbling louder and louder. A few heavy flies were buzzing in the foolish and premature belief that it was already noon, and the summer heat was gradually becoming palpable.

The district captain halted in the middle of the room, his cocked hat on his right hip, his left hand, dazzling white, on the gold hilt of the sword, his face rigidly set toward the door of the room where the Kaiser was sitting. Thus he stood for perhaps two minutes. The golden strokes of clocks on distant turrets came wafting through the open windows.

All at once, the double door split apart. Stretching his head and walking cautiously, noiselessly, yet with a firm tread, the district captain stepped forward. He executed a low bow, remaining in that position for several seconds, his face toward the parquet, his mind blank. By the time he straightened up, the door had closed behind him. In front of him, behind the desk, stood Kaiser Franz Joseph, and the district captain felt as if his older brother were standing behind the desk. Yes, Franz Joseph's whiskers were somewhat yellowish, especially around the mouth, but otherwise they were as white as Herr von Trotta's whiskers. The Kaiser wore a general's uniform, and Herr von Trotta a district captain's uniform. And they were like two brothers, one of whom had become a Kaiser, the other a district captain.

As human as the rest of the audience (which was never recorded in the archives) was the Kaiser's gesture at this very moment: fearing that a drop might be dangling from his nose, he drew his handkerchief from his trouser pocket and wiped his moustache. Then he glanced at the file. Aha, Trotta! he thought. Yesterday the need for this sudden audience had been explained to him, but he had not listened carefully. The Trottas had not stopped haunting him for months now. He recalled speaking to the youngest offspring of this family at the maneuvers. That had been a lieutenant, a strangely pale lieutenant. This man had to be his father. The Kaiser had already forgotten whether it was the lieutenant's grandfather or father who had saved his life at the Battle of Solferino. Had the Hero of Solferino suddenly become a district captain? Or was he the son of the Hero of Solferino? The Emperor propped his hands on the desk.

"Well, my dear Trotta?" he asked. For it was his imperial duty to stun his visitors by knowing their names.

"Your Majesty!" said the district captain and bowed deeply once again. "I beg for clemency for my son!"

"What kind of a son do you have?" asked the Kaiser, to gain time and avoid letting on that he was not versed in the background of the Trotta family.

"My son is a lieutenant with the riflemen in B," said Herr von Trotta.

"Ah, I see, I see!" said the Kaiser. "That's the young man I saw at the most recent maneuvers. A fine fellow!" And because his thoughts were slightly scrambled, he added, "He nearly saved my life. Or was that you?"

"Your Majesty, it was my father, the Hero of Solferino!" the district captain remarked, bowing yet again.

"How old is he now?" asked the Kaiser. "The Battle of Solferino. That was the man with the primer, wasn't it?"

"Yes, Your Majesty!" said the district captain.

And all at once the Kaiser clearly recalled the strange captain's audience. And just as he done when the bizarre captain had appeared in this study, Franz Joseph I came out from behind the desk, walked several steps toward the visitor, and said, "Come closer!"

The district captain came closer. The Kaiser stretched out his thin, trembling hand, an old man's hand with tiny blue veins and with nodules on the knuckles. The district captain took the Kaiser's hand and bowed. He wanted to kiss it. He did not know whether he should venture to hold it or to place his own hand in the Kaiser's so that the sovereign could withdraw it at any time. "Your Majesty!" the district captain said a second time. "I beg for clemency for my son!"

They were like two brothers. A stranger seeing them at this moment could have easily mistaken them for two brothers. Their white whiskers, their narrow, sloping shoulders, their equal physical size made each of them feel he was facing his own reflection. And one thought he had changed into a district captain. And the other thought he had changed into the Kaiser. To the Kaiser's left and Herr von Trotta's right, the two huge windows of the room were open, but likewise still shrouded by sunny yellow curtains.

"Nice weather today!" Franz Joseph suddenly said.

"Wonderful weather today!" the district captain said.

And while the Kaiser pointed his left hand at the window, the district captain stretched his right hand in the same direction. And the Kaiser felt he was standing in front of his own mirror image.

All at once the Kaiser realized he still had a lot to do before leaving for Ischl. So he said, "Fine! It'll all be taken care of! What's he done anyway, gotten in debt? It'll be taken care of! My best to your papá!"

"My father is dead, Your Majesty," said the district captain.

"I see, dead," said the Kaiser. "Too bad, too bad!" Lost in memories of the Battle of Solferino, he returned to his desk, sat down, pressed the buzzer, and did not see the district captain leaving, with his head bowed, the sword hilt on his left hip, the cocked hat on his right hip.

The morning birdsong flooded the room. Much as the Kaiser valued birds as creatures privileged by God, so to speak, he nevertheless fairly distrusted them from the bottom of his heart, just as he distrusted artists. And during the past few years, experience had taught him that the twittering birds were always to blame for his minor lapses of memory. That was why he quickly jotted *Trotta Affair* on the file.

Then he waited for his comptroller's daily visit. The clock was already striking nine. Now he came.

Chapter 19

LIEUTENANT TROTTA'S AWKWARD problem was buried in solicitous silence. Major Zoglauer said only, "Your affair has been
settled on the highest level. Your papá has sent the money.
There's nothing more to say about it."

Trotta thereupon wrote to his father. He reported that the
threat to his honor had been averted on the highest level. He
begged forgiveness for maintaining a blasphemously long silence
and not answering the district captain's letters. He was touched
and moved. And he tried to describe how touched he was. But
he found no words for regret, melancholy, and longing in his
meager vocabulary. It was a bitter drudgery. After he signed the
letter, a sentence crossed his mind: "I am planning to apply for a
furlough soon so I can ask your forgiveness in person." For
formal reasons this felicitous sentence could not be added as a
postscript. So the lieutenant set about rewriting the entire letter.
One hour later he was done. The style had only improved in the
new final draft. And thus he felt that everything was taken care
of—the whole disgusting business.

He himself marveled at his "phenomenal luck." The grandson
of the Hero of Solferino could count on the old Kaiser, come
what may. No less delightful was the demonstrated fact that Carl
Joseph's father had money. Now that the threat of dishonorable
discharge had been sidestepped, he could, if he liked, resign
voluntarily, live with Frau von Taussig in Vienna, perhaps get a
government job, and wear civvies. He hadn't been in Vienna for a
long time. He hadn't heard from the woman. He missed her. He
drank a 180 Proof and missed her even more—and he reached
that beneficial degree of longing which permits a little weeping.
Recently his tears had flowed quite readily. Lieutenant Trotta had

another pleasurable look at the letter, his successful handiwork; then he slipped it into an envelope and cheerfully scrawled the address. To reward himself he ordered a double 180 Proof.

Herr Brodnitzer personally brought the drink and said, "Kapturak is gone!"

A happy day, no doubt about it. The little man who could have always reminded the lieutenant of one of his worst times had likewise been eliminated.

"How come?"

"He was simply deported!"

Yes, that was how far Franz Joseph's arm reached—the arm of the old man who had spoken to Lieutenant Trotta with a glistening drop on the imperial nose. And that was how far their memory of the Hero of Solferino reached.

Within a week after the district captain's audience, Kapturak had been gotten rid of. Upon receiving an august hint, the local civil authorities also closed down Brodnitzer's casino. No further mention was made of Captain Jedlicek. He submerged into that mute and enigmatic oblivion from which a man could no more return than from the beyond. He vanished inside the military remand prisons of the old monarchy, the "lead chambers" of Austria. If ever his name drifted into an officer's mind, he instantly shooed it away. Most of them succeeded in doing so, thanks to their natural ability to forget everything.

A new captain arrived—his name was Lorenz—a plump, stocky, good-natured man who tended to be uncontrollably casual in matters of dress and bearing, always ready to take off his tunic, although it was prohibited, and play a round of pool. The shirtsleeves he revealed at such times were short, patched, and a bit sweaty. He was the father of three children and the husband of a careworn woman. He quickly felt at home here. People got used to him at once. All three children, as alike as triplets, would call for him at the café.

Gradually the various dancing nightingales disappeared—the ones from Olomouc, Hernals, and Mariahilf. Now the café band performed only twice a week. But it lacked verve and fire; for want of dancers it turned classical and seemed to grieve for bygone days rather than play music. The officers grew bored again if they weren't drinking. But when they drank they wallowed in melancholy and in profound self-pity.

The summer was very sultry. During morning drills, the soldiers had two breaks. Troops and rifles sweated. The notes emerging from the bugles were dull and lifeless as they struck the heavy air. A thin fog evenly covered the sky—a veil of silvery lead. It also clung to the swamps, dampening even the ever-cheery croaking of the frogs. The willows never stirred. Everyone waited for a wind. But all winds were asleep.

This year Chojnicki hadn't returned home. Everyone resented this, as though he were an entertainer who had broken his perennial summer contract with the army. So in order to lend new glamour to life in this godforsaken garrison, Rittmaster Count Zschoch of the dragoons hit on the brilliant idea of mounting a huge summer festival. This idea was brilliant simply because the festival could be a dry run for the regiment's great centennial celebration. The hundredth birthday of the dragoon regiment was a year away, but the dragoons seemed unable to contain themselves for a whole ninety-nine years without some kind of merrymaking.

Everyone agreed that the idea was brilliant. Colonel Festetics said so too and even fancied that he alone had come up with it. After all, several weeks earlier he had also begun preparing for the great centennial celebration. Every day, he spent his spare time in the regimental office, dictating the humble invitation that was to be dispatched six months later to the honorary commander of the regiment, a minor German prince from an, alas, neglected collateral branch. The mere stylistics of this courtly missive occupied two men, Colonel Festetics and Rittmaster Zschoch. Sometimes they got into violent arguments about stylistic niceties. For instance, the colonel found the phrase "And the Regiment most humbly takes the liberty" acceptable, while the rittmaster was of the opinion that the "And" was inappropriate and the "most humbly" not quite comme il faut. They had decided to indite two sentences a day, and they succeeded in doing so. Each of them dictated to a secretary: the rittmaster to a corporal, the colonel to a platoon leader. Then they compared the results. They gushed over each other. The colonel thereupon locked away these two drafts in the regiment office's large cabinet, to which he alone had the key. He added them to the plans he had already made regarding the grand review and the gymnastic displays of officers and troops. The plans were all stored next to the huge, mysterious, sealed envelopes containing the secret orders in the event of mobilization.

So after Rittmaster Zschoch announced his brilliant idea, they interrupted the composition of the letter to the prince and set about dispatching identical invitations to the four corners of the world. Since these plain texts demanded less literary effort, they were completed within days. The few discussions focused on questions of precedence for, unlike Colonel Festetics, Count Zschoch was of the opinion that the invitations had to be sent in the proper sequence, first to the most noble, then to the less noble.

"All at the same time!" said the colonel. "That's an order!"

And although the Festetics family was one of the best in Hungary, Count Zschoch believed that the colonel's order implied a democratic leaning inspired by his Hungarian blood. He wrinkled his nose and dispatched the invitations all at the same time.

The superintendent was called in. He had the addresses of each and every reserve officer and retired officer. All were invited. So were the close relatives and friends of the dragoon officers. This, they were informed, was a dress rehearsal for the centennial celebration. It was a way of letting them know that they might personally meet the honorary commander, the German prince from an, alas, not very respectable collateral branch. Some of the invitees were of older stock than the honorary corporal. Nevertheless they placed some value on contact with a mediatized prince.

The organizers decided that since it was to be a summer festival they would try to use Count Chojnicki's Little Forest. The Little Forest differed from his other forests in that it seemed destined by nature and by its owner to serve as a site for parties. The Little Forest was young. Consisting as it did of jolly little pine saplings, it offered shade and coolness, leveled paths, and a few small clearings that plainly were fit for nothing but being converted into dance floors. So the Little Forest was rented. On this occasion, they again regretted Chojnicki's absence. But they invited him all the same, hoping he would be unable to resist an invitation to the dragoon festival and might even "bring along a few charming people," as Festetics put it.

They also invited the Hulins and the Kinskys, the Podstatzkis and the Schönborns, the family of Albert Tassilo Larisch, the Kirchbergs, the Weissenhorns, and the Babenhausens, the Sennyis, the Benkyös, the Zuschers, and the Dietrichsteins. Each of them had some connection with this dragoon regiment. When Rittmaster Zschoch checked through the guest list once again, he said, "Well, I'll be damned and double damned!" And he repeated this original remark several times. It was unfortunate but unavoidable that they also had to invite the ordinary officers of the rifle battalion to this grand festival. We'll keep them in their places! thought Colonel Festetics. Rittmaster Zschoch had the very same thought. While formulating the invitations for the officers of the rifle battalion, dictating them respectively to the corporal and the platoon leader, they exchanged grim looks. And each of them made the other responsible for inviting the rifle battalion. However, their faces brightened at the mention of the name of Baron von Trotta und Sipolje.

"Battle of Solferino," the colonel casually tossed in.

"Ah!" said Rittmaster Zschoch. He was convinced that the Battle of Solferino had taken place in the sixteenth century.

All the regimental clerks made garlands out of green and red paper. The orderlies clung to the slender trunks in the Little Forest, hanging wires from pine to pine. Three days a week the dragoons did not drill. Instead they attended "school" in the barracks. Here they were instructed in the fine art of how to behave in the presence of illustrious guests. Half a squadron was temporarily assigned to KP. Here the peasants learned how to polish kettles, serve on trays, hold wineglasses, and turn a spit. Every morning Colonel Festetics rigorously inspected kitchen, cellar, and mess hall. White cotton gloves had been issued to every single private who had even the slightest prospect of coming into any sort of contact with the guests. Every morning these dragoons had to hold out their white-clad hands, splaying all their fingers, for the colonel's perusal—a harsh distinction they owed to a whim of the master-at-arms. The colonel inspected the fit and cleanliness of the gloves and the sturdiness of their seams. He was in high spirits, radiant with a special hidden inner sun. He admired his own energy, praised it, and demanded admiration. He developed an unwonted imagination. Every day it gifted him with at least ten ideas, whereas earlier he had gotten along quite nicely on just one a week. And these flashes of insight pertained not only to the celebration but also to the great issues of life: say, the rules of drilling, proper attire, and even military tactics. During these days it became clear to Colonel Festetics that he could make general—as easy as pie.

Now the wires were stretched from trunk to trunk, and then the garlands had to be attached to the wires. So they were hung experimentally. The colonel reviewed them. There was no denying the necessity of adding Chinese lanterns. But since despite fog and sultriness it hadn't rained in a long time, they expected a surprise storm any day now. The colonel therefore posted sentries in the Little Forest, their assignment being to take down the lanterns at the slightest hint of a brewing storm.

"The wires too?" he prudently asked the rittmaster. For he knew that great men listen to advice from their lesser helpers.

"Nothing'll happen to the wires," said the rittmaster.

So they were left on the trees.

No storms came. The air remained heavy and sultry. On the other hand, they learned from some of the refusals that a well-known aristocratic club in Vienna had scheduled a party on the same Sunday as the dragoons. Some of the invitees were torn between their desire to hear all the latest society news (which was possible only at the club ball) and the adventurous pleasure of visiting the almost legendary border. This exoticism was just as seductive as the gossip, as the opportunity to spot a favorable or hateful attitude, grant favors that were requested, or obtain favors that were needed. A few people promised to cable—at the last moment, however. Such responses and the prospect of telegrams almost totally destroyed the sense of security that Colonel Festetics had developed during the past few days.

"It's disastrous!" he said.

"It's disastrous!" the rittmaster repeated.

And their heads drooped.

How many room should be prepared? A hundred or only fifty? And where, at the hotel? In Chojnicki's home? Unfortunately, he wasn't here and he hadn't even replied!

"He's crafty, that Chojnicki, I've never trusted him!" said the rittmaster.

"I couldn't agree more!" the colonel confirmed.

There was a knock, and the orderly announced Count Chojnicki.

"A fabulous fellow!" both officers cried in unison.

They welcomed him exuberantly. The colonel privately felt that his own genius was failing him and needed help. They took turns embracing the guest, each man three times. And each man waited impatiently for the other to finish his embrace. Then they ordered drinks.

All their deep anxieties suddenly turned into charming, graceful ideas. When, say, Chojnicki cried, "Then we'll order a hundred rooms, and if fifty stay empty who cares?", both officers chorused as if in one voice, "Brilliant!" And they again threw their exuberant arms around the guest.

During the final week before the celebration, there was no rain. All the garlands remained aloft, all the lanterns. At times the junior officer and the four privates camping like an outpost on the outskirts of the Little Forest and peering westward, in the direction of the heavenly foe, were frightened by a distant rumble, an echo of distant thunder. At times some pale sheet lightning flamed in the evening over the gray-blue fog thickening on the western horizon, where it gently cushioned the declining red sun. The storms might be breaking far from here, as if in a different world. But the mute Little Forest crackled with dry needles and the parched bark of the pine trunks. The birds peeped, dull and drowsy. The soft, sandy ground between the trunks was aglow. No storm came. The garlands remained on the wires.

On Friday a few guests arrived. They had been announced by telegrams. The officer on duty picked them up at the station. The excitement in both barracks mounted by the hour. In Brodnitzer's café, dragoons and riflemen conferred, the pretexts flimsy, the goal being purely to intensify the nervousness. Nobody was able to stay alone. Impatience drove them together. They whispered; they suddenly knew lots of bizarre secrets that they had hushed up for years. They trusted one another unreservedly, they loved one another. They sweated harmoniously, in joint expectation. The celebration eclipsed the horizon like a huge festive mountain. They were all convinced that this was no mere diversion; it was a radical transformation of their lives. In the last moment they had qualms about their own work. The celebration, of its own accord, started beckoning amiably and threatening dangerously. It darkened the sky, it brightened the sky. The men brushed and ironed their dress uniforms. Not even Captain Lorenz dared to play pool in these days. The easygoing coziness in which he had made up his mind to spend the rest of his military life was destroyed. He eyed his dress tunic suspiciously; it looked like a fat drayhorse that is suddenly forced to run a harness race after years of standing in the cool shade of a stable.

Sunday dawned at last. They counted fifty-four guests. "Well I'll be damned and double damned!" Count Zschoch said a couple of times. He knew the kind of regiment he was serving in, but at the sight of the fifty-four exalted names on the guest list he decided that all these years he had not been proud enough of this regiment.

The celebration began at 1 P.M. with an hour-long parade on the drilling grounds. They had borrowed two military bands from larger garrisons. They performed in two round, open, wooden malls in the Little Forest. The ladies sat in canvas-covered baggage wagons, wearing summer frocks over stiff corsets and wheel-size hats on which stuffed birds nested. Although the ladies were hot they smiled, each lady a cheerful breeze. They smiled with lips and eyes, with breasts trapped in airy tight-hooked frocks, with ajourisé lace gloves that reached up to their elbows, with tiny handkerchiefs that they held in their hands, sometimes dabbing their noses—but gently, gently to avoid tattering the lace. Vendors sold candy, champagne, and tickets for the wheel of fortune, which was handled personally by the superintendent, and colored pouches of confetti, which was poured on all of them and which they tried to puff away by coquettishly pursing their lips. Nor was there any lack of paper streamers. They coiled around necks and legs and dangled from the trees, instantly turning all natural pines into man-made ones. For they were denser and more convincing than the green of nature.

Meanwhile the long-awaited clouds had gathered in the sky above the forest. The thunder drew closer and closer, but it was drowned out by the army bands. When the evening set in over tents, carriages, confetti, and dancing, the lanterns were lit, and no one noticed that they were shaken harder by sudden gusts than was proper for festive lanterns. For a long time the sheet lightning that flamed more and more intensely in the sky could not compete with the fireworks that the troops set off behind the forest. And most of these people assumed that any flashes of lightning that they happened to notice were merely fizzled rockets. All at once somebody exclaimed, "A storm's coming!" And the rumor of the storm began spreading through the forest.

So they got ready to leave, and on foot, on horseback, and in carriages they headed toward Chojnicki's home. All the windows were open. The radiance of the candles poured freely, a powerful flickering that fanned out into the broad avenue, gilding the ground and the trees, making the leaves look like metal. It was still early but already dark, because of the hosts of clouds moving in on all sides, joining forces, uniting in a single mass. Outside the entrance to the castle, in the broad avenue and on the gravel-strewn oval in front of the gates, the horses, carriages, and guests now gathered, the colorful ladies and the even more colorful officers. The mounts, which privates held at the bit, and the carriage horses, barely reined in by the coachmen, grew impatient: the wind stroked their glossy coats like an electric comb; the frightened horses whinnied for their stables, scraping the gravel with trembling hooves.

The humans seemed to share the agitation of nature and animals. The excited shouts accompanying their ball games just minutes ago now died out. They all peered, somewhat nervously, at the doors and windows. The huge double door flew open, and groups of people began approaching the entrance. Either they were too preoccupied with the not unusual but nevertheless constant agitation of the storm or else they were distracted by the confused sounds of the two military bands, which had already started tuning their instruments inside the house. But whatever the reason, no one caught the rapid gallop of the orderly who now sprang over to the gates and sharply reined in his horse; in his service uniform, with a sparkling helmet, a rifle slung across his back and a cartridge belt on his waist, the orderly, surrounded by the flickers of white lightning and the gloom of violet clouds, was not unlike a theatrical messenger of war.

The dragoon dismounted and asked for Colonel Festetics. The colonel, he was told, was already inside. An instant later, Festetics came out, was handed a letter by the orderly, and went back indoors.

He halted in the circular vestibule, which had no ceiling light. A footman stepped behind him, clutching a candelabrum. The colonel tore open the envelope. The footman, although trained since earliest childhood in the great art of serving, could not keep his hand from suddenly trembling. The candles he held began guttering wildly. He made no attempt to read over the colonel's shoulder, but nevertheless the text of the letter passed within sight of his well-trained eyes: a lone sentence made up of huge and very distinct words scrawled in blue pencil. Had his lids been closed, he would have still been unable to avoid sensing the lightning that now flashed more and more often in all parts of the sky, and likewise he could not possibly have removed his eyes from the big, blue, dreadful script. HEIR TO THRONE RUMORED ASSASSINATED IN SARAJEVO, said the capital letters.

The text plunged as one word, without breaks, into the colonel's mind and into the footman's eyes behind him. The colonel dropped the envelope. The footman, his left hand clutching the candelabrum, bent down to retrieve the envelope with his right hand. Standing up again, he peered directly into the face of Colonel Festetics, who had turned toward him. The footman stepped back. He held the candelabrum in one hand, the envelope in the other, and both his hands trembled. The glow of the candles flickered over the colonel's face, alternately brightening and darkening it. His normally reddish face, decorated with a big grayish-blond moustache, kept turning violet or chalk white. His lips quivered slightly, and his moustache twitched. Aside from the footman and the colonel, the vestibule was deserted. From the interior rooms they could already hear the first muffled waltz of the two army bands, the clinking of glasses, and the murmuring of voices. Through the vestibule door, they saw the reflections of distant lightning, they heard the faint echoes of distant thunder.

The colonel eyed the footman. "Did you read it?"

"Yessir, Herr Colonel."

"Keep your mouth shut!" said Festetics, putting his finger to his lips. He walked off. He reeled slightly. Perhaps it was the flickering candlelight that made his gait look unsteady.

The inquisitive footman, as agitated by the colonel's gag order as by the gory news that he had just learned, waited for a colleague who would take over his candelabrum; the footman wanted to go into the rooms and perhaps get some details. Although a sensible and enlightened middle-aged man, he suddenly got the creeps in this vestibule, which he could illuminate only meagerly with his candles as it sank into an even deeper brown darkness after each vehement streak of bluish-white lightning. Heavy billows of charged air came through the room. The storm hesitated. The footman saw a supernatural link between the chance arrival of the storm and the terrible news. He felt that the moment had finally come when the supernatural forces of the world were clearly trying to announce their dreadful coming. And he crossed himself, his left hand clutching the candelabrum. At that instant, Chojnicki emerged, gaped at him in surprise, and asked if he was really that frightened of the storm. It wasn't the storm, the footman replied. For while he had promised to keep mum, he was no longer able to bear the burden of his complicity.

"Then what are you scared of?" asked Chojnicki.

Colonel Festetics had received some horrible news, said the footman. And he quoted the text.

All the windows were already shut because of the storm, and Chojnicki told his servants to draw the thick curtains as well and then to prepare his carriage. He wanted to drive to town. While the horses were being harnessed, a droshky pulled up, with its unrolled hood dripping, so you could tell it came from an area where the storm had already broken. Out stepped that cheery district commissioner who had tried to quell the demonstration of the striking bristle workers; he had a briefcase under his arm. First, as if this were his main reason for coming, he reported that it was raining in the little town. Next he informed Chojnicki that the heir to the throne of the Austro-Hungarian monarchy had probably been shot to death in Sarajevo. Travelers who had arrived three hours ago had been the first to spread the news. Then a mutilated, encoded wire from the governor's office had arrived. Obviously, he said, telegraph communication had been disrupted by the storm, as a request for particulars had so far gone unanswered. Furthermore this was Sunday, and there was almost nobody in the offices. The agitation in town and even in the villages was, he said, rising steadily, and despite the storm people were out in the streets.

While the commissioner spoke in hasty whispers, they could hear the shuffling of the dancers in the rooms, the sharp clinking of glasses, and, from time to time, the deep laughter of men. Chojnicki decided to gather a few of his guests in a separate room—people he viewed as influential, discreet, and still sober. Resorting to all kinds of pretexts, he steered now one, now another into the selected room, introduced the district commissioner, and reported the news. These chosen few included the colonel of the dragoon regiment and the major of the rifle battalion with their aides, several bearers of illustrious names, and, representing the officers of the rifle battalion, Lieutenant Trotta. The room they were in was short on seating, so a couple of the men had to lean against the walls while a few unsuspecting and exuberant souls, not knowing what had occurred, sat cross-legged on the carpet. But as it soon turned out, they remained where they were even after hearing the news. Several may have been paralyzed by the shock, others were simply drunk. A third group, however, was by nature indifferent to all events in the world and, so to speak, paralyzed out of innate refinement, and they felt it would not do for them to inconvenience their bodies merely because of a catastrophe. Some had not even removed the gaudy shreds of streamers and the round confetti bits from their necks, heads, and shoulders. And these clownish insignia lent even greater horror to the news.

The small room became hot within minutes. "Let's open a window!" someone said. Someone else unlatched one of the high narrow windows, leaned out, and bounced back a second later. An unusually violent bolt of white-hot lightning struck the park beyond the window. They couldn't tell where it had landed, but they heard the splintering of felled trees. Their roaring crowns toppled, black and heavy. And even the exuberant squatters, normally indifferent, leaped up; the tipsy guests began to stagger; and everyone blanched. They were amazed that they were still alive. They held their breath, gawked wide-eyed at one another, and waited for the thunder. It followed within seconds. But between lightning and thunder, eternity itself was crammed in. They all tried to huddle together. They formed a clump of heads and bodies around the table. For an instant their faces, however diverse the features, showed a fraternal resemblance. They acted as if this were their first storm. In fear and awe they waited for the terse clap of cracking thunder. Then they breathed sighs of relief. And while outside the windows the heavy clouds sliced up by the lightning foamed together in a jubilant tumult, the men began returning to their places.

"We have to break up the party!" said Major Zoglauer.

Rittmaster Zschoch, with some confetti stars in his hair and a scrap of pink streamer around his neck, leaped up. He was offended: as a count, as a rittmaster, as a dragoon in particular, as a cavalryman in general, and very particularly as himself, an extraordinary individual—in a word, as Zschoch. His short thick eyebrows bristled, their stiff tiny spikes forming two menacing hedges against Major Zoglauer. His big, bright, silly eyes, which always mirrored everything they might have picked up years ago but rarely what they saw at the moment, now seemed to express the arrogance of his ancestors, an arrogance from the fifteenth century. He had nearly forgotten the lightning, the thunder, the dreadful news—all the events of the past few minutes. His mind retained only the arduous efforts he had gone to for the celebration, his brainchild. Nor could he hold liquor—he had drunk champagne, and his tiny saddlenose was perspiring slightly.

"The news isn't true," he said. "It's simply not true. Let someone prove to me that it's true. A stupid lie—you can tell just from the words 'rumored' or 'probably' or whatever the political gobbledygook!"

"A rumor is enough!" said Zoglauer.

Now Herr von Babenhausen, reserve rittmaster, joined the argument. He was tipsy and kept fanning himself with his handkerchief, either sticking it into his sleeve or pulling it out again. He detached himself from the wall, stepped over to the table, and squinted.

"Gentlemen," he said, "Bosnia is far away. We don't give a damn about rumors. As far as I'm concerned, to hell with them! If it's true, we'll find out soon enough."

"Bravo!" cried Baron Nagy Jenö, the one from the hussars.

Although he undeniably had a Jewish grandfather in Bogumin and although his father had purchased his baronage, he considered the Magyars one of the noblest races in the monarchy—nay, the world!—and he managed to forget his Semitic background by taking on all the defects of the Hungarian gentry.

"Bravo!" he repeated. He had succeeded in respectively loving or hating anything that seemed favorable or detrimental to Hungary's nationalist policies. He had spurred his heart to loathe the heir to the monarchy's throne because it was generally said that Franz Ferdinand was partial to the Slavic peoples and hostile to the Hungarians. Baron Nagy had not traveled all the way to a party on the godforsaken border just to have it disrupted by some incident. He considered it a betrayal of the whole Magyar nation if some rumor prevented one of its members from dancing a czardas, which he felt racially obligated to do. Wedging his monocle in tighter as he always did when he had to feel nationalistic, the way an old man clutches his cane harder when he starts out on a hike, the baron said in the German of the Hungarians, which sounded vaguely like a process of whiny orthography, "Herr von Babenhausen is right, absolutely right! If the heir to the throne has been assassinated, then there are other heirs left!"

Herr von Senny, more Magyar by blood than Herr von Nagy, was filled with sudden dread that someone of a Jewish background might outdo him in Hungarian nationalism; rising to his feet, he said, "If the Herr heir to the throne has been assassinated, well, first of all, we know nothing for certain, and secondly, it doesn't concern us in the least!"

"It does concern us to some extent," said Count Benkyö, "but he hasn't been assassinated at all. It's just a rumor!"

Outside the rain gushed on steadily. The bluish white flashes grew rarer and rarer; the thunder moved away.

First Lieutenant Kinsky, who had grown up on the banks of the Moldau, claimed that in any case the heir to the throne had been a highly precarious choice for the monarchy—assuming one could even use the word "been." He himself, the first lieutenant, agreed with the men who had spoken before him: the news of the assassination of the heir to the throne had to be treated as a false rumor. They were so far away from the scene of the alleged crime that there was no way they could verify anything. And in any case they wouldn't find out the whole truth until long after the party.

Count Battyanyi, who was drunk, hereupon began speaking Hungarian to his compatriots. The others didn't understand a word. They remained silent, glancing at each speaker in turn and waiting, a bit stunned all the same. But the Hungarians seemed determined to go merrily along for the rest of the evening; perhaps it was a national custom. While the non-Hungarians were far from grasping even a syllable, they could tell by the faces of the Magyars that they were gradually starting to forget that anyone else was present. Sometimes they laughed in unison. The others were offended, not so much because laughter seemed inappropriate at this moment as because they couldn't ascertain its cause.

Jelacich, a Slovene, hit the ceiling. He hated the Hungarians as much as he despised the Serbs. He loved the monarchy. He was a patriot. And there he stood, love of Fatherland in his helplessly outspread hands, like a flag you have to plant somewhere but can't find a roof for. A number of his fellow Slovenes and his cousins, the Croats, lived directly under Hungarian rule. The whole of Hungary separated Rittmaster Jelacich from Austria and from Vienna and from Kaiser Franz Joseph. The heir to the throne had been killed in Sarajevo, practically Jelacich's homeland, and perhaps by a Slovene, such as the rittmaster himself was. If the rittmaster now began defending the victim against blasphemy from the Hungarians (he was the only non-Hungarian here to understand their language), they could retort that the assassins were his compatriots. And he did feel a wee bit guilty. He didn't know why. For some hundred and fifty years his family had been serving the Hapsburgs with sincerity and devotion. But both his teenage sons were already talking about independence for all southern Slavs, and they had pamphlets that they concealed from him—pamphlets that might come from a hostile Belgrade. Yet he loved his sons! Every afternoon at thirteen hundred hours, when his regiment passed the high school, his sons dashed over to him, fluttering out of the huge brown door of the school, their hair tousled, laughter pouring from their open mouths, and paternal tenderness compelled him to dismount and hug his children. He shut his eyes when he saw them reading suspicious newspapers, and he closed his ears when he heard them making suspicious remarks. He was intelligent and he knew that he stood powerless between his forebears and his offspring, who were destined to become the ancestors of a brand-new race. They had his features, his hair color, and his eyes, but their hearts beat to a new rhythm, their heads gave birth to strange thoughts, their throats sang new and strange songs that he had never heard. And though he was only forty, the rittmaster felt like an old man, and his sons seemed liked incomprehensible great-grandchildren.

None of that matters, he thought now, and he went over to the table and slapped it with his flat hand. "Gentlemen," he said, "may we request that you continue the conversation in German."

Benkyö, who was speaking, broke off and replied, "I will say it in German. We are in agreement, my countrymen and I: we can be glad the bastard is gone!"

Everyone leaped up. Chojnicki and the cheery district commissioner left the room. The guests remained alone. They had been informed that no witness would be tolerated during internal army quarrels. Lieutenant Trotta stood by the door. He had drunk a lot. His face was ashen, his limbs were slack, his palate was dry, his heart hollow. He felt intoxicated, but to his amazement he missed the familiar beneficent fog in front of his eyes.

Instead he appeared to see everything more distinctly, as if through clear, shiny ice. Although he had never seen these faces before, he felt he had known them a long time. Indeed, this whole occasion seemed utterly familiar, the realization of something he had often dreamed of. The Fatherland of the Trottas was splintering and crumbling.

At home, in the Moravian district seat of W, Austria might still exist. Every Sunday Herr Nechwal's band played "The Radetzky March." Austria existed once a week, on Sundays. The Kaiser, that forgetful old man with the white beard and the drop gleaming on his nose, and old Herr von Trotta were Austrians. Old Jacques was dead. The Hero of Solferino was dead. Regimental Physician Dr. Demant was dead. "Leave the army!" he had said. I'm going to leave the army, the lieutenant thought. My grandfather left it too. I'm gonna tell them, he thought. He felt compelled to do something, just as he had felt years ago in Frau Resi's establishment. Was there no painting to rescue here? He felt his grandfather's dark gaze on the back of his neck. He took a step toward the center of the room. He didn't quite know what he wanted to say. A few of the men looked at him.

"I know," he began and still knew nothing. "I know," he repeated, taking another step forward, "that His Imperial-Royal Highness, the Archduke and Heir Apparent, has really been assassinated."

He fell silent. He pressed his lips together. They formed a thin pale-pink strip. A clear, almost white light gleamed in his small dark eyes. His black, tangled hair overshadowed his low forehead, darkening the cleft between the eyebrows, the cavern of anger, the Trotta legacy. He kept his head down. His clenched fists hung on his slack arms. They all stared at his hands. Had they been acquainted with the portrait of the Hero of Solferino, they would have believed that old Trotta had returned from the grave.

"My grandfather," the lieutenant resumed, still feeling the old man's gaze on the back of his neck, "my grandfather saved the Kaiser's life. And I, his grandson, will not allow anyone to insult the House of our Supreme Commander in Chief. These gentlemen are behaving scandalously." He raised his voice. "Scandal!" he shouted. This was the first time he had ever heard himself shout. Unlike his fellow officers, he never shouted at his men. "Scandal!" he repeated. The echo of his voice reverberated in his ears. The drunken Count Benkyö took a staggering step toward the lieutenant.

"Scandal!" the lieutenant repeated once again.

"Scandal!" Rittmaster Jelacich echoed.

"If anyone else says another word against the dead man," the lieutenant went on, "I'll shoot him down!" He reached into his pocket. Since the drunken Count Benkyö was starting to murmur something, Trotta shouted "Silence!" in a voice that sounded borrowed, a thundering voice—perhaps it was the voice of the Hero of Solferino. He felt as one with his grandfather. He himself was the Hero of Solferino. That was his own portrait blurring under the ceiling of his father's den.

Colonel Festetics and Major Zoglauer stood up. For the first time in the history of the Austrian army a lieutenant was ordering rittmasters, majors, and colonels to shut up. No one now believed that the assassination of the heir to the throne was merely a rumor. They could see him lying in a steaming pool of red blood. They feared they would see blood here too, in this room, any second now. "Order him to keep quiet," Colonel Festetics whispered.

"Herr Lieutenant," said Zoglauer, "leave us!"

Trotta turned toward the door. At that instant, it burst open. Countless guests poured in, with confetti and streamers clinging to their heads and shoulders. The door stayed open. They heard the women laughing in the other rooms and the music and the shuffling of the dancers.

Someone yelled, "The heir to the throne has been assassinated!"

"The Funeral March!" shouted Benkyö.

"The Funeral March!" several voices repeated.

They poured out the door. In the two huge rooms where the guests had been dancing, both military bands, led by their bright-red, smiling bandmasters, played Chopin's Funeral March. All around, a few guests were circling, circling to the beat of the music. Gaudy streamers and confetti stars clung to their hair and shoulders. Men in uniform or in mufti escorted ladies. Their feet unsteadily obeyed the macabre and stumbling rhythm. For the bands were playing without scores, not conducted but accompanied by the slow loops that the black batons traced in the air. Sometimes one band lagged behind the other and then tried to catch up with the hastier one by skipping a few measures.

The guests walked in a circle around the empty, mirrorlike parquet floor. They circled round and round, each person a mourner behind the corpse of the one in front of him, and, at the center of the room, the invisible corpses of the heir apparent and the monarchy. Everyone was drunk. And if someone hadn't drunk enough, his head spun anyway from the indefatigable circling.

Gradually the bands accelerated the beat, and the legs of the walkers began to march. The drummers drummed incessantly, and the heavy sticks began pelting the bass drum like lively young drumsticks. The intoxicated drummer struck a silver triangle, and Count Benkyö pranced for joy. "The bastard's gone!" the count yelled in Hungarian. But everyone understood him as if he had spoken German. Suddenly a few guests began to hop; the bands boomed out the Funeral March faster and faster. In between, the triangle smiled, sharp, silvery, and drunk.

Eventually Chojnicki's footmen began clearing away the instruments. The smiling musicians put up with it. The violinists stared googly-eyed after their violins, the cellists after their cellos, the horn players after their horns. A couple of string players were still sliding their bows over the deaf-and-dumb cloth of their sleeves, with their heads swaying to the strains of inaudible melodies that were simmering in their drunken minds. When the drummer's percussions were hauled away, he kept brandishing his sticks in the air. Eventually, the bandleaders, having drunk the most, were dragged away like the instruments, each by two footmen. The guests laughed. Then the rooms grew still. No one uttered a sound. They all remained wherever they stood or sat and did not budge. After the instruments the bottles were cleared away, and any half-full glass remaining in anyone's hand was removed.

Lieutenant Trotta left the house. On the steps leading to the entrance sat Colonel Festetics, Major Zoglauer, and Rittmaster Zschoch. The rain had stopped. Every now and then drops fell from the thinning clouds and from the eaves. Huge white sheets had been draped over the stones for the three men to sit on. They looked as if they were sitting on their own shrouds. Large jagged splotches of rain gaped from their dark-blue backs. The wet tatters of a streamer now clung permanently around the rittmaster's neck.

The lieutenant halted before them. They didn't stir. Their heads stayed down. They recalled a group of military dummies in a waxworks.

"Herr Major," said Trotta to Zoglauer, "tomorrow I'm going to apply for my discharge from the army!"

Zoglauer stood up. He held out his hand, tried to speak, but was tongue-tied. The sky was gradually turning light. A gentle breeze tore the clouds apart; the faces could be seen distinctly in the shimmering silver of the brief night, which already contained an inkling of morning. Everything was astir in the major's haggard face. The tiny creases shifted into one another, the skin twitched, the jaw wandered to and fro, it seemed to be almost swinging, a few tiny muscles rippled around the cheekbones, the eyelids fluttered, and the cheeks quivered. Everything was astir because of the turmoil unleashed by the confused words, unspoken and unspeakable, inside the mouth. A hint of madness flickered across this face. Zoglauer squeezed Trotta's hand for a few seconds—eternities. Festetics and Zschoch were still squatting motionless on the steps. They could smell the strong scent of elder. They heard the gentle dripping of the rain and the delicate rustling of wet trees, and now the voices of animals, which had gone silent before the storm, began timidly awakening. The music inside the house had faded. Human speech was all that drifted through the closed and curtained windows.

"Maybe you're doing the right thing, you're young!" Zoglauer finally said. It was the most meager, the most ludicrous fraction of what he had been thinking during those seconds. He swallowed the rest of his thoughts, a huge tangled coil.

It was long past midnight. But in the small town the people were still standing in front of their houses, talking on the wooden sidewalks. They fell silent when the lieutenant walked past.

By the time he reached the hotel, day was dawning. He opened his closet. He put two uniforms, the civilian suit, the underclothes, and Max Demant's sword into the trunk. He worked slowly in order to fill out the time. He clocked the length of each motion. He stretched out his movements. He feared the empty time remaining until his report.

Morning had come. Onufrij brought the dress uniform and the glossy waxed boots.

"Onufrij," said the lieutenant, "I'm leaving the army."

"Yessir, Herr Lieutenant," said Onufrij. He went out, along the corridor, down the stairs, into his room, packed his belongings in a colored handkerchief, tied it to the thick end of his stick, and placed everything on the bed. He decided to return home, to Burdlaki; the harvesting would be starting soon. Now there was nothing to keep him in the Imperial and Royal Army. This was known as "deserting," and you could be shot. But the constables reached Burdlaki only once a week, and he could hide. How many others had already done the same! Panterleimon, Ivan's son; Grigorii, Nikolai's son; pockmarked Pavel; red-haired Nikofor. Only one man had been caught and condemned, but that had been a long time ago.

As for Lieutenant Trotta, he submitted his discharge request during his report. He was instantly furloughed. He took leave of his fellow officers on the drilling grounds. They didn't know what to say to him. They surrounded him in a loose circle until Zoglauer finally hit on the right wording. It was extremely simple—"Good luck!"—and everyone repeated it.

The lieutenant went to see Chojnicki.

"There's room here any time," said the count. "By the way, let me pick you up!"

For a second, Trotta thought of Frau von Taussig.

Chojnicki read his mind and said, "She's with her husband. His current attack is going to last for a long time. He may stay there for good. And he's right. I envy him. Incidentally, I've visited her. She's grown old, dear friend, she's grown old!"

The next morning at ten, Lieutenant Trotta entered the district headquarters. His father was sitting in his den. As soon as the lieutenant opened the door, he saw him. His father sat opposite the door, next to the window. Through the green blinds the sun traced thin stripes on the dark-red carpet. A fly buzzed, a clock ticked on the wall. The room was cool, shady, and filled with summery hush, as it had been long ago during vacations. Nevertheless a vague new glow clung to all the objects here. One couldn't tell where it came from. The district captain stood up. He himself emanated the new shimmer. The pure silver of his beard tinged the greenish light of the day and the reddish glow of the carpet. It exhaled the radiant mildness of an unknown, perhaps otherworldly day that was already dawning in the midst of Herr von Trotta's earthly life, just as the mornings of this world begin to dawn while the stars of the night are still shining. Many years ago, when the boy had come from Hranice to spend his vacation, his father's whiskers had been a small black cloud divided in two.

The district captain remained standing at his desk. He let his son approach, placed his pince-nez on the documents, and held out his arms. They kissed quickly.

"Sit down!" said the old man, pointing to the armchair where Carl Joseph had sat as a cadet on those Sundays, from 9 to 12 A.M., his cap on his knees and his radiant snow-white gloves on the cap.

"Father," Carl Joseph began, "I'm leaving the army."

He waited. He instantly sensed that he could explain nothing while sitting. So he got up, stood facing his father at the other end of the desk, and looked at the silvery whiskers.

"After this disaster," said the father, "that struck us two days ago, such an act amounts to . . . to . . . desertion."

"The whole army has deserted," Carl Joseph replied. He left the desk. He began walking up and down the room, his left hand on his back, his right hand accompanying his words. Many years ago, that was how the old man had walked through the room.

A fly buzzed, the clock ticked. The sunny stripes on the carpet grew brighter and brighter. The sun was rising quickly; it must be very high by now. Carl Joseph broke off and glanced at the district captain. The old man sat there. Both hands dangled limply, half hidden in the stiff, round, shiny cuffs on the arms of the chair. His head sank to his chest, and his whiskers rested on his lapels. He's young and foolish, the son thought. He's a dear young fool with white hair. Perhaps I'm his father, the Hero of

Solferino. I've grown old; he has merely lived for many years." Carl Joseph walked up and down, explaining.

"The monarchy is dead, it's dead!" he cried and halted.

"Probably," murmured the district captain.

He rang for his assistant. "Tell Fräulein Hirschwitz that we are lunching twenty minutes later today."

Then he said, "Come on," stood up, and took his hat and cane. They walked to the town park.

"Fresh air can't hurt," said the district captain. They avoided the pavilion where the blond girl served soda water with raspberry syrup. "I'm tired!" said the district captain. "Let's sit down!" For the first time since he had begun serving in this town, Herr von Trotta sat on an ordinary bench in the park. With his cane tracing aimless lines and figures on the ground, he said, "I went to see the Kaiser. Actually I didn't want to tell you. The Kaiser himself took care of your problem. Not another word about it!"

Carl Joseph slipped his hand under his father's arm. He now felt the old man's thin arm as he had felt it years ago during an evening stroll in Vienna. This time he didn't remove his hand. They stood up together. They went home arm in arm.

Fräulein Hirschwitz came in her Sunday gray silk frock. A narrow strip of her lofty hairdo over the forehead had taken on the color of her festive garment. Despite the short notice she had managed to whip up a Sunday dinner: noodle soup, garnished roast, and cherry dumplings.

But the district captain didn't waste a single word on the menu. It was as if he were eating a run-of-the-mill schnitzel.

Chapter 20

ONE WEEK LATER Carl Joseph left his father. They hugged in the vestibule before climbing into the fiacre. In old Herr von Trotta's opinion, shows of affection should not take place on the railroad platform in front of chance witnesses. Their embrace was swift as usual, in the damp shade of the vestibule and the cool breath of the flagstones. Fräulein Hirschwitz was waiting on the balcony, as self-controlled as a man. Herr von Trotta had uselessly tried to explain to her that she need not wave. Apparently she considered it a duty. Although it wasn't raining, Herr von Trotta opened his umbrella. A slight overcast struck him as reason enough. Shielded by the umbrella, he mounted the fiacre. Fräulein Hirschwitz couldn't see him from the balcony. He didn't say a word. It was only when his son was standing in the train that the old man raised his hand and pointed his forefinger.

"It would be good," he said, "if you could get a medical discharge. One doesn't leave the army without good grounds!"

"Yessir, Papá!" said the lieutenant.

Just before the departure of the train, the district captain left the platform. Carl Joseph saw him walking away, his back rigid and, under his arm, the rolled-up umbrella pointing aloft like a drawn sword. He did not look back, old Herr von Trotta.

Carl Joseph received his discharge.

"What d'you wanna do now?" the other officers asked.

"I have a position!" said Trotta, and they delved no further.

He inquired after Onufrij. The regimental office told him that the orderly Kolohin had deserted.

Lieutenant Trotta went to the hotel. He slowly changed clothes. First he unbuckled his sword, the weapon and emblem of his honor. He had dreaded this moment. He was surprised that he felt no melancholy. A bottle of 180 Proof stood on the table, but he didn't need a drink. Chojnicki came to pick him up. His riding crop cracked downstairs—and now he was in the room. He sat and watched. It was afternoon, the church clock struck three. All the mellow voices of summer poured in through the open window. Summer itself was calling Lieutenant Trotta. Chojnicki, in a light-gray suit with yellow stripes, his yellow crop in his hand, was an envoy of summer. The lieutenant rubbed his sleeve across the dull scabbard, drew the sword, puffed on it, wiped the steel with his handkerchief, and placed the weapon in a case. It was like preparing a corpse for its funeral. Before strapping the sword case to the trunk, he balanced it once again on his palm. Then he buried Max Demant's sword next to it. He read the inscription scratched under the hilt. "Leave the army!" Demant had said. Now he was leaving. . . .

The frogs were croaking, the crickets were chirping. Chojnicki's chestnuts were neighing under the window, softly tugging on the light carriage; its axles were groaning. The lieutenant stood there, his tunic unbuttoned, the black rubber neckband between the open green lapels of the blouse. He turned around and said, "The end of a career!"

"The career has ended," Chojnicki remarked. "The career itself has come to an end!"

Now Trotta took off his tunic, the Kaiser's tunic. He spread the blouse flat across the table as he had learned to do at the military academy. First he pushed back the stiff collar, then folded the sleeves across it and put them into the cloth. Next he folded the lower half of the blouse. It was already a small package. The gray moiré lining was iridescent. Next came the trousers, folded twice. Now Trotta put on his gray civilian suit, but he kept the belt—the last reminder of his career (he had never understood how to deal with suspenders).

"One day my grandfather," he said, "must have packed up his military personality in much the same way."

"Probably," Chojnicki confirmed.

The trunk was still open. Trotta's military personality lay inside it, a corpse folded according to army regulations. It was time to close the trunk. Now the lieutenant felt a sudden stab of pain. His throat tightened, and tears came to his eyes; he turned to Chojnicki, trying to speak. At the age of seven Trotta had started boarding school, at ten military school. He had been a soldier all his life. Trotta the soldier had to be buried and mourned. You didn't lower a corpse into the ground without weeping. It was good that Chojnicki was there.

"Let's have a drink," said Chojnicki. "You're getting melancholy."

They drank. Then Chojnicki stood up and closed the lieutenant's trunk.

Brodnitzer himself carried the trunk down to the carriage. "You were a cherished tenant, Herr Baron," said Brodnitzer. He stood, hat in hand, beside the carriage. Chojnicki was already holding the reins. Trotta felt a burst of affection for Brodnitzer. Farewell! he wanted to say. But Chojnicki clicked his tongue, and the horses tugged at the reins, lifting their heads and tails simultaneously, and the high light wheels of the small carriage crunched across the sand of the street as if rolling through a soft bed.

They drove along between the swamps, which resonated with the din of the frogs.

"This is where you'll live," said Chojnicki.

It was a lodge on the edge of the Little Forest; it had green blinds like those on the windows of the district headquarters. The lodge was inhabited by Jan Stepaniuk, an assistant forester, an old man with a long drooping moustache of tarnished silver. He had served in the military for twelve years. Coming home to his army mother tongue, he addressed Trotta as "Herr Lieutenant." He wore a coarse linen shirt with a narrow collar embroidered in blue and red. The wind billowed the broad sleeves of the shirt, making his arms look like wings.

And here Lieutenant Trotta remained.

He was determined not to see any of his fellow officers. In his wooden room, by the glow of the flickering candle, he wrote letters to his father on yellowish, fibrous official stationery, the salutation four fingers from the top, the text two fingers from the side. All the letters were as alike as timetables.

He had little to do. He entered the names of the day laborers into the huge black-and-green ledgers, the salaries, the requirements of Chojnicki's guests. He added up the figures, with good intentions but incorrectly; reported on the state of the poultry, the pigs, the fruit that was sold or kept, the small plot where the yellow hops grew, and the kiln, which was leased to a commissioner every year.

He now spoke the local vernacular. He could pick up some of what the peasants said. He dealt with the red-haired Jews, who were already buying wood for the winter. He learned the different values of birches, pines, firs, oaks, lindens, and maples. He pinched pennies. Just like his grandfather, the Hero of Solferino, the Knight of Truth, he counted out hard silver coins with gaunt, hard fingers whenever he came to town for the Thursday pig market to purchase saddles, horse collars, yokes, and scythes, grindstones, sickles, rakes, and seed. If he spotted an officer walking by, he lowered his head. It was an unnecessary precaution. His moustache had grown and thickened; the stubble on his cheeks bristled hard, black, and dense. You could scarcely recognize him.

Everyone was preparing for the harvest. The peasants stood outside their huts, whetting their scythes on the round brick-red grindstones. Throughout the countryside, stone whirred against steel, drowning out the chant of the crickets. At night the lieutenant sometimes heard music and clamor from Chojnicki's New Castle. He absorbed those voices into his sleep, along with the nocturnal crowing of roosters and the barking of dogs at the full moon. He finally felt content, lonesome, and at peace. It was as if he had never led any other life. Whenever he couldn't sleep, he would get up, take his stick, walk across the fields, through the many-voiced chorus of the night, wait for morning, greet the red sun, breathe the dew and the gentle singing of the wind that ushers in the day. He felt as fresh as if he had slept all night.

Each morning he strolled through the adjacent villages. "Praised be Jesus Christ!" said the peasants. "Forever. Amen!" Trotta replied. Like them he walked with slightly bent knees. That was how the peasants of Sipolje had walked.

One day he passed through the village of Burdlaki. The tiny church spire stood—a finger of the village—against the blue sky. The afternoon was quiet. The roosters crowed drowsily. The mosquitoes hummed and capered along the village road. Suddenly a peasant with black hair and a full beard emerged from his hut, stood in the middle of the road, and greeted him.

"Praised be Jesus Christ!"

"Forever. Amen!" said Trotta, about to move on.

"Herr Lieutenant, I'm Onufrij!" said the bearded peasant. The beard, a dense, black, outspread fan, camouflaged his face.

"Why did you desert?" asked Trotta.

"I only wen' home," said Onufrij.

It made no sense asking such foolish questions. He understood Onufrij. He had served the lieutenant just as the lieutenant had served the Kaiser. There was no more Fatherland. It was crumbling, splintering.

"Aren't you afraid?" asked Trotta.

Onufrij was not afraid. He lived with his sister. The constables went through the village every week without checking anything. Besides, they were Ukrainians, peasants like Onufrij himself. If no one filed a written complaint with the sergeant-major, Onufrij had nothing to worry about. And in Burdlaki no one filed complaints.

"Goodbye and good luck, Onufrij!" said Trotta. He walked up the winding road, which unexpectedly opened into the vast fields. Onufrij followed him as far as the bend. Trotta heard the thumping of the hobnailed military boots on the gravel of the road. Onufrij had taken along his army boots.

Trotta went to the village tavern owned by the Jew Avramtshik. You could buy curd soap here, liquor, cigarettes, tobacco, and postage stamps. The Jew had a fiery red beard. He sat outside the arched entrance of his tavern, shining far and wide, over more than a mile of the road. When he grows old, thought the lieutenant, he'll be a white-bearded Jew like Max Demant's grandfather.

Trotta had a drink, bought tobacco and stamps, and left. From Burdlaki the road led past Oleksk to the village of Sosnov, then Bytók, Leshnitz, and Dombrova. He took this route every day. He crossed the railroad tracks twice—two nondescript black-

and-yellow gates and the glassy signals ringing incessantly in the booths. Those were the merry voices of the great world, voices that no longer concerned Baron Trotta. The great world was snuffed out. His years in the military were snuffed out as if he had been walking across fields and along country roads all his life, stick in hand and never with sword at hip. He lived like his grandfather, the Hero of Solferino, and like his great-grandfather, the retired veteran in the castle park of Laxenburg, and perhaps like his nameless, unknown ancestors, the peasants of Sipolje. Always the same route, always past Oleksk, toward Sosnow, toward Bytók, toward Leshnitz and Dombrova. These villages lay around Chojnicki's castle; they all belonged to him. From Dombrova a willow-lined path led to Chojnicki. It was still early. If Trotta strode faster he would reach the castle by six without running into any of his former comrades. Trotta lengthened his stride. Now he stood under the windows. He whistled. Chojnicki appeared at the window, nodded, and emerged.

"It's finally come!" said Chojnicki. "The war's begun. We've been expecting it for a long time. But it will still catch us unprepared. I don't think any Trotta is destined to live very long in freedom. My uniform is ready. I assume we'll both be marching off in a week or two."

To Trotta it seemed as if nature had never been so peaceful as at this moment. You could look straight into the sun, it was sinking westward with visible haste. Receiving the sun, a stiff wind came, curling the white cloudlets in the sky, rippling the wheat and rye stalks on the earth, and caressing the red faces of the poppies. A blue shadow floated across the green meadows. In the east the Little Forest sank into dusky violet. Stepaniuk's white lodge, where Trotta was residing, shone at the edge of the forest, the melting sunlight burned in the windows. The crickets chirped louder. The wind carried their voices far away. There was a moment of hush; he could hear the breathing of the earth. Suddenly a faint, hoarse shrieking came from above, under the sky. Chojnicki raised his arm.

"Do you know what that is? Wild geese! They're leaving us earlier than usual. The summer's only half over. They can already hear the gunfire. They know what they're doing!"

It was Thursday, the day of the "small soiree." Chojnicki turned around. Trotta slowly walked toward the glittering windows of his lodge.

That night he got no sleep. At midnight he heard the hoarse shrieks of the wild geese. He dressed. He stepped outdoors. Stepaniuk, in his shirt, lay in front of the threshold, his pipe gleaming reddish. He lay flat on the ground and said without moving, "Can't sleep tonight."

"The geese!" said Trotta.

"That's right, the geese," Stepaniuk confirmed. "I've never heard them this early in all my life. Listen, listen!"

Trotta looked at the sky. The stars were twinkling as usual. Nothing else could be seen up there. Yet the hoarse shrieks persisted under the stars.

"They're practicing," said Stepaniuk. "I've been lying out here for a long time. Sometimes I can see them. They're only a gray shadow. Look!"

Stepaniuk stretched his gleaming pipe toward the sky. At that instant, they saw the tiny gray shadow of the wild geese under the cobalt blue. They wafted away, a small clear veil, among the stars.

"That's not all!" said Stepaniuk. "This morning I saw hundreds of ravens, a lot more than usual. Foreign ravens, they're coming from foreign parts. I think they're from Russia. Around here people say that the ravens are the prophets among the birds."

A broad silver stripe ran along the northeastern horizon. It grew visibly brighter. A wind arose. It brought a hubbub of sounds from Chojnicki's castle. Trotta lay down next to Stepaniuk. He drowsily gazed at the stars, listened to the shrieking of the geese, and fell asleep.

He awoke at sunrise. He felt as if he had napped only half an hour, but at least four hours must have slipped by. Instead of the familiar twittering of birds that greeted every new morning, he heard the black croaking of hundreds of ravens. Stepaniak got up at Trotta's side. His pipe had grown cold while he slept; he took it out of his mouth and pointed the stem at the surrounding trees. The large black birds sat rigid on the branches—sinister fruit fallen from the air. They sat motionless, the black birds, only croaking. Stepaniuk tossed stones at them, but the ravens merely flapped their wings a few times. They clung to the branches like fruit.

"I'm gonna shoot," said Stepaniuk.

He went indoors, he got his rifle, he shot. A few birds tumbled down, the rest seemed not to have heard the blast. They all remained on the branches. Stepaniuk picked up the black corpses. He had bagged a good dozen; he held his quarry in both hands and carried it indoors, blood dripping on the grass.

"Strange ravens," he said. "They don't stir. They are the prophets among the birds."

It was Friday. In the afternoon Carl Joseph walked through the villages as usual. The crickets weren't chirping, the frogs weren't croaking, only the ravens were shrieking. They perched everywhere, on the lindens, the oaks, the birches, the willows. Perhaps they always come before the harvest, thought Trotta. They hear the peasants sharpening the scythes, and then they simply gather.

He walked through the village of Burdlaki, secretly hoping that Onufrij would reappear. But Onufrij did not come. The peasants stood outside their huts, grinding the steel on the reddish whetstones. Now and then they looked up. They were worried by the croaking of the ravens and they fired black curses at the black birds.

Trotta walked past Avramtshik's tavern; the red-haired Jew sat at the entrance, his beard shining. Avramtshik stood up. He tipped his black velvet cap, pointed aloft, and said, "Ravens have come! They've been shrieking all day. Wise birds! We'd better watch out!"

"Maybe, yes, maybe you're right," said Trotta and walked on, along the familiar willow-lined path, to Chojnicki's home. Now Trotta stood under the windows. He whistled. No one came.

Chojnicki must have gone to town. Trotta headed there, taking the route across the swamps to avoid running into anyone. Only the peasants used this path A few came toward him. The path was so narrow they couldn't go past one another. One person had to stand and let the other squeeze by. All the people who came toward Trotta seemed to be walking faster than usual. They greeted more hastily than usual. They took longer strides. They walked with bent heads like people absorbed in a single weighty thought. And all at once, Trotta spotted the tollgate marking the town limit. There were more people out, a group of twenty or more, now walking in single file.

Trotta halted. He saw they must be workers, bristle workers returning to their villages. Perhaps some of them were people he had fired at. He halted to let them pass. They hurried by mutely, one after another, each with a small bundle on a shouldered stick. The evening seemed to gather more swiftly, as if the hastening people were increasing the darkness. The sky was faintly overcast; the sun was setting red and small; the silvery-gray fog rising over the swamps was an earthly brother of the clouds, striving toward his sisters.

Suddenly all the bells in town began to toll. The wayfarers paused for a moment, listened, and then strode on. Trotta stopped one of the last to ask why the bells were tolling.

"It's because of the war," the man replied without looking up.

"Because of the war," Trotta repeated. It was obvious: war. He felt he had known it since daybreak, since last night, since the day before yesterday, since weeks ago, since his discharge and the ill-fated celebration of the dragoons. Here was the war for which he had prepared himself since the age of seven. It was his war, the grandson's war. The days and the heroes of Solferino were returning.

The bells tolled endlessly. Now the customs barriers came. The sentry with the wooden leg stood outside his booth, surrounded by people; a radiant black-and-yellow poster hung on the door. The first few words, black on yellow, could be read even from far away. Like heavy beams they loomed over the heads of the assembled onlookers: TO MY PEOPLES!

Peasants in short odorous sheepskins, Jews in fluttering black-and-green gaberdines, Swabian farmers from the German colonies wearing green loden coats, Polish burghers, merchants,

craftsmen, and government officials surrounded the customs
officer's booth. On each of the four bare walls a huge poster was
pasted, each in a different tongue and starting with the Kaiser's
salutation: TO MY PEOPLES! Those who were literate read the
text aloud. Their voices mingled with the booming chant of the
bells. Some onlookers went from wall to wall, reading the text
in each language. Whenever one bell died out, another instantly
started booming. Throngs poured from the little town, surging
into the broad street that led to the railroad station. Trotta
walked toward them into town.

Evening had set in, and since it was Friday, the candles were
burning in the small Jewish cottages, illuminating the sidewalks.
Each cottage was like a small tomb. Death himself had lit the
candles. Louder than on other holy days, the chanting emerged
from the Jewish prayer houses. They were ushering in an
extraordinary, a bloody Sabbath. The Jews streamed from the
houses in black, hasty throngs, gathering on the crossroads, and
soon their laments arose for the soldiers among them, who had
to march off the next day. They clasped hands, they kissed one
another on the cheeks, and whenever two of them embraced,
their red beards tangled in a special farewell and they had to
untangle their beards with their fingers. The bells tolled over
their heads. Between their tolling and the shouts of the Jews
came the cutting voices of the bugles in the barracks. They were
sounding taps, the final lights-out. Night had come. No star
could be seen. The sky hung low, flat, and dreary over the little
town.

Trotta turned around. He tried to find a carriage—there was
none. He walked to Chojnicki's home with long, swift strides.
The door was open, and all the rooms were illuminated as they
were for the grand parties. In the antechamber Chojnicki came
toward him, wearing a uniform with a helmet and cartridge
pouches. He ordered a carriage. His garrison was twelve miles
away, and he wanted to travel that night.

"Wait a moment!" he said. This was the first time he used the
familiar form with Trotta, perhaps out of carelessness, perhaps
because he was already in uniform. "I'll drive you home and
then back to town."

They pull up at Stepaniuk's lodge. Chojnicki sits down. He watches Trotta doffing his civvies and donning his uniform, piece by piece. Several weeks ago—why, how long ago that was!—in Brodnitzer's hotel, he watched Trotta taking off his uniform. Trotta is returning to his military garb, to his homeland. He takes the saber from its case. He straps on his officer's sash, the gigantic black-and-yellow tassels gently caress the shimmering metal of the sword. Now Trotta shuts the trunk.

They have very little time for farewells. They pull up at the riflemen's barracks.

"Adieu!" says Trotta. Their handshake is a long one. Time passes almost audibly behind the coachman's broad, motionless back. A handshake seems inadequate. They feel they ought to do more.

"We usually kiss," says Chojnicki.

So they embrace and exchange a rapid kiss. Trotta gets out. The sentry at the barracks presents arms. The horses tug at the reins. The barracks gate falls shut behind Trotta. He stands for an instant, listening to Chojnicki's carriage drive away.

Chapter 21

THAT SAME NIGHT the rifle battalion headed northeast toward the border area of Woloczyska. It began drizzling gently, then raining harder and harder, and the white dust on the road turned into silvery-gray slime. The mire slapped against the boots of the soldiers and splattered the impeccable uniforms of the officers, who were marching to their death in regulation regalia. The long sabers got in their way, and the splendid long-fringed tassels of their black-and-gold sashes dropped on their hips, soaked, snarled, and spotted with a thousand tiny clots of mud. By dawn, the battalion reached its destination, joining with two other infantry regiments and forming skirmish lines.

They waited there for two days, with no sign of the war. At times they heard stray firing from far away, to their right. It came from minor border scrimmages between mounted squads. Sometimes they saw wounded customs officials and occasionally a dead border constable. Ambulance men whisked both the wounded and the dead past the waiting soldiers. The war refused to start. It wavered, just as a storm may brew for days before erupting.

The third day brought orders to retreat, and the battalion formed to march off. Both officers and men were disappointed. It was rumored that an entire dragoon regiment had been wiped out nine miles to the east. Supposedly Cossacks had invaded the country. Silent and grumpy, the Austrians marched west. They soon realized that no one had prepared the retreat, for they came upon a confused donnybrook of the most disparate military branches at highway crossings and in villages and small towns. Innumerable and conflicting directives poured in from army headquarters.

Most of these orders pertained to the evacuation of villages and towns and the treatment of pro-Russian Ukrainians, clerics, and spies. Hasty court-martials in villages passed hasty sentences. Secret informers delivered unverifiable reports on peasants, Orthodox priests, teachers, photographers, officials. There was no time. The army had to retreat swiftly but also punish the traitors swiftly. And while ambulances, baggage columns, field artillery, dragoons, riflemen, and infantrists formed abrupt and helpless clusters on the sodden roads, while couriers galloped to and fro, while inhabitants of small towns fled westward in endless throngs, surrounded by white terror, loaded down with red-and-white featherbeds, gray sacks, brown furniture, and blue kerosene lamps, the shots of hasty executioners carrying out hasty sentences rang from the church squares of hamlets and villages, and the somber rolls of drums accompanied the monotonous decisions of judges, and the wives of victims lay shrieking for mercy before the mud-caked boots of officers, and red and silver flames burst from huts and barns, stables and hayricks. The Austrian army's war had begun with court-martials. For days on end genuine and supposed traitors hung from the trees on church squares to terrify the living.

The living, however, had fled far and wide. Fires surrounded the corpses dangling from trees, and the leaves were already crackling, and the fire was more powerful than the steady, widespread gray drizzle heralding the bloody autumn. The old bark of ancient trees slowly charred, tiny, silvery, swelling sparks crept up along the fissures like fiery worms, reaching the foliage, and the green leaves curled, turned red, then black, then gray; the ropes broke, and the corpses plunged to the ground, their faces black, their bodies unscathed.

One day the soldiers halted in the village of Krutyny. They arrived in the afternoon, they were supposed to continue westward in the morning, before sunrise. By now the steady widespread rain had paused and the late-September sun wove a benevolent silvery light across the vast fields, which were still filled with grain, the living bread that would never be eaten. Gossamer drifted very slowly through the air. Even the crows and ravens kept still, inveigled by the fleeting peace of this day and with no hope of finding the expected carrion.

The officers hadn't taken off their clothes for a week. Their boots were waterlogged, their feet swollen, their knees stiff, their calves sore, their backs couldn't bend. They were billeted in huts. They tried to fish dry clothes out of the trunks and wash at the meager wells. In the clear, still night, with the abandoned and forgotten dogs in scattered farmyards howling in fear and hunger, the lieutenant couldn't sleep, and he left the hut where he was quartered. He walked down the long village street toward the church spire, which loomed against the stars with its twofold Greek cross. The church with its shingle roof stood in the middle of the small churchyard, surrounded by slanting wooden crosses that seemed to caper in the nocturnal light. Outside the huge gray wide-open gates of the graveyard three corpses were dangling: a bearded priest flanked by two young peasants in sandy-yellow smocks, with coarse-plaited raffia shoes on their unstirring feet. The black cassock of the priest hung down to his shoes. And sometimes the night wind nudged his feet so that they struck the circle of his priestly garment like dumb clappers in a deaf-and-dumb bell; they seemed to be tolling without evoking a sound.

Lieutenant Trotta approached the hanged men. He peered at their bloated faces. And he thought he recognized some of his own soldiers in these three victims. These were the faces of the peasants he had drilled with every day. The priest's black, fanning beard reminded him of Onufrij's beard. That was his parting image of Onufrij. And who could say? Perhaps Onufrij was the brother of this hanged priest. Lieutenant Trotta looked around. He listened. No human sound was to be heard. The bats rustled in the belfry of the church. Abandoned dogs howled in abandoned farms. The lieutenant drew his sword and cut down the three hanged men, one by one. Then he slung the corpses, one by one, over his shoulder and carried all of them, one by one, to the graveyard. Then, with his bare sword, he began loosening the soil on the paths between graves until he felt he had room enough for three corpses. Then he put all three of them in, shoveled the soil over them with sword and scabbard, and trampled on the ground till it was solid. Then he made the sign of the cross. He hadn't crossed himself since the final mass at the military academy in Hranice. He wanted to recite the Lord's Prayer, but his lips moved without producing a sound. Some nocturnal bird shrieked. The bats rustled. The dogs howled.

The next day, before sunrise, they marched on. The silvery mists of the autumn morning shrouded the world. But soon the sun climbed out of them, glowing as at the height of summer. They were thirsty. They marched through a desolate sandy area. At times they thought they heard water gurgling somewhere. A few soldiers ran toward where the gurgling seemed to come from, but then they instantly doubled back. No brook, no pond, no well. They marched through a couple of villages, but the wells were stuffed with corpses of people who had been shot or strung up. The corpses, some crumpled over in the middle, dangled from the wooden rims of the well. The soldiers didn't look into the depths. They rejoined the others. They marched on.

Their thirst grew fiercer. Noon came. They heard shots and lay flat on the ground. The enemy must have overtaken them. They now wormed their way along the ground. Soon they noticed that the road was widening. A deserted railroad station shone nearby. That was where the tracks began. The battalion ran to the station—they were safe here; for a few miles they would be covered on either side by the embankments. The enemy, perhaps a sotnia of galloping Cossacks, must be across from them on the other side. Silent and dejected, they marched between the embankments.

All at once someone shouted, "Water!" And a second later they had all spotted the well next to a signal booth on the ridge of the slope.

"Stay here!" Major Zoglauer commanded.

"Stay here!" the officers repeated.

But the parched men couldn't be stopped. Several individuals, then whole groups, scrambled up the slope. Shots rang out and the men dropped. Enemy horsemen on the other side of the embankment were firing at the parched soldiers, and more and more thirsty men were running toward the deadly well. By the time the second platoon of the second company approached the well, a dozen corpses were sprawling on the green slope.

"Platoon—halt!" Lieutenant Trotta commanded. Stepping out, he said, "I'll get you water! No one move! Wait here! Hand me a pail!"

They brought him two watertight canvas pails from the machine-gun section. He took a pail in each hand. And he climbed up the slope, toward the well. Bullets whistled around him, struck the soil at his feet, whizzed past his ears and his legs and above his head. He leaned over the well. Beyond the slope, on the other side, he saw the two lines of aiming Cossacks. He was not afraid. It never occurred to him that he could be hit like the others. He heard the shots before they were fired and also the opening drumbeats of "The Radetzky March." He was standing on the balcony of his father's house. The army band was playing down below. Now Nechwal raised the black ebony baton with the silver knob. Now Trotta lowered the second pail into the well. Now the cymbals clashed. Now he lifted the pail high. With an overflowing pail in each hand, amid whizzing bullets, he put down his left foot in order to descend. Now he took two steps. Now his head just barely loomed over the edge of the slope.

Now a bullet hit his skull. He took one more step and collapsed. The brimming pails shook, plunged, and poured water on him. Warm blood ran from his head to the cool soil of the slope. From below the Ukrainian peasants in his platoon chorused, "Praised be Jesus Christ!"

Forever. Amen! he wanted to say. Those were the only Ruthenian words he knew. But his lips didn't stir. His mouth gaped. His white teeth shone against the blue autumn sky. His tongue slowly turned blue; he felt his body grow cold. Then he died.

That was the end of Lieutenant Carl Joseph, Baron von Trotta.

The end of the grandson of the Hero of Solferino was a commonplace end, not suitable for textbooks in the elementary schools and high schools of Imperial and Royal Austria. Lieutenant Trotta died holding not a weapon but two pails.

Major Zoglauer wrote to the district captain. Old Trotta read the letter several times; then his hands sank. The letter dropped, fluttering down to the reddish carpet. Herr von Trotta did not remove his pince-nez. His head trembled, and the wobbly pince-nez with its oval lenses fluttered on the old man's nose like a glass butterfly. Two heavy crystal drops dripped simultaneously, dimmed the lenses, and ran down into the whiskers. Herr von Trotta's entire body remained calm, only his head waggled from back to front and from left to right, while the glass wings of the pince-nez kept fluttering.

For an hour or more the district captain remained at his desk. Then he stood up and walked home at his usual pace. He took the black suit out from his closet, and the black tie and the black crepe bands he had worn on his hat and his arm after his father's death. He changed clothes. He didn't look into the mirror while changing. His head was still waggling. He tried to steady his unruly skull. But the greater his effort, the more his head shook. The pince-nez was still fluttering on his nose. Finally the district captain gave up trying and let his skull waggle.

In his black suit, with the black band around his arm, he went to Fräulein Hirschwitz's room, halted at the door, and told her, "My son is dead, madam!"

He quickly shut the door, went to his headquarters, walked from office to office, stuck his waggling head through the door, and announced everywhere, "My son is dead, Herr So-and-so! My son is dead, Herr So-and-so!"

Then he took his hat and cane and went outdoors. All the people greeted him, surprised at his waggling head. Now and then the district captain stopped someone and announced, "My son is dead!" And he did not wait for the stunned man's condolence; instead he kept walking, toward Dr. Skowronnek. Dr. Skowronnek was in uniform, a medical colonel, at the garrison hospital in the morning, at the café in the afternoon. He rose when the district captain entered, saw the old man's waggling head, the band on his sleeve, and he knew everything. He took the district captain's hand and gazed at the trembling head and the fluttering pince-nez.

"My son is dead!" Herr von Trotta repeated.

Skowronnek held his friend's hand for a long time, for several minutes. Both remained standing, hand in hand. The district captain sat down, Skowronnek put the chessboard on a different table.

When the waiter came, the district captain announced, "My son is dead!" And the waiter bowed very low and brought him a cognac.

"Another one!" the district captain said. He finally removed his pince-nez. He remembered that the announcement of his son's death had been left on the carpet of his office. The district captain stood up and headed back to the district headquarters. Dr. Skowronnek walked after him. Herr von Trotta didn't seem to notice. Nor was he the least bit surprised when Skowronnek, without knocking, opened the door to the office, stepped inside, and halted. "Here is the letter!" said the district captain.

That night and many thereafter, old Herr von Trotta did not sleep. His head trembled and waggled on the pillows. Sometimes the district captain dreamt about his son. Lieutenant Trotta was standing in front of his father, his officer's cap filled with water, and he said, "Drink, Papá, you're thirsty!"

This dream kept recurring, more and more often. And gradually the district captain managed to call his son every night, and on some nights Carl Joseph showed up several times. Herr von Trotta began longing for night and bed, the day made him impatient. And when spring came and the days grew longer, the district captain darkened the rooms in the morning and the evening, prolonging his nights artificially. His head never stopped trembling. And he himself and everyone else got used to the constant trembling of his head.

The war scarcely seemed to trouble Herr von Trotta. He picked up a newspaper only to conceal his trembling skull. He and Dr. Skowronnek never talked about victories or defeats. Mostly they played chess without exchanging a word. But sometimes one would say to the other, "Do you remember? That game two years ago? You were as unfocused as you are today." It was as if they were talking about events that had occurred decades earlier.

A long time had passed since the news of the son's death, the seasons had replaced one another, according to the ancient, steadfast laws of nature, yet were barely perceptible under the red veil of war—least of all to the district captain. His head still trembled constantly like a huge but light fruit on an all-too-thin stem. Lieutenant Trotta had long since rotted or been gobbled up by ravens, which circled over the deadly embankments in those days; but old Herr von Trotta still felt as if he had received the news of his son's death only yesterday. And the letter from Major Zoglauer, who had likewise already died, remained in the district captain's breast pocket; it was read anew every day and maintained in its dreadful freshness, the way a grave mound is maintained by loving hands.

What did old Herr von Trotta care about the hundred thousand new corpses that had meanwhile followed his son? What did he care about the hasty and confused directives that came from his superiors week after week? And what did he care about the end of the world, which he now saw coming more clearly than the prophetic Chojnicki had once seen it? His son was dead. His office was terminated. His world had ended.

Epilogue

OUR SOLE REMAINING task is to describe the district captain's final days. They slipped by virtually like one day. Time flowed past him, a broad, even river, murmuring monotonously. The war communiqués and the governor's extraordinary decrees and directives barely ruffled the district captain's mind. He would have retired long since anyhow. He remained in office only because of the war. And so at times he felt he was merely living a second, paler life, long after completing his first and real life. His days did not seem to be hurrying toward the grave like the days of all other people. Petrified like his own gravestone, the district captain stood on the brink of days. Never had Herr von Trotta so closely resembled Kaiser Franz Joseph. At times he even dared to compare himself to the Kaiser. He thought of his audience at Schönbrunn, and in the manner of simple old men who talk about a catastrophe that has struck both of them, he would mentally say to Franz Joseph, What? If only someone had told us at the time! Told us two old men! . . .

Herr von Trotta slept very little. He ate without noticing what was put before him. He signed documents that he hadn't carefully read. At times, he would appear at the café in the afternoon, before Dr. Skowronnek arrived. Herr von Trotta would then pick up a three-day-old newspaper and read something he was long familiar with. But if Dr. Skowronnek spoke about the latest events, the district captain would merely nod as if he had learned the news long ago.

One day he received a letter. A woman he had never heard of, Frau von Taussig, now a voluntary nurse at the Steinhof Insane Asylum in Vienna, informed Herr von Trotta that Count Chojnicki had returned from the front, insane, several months ago and that he spoke about the district captain very frequently: in his confused utterances, he kept reiterating that he had important information for Herr von Trotta. And if the district captain happened to be planning a trip to Vienna, his visit with the patient might unexpectedly restore his sanity, as had occurred in similar cases now and then. The district captain consulted Dr. Skowronnek.

"Anything is possible," said Skowronnek. "If you can stand it—I mean, stand it easily. . . ."

Herr von Trotta said, "I can stand anything."

He decided to leave immediately. Perhaps the patient knew something important about the lieutenant. Perhaps he had something of the son's to give the father. Herr von Trotta went to Vienna.

He was taken to the military section of the asylum. It was late autumn, a dreary day; the asylum was shrouded in a gray, persistent rain that had been pouring over the world for days now. Herr von Trotta sat in the dazzling white corridor, peering through the barred window at the denser and softer bars of rain, and thought of the embankment slope where his son had died. Now he's getting soaked, thought the district captain, as if the lieutenant had died only today or yesterday and the corpse were still fresh.

Time wore by slowly. He saw people shuffling by with deranged faces and gruesomely contorted limbs, but for the district captain madness held little terror, even though this was his first visit to an insane asylum. Only death was terrible. Too bad! thought Herr von Trotta. If Carl Joseph had gone crazy instead of dying in action, I would have brought him back to his senses. And if I hadn't succeeded, then I would have come to see him every day! Perhaps he would have contorted his arm as horribly as this lieutenant here that they're walking past me. But it would have been only his arm, and you can caress a contorted arm. You can also look into twisted eyes! So long as they're my son's eyes. Happy the fathers whose sons are crazy!

Frau von Taussig came at last, a nurse like any other. He saw only her uniform—what did he care about her face? But she gazed and gazed at him and then said, "I knew your son!"

Only now did the district captain look at her face. It was the face of a woman who had grown old but was still beautiful. Indeed, the nurse's coif rejuvenated her, as it does all women, because it is in their nature to be rejuvenated by kindness and compassion and also by the external insignia of compassion. She comes from high society, thought Herr von Trotta.

"How long ago," he asked, "did you know my son?"

"It was before the war," said Frau von Taussig. Then she took the district captain's arm, led him down the corridor as she was accustomed to escorting patients, and murmured, "We were in love, Carl Joseph and I."

The district captain asked, "Forgive me, but was that foolish scrape because of you?"

"Partly because of me," said Frau von Taussig.

"I see, I see," said Herr von Trotta. "Partly because of you." Then he squeezed the nurse's arm slightly and went on. "I wish Carl Joseph could still get into foolish scrapes because of you!"

"Now let's go to the patient," said Frau von Taussig. For she felt tears welling up, and she believed that she mustn't weep.

Chojnicki sat in a bare room from which all objects had been removed because he sometimes had fits. He sat in a chair whose four feet were screwed into the floor. When the district captain entered, the count stood up, walked toward the guest, and said to Frau von Taussig, "Leave the room, Vally! We have something important to discuss!"

Now they were alone. The door had a peephole. Chojnicki went over to the door, covered the peephole with his back, and said, "Welcome to my home!"

For some unfathomable reason his bald head looked even balder. The patient's large, blue, somewhat bulging eyes seemed to emanate an icy wind, a frost blasting over the gaunt and bloated yellow face and the wasteland of the skull. From time to time the right-hand corner of Chojnicki's mouth twitched. It was as if he were trying to smile with that side. His ability to smile had simply lodged in that corner, abandoning the rest of the mouth forever.

"Sit down!" said Chojnicki. "I sent for you in order to give you some important information. Not a word to anyone else!

Nobody but you and me must know about it: the Old Man is dying!''

"How do you know?" asked Herr von Trotta.

Chojnicki, still at the door, pointed his finger at the ceiling, then put it to his lips, and said, "From a higher source!"

Next he turned around, opened the door, cried "Nurse Vally!" and said to Frau von Taussig, who instantly appeared, "The audience is over!"

He bowed. Herr von Trotta left.

He walked down the long corridor, accompanied by Frau von Taussig, and descended the wide steps.

"Perhaps it worked," she said.

Herr von Trotta took his leave and went to see Railroad Councilor Stransky. He didn't quite know why. He went to see Stransky, who had married a Koppelmann. The Stranskys were at home. They didn't recognize the district captain right off. Then they greeted him, embarrassed and nostalgic and aloof at once—so it seemed to him. They served him coffee and cognac.

"Carl Joseph!" said Frau Stransky, née Koppelmann. "When he made lieutenant, he came to see us right away. He was a dear boy!"

The district captain stroked his whiskers silently. Then the Stransky son came in. He limped, it was unsightly. He limped quite severely. Carl Joseph did not limp! the district captain thought.

"They say the Old Man's dying," Railroad Councilor Stransky suddenly said.

The district captain instantly rose and left. After all, he knew the Old Man was dying. Chojnicki had told him, and Chojnicki had always known everything. The district captain went to see his boyhood friend Smetana at the Royal Comptroller's office. "The Old Man's dying!" said Smetana.

"I'd like to go to Schönbrunn!" said Herr von Trotta. And he went to Schönbrunn.

The thin, relentless drizzle shrouded the castle of Schönbrunn just as it did the Steinhof Insane Asylum. Herr von Trotta walked up the garden lane, the same lane he had followed long, long ago, to the secret audience about his son. His son was dead.

And the Kaiser was dying too. And for the first time since learning of his son's death Herr von Trotta believed he knew that his son had not died by chance. The Kaiser cannot outlive the Trottas! the district captain thought. He cannot outlive them! They saved his life, and he will not outlive the Trottas.

He remained outside. He remained outside among the people of lower ranks. A gardener in a green apron and with a spade in his hand came from Schönbrunn Park and asked the onlookers, "How's he doing?" And the onlookers—foresters, coachmen, minor officials, janitors, and war veterans like the father of the Hero of Solferino—replied: "No news. He's dying!"

The gardener took off, went with his spade to dig up the flower beds, the eternal earth.

Rain was falling, quiet, dense, and increasingly denser. Herr von Trotta doffed his hat. The lower court officials standing there took him for one of their own or for a mailman from the Schönbrunn Post Office. And one or another of them asked the district captain, "Did you know him, the Old Man?"

"Yes," replied Herr von Trotta. "He once spoke to me."

"Now he's dying!" said a forester.

At that moment the priest entered the Kaiser's bedroom with the Most Holy Sacrament.

Franz Joseph's temperature was 102.9; it had just been taken.

"I see, I see," he said to the Capuchin monk. "So this is death!" He sat up in the pillows. He heard the relentless rain outside the windows and now and then the grinding of feet walking across the gravel. To the Kaiser these noises sounded alternately very far and very near. At times he realized that the rain was causing the gentle trickle outside the window. But then he soon forgot that it was the rain. And he asked his physician several times, "Why is it whispering like that?" For he could no longer pronounce the word *trickle* although it was on the tip of his tongue. But after inquiring about the cause of the whispering, he truly believed that all he heard was a whispering. The rain was whispering. The footfalls of people walking by were also whispering. The word and the sounds it signified for him appealed to the Kaiser more and more. Besides, it didn't matter what he asked, for they couldn't hear him. He only moved his lips, but he believed he was speaking, his voice audible if a bit soft, but no different than in the past few days. At times he was surprised that no one responded. But then he promptly forgot both his questions and his surprise at the muteness of the listeners. And once again he surrendered to the gentle whispering of the world, which lived around him while he lay dying— and he resembled a child that gives up all resistance to sleep, compelled by the lullaby and wrapped up in it.

He closed his eyes. But after a while he reopened them and saw the plain silver cross and, on the table, the blinding candles waiting for the priest. And now he knew that the priest would be coming soon. And he moved his lips and began reciting what he had been taught as a boy:

"In contrition and humility I confess my sins!"

But that too went unheard. Besides, he instantly saw that the Capuchin was already here.

"I've had to wait a long time!" he said. Then he thought about his sins. "Pride" occurred to him. "I was proud!" he said.

He went through sin after sin, as listed in the catechism. I was emperor for too long! he mused. But he thought he had said it aloud. "Everyone has to die. The Kaiser dies too." And he felt as if at the same time, somewhere, far from here, that part of him that was imperial was dying. "War is also a sin!" he said aloud. But the priest didn't hear him. Franz Joseph was again surprised. Every day brought casualty lists; the war had been raging since 1914. "Let it end!" said Franz Joseph. No one heard him. "If only I'd been killed at Solferino!" he said. No one heard him. Perhaps, he thought, I'm already dead and I'm talking as a dead man. That's why they don't understand me. And he fell asleep.

Outside, among the lower ranks, Herr von Trotta waited, the son of the Hero of Solferino, holding his hat, in the persistently trickling rain. The trees in Schönbrunn Park sighed and soughed; the rain whipped them, gentle, patient, lavish. The evening came. Curiosity-seekers came. The park filled up. The rain wouldn't stop. The onlookers spelled one another; they came, they went. Herr von Trotta remained. The night set in, the steps were empty, the people went home to bed. Herr von Trotta pressed against the gate. He heard carriages draw up;

sometimes a window was unlatched over his head. Voices called. The gate was opened, the gate was closed. He was not seen. The rain trickled, gentle, relentless; the trees soughed and sighed.

At last the bells began to toll. The district captain walked away. He went down the flat steps, along the lane to the iron gate. It was open tonight. He walked the whole long way back to the city, bare-headed, clutching his hat; he encountered no one. He walked very slowly as if following a hearse. Day was dawning when he reached the hotel.

He went home. It was also raining in the district seat of W. Herr von Trotta sent for Fräulein Hirschwitz and said, "I'm going to bed, madam. I'm tired." And for the first time in his life he went to bed during the day.

He couldn't fall asleep. He sent for Dr. Skowronnek.

"Dear Dr. Skowronnek," he said, "would you tell them to bring me the canary." They brought the canary from old Jacques's cottage. "Give it a piece of sugar!" said the district captain. And the canary got a piece of sugar.

"The dear creature!" said the district captain.

Dr. Skowronnek repeated, "A dear creature!"

"It will outlive us all," said Trotta. "Thank goodness!"

Then the district captain said, "Send for the priest. But come back!"

Dr. Skowronnek waited for the priest. Then he came back. Old Herr von Trotta lay silently in the pillows. His eyes were half shut. He said, "Your hand, dear friend! Would you bring me the picture?"

Dr. Skowronnek went to the den, climbed on a chair, and unhooked the portrait of the Hero of Solferino. By the time he came back, holding the picture in both hands, Herr von Trotta was no longer able to see it. The rain drummed softly on the windows.

Dr. Skowronnek waited with the portrait of the Hero of Solferino on his lap. After a few minutes he stood up, took hold of Herr von Trotta's hand, leaned over the district captain's chest, breathed deeply, and shut the dead man's eyes.

This was the day on which the Kaiser was buried in the Capuchin Vault. Three days later Herr von Trotta's corpse was lowered into the grave. The mayor of the town of W spoke. His funeral oration, like all speeches during that period, began with the war. The mayor went on to say that though the district captain had given his only son to the Kaiser he had nevertheless gone on living and serving. Meanwhile the tireless rain washed over all the bared heads of the mourners gathered at the grave, and it sighed and soughed all around from the wet shrubs, wreaths, and flowers. Dr. Skowronnek, in a uniform that was unfamiliar to him, that of a home reserve medical corporal, did his best to stand at attention with a very military bearing, although he by no means considered that a crucial expression of piety, civilian that he was. After all, death is no staff surgeon! thought Dr. Skowronnek.

He then was one of the first to approach the grave. He waved off the spade offered him by a gravedigger; instead he bent down and broke off a clod of wet soil and crumbled it in his left hand and his right hand tossed the individual crumbs upon the coffin. Then he stepped back. It occurred to him that it was afternoon, chess time was approaching. He had no one to play with now; but he decided to go to the café anyhow.

When they left the graveyard, the mayor invited him into his carriage. Dr. Skowronnek got in.

"I would like to have added," said the mayor, "that Herr von Trotta could not outlive the Kaiser. Don't you agree, Herr Doctor?"

"I don't know," Dr. Skowronnek replied. "I don't think either of them could have outlived Austria."

Dr. Skowronnek told the coachman to drop him off at the café. He went to his usual table as on any other day. The chessboard lay there as if the district captain hadn't died. The waiter came to clear it away, but Skowronnek said, "Leave it!" And he played a game against himself, smirking, occasionally looking at the empty chair across the table, his ears filled with the gentle noise of the autumn rain, which was still running tirelessly down the panes.

ABOUT THE TRANSLATOR

JOACHIM NEUGROSCHEL is the translator of over 130 books, including works by George Bataille, Franz Kafka and Elias Canetti. He has won numerous awards, including three PEN translation prizes.

ABOUT THE INTRODUCER

ALAN BANCE is Professor of German at the University of Southampton and a specialist in twentieth-century German literature. He has edited *Weimar Germany: Writers and Politics* and is the author of *Theodor von Fontane: The Major Novels*. He has also edited a number of German novels, including Roth's *Die Kapuzinergruft*.

CHINUA ACHEBE
Things Fall Apart

THE ARABIAN NIGHTS
(2 vols, tr. Husain Haddawy)

AUGUSTINE
The Confessions

JANE AUSTEN
Emma
Mansfield Park
Northanger Abbey
Persuasion
Pride and Prejudice
Sanditon and Other Stories
Sense and Sensibility

HONORÉ DE BALZAC
Cousin Bette
Eugénie Grandet
Old Goriot

SIMONE DE BEAUVOIR
The Second Sex

SAUL BELLOW
The Adventures of Augie March

HECTOR BERLIOZ
The Memoirs of Hector Berlioz

WILLIAM BLAKE
Poems and Prophecies

JORGE LUIS BORGES
Ficciones

JAMES BOSWELL
The Life of Samuel Johnson
The Journal of a Tour to
the Hebrides

CHARLOTTE BRONTË
Jane Eyre
Villette

EMILY BRONTË
Wuthering Heights

MIKHAIL BULGAKOV
The Master and Margarita

SAMUEL BUTLER
The Way of all Flesh

ITALO CALVINO
If on a winter's night a traveler

ALBERT CAMUS
The Outsider

MIGUEL DE CERVANTES
Don Quixote

RAYMOND CHANDLER
The novels (2 vols)
Collected Stories

GEOFFREY CHAUCER
Canterbury Tales

ANTON CHEKHOV
My Life and Other Stories
The Steppe and Other Stories

KATE CHOPIN
The Awakening

CARL VON CLAUSEWITZ
On War

S. T. COLERIDGE
Poems

WILKIE COLLINS
The Moonstone
The Woman in White

CONFUCIUS
The Analects

JOSEPH CONRAD
Heart of Darkness
Lord Jim
Nostromo
The Secret Agent
Typhoon and Other Stories
Under Western Eyes
Victory

THOMAS CRANMER
The Book of Common Prayer

DANTE ALIGHIERI
The Divine Comedy

DANIEL DEFOE
Moll Flanders
Robinson Crusoe

CHARLES DICKENS
Bleak House
David Copperfield
Dombey and Son
Great Expectations
Hard Times
Little Dorrit
Martin Chuzzlewit
Nicholas Nickleby
The Old Curiosity Shop

This book is set in BEMBO which was cut
by the punch-cutter Francesco Griffo
for the Venetian printer-publisher
Aldus Manutius in early 1495
and first used in a pamphlet
by a young scholar
named Pietro
Bembo.